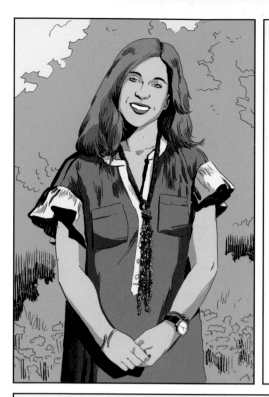

LAUREN TARSHIS'S

NEW YORK TIMES BESTSELLING I SURVIVED SERIES TELLS STORIES OF YOUNG PEOPLE AND THEIR RESILIENCE AND STRENGTH IN THE MIDST OF UNIMAGINABLE DISASTERS AND TIMES OF TURMOIL. LAUREN HAS BROUGHT HER SIGNATURE WARMTH, INTEGRITY, AND EXHAUSTIVE RESEARCH TO TOPICS SUCH AS THE BATTLE OF D-DAY, THE AMERICAN REVOLUTION, HURRICANE KATRINA, THE BOMBING OF PEARL HARBOR, AND OTHER WORLD EVENTS. LAUREN LIVES IN CONNECTICUT WITH HER FAMILY, AND CAN BE FOUND ONLINE AT LAURENTARSHIS.COM.

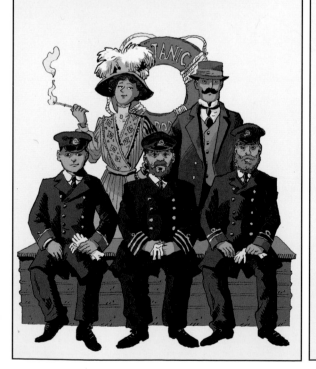

HAUS STUDIO

WAS FOUNDED IN 1997 BY A GROUP OF FRIENDS WHO SELF-PUBLISHED THEIR OWN COMICS. THEY ARE LOCATED IN BUENOS AIRES, ARGENTINA, BUT COLLABORATE WITH WRITERS AND PUBLISHERS AROUND THE WORLD. IN ADDITION TO THEIR ILLUSTRATION WORK, THE TEAM RUNS AN ART SCHOOL AND HAS ORGANIZED COMIC BOOK CONVENTIONS AND OTHER EXHIBITIONS IN LATIN AMERICA. HAUS STUDIO ARTISTS CONSIDER THEMSELVES STORYTELLERS MORE THAN ARTISTS, AND THEREFORE LOVE WORKING ON PROJECTS WITH RICH STORIES TO TELL.

DISCOVER THE SERIES THAT STARTED IT ALL!

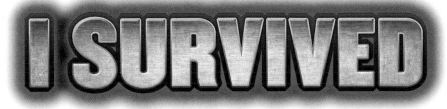

WHEN DISASTER STRIKES, HEROES ARE MADE.

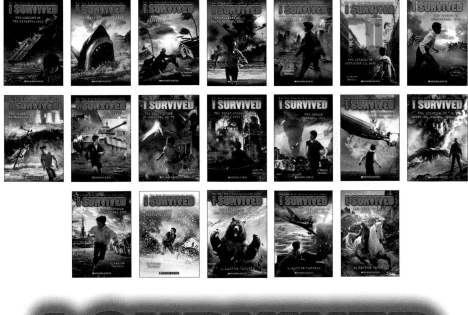

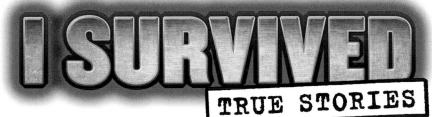

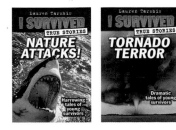

REAL KIDS. REAL DISASTERS.

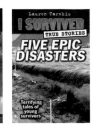

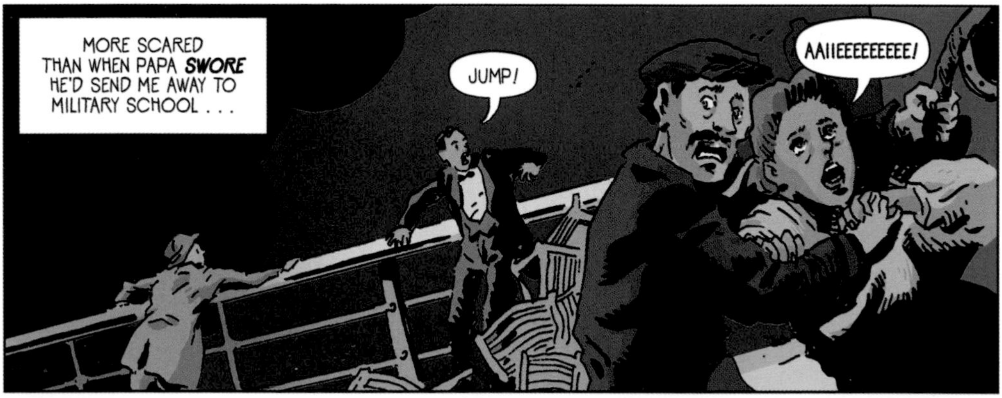
MORE SCARED THAN WHEN PAPA **SWORE** HE'D SEND ME AWAY TO MILITARY SCHOOL . . .
JUMP!
AAIIEEEEEEEEEE!

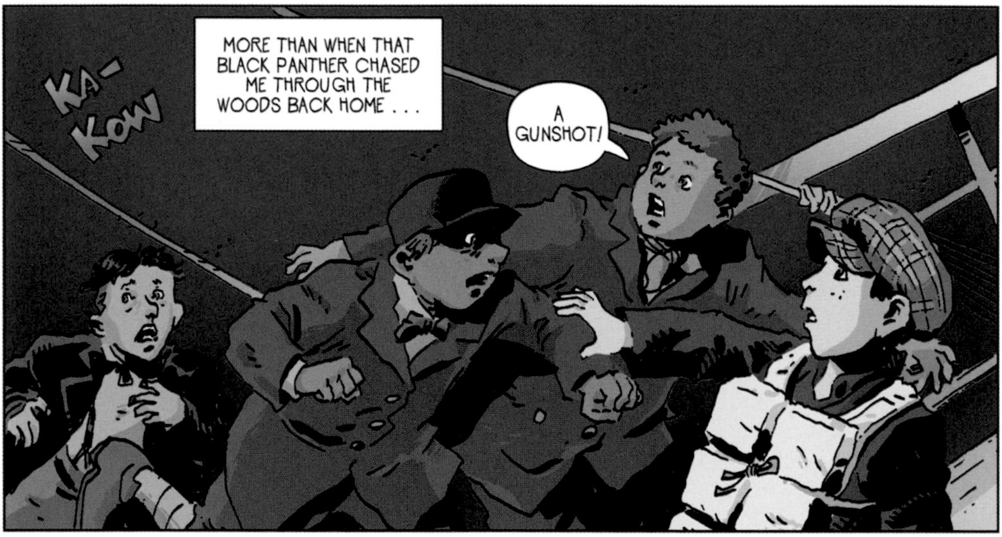
KA-KOW
MORE THAN WHEN THAT BLACK PANTHER CHASED ME THROUGH THE WOODS BACK HOME . . .
A GUNSHOT!

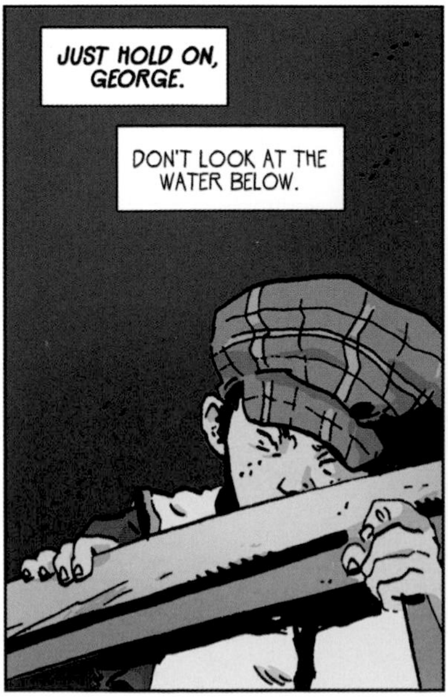
JUST HOLD ON, GEORGE.
DON'T LOOK AT THE WATER BELOW.

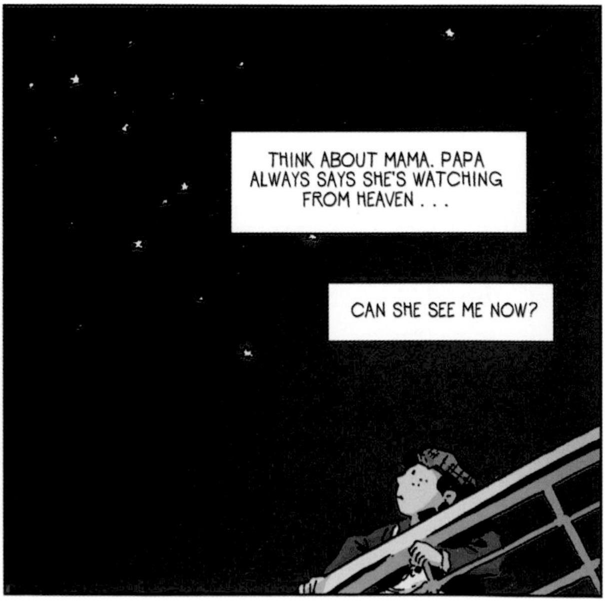
THINK ABOUT MAMA. PAPA ALWAYS SAYS SHE'S WATCHING FROM HEAVEN . . .
CAN SHE SEE ME NOW?

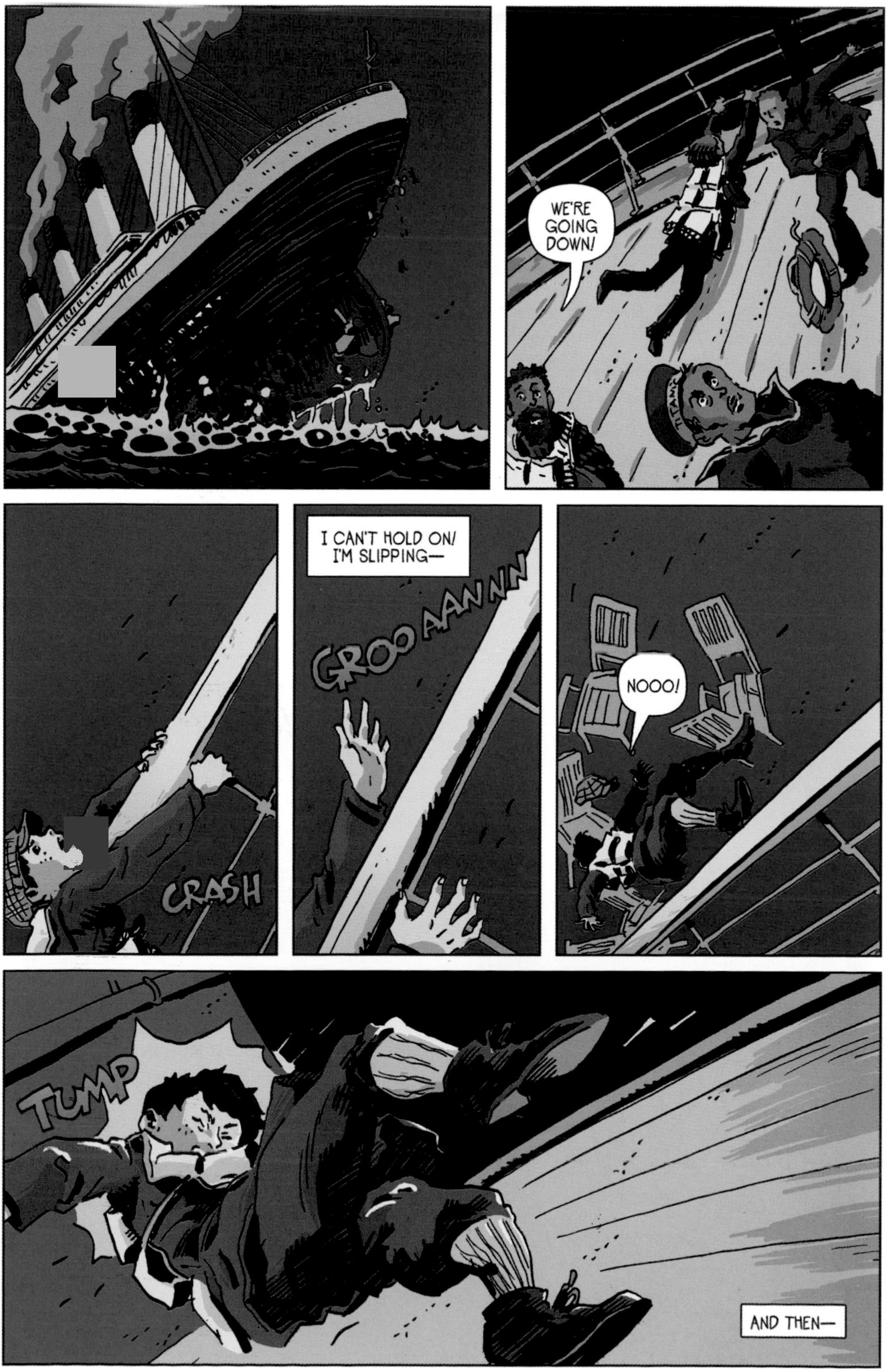
WE'RE GOING DOWN!
CRASH
I CAN'T HOLD ON! I'M SLIPPING—
GROOAANNN
NOOO!
TUMP
AND THEN—

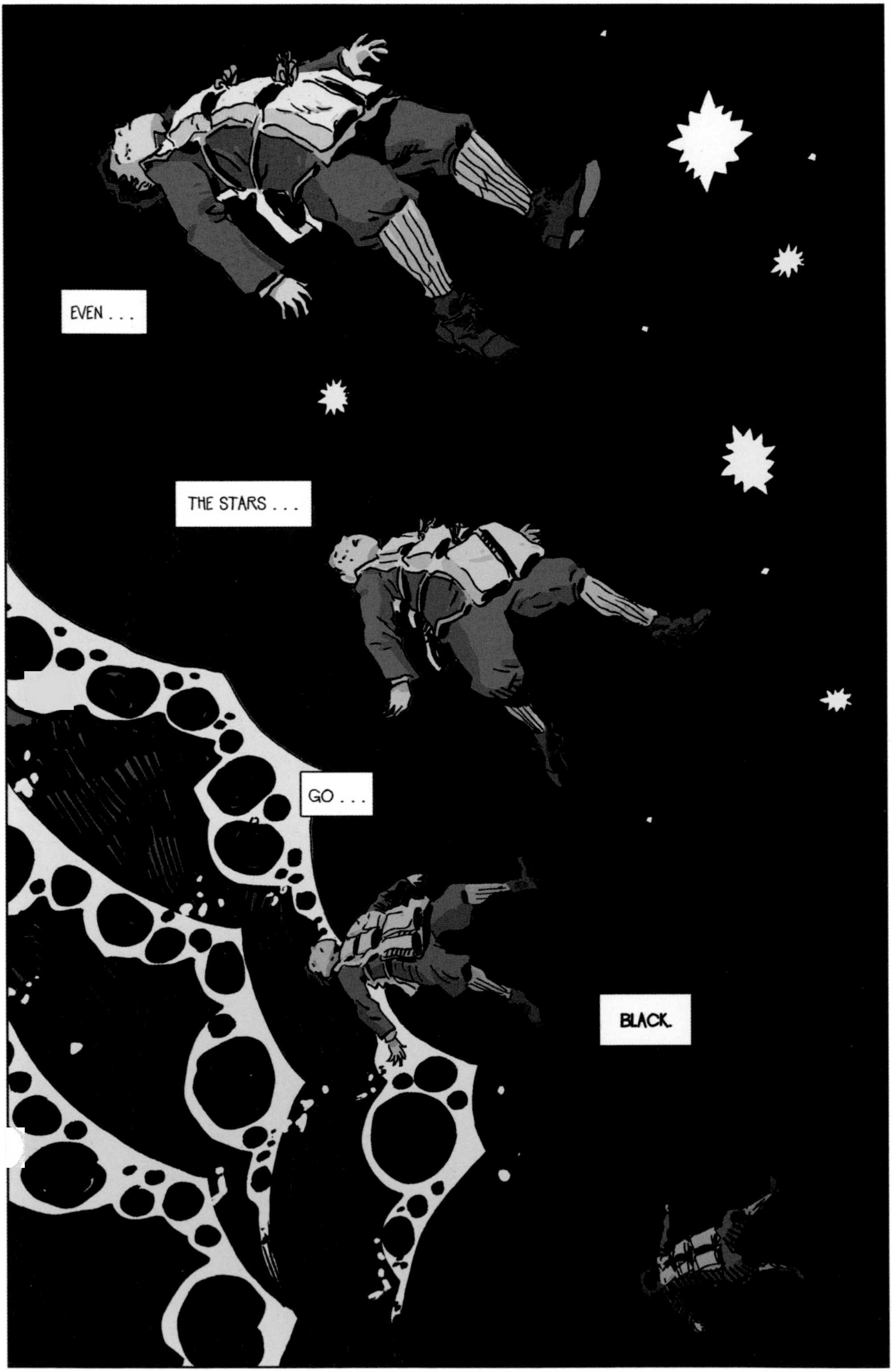
EVEN . . .
THE STARS . . .
GO . . .
BLACK.

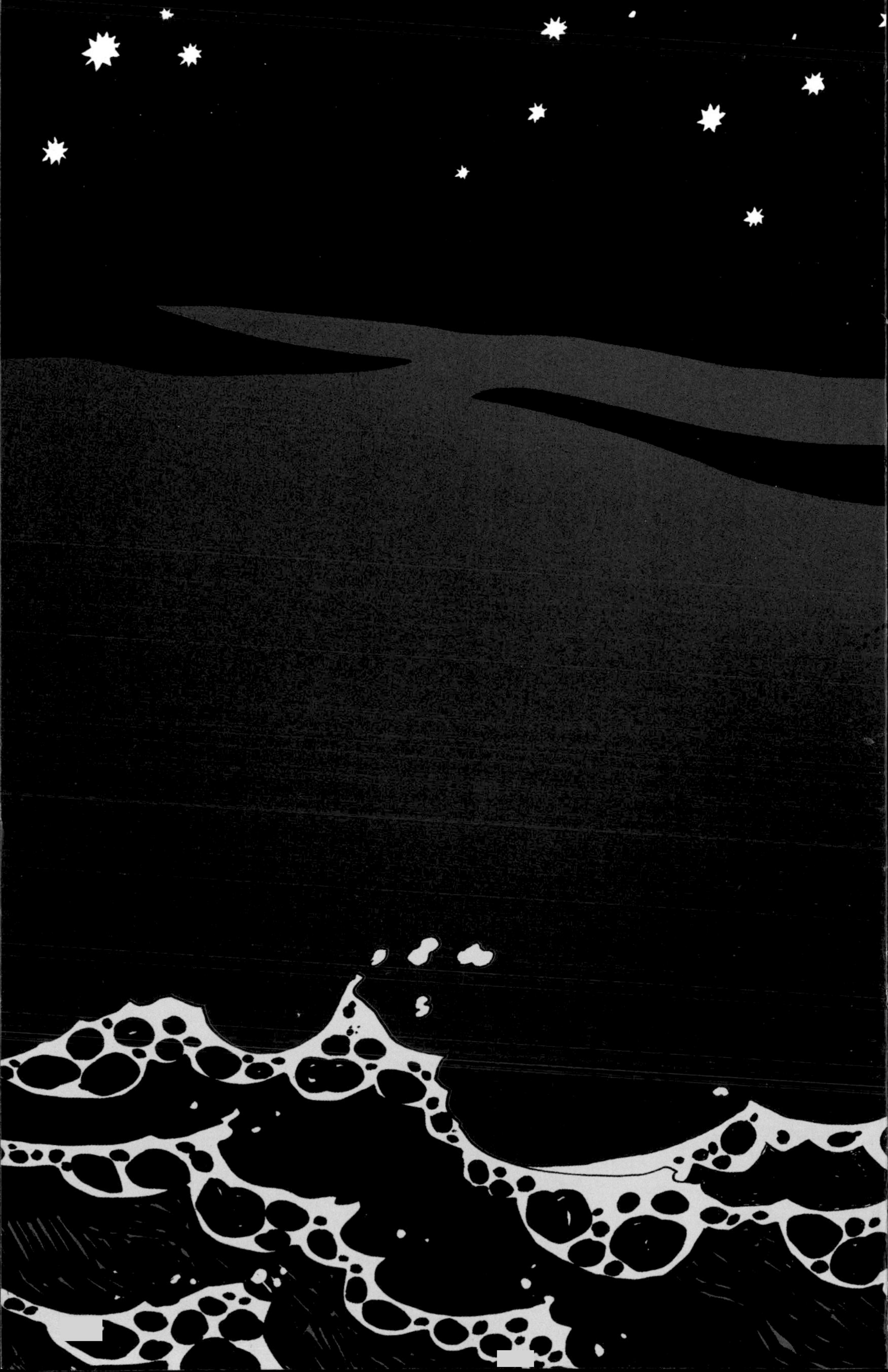

THE SINKING OF THE *TITANIC*, 1912

BASED ON THE NOVEL IN THE *NEW YORK TIMES*
BESTSELLING SERIES BY LAUREN TARSHIS

ADAPTED BY GEORGIA BALL
WITH ART BY HAUS STUDIO
PENCILS BY GERVASIO
INKS BY JOK AND CARLOS AÓN
COLORS BY LARA LEE
ART ASSISTANCE BY DARIO BRABO
LOGO AND FONTS BY CARLOS AÓN

graphix
AN IMPRINT OF
SCHOLASTIC

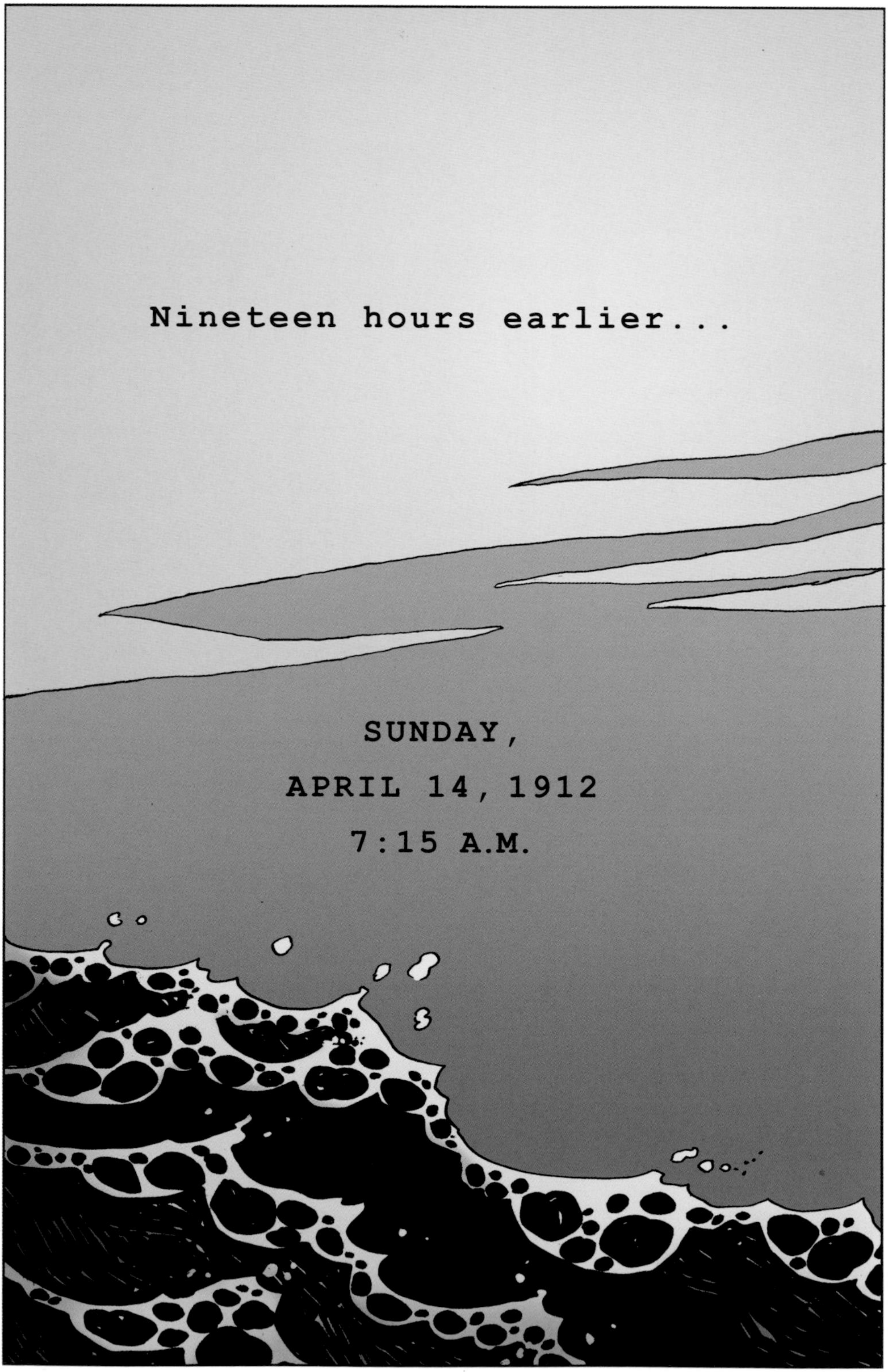
Nineteen hours earlier...
SUNDAY,
APRIL 14, 1912
7:15 A.M.

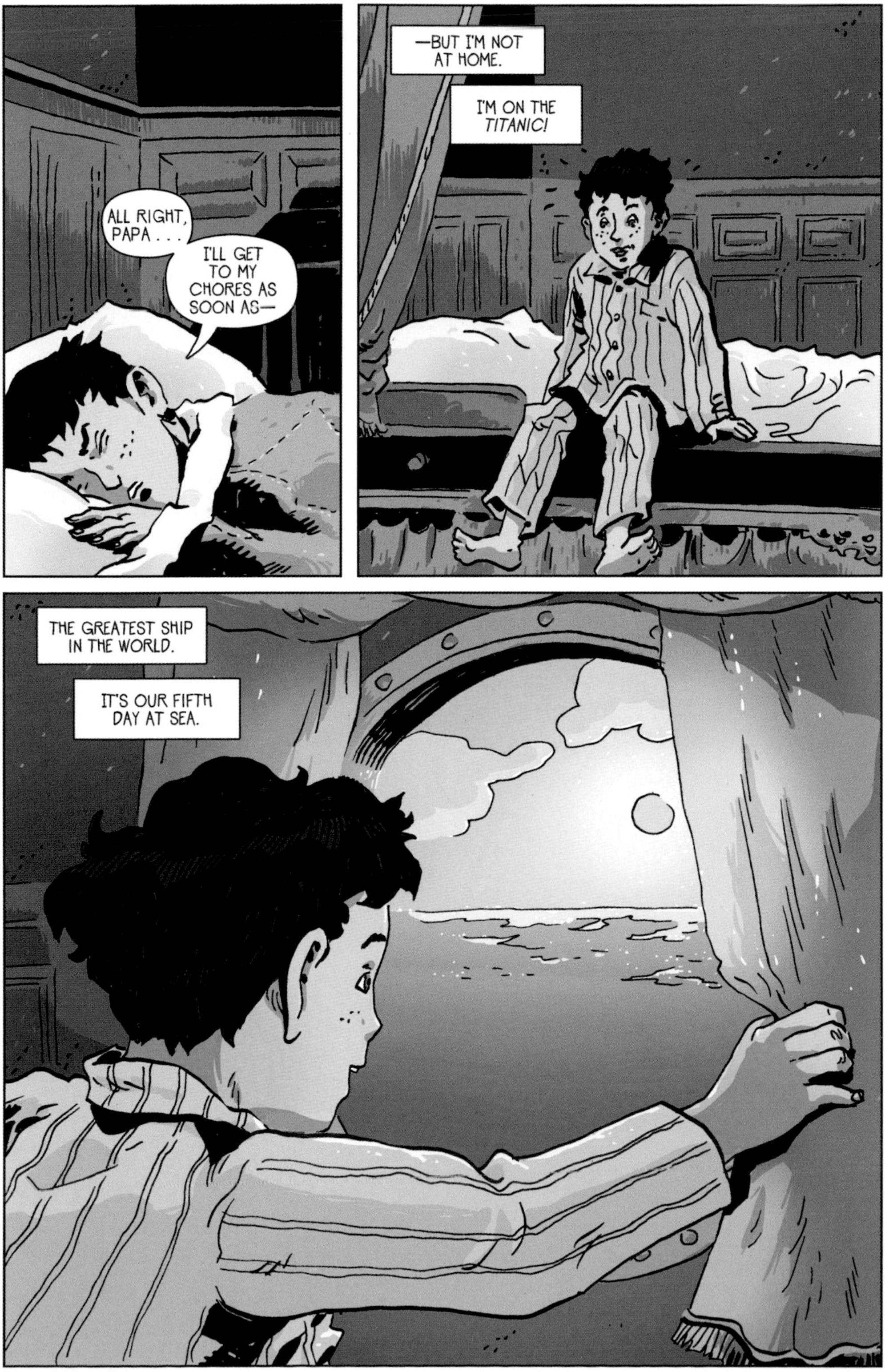
ALL RIGHT, PAPA . . .
I'LL GET TO MY CHORES AS SOON AS—
—BUT I'M NOT AT HOME.
I'M ON THE *TITANIC!*
THE GREATEST SHIP IN THE WORLD.
IT'S OUR FIFTH DAY AT SEA.

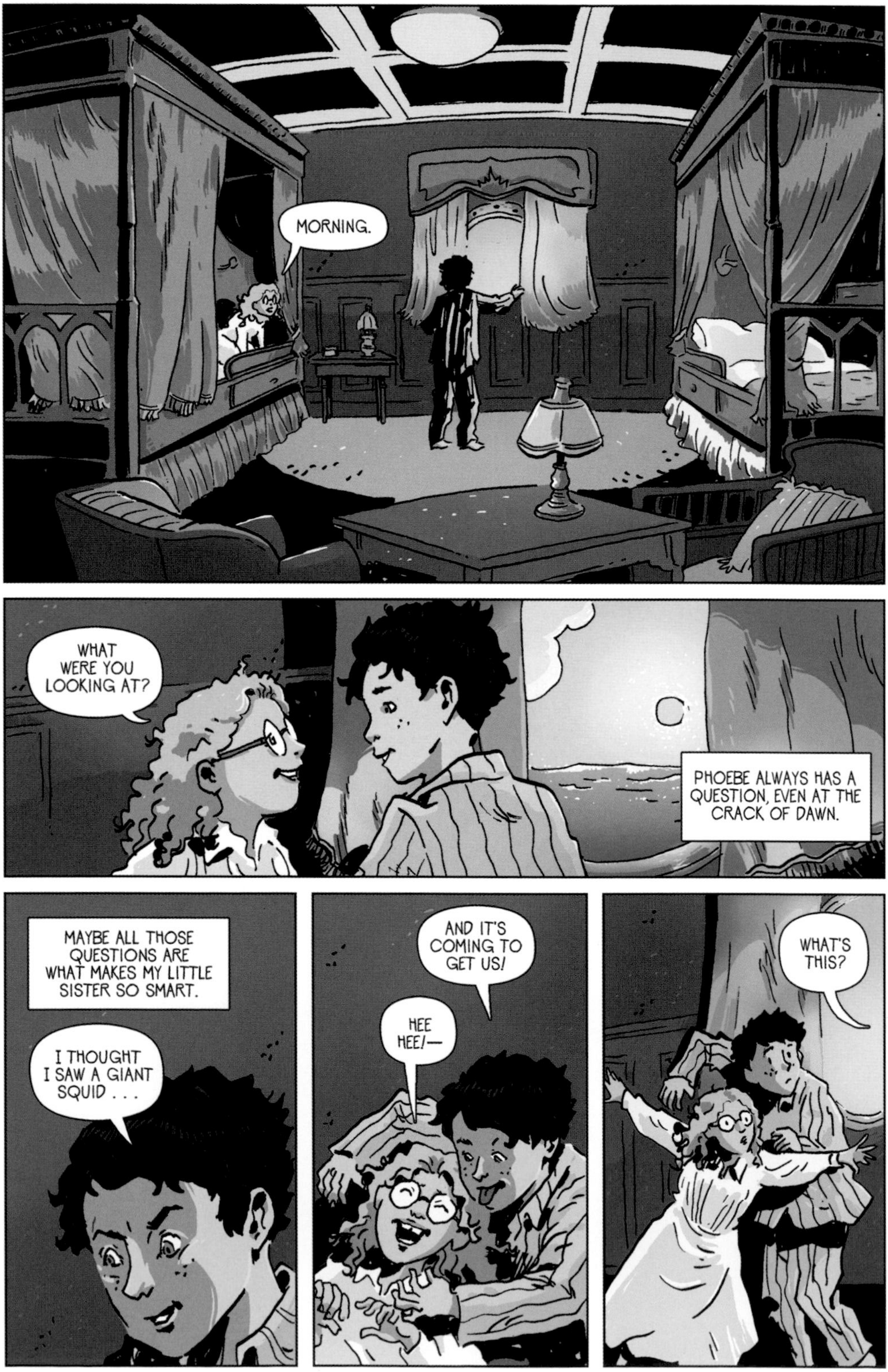
MORNING.
WHAT WERE YOU LOOKING AT?
PHOEBE ALWAYS HAS A QUESTION, EVEN AT THE CRACK OF DAWN.
MAYBE ALL THOSE QUESTIONS ARE WHAT MAKES MY LITTLE SISTER SO SMART.
I THOUGHT I SAW A GIANT SQUID . . .
AND IT'S COMING TO GET US!
HEE HEE!—
WHAT'S THIS?

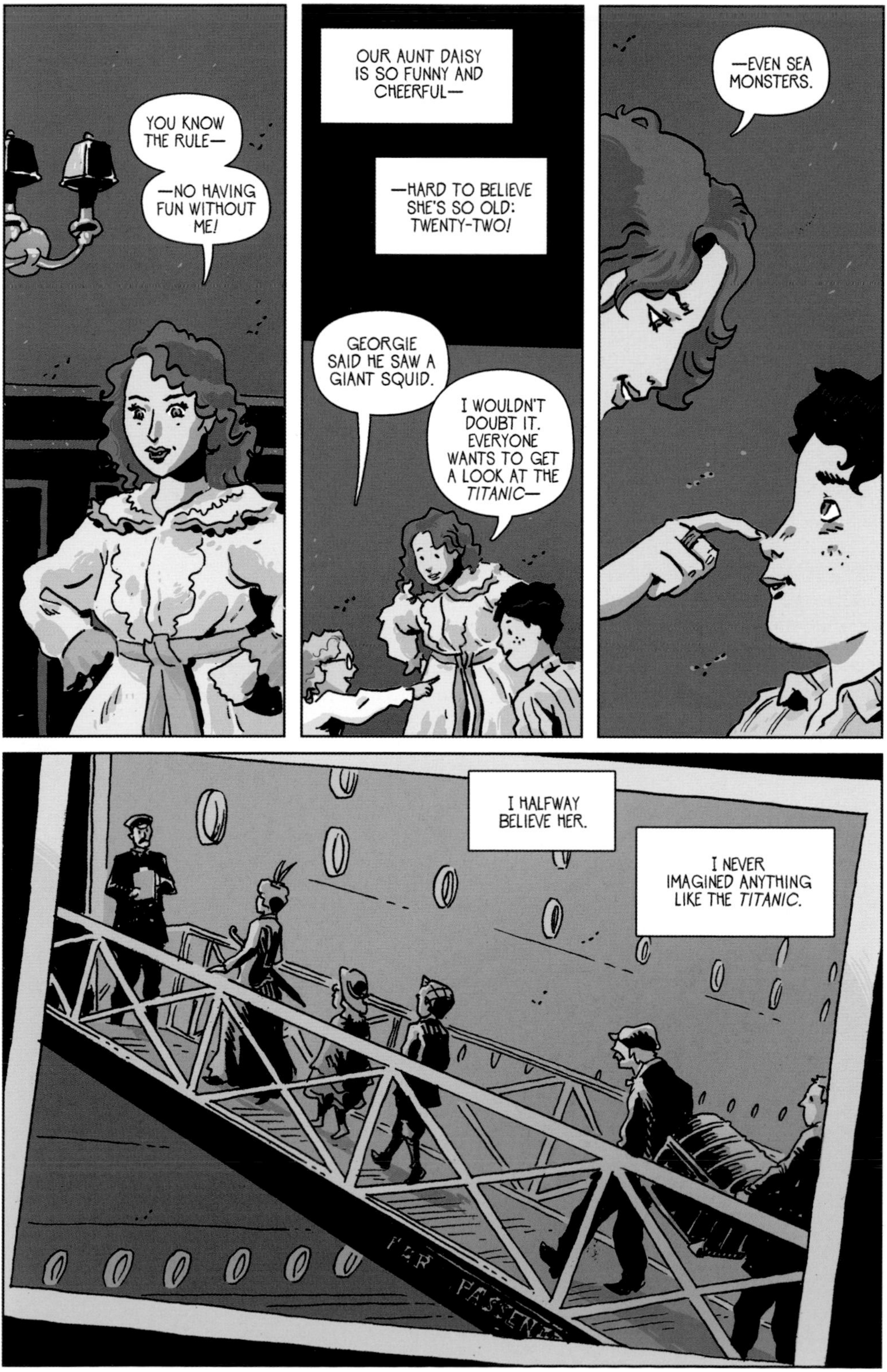
YOU KNOW THE RULE—
—NO HAVING FUN WITHOUT ME!
OUR AUNT DAISY IS SO FUNNY AND CHEERFUL—
—HARD TO BELIEVE SHE'S SO OLD: TWENTY-TWO!
GEORGIE SAID HE SAW A GIANT SQUID.
I WOULDN'T DOUBT IT. EVERYONE WANTS TO GET A LOOK AT THE *TITANIC*—
—EVEN SEA MONSTERS.
I HALFWAY BELIEVE HER.
I NEVER IMAGINED ANYTHING LIKE THE *TITANIC*.

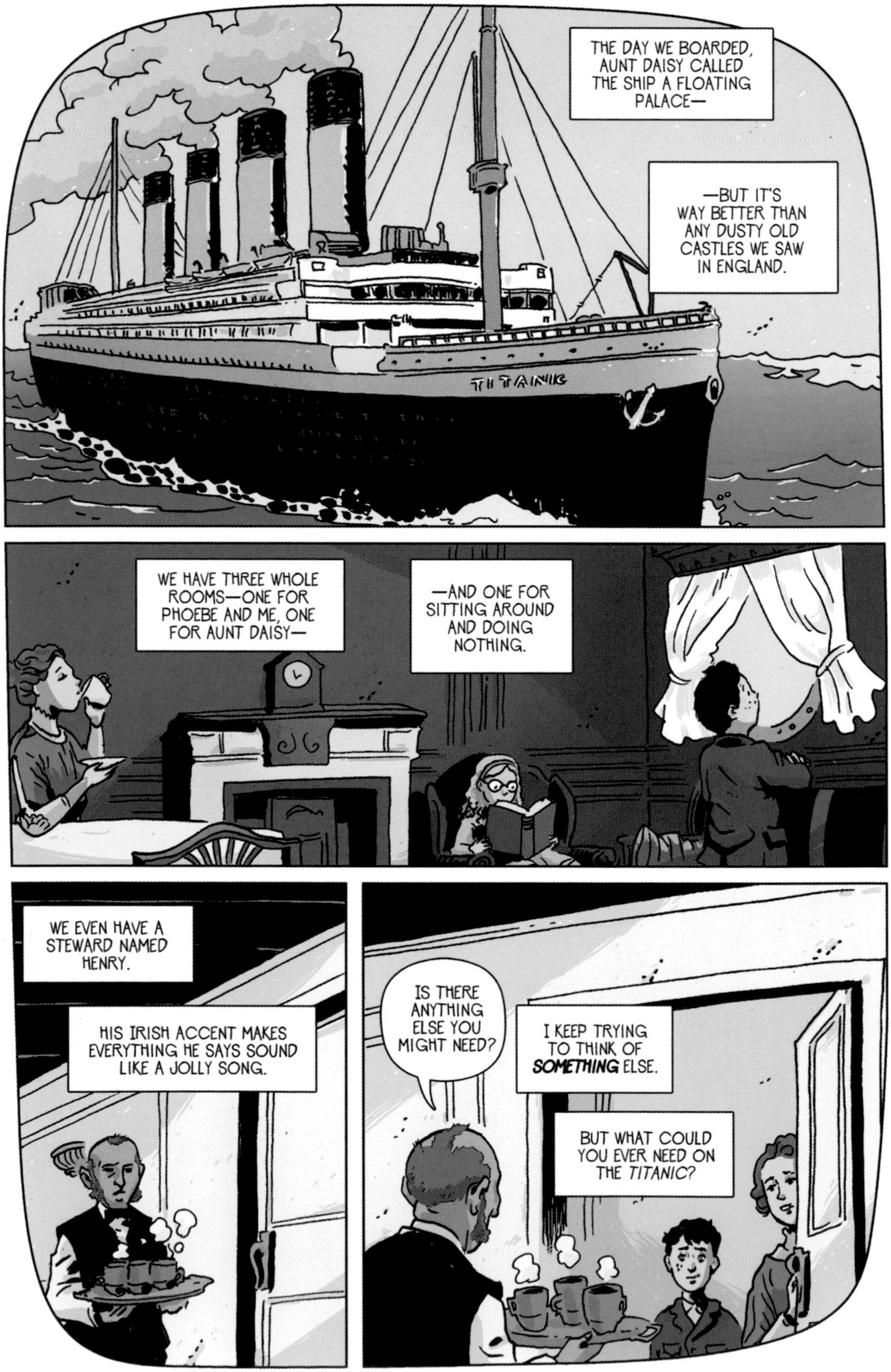
THE DAY WE BOARDED, AUNT DAISY CALLED THE SHIP A FLOATING PALACE—
—BUT IT'S WAY BETTER THAN ANY DUSTY OLD CASTLES WE SAW IN ENGLAND.
TITANIC
WE HAVE THREE WHOLE ROOMS—ONE FOR PHOEBE AND ME, ONE FOR AUNT DAISY—
—AND ONE FOR SITTING AROUND AND DOING NOTHING.
WE EVEN HAVE A STEWARD NAMED HENRY.
HIS IRISH ACCENT MAKES EVERYTHING HE SAYS SOUND LIKE A JOLLY SONG.
IS THERE ANYTHING ELSE YOU MIGHT NEED?
I KEEP TRYING TO THINK OF ***SOMETHING*** ELSE.
BUT WHAT COULD YOU EVER NEED ON THE *TITANIC*?

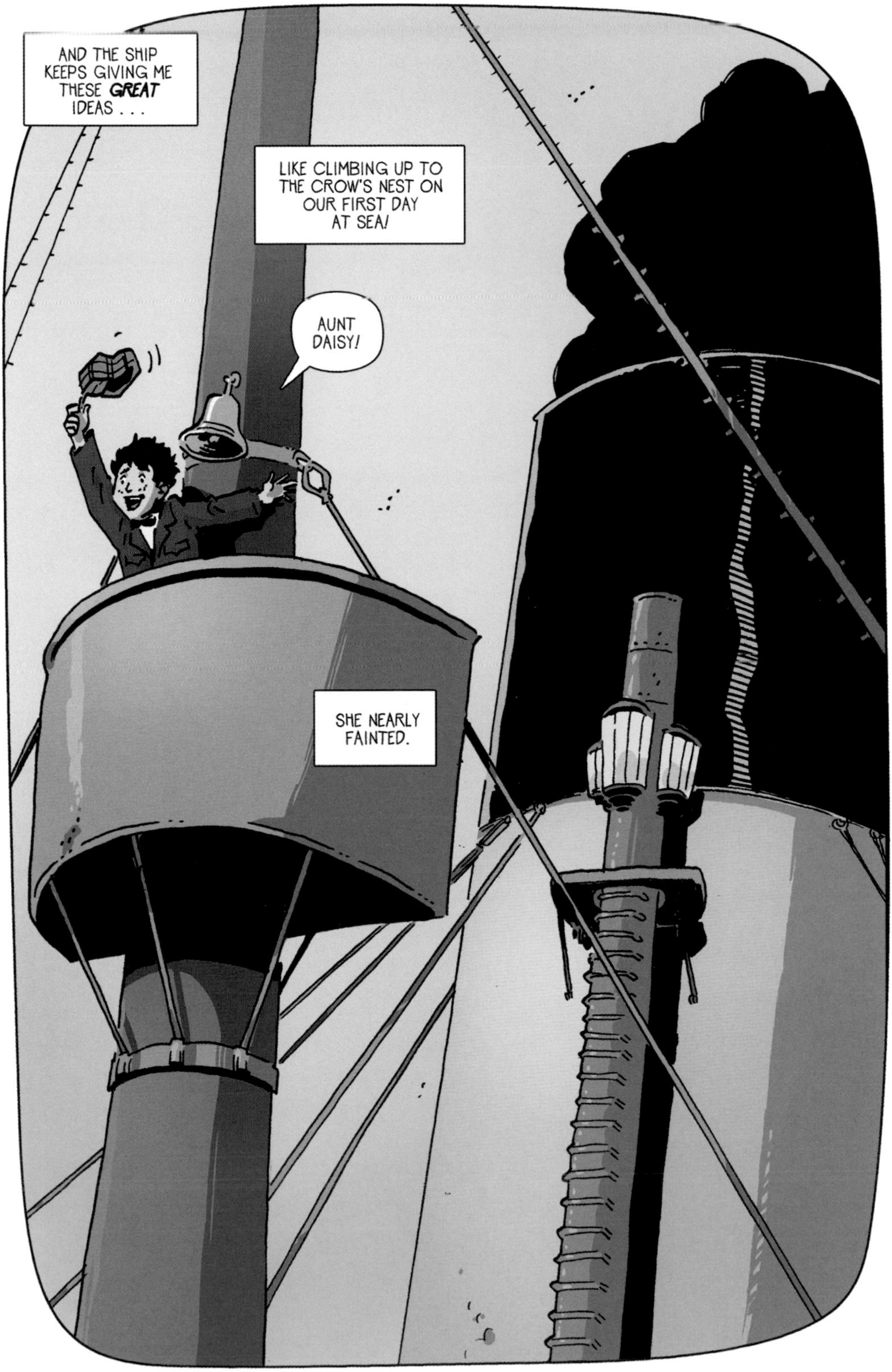
AND THE SHIP KEEPS GIVING ME THESE **GREAT** IDEAS . . .
LIKE CLIMBING UP TO THE CROW'S NEST ON OUR FIRST DAY AT SEA!
AUNT DAISY!
SHE NEARLY FAINTED.

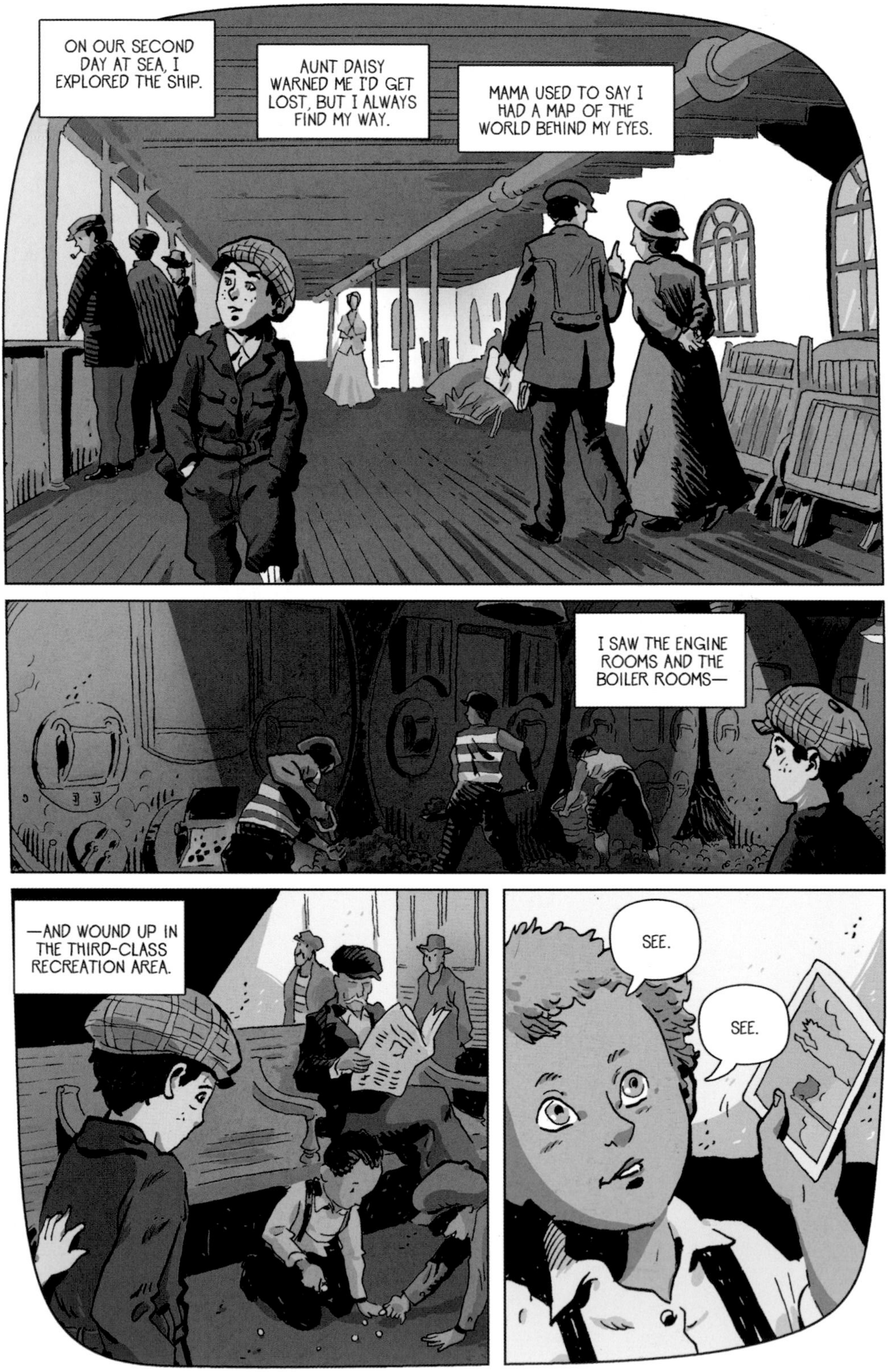
ON OUR SECOND DAY AT SEA, I EXPLORED THE SHIP.
AUNT DAISY WARNED ME I'D GET LOST, BUT I ALWAYS FIND MY WAY.
MAMA USED TO SAY I HAD A MAP OF THE WORLD BEHIND MY EYES.
I SAW THE ENGINE ROOMS AND THE BOILER ROOMS—
—AND WOUND UP IN THE THIRD-CLASS RECREATION AREA.
SEE.
SEE.

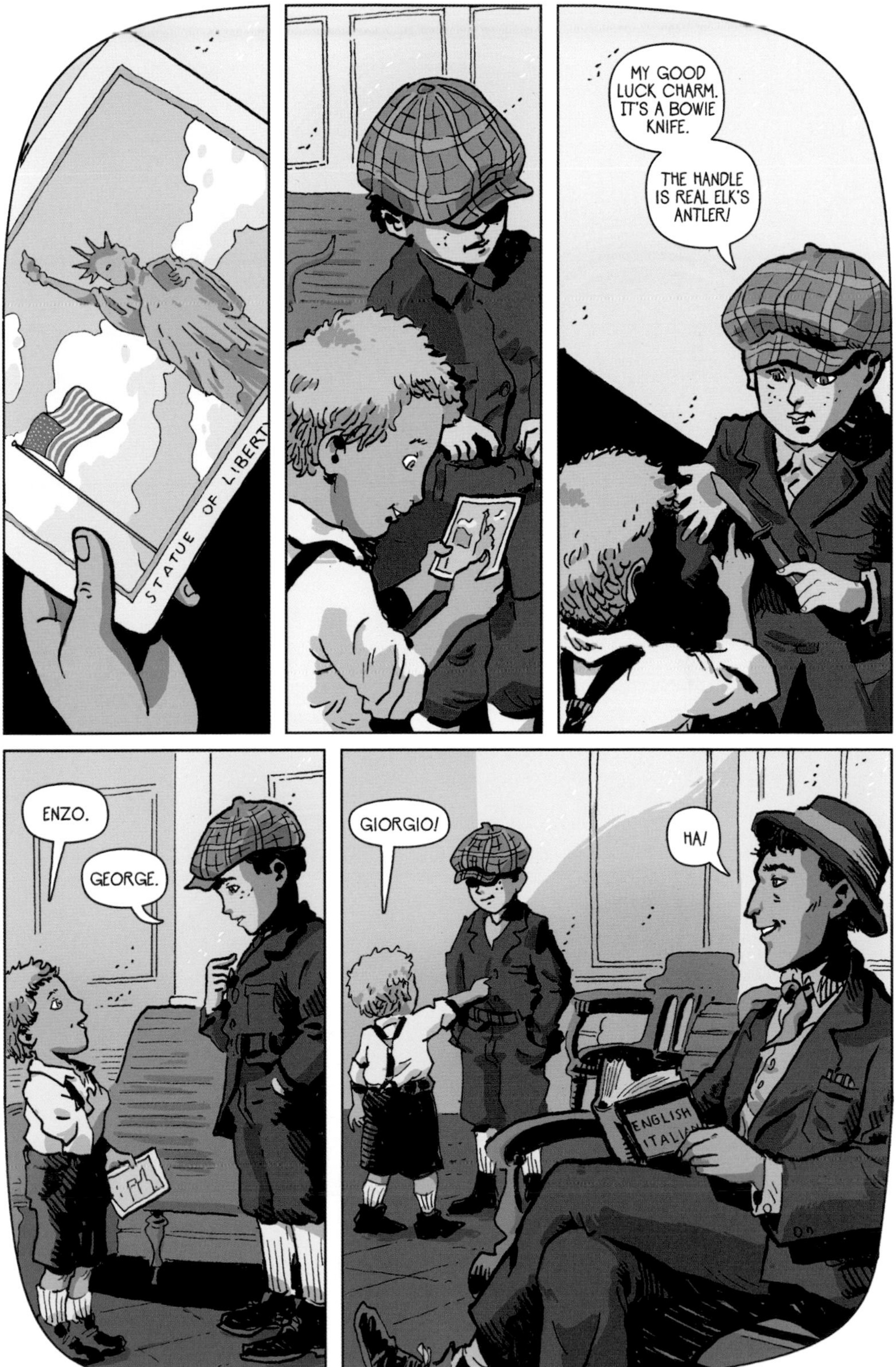
STATUE OF LIBERTY
MY GOOD LUCK CHARM. IT'S A BOWIE KNIFE.
THE HANDLE IS REAL ELK'S ANTLER!
ENZO.
GEORGE.
GIORGIO!
HA!
ENGLISH ITALIAN

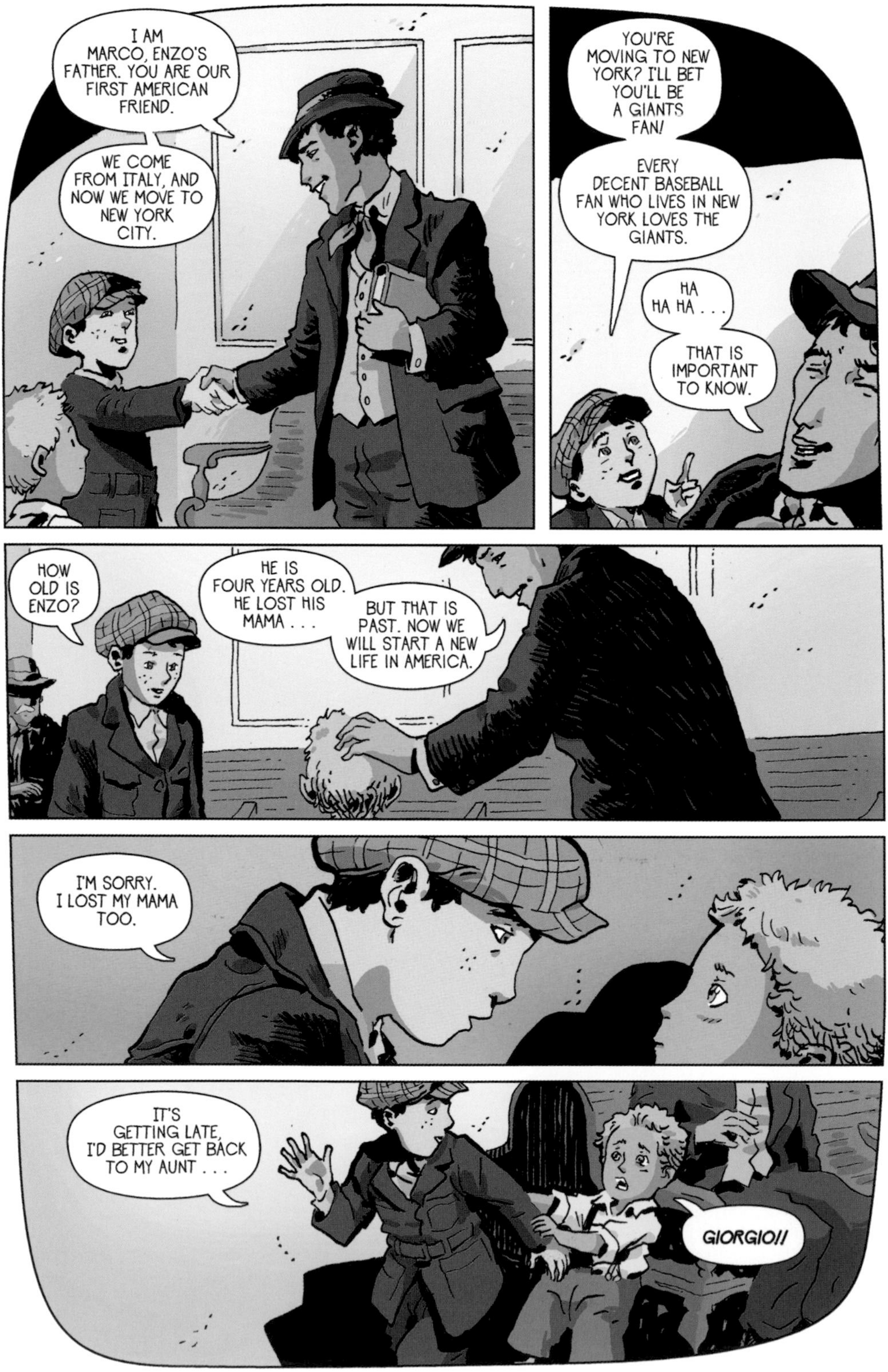
I AM MARCO, ENZO'S FATHER. YOU ARE OUR FIRST AMERICAN FRIEND.
WE COME FROM ITALY, AND NOW WE MOVE TO NEW YORK CITY.
YOU'RE MOVING TO NEW YORK? I'LL BET YOU'LL BE A GIANTS FAN!
EVERY DECENT BASEBALL FAN WHO LIVES IN NEW YORK LOVES THE GIANTS.
HA HA HA . . .
THAT IS IMPORTANT TO KNOW.
HOW OLD IS ENZO?
HE IS FOUR YEARS OLD. HE LOST HIS MAMA . . .
BUT THAT IS PAST. NOW WE WILL START A NEW LIFE IN AMERICA.
I'M SORRY. I LOST MY MAMA TOO.
IT'S GETTING LATE, I'D BETTER GET BACK TO MY AUNT . . .
GIORGIO!!

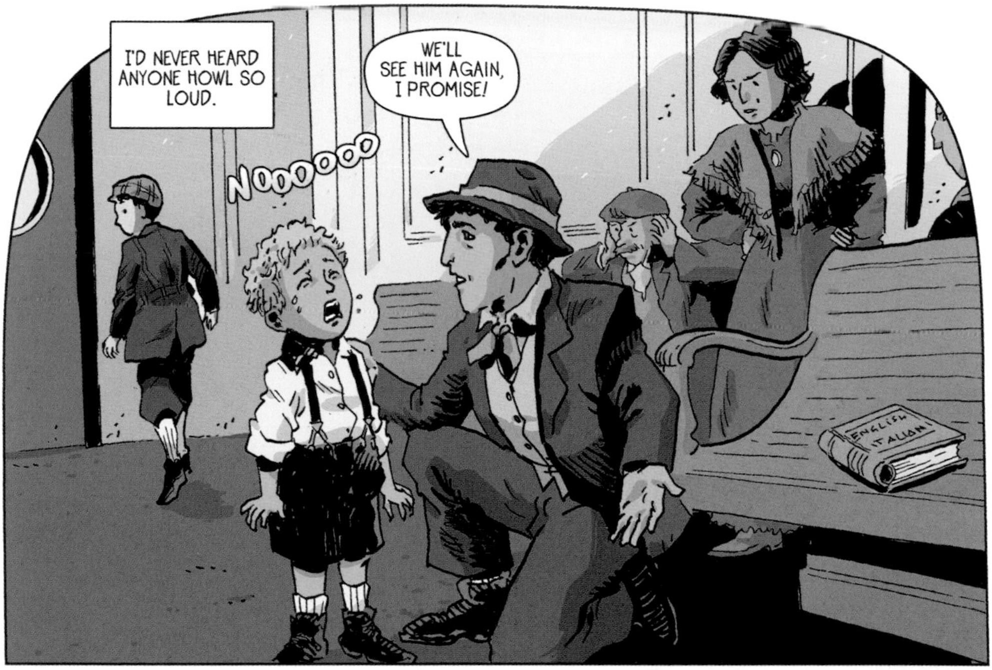
I'D NEVER HEARD ANYONE HOWL SO LOUD.
WE'LL SEE HIM AGAIN, I PROMISE!
NOOOOOO
ENGLISH ITALIAN

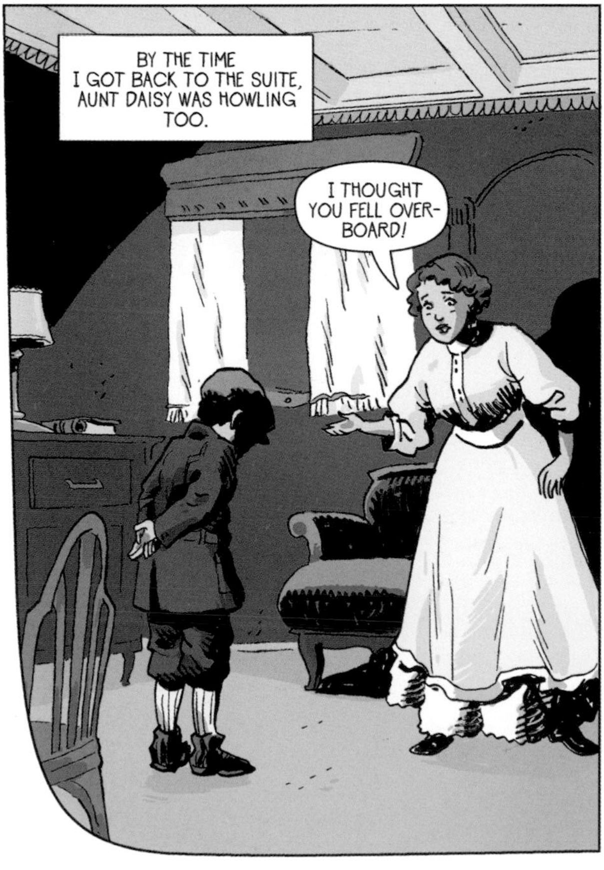
BY THE TIME I GOT BACK TO THE SUITE, AUNT DAISY WAS HOWLING TOO.
I THOUGHT YOU FELL OVER-BOARD!

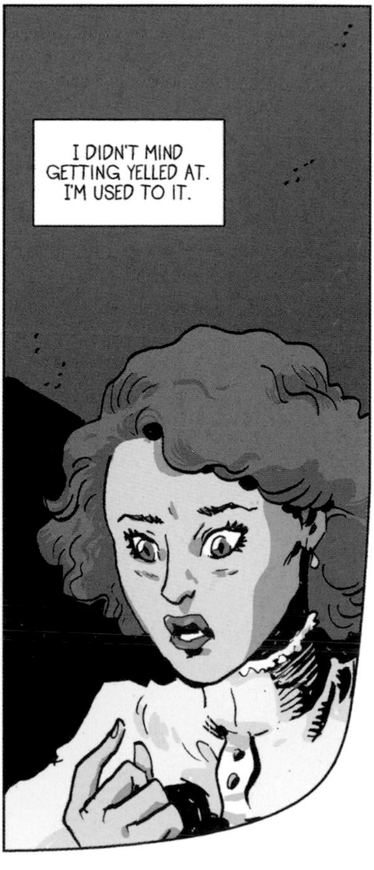
I DIDN'T MIND GETTING YELLED AT. I'M USED TO IT.

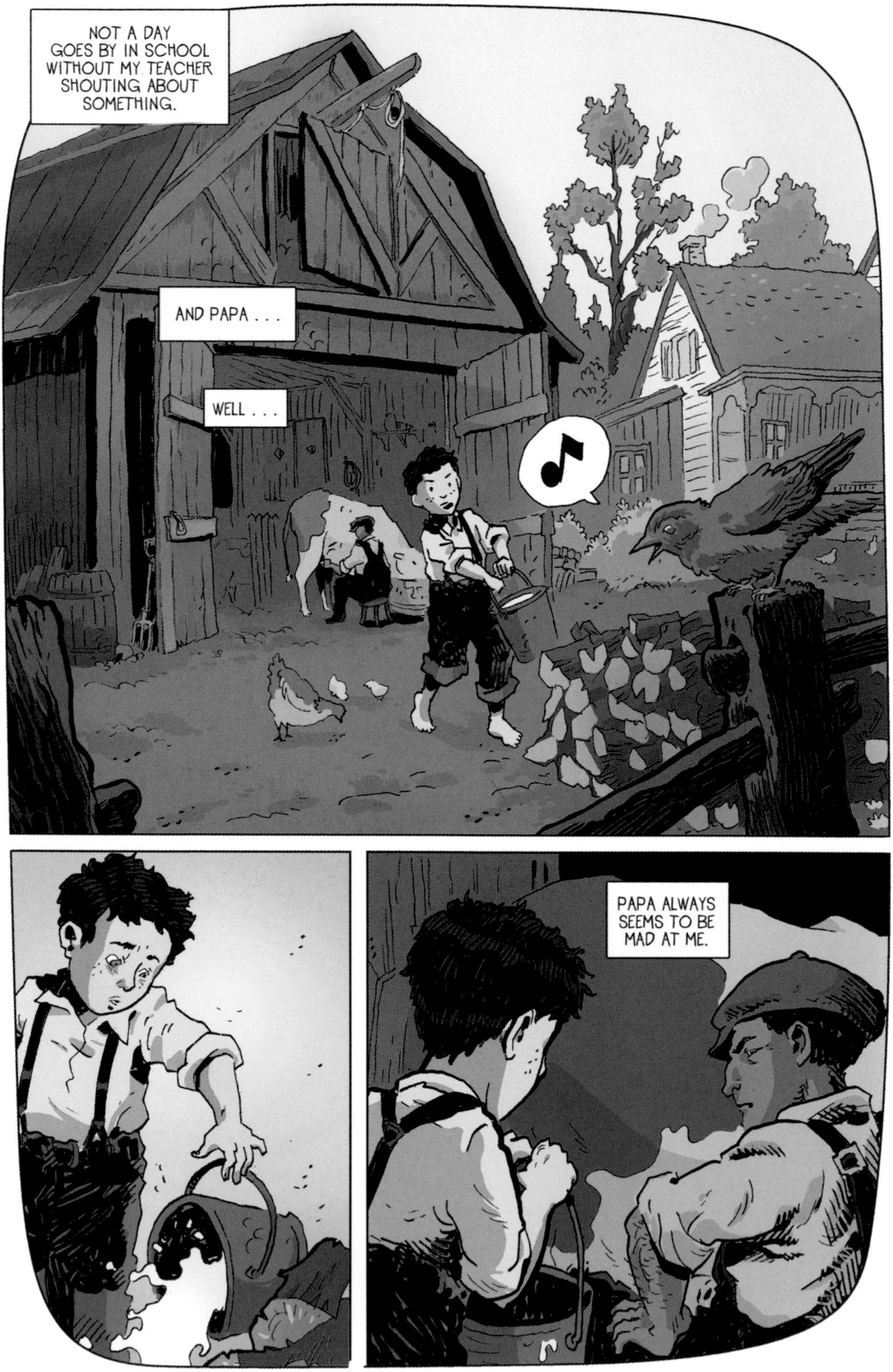
NOT A DAY GOES BY IN SCHOOL WITHOUT MY TEACHER SHOUTING ABOUT SOMETHING.
AND PAPA . . .
WELL . . .
PAPA ALWAYS SEEMS TO BE MAD AT ME.

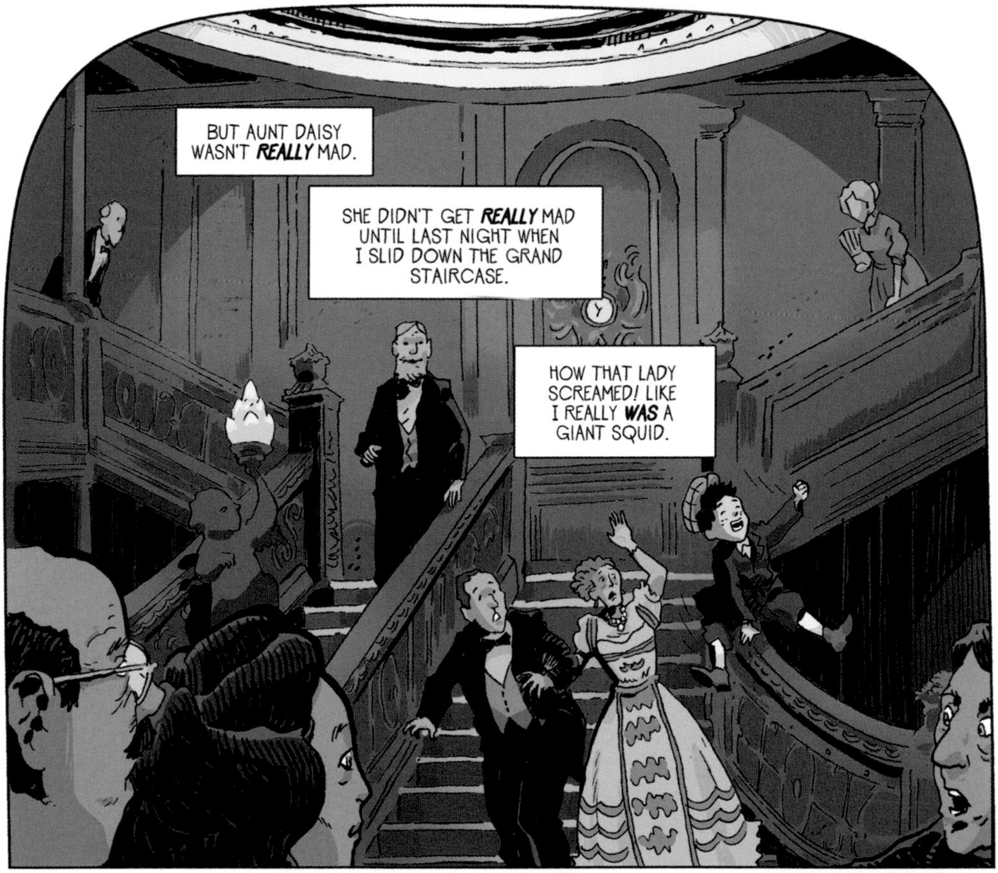
BUT AUNT DAISY WASN'T **REALLY** MAD.
SHE DIDN'T GET **REALLY** MAD UNTIL LAST NIGHT WHEN I SLID DOWN THE GRAND STAIRCASE.
HOW THAT LADY SCREAMED! LIKE I REALLY **WAS** A GIANT SQUID.

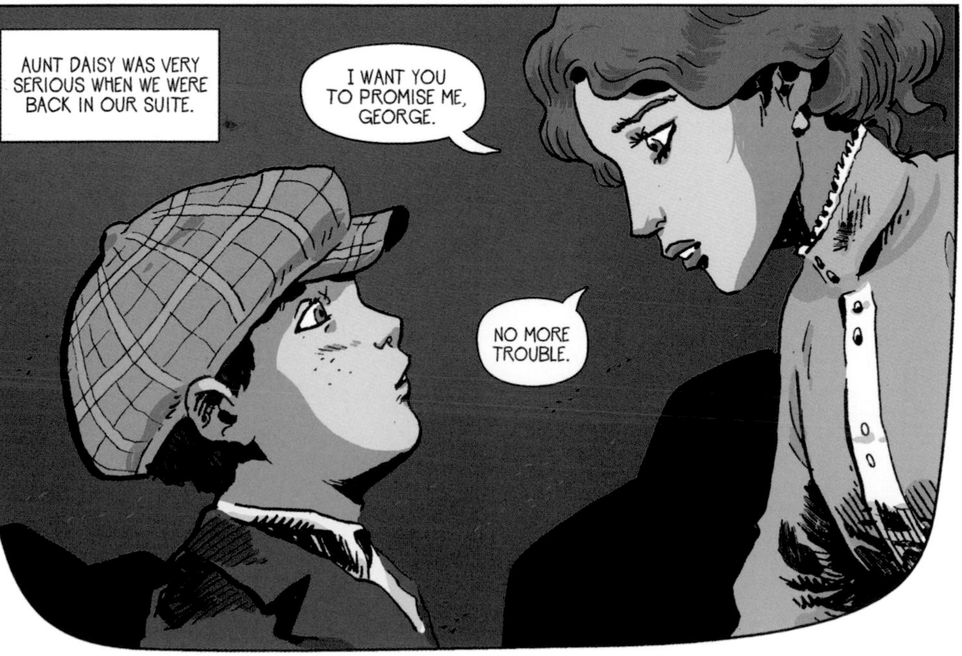
AUNT DAISY WAS VERY SERIOUS WHEN WE WERE BACK IN OUR SUITE.
I WANT YOU TO PROMISE ME, GEORGE.
NO MORE TROUBLE.

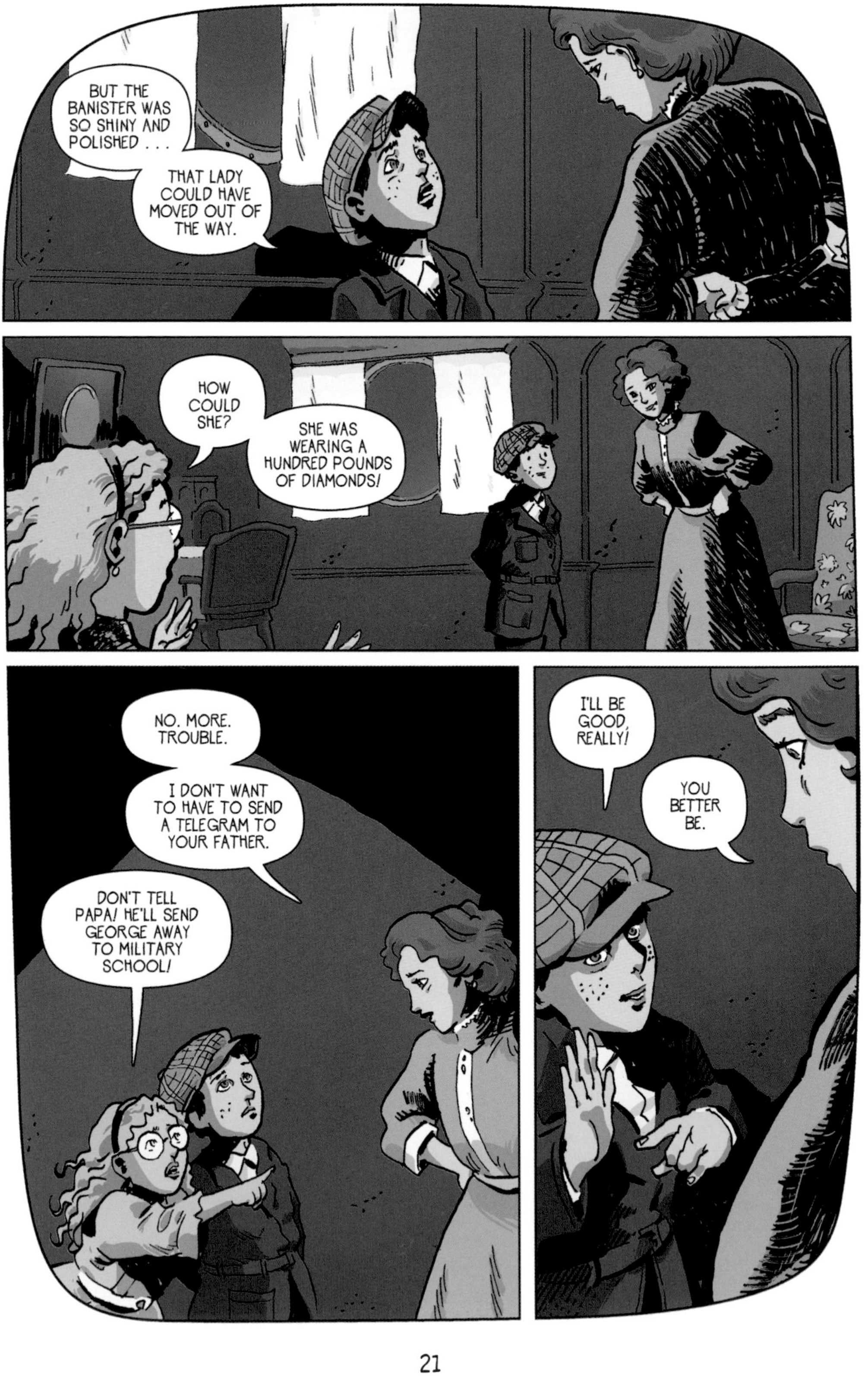
BUT THE BANISTER WAS SO SHINY AND POLISHED . . .
THAT LADY COULD HAVE MOVED OUT OF THE WAY.
HOW COULD SHE?
SHE WAS WEARING A HUNDRED POUNDS OF DIAMONDS!
NO. MORE. TROUBLE.
I DON'T WANT TO HAVE TO SEND A TELEGRAM TO YOUR FATHER.
DON'T TELL PAPA! HE'LL SEND GEORGE AWAY TO MILITARY SCHOOL!
I'LL BE GOOD, REALLY!
YOU BETTER BE.

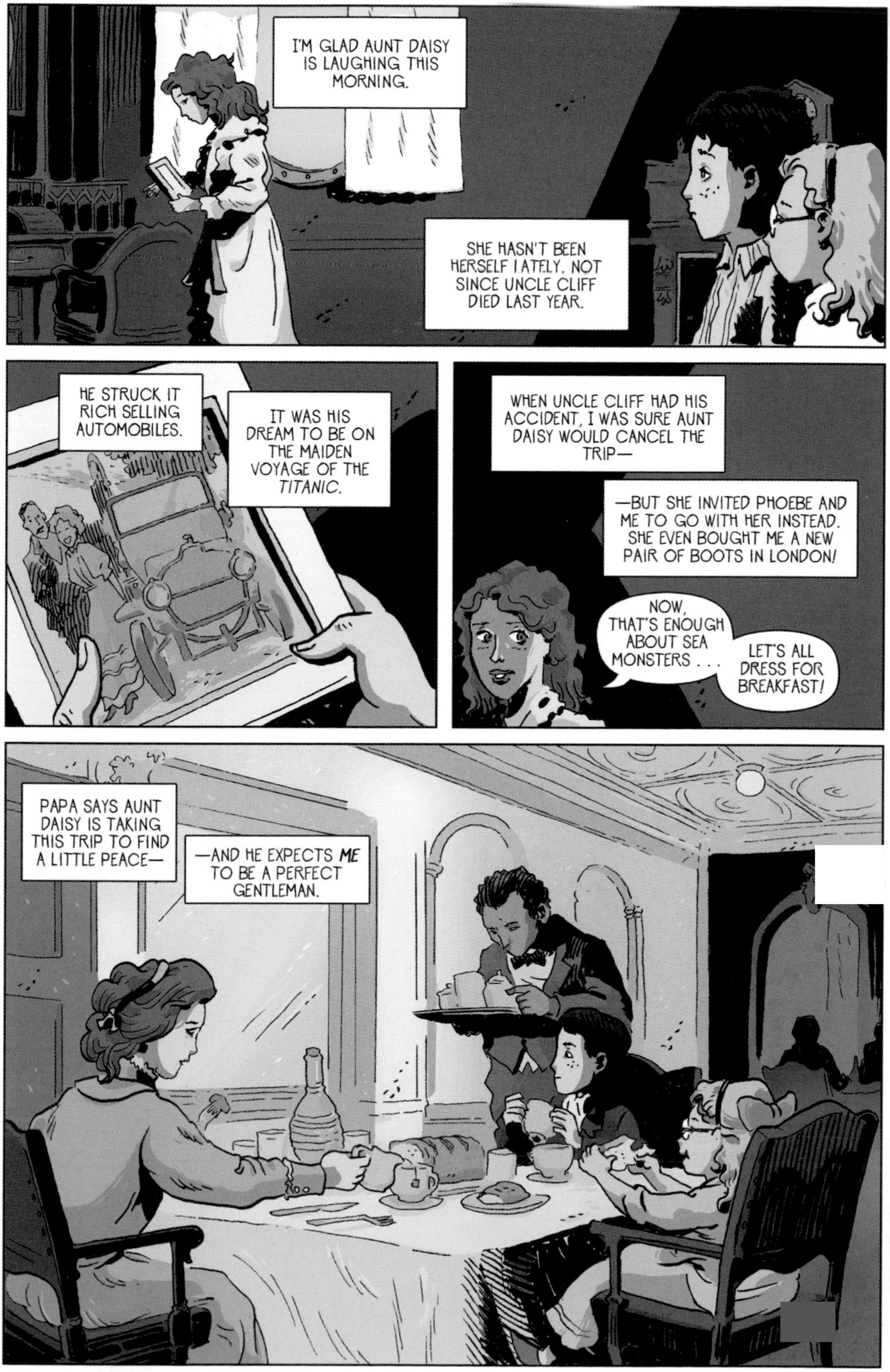
I'M GLAD AUNT DAISY IS LAUGHING THIS MORNING.
SHE HASN'T BEEN HERSELF LATELY. NOT SINCE UNCLE CLIFF DIED LAST YEAR.
HE STRUCK IT RICH SELLING AUTOMOBILES.
IT WAS HIS DREAM TO BE ON THE MAIDEN VOYAGE OF THE *TITANIC*.
WHEN UNCLE CLIFF HAD HIS ACCIDENT, I WAS SURE AUNT DAISY WOULD CANCEL THE TRIP—
—BUT SHE INVITED PHOEBE AND ME TO GO WITH HER INSTEAD. SHE EVEN BOUGHT ME A NEW PAIR OF BOOTS IN LONDON!
NOW, THAT'S ENOUGH ABOUT SEA MONSTERS . . .
LET'S ALL DRESS FOR BREAKFAST!
PAPA SAYS AUNT DAISY IS TAKING THIS TRIP TO FIND A LITTLE PEACE—
—AND HE EXPECTS ***ME*** TO BE A PERFECT GENTLEMAN.

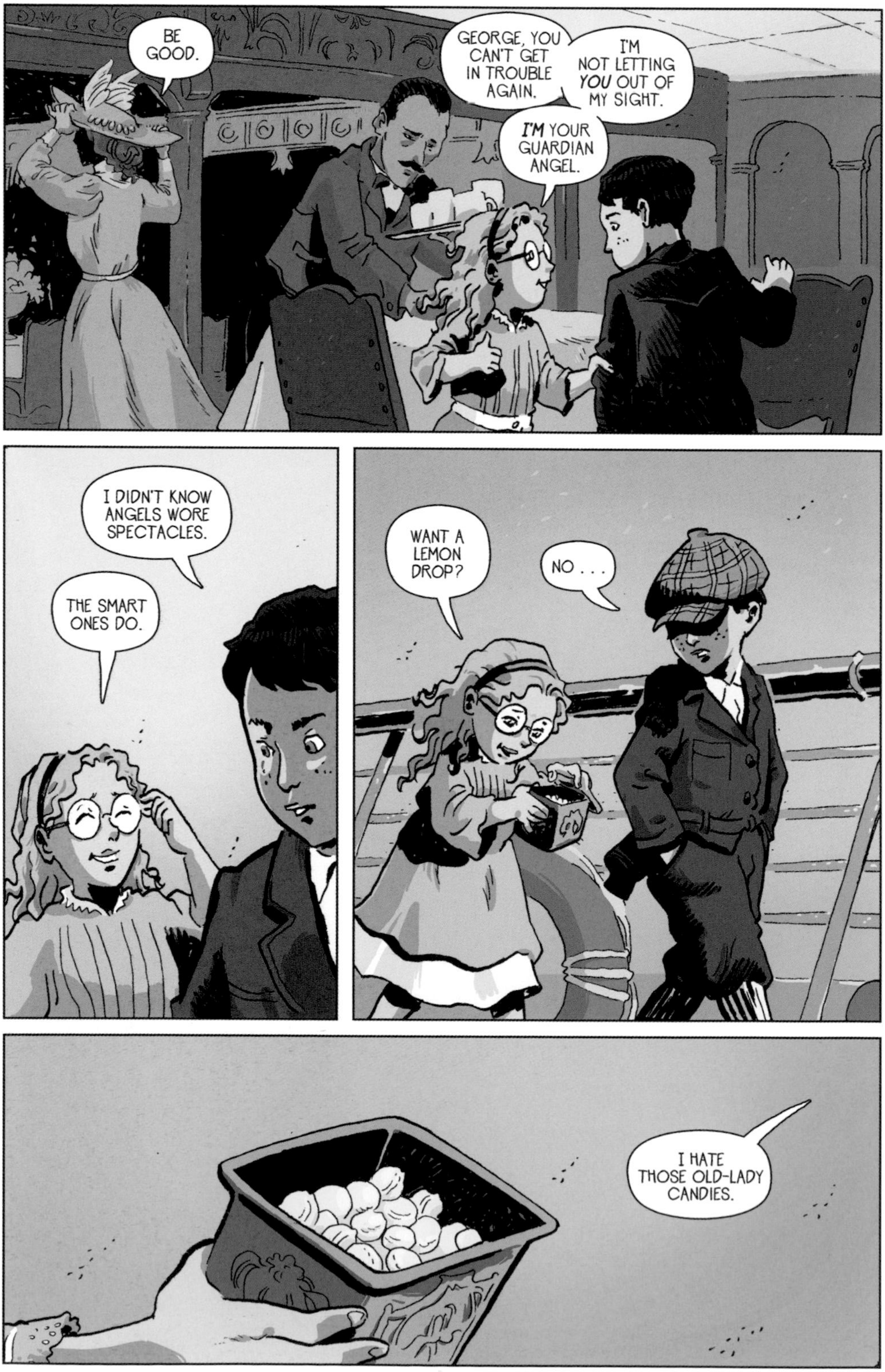
BE GOOD.
GEORGE, YOU CAN'T GET IN TROUBLE AGAIN.
I'M NOT LETTING *YOU* OUT OF MY SIGHT.
I'M YOUR GUARDIAN ANGEL.
I DIDN'T KNOW ANGELS WORE SPECTACLES.
THE SMART ONES DO.
WANT A LEMON DROP?
NO . . .
I HATE THOSE OLD-LADY CANDIES.

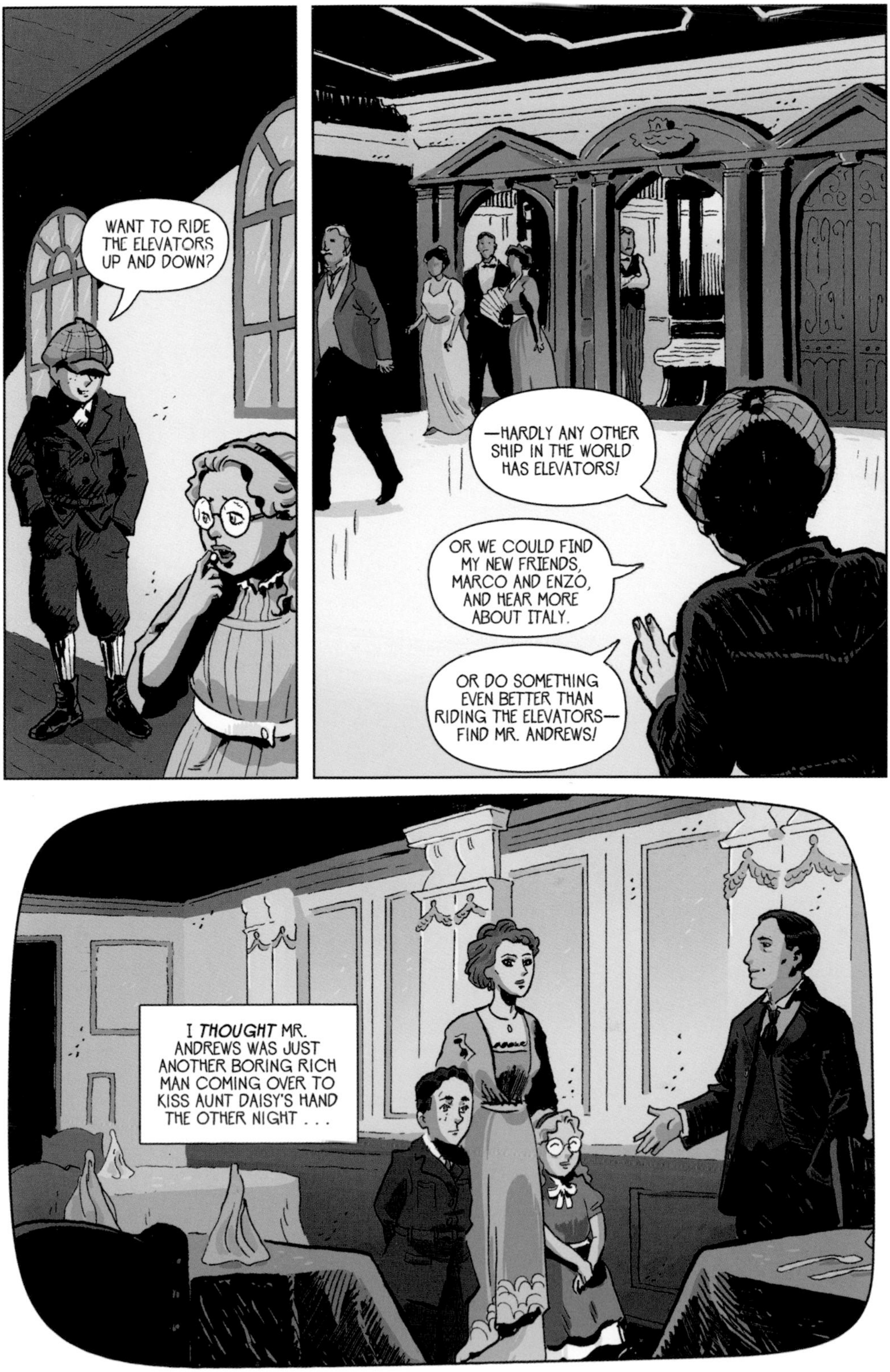
WANT TO RIDE THE ELEVATORS UP AND DOWN?
—HARDLY ANY OTHER SHIP IN THE WORLD HAS ELEVATORS!
OR WE COULD FIND MY NEW FRIENDS, MARCO AND ENZO, AND HEAR MORE ABOUT ITALY.
OR DO SOMETHING EVEN BETTER THAN RIDING THE ELEVATORS— FIND MR. ANDREWS!
I *THOUGHT* MR. ANDREWS WAS JUST ANOTHER BORING RICH MAN COMING OVER TO KISS AUNT DAISY'S HAND THE OTHER NIGHT . . .

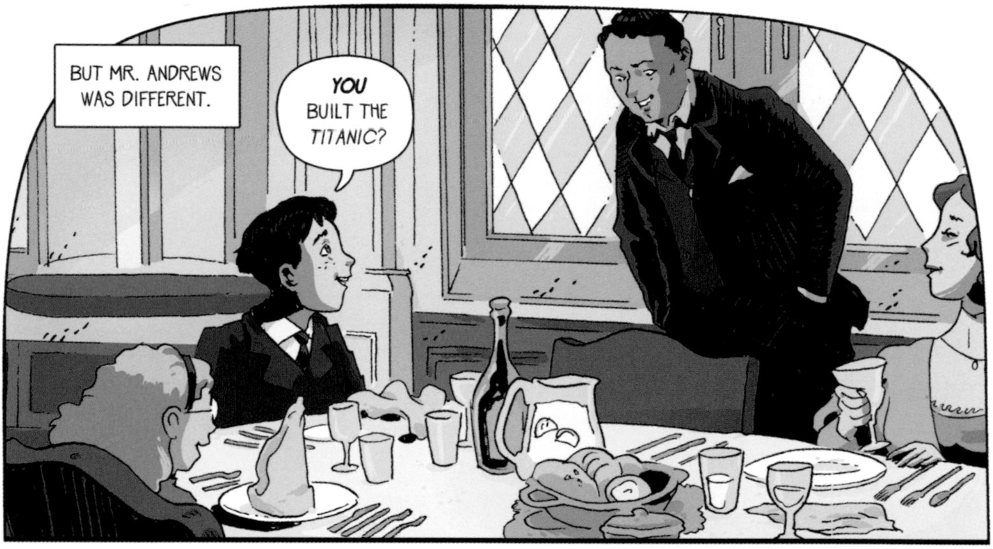
BUT MR. ANDREWS WAS DIFFERENT.
YOU BUILT THE *TITANIC?*

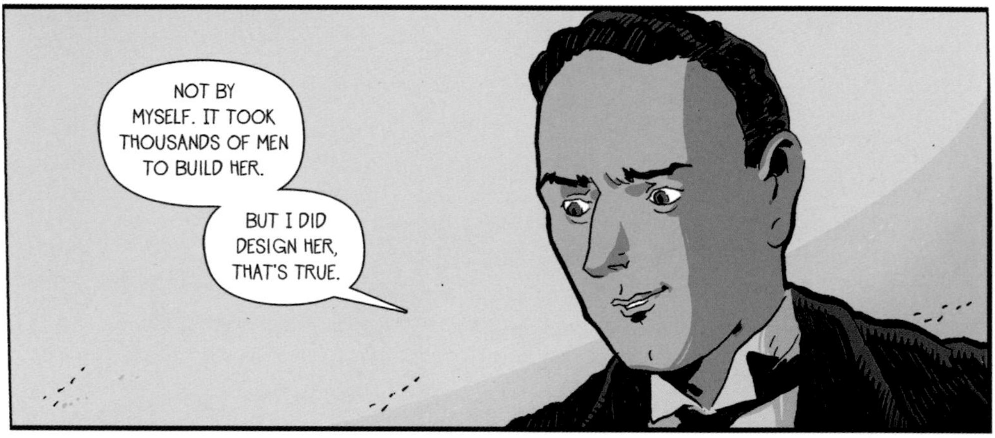
NOT BY MYSELF. IT TOOK THOUSANDS OF MEN TO BUILD HER.
BUT I DID DESIGN HER, THAT'S TRUE.

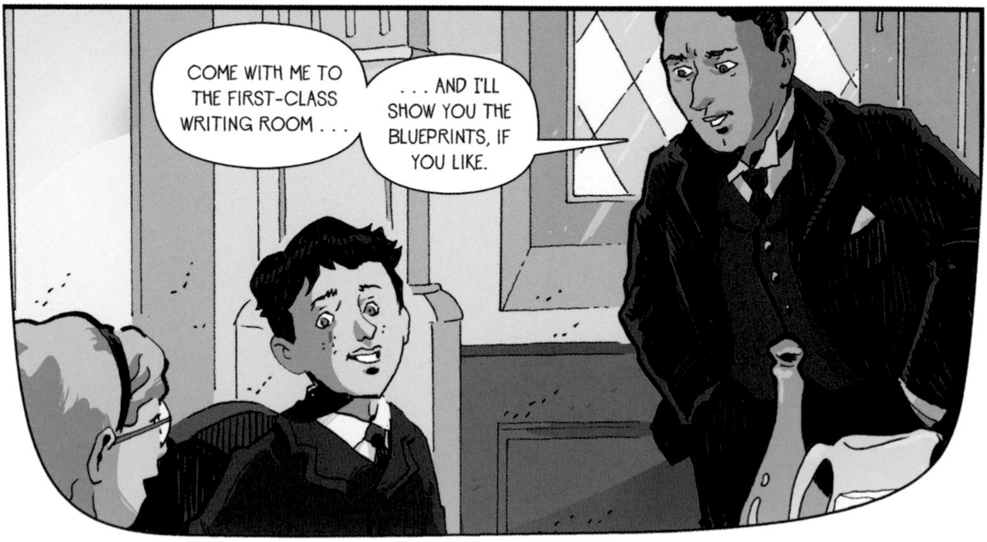
COME WITH ME TO THE FIRST-CLASS WRITING ROOM . . .
. . . AND I'LL SHOW YOU THE BLUEPRINTS, IF YOU LIKE.

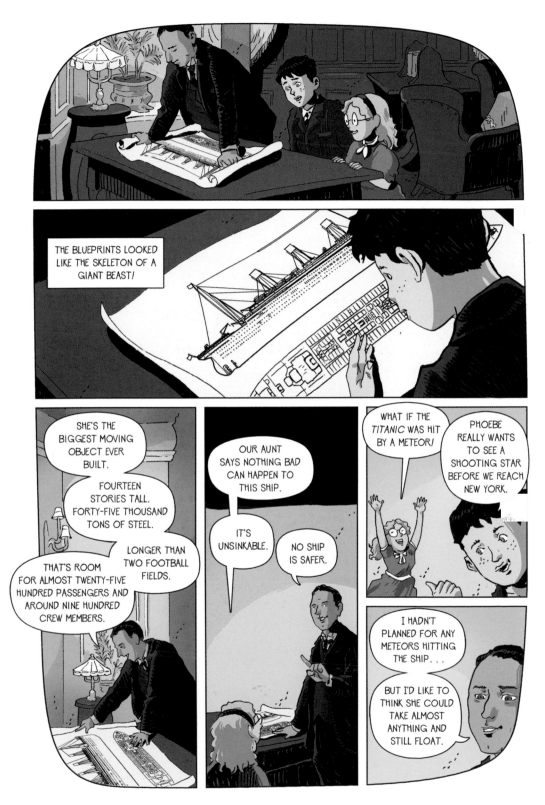

THE BLUEPRINTS LOOKED LIKE THE SKELETON OF A GIANT BEAST!

SHE'S THE BIGGEST MOVING OBJECT EVER BUILT.

FOURTEEN STORIES TALL. FORTY-FIVE THOUSAND TONS OF STEEL.

LONGER THAN TWO FOOTBALL FIELDS.

THAT'S ROOM FOR ALMOST TWENTY-FIVE HUNDRED PASSENGERS AND AROUND NINE HUNDRED CREW MEMBERS.

OUR AUNT SAYS NOTHING BAD CAN HAPPEN TO THIS SHIP.

IT'S UNSINKABLE.

NO SHIP IS SAFER.

WHAT IF THE *TITANIC* WAS HIT BY A METEOR!

PHOEBE REALLY WANTS TO SEE A SHOOTING STAR BEFORE WE REACH NEW YORK.

I HADN'T PLANNED FOR ANY METEORS HITTING THE SHIP. . .

BUT I'D LIKE TO THINK SHE COULD TAKE ALMOST ANYTHING AND STILL FLOAT.

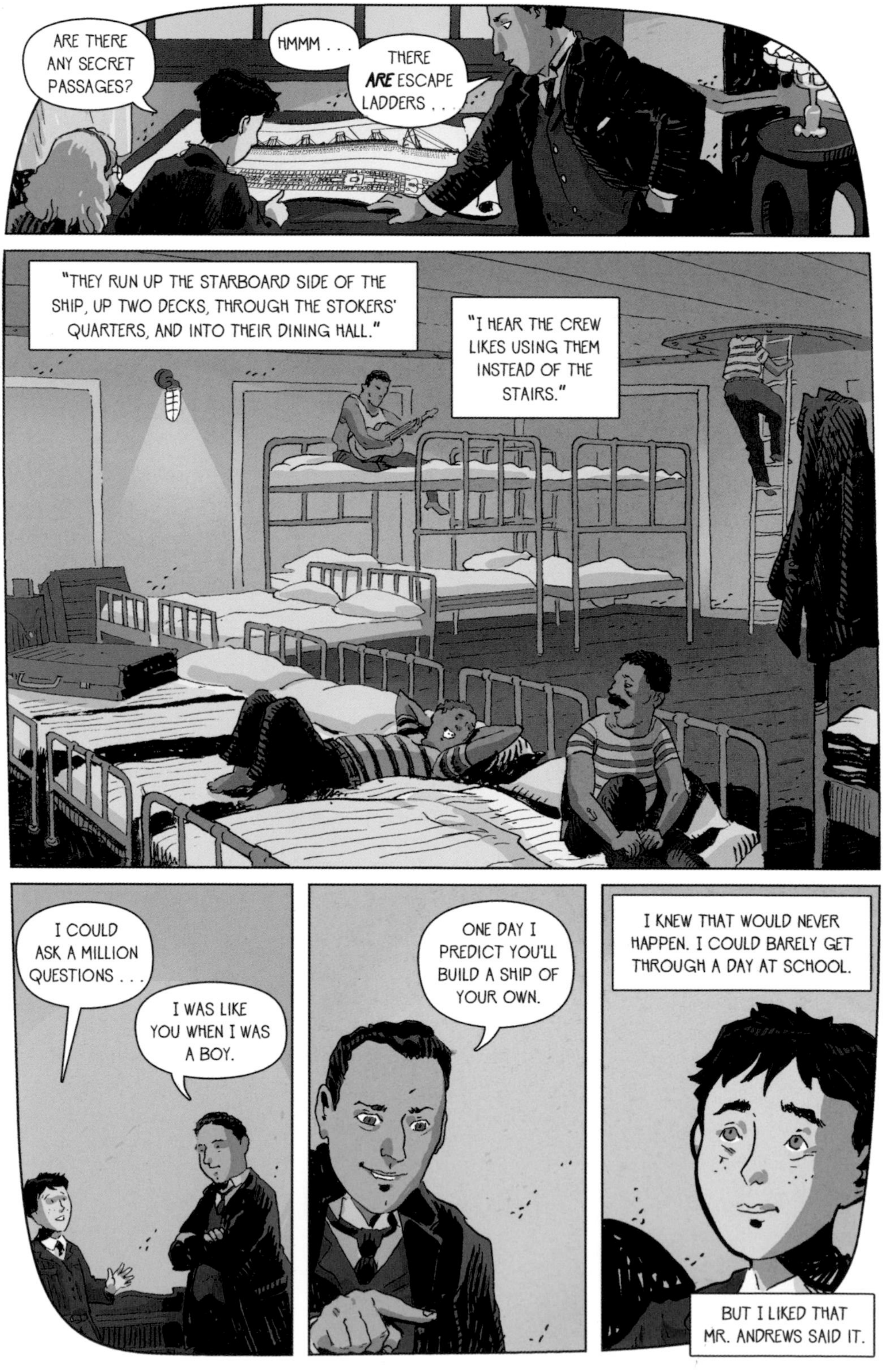
ARE THERE ANY SECRET PASSAGES?
HMMM . . .
THERE **ARE** ESCAPE LADDERS . . .
"THEY RUN UP THE STARBOARD SIDE OF THE SHIP, UP TWO DECKS, THROUGH THE STOKERS' QUARTERS, AND INTO THEIR DINING HALL."
"I HEAR THE CREW LIKES USING THEM INSTEAD OF THE STAIRS."
I COULD ASK A MILLION QUESTIONS . . .
I WAS LIKE YOU WHEN I WAS A BOY.
ONE DAY I PREDICT YOU'LL BUILD A SHIP OF YOUR OWN.
I KNEW THAT WOULD NEVER HAPPEN. I COULD BARELY GET THROUGH A DAY AT SCHOOL.
BUT I LIKED THAT MR. ANDREWS SAID IT.

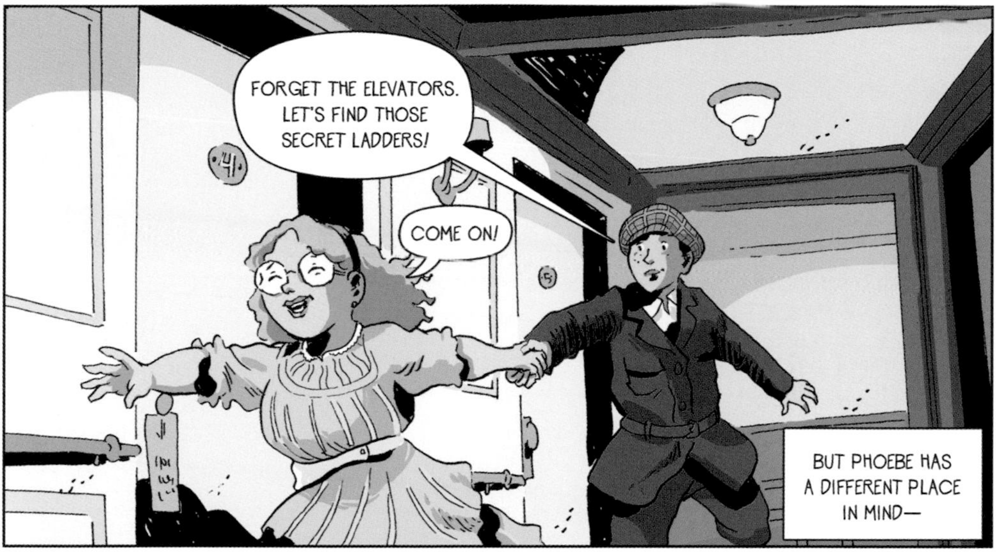
FORGET THE ELEVATORS. LET'S FIND THOSE SECRET LADDERS!
COME ON!
BUT PHOEBE HAS A DIFFERENT PLACE IN MIND—

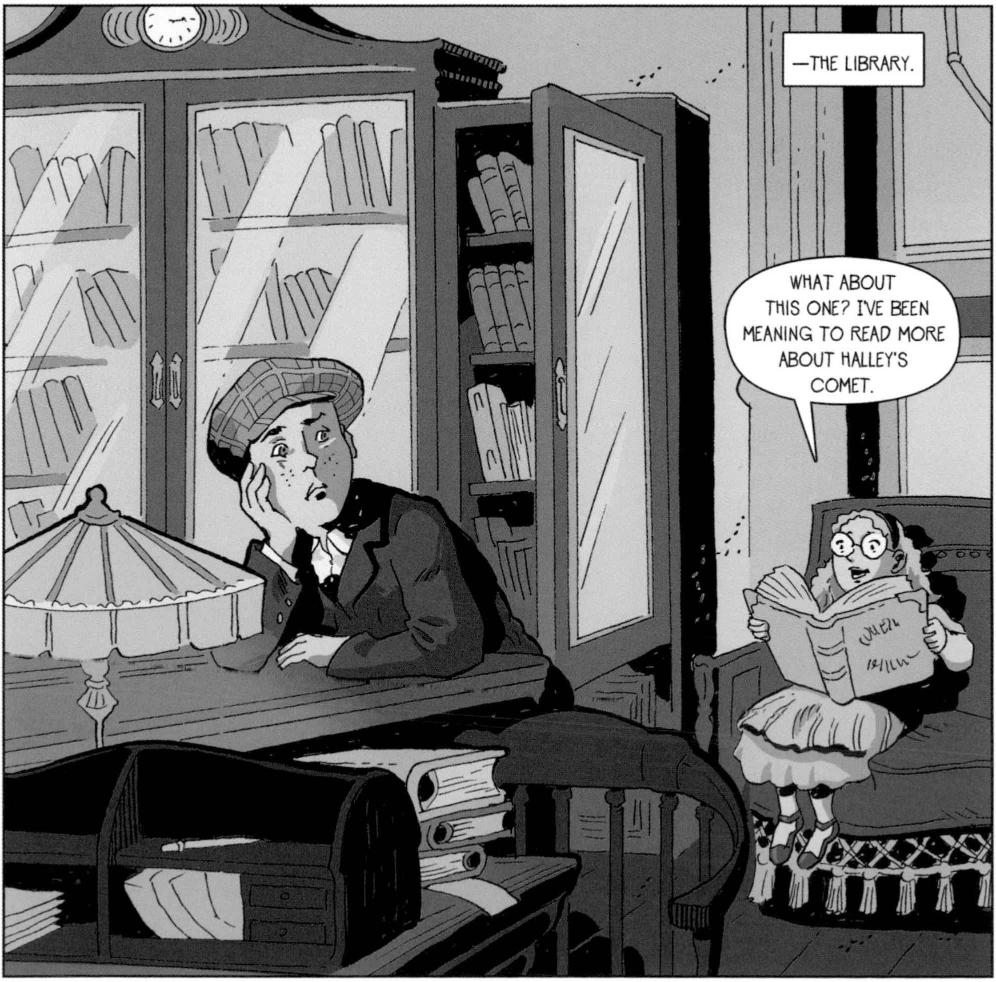
—THE LIBRARY.
WHAT ABOUT THIS ONE? I'VE BEEN MEANING TO READ MORE ABOUT HALLEY'S COMET.

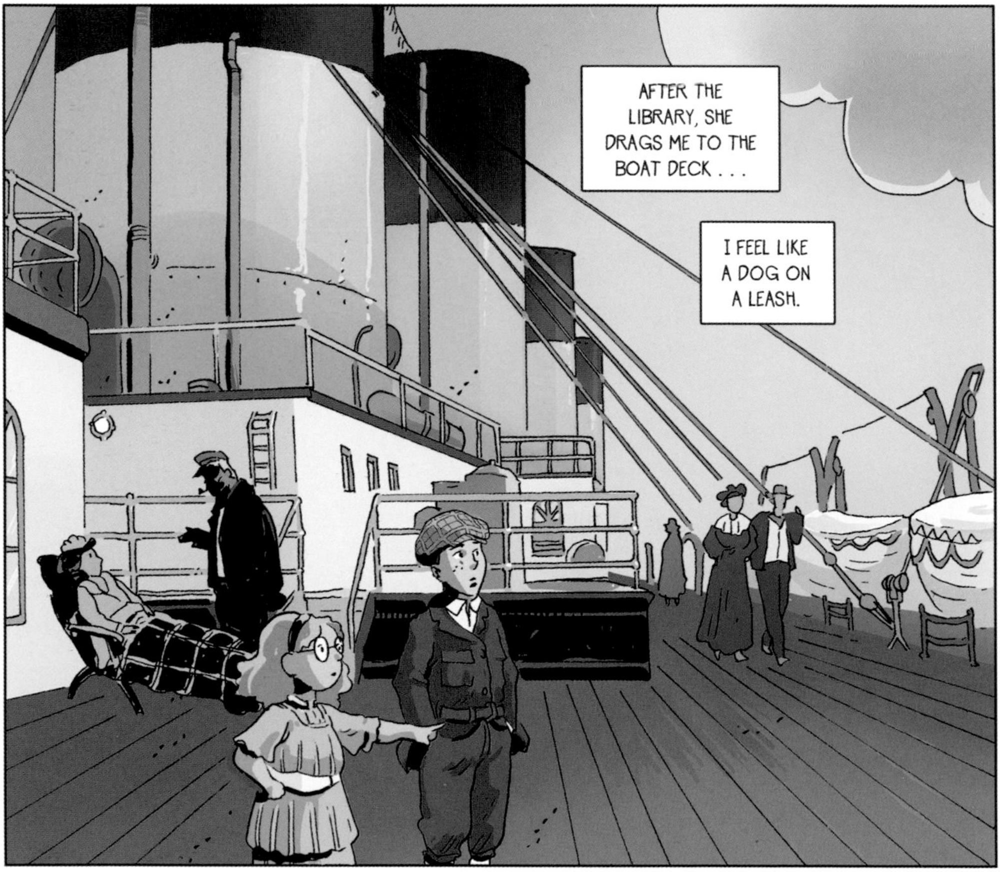
AFTER THE LIBRARY, SHE DRAGS ME TO THE BOAT DECK . . .
I FEEL LIKE A DOG ON A LEASH.

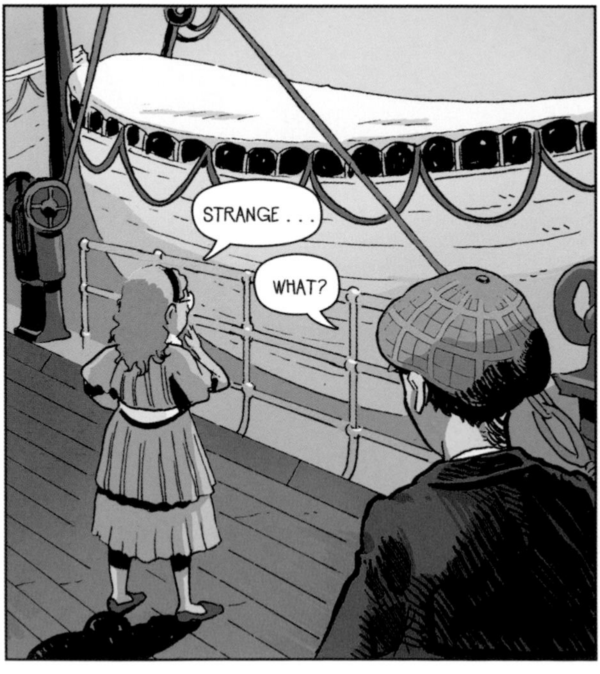
STRANGE . . .
WHAT?

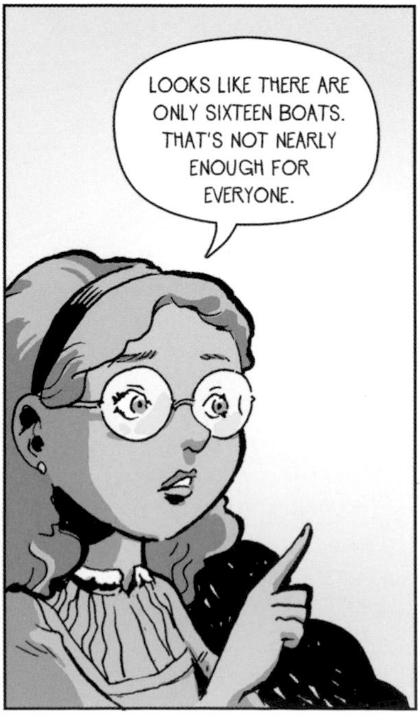
LOOKS LIKE THERE ARE ONLY SIXTEEN BOATS. THAT'S NOT NEARLY ENOUGH FOR EVERYONE.

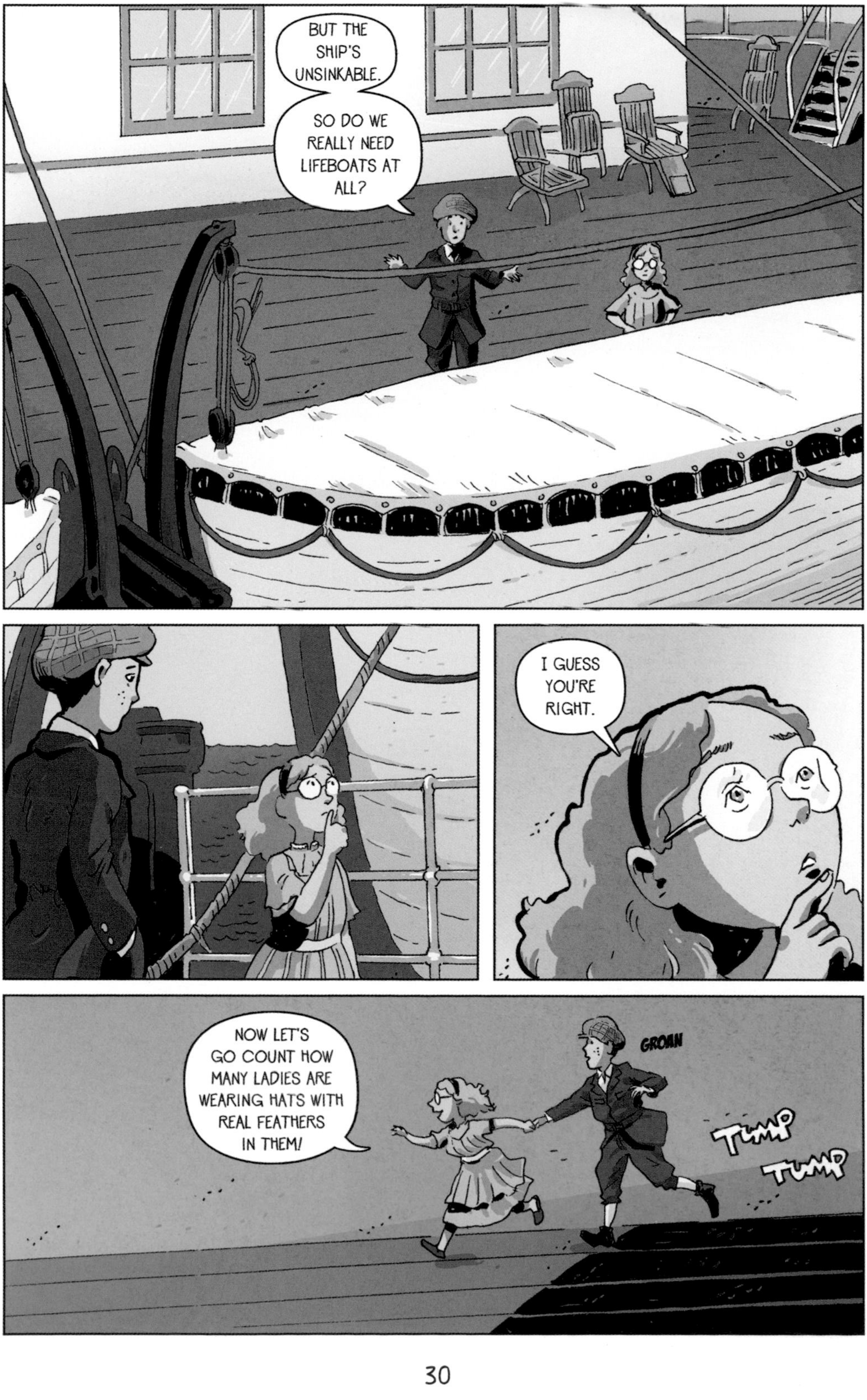
BUT THE SHIP'S UNSINKABLE.
SO DO WE REALLY NEED LIFEBOATS AT ALL?
I GUESS YOU'RE RIGHT.
NOW LET'S GO COUNT HOW MANY LADIES ARE WEARING HATS WITH REAL FEATHERS IN THEM!
GROAN
TUMP
TUMP

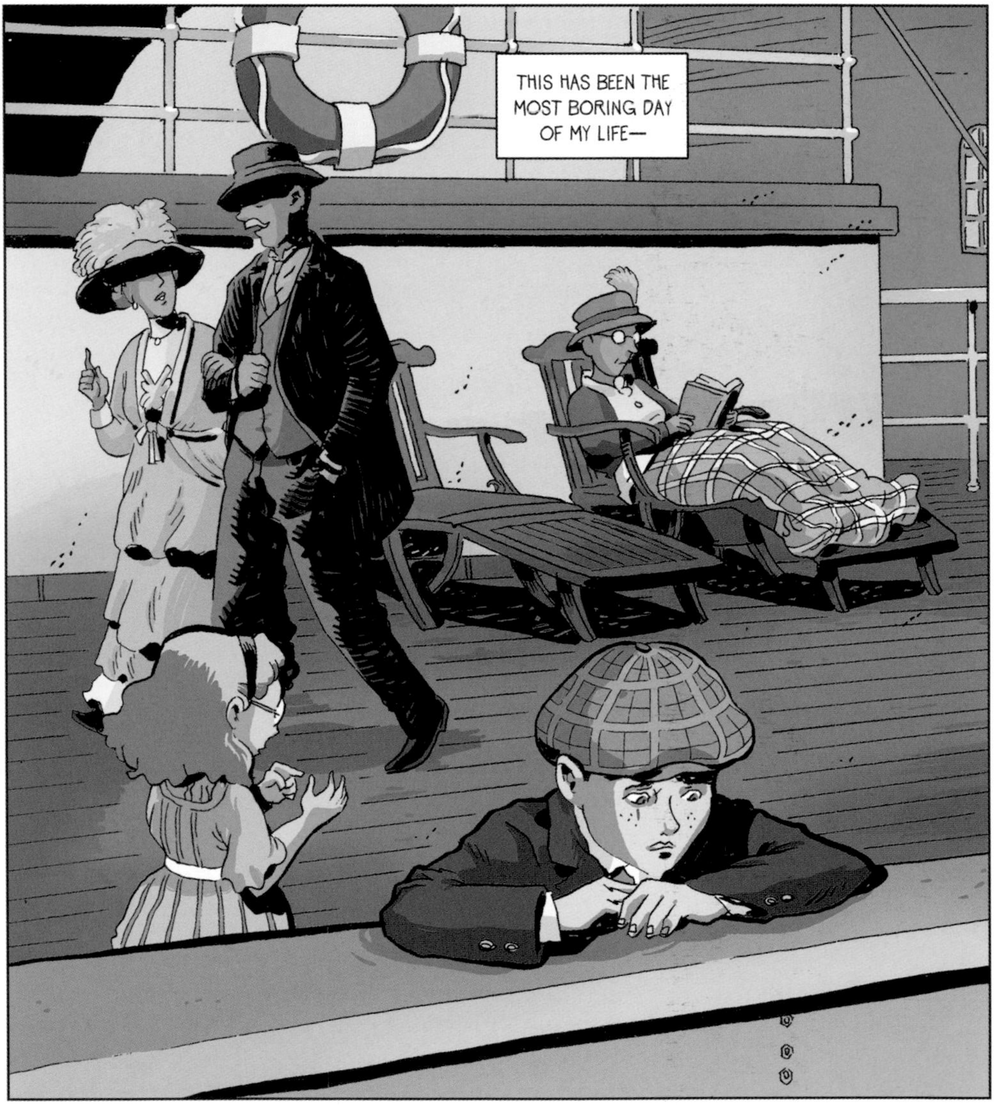
THIS HAS BEEN THE MOST BORING DAY OF MY LIFE—
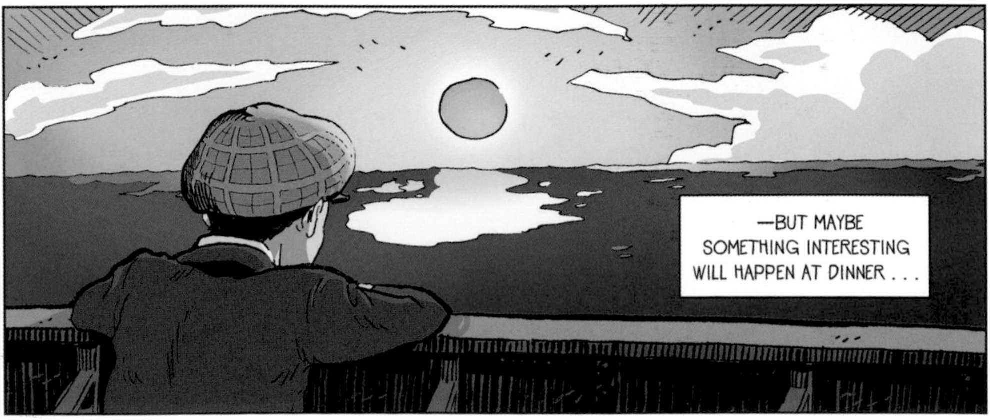
—BUT MAYBE SOMETHING INTERESTING WILL HAPPEN AT DINNER . . .

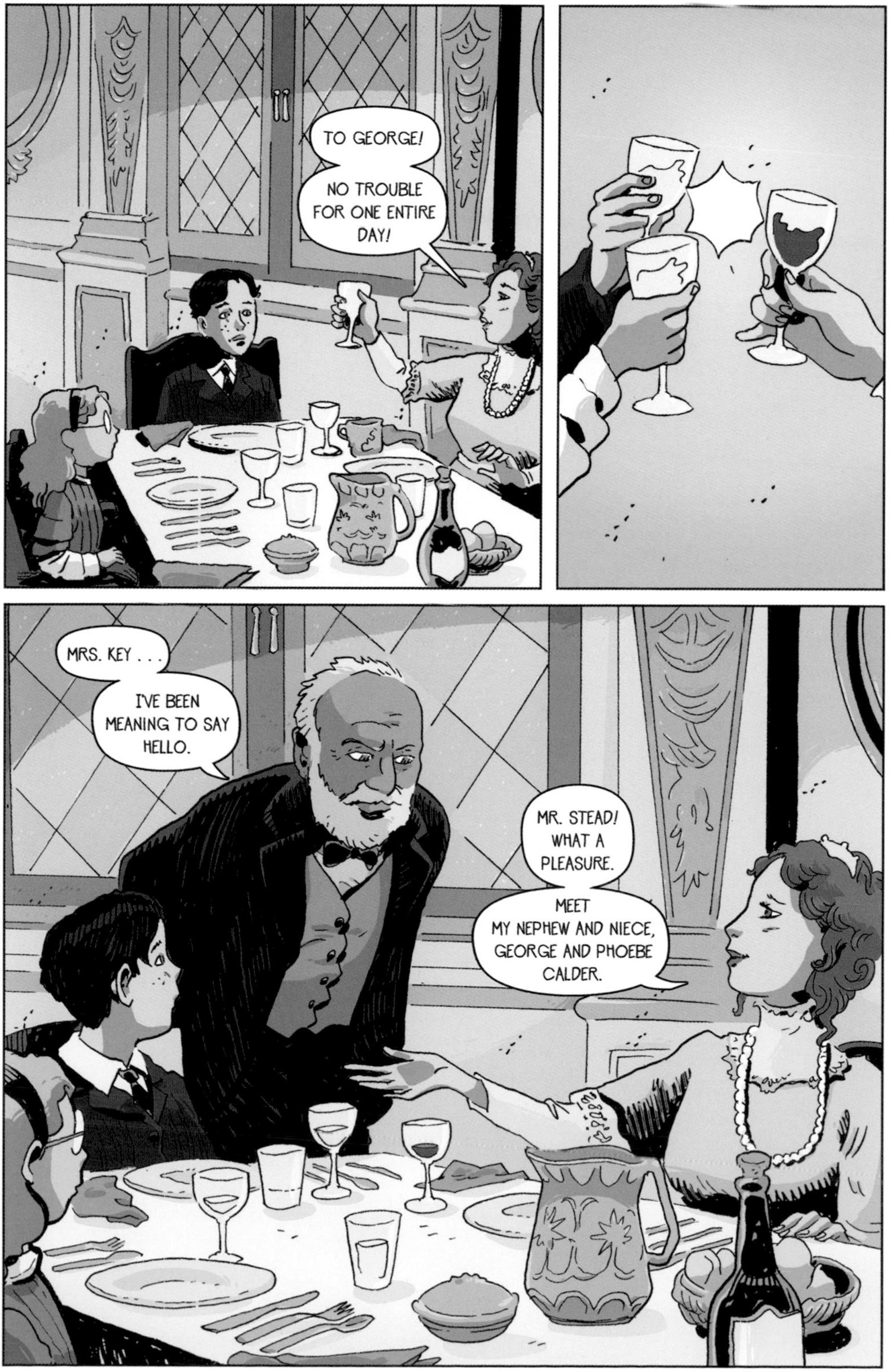
TO GEORGE!
NO TROUBLE FOR ONE ENTIRE DAY!
MRS. KEY . . .
I'VE BEEN MEANING TO SAY HELLO.
MR. STEAD! WHAT A PLEASURE.
MEET MY NEPHEW AND NIECE, GEORGE AND PHOEBE CALDER.

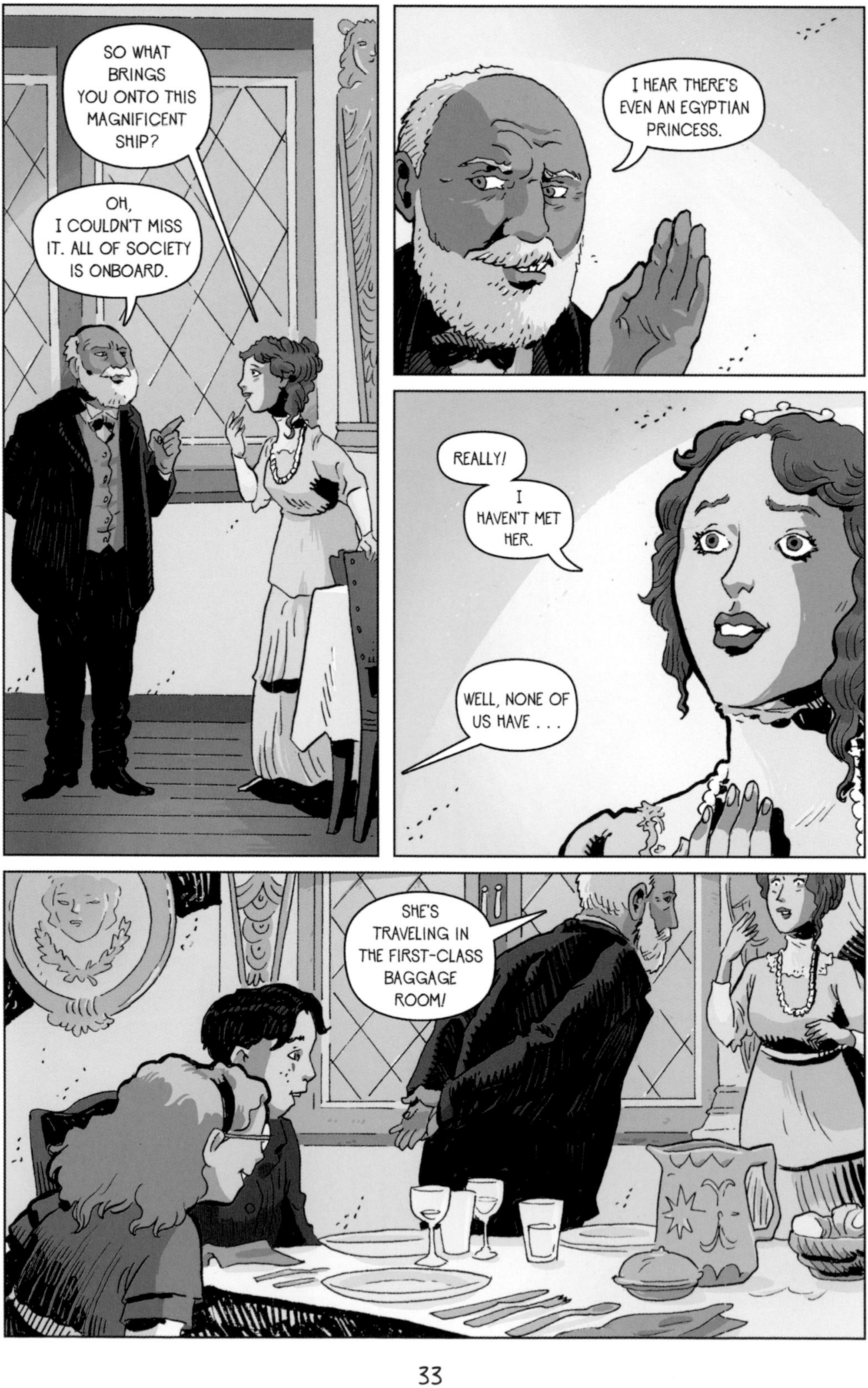
SO WHAT BRINGS YOU ONTO THIS MAGNIFICENT SHIP?
OH, I COULDN'T MISS IT. ALL OF SOCIETY IS ONBOARD.
I HEAR THERE'S EVEN AN EGYPTIAN PRINCESS.
REALLY!
I HAVEN'T MET HER.
WELL, NONE OF US HAVE . . .
SHE'S TRAVELING IN THE FIRST-CLASS BAGGAGE ROOM!

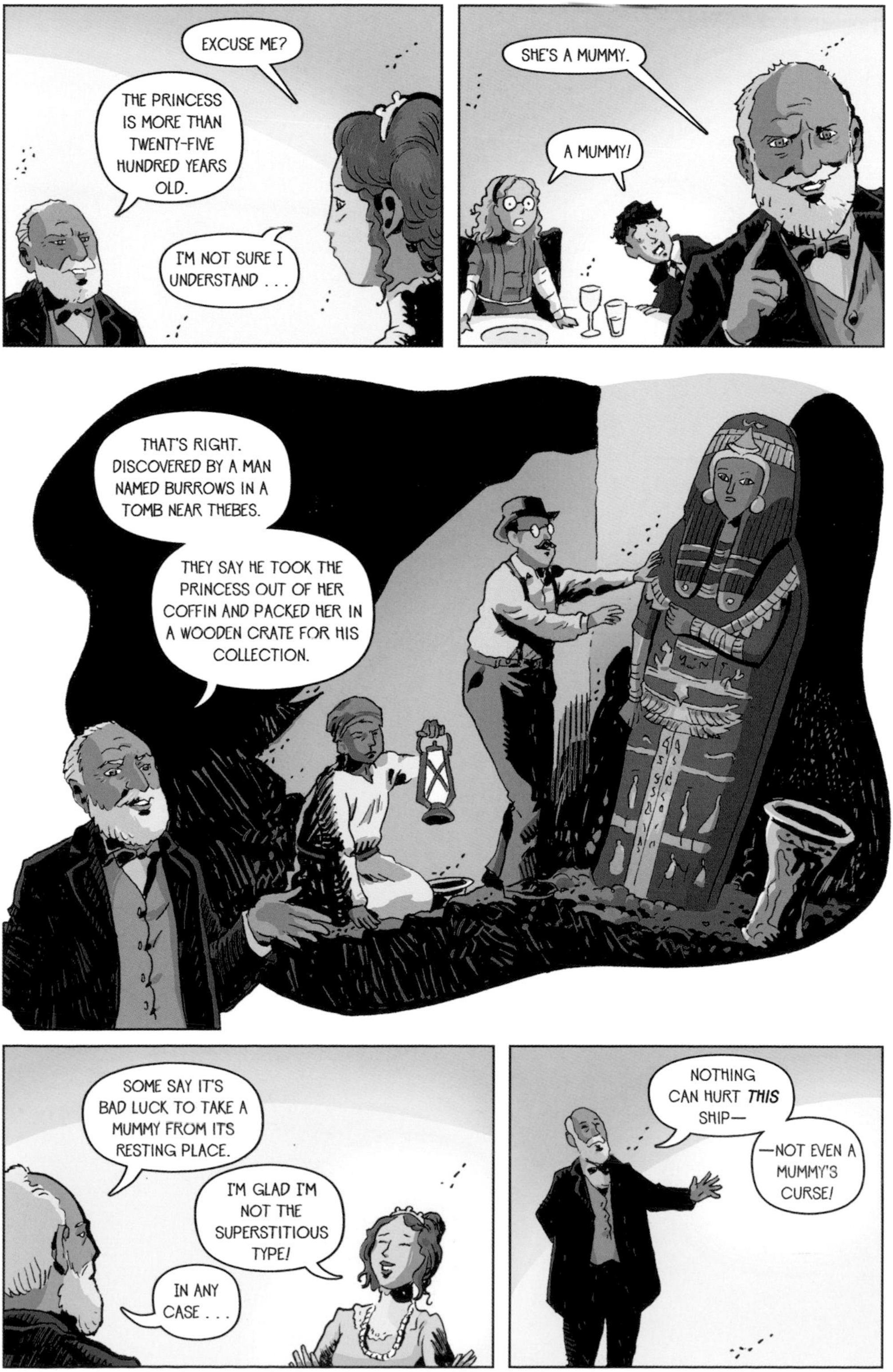
EXCUSE ME?
THE PRINCESS IS MORE THAN TWENTY-FIVE HUNDRED YEARS OLD.
I'M NOT SURE I UNDERSTAND . . .
SHE'S A MUMMY.
A MUMMY!
THAT'S RIGHT. DISCOVERED BY A MAN NAMED BURROWS IN A TOMB NEAR THEBES.
THEY SAY HE TOOK THE PRINCESS OUT OF HER COFFIN AND PACKED HER IN A WOODEN CRATE FOR HIS COLLECTION.
SOME SAY IT'S BAD LUCK TO TAKE A MUMMY FROM ITS RESTING PLACE.
I'M GLAD I'M NOT THE SUPERSTITIOUS TYPE!
IN ANY CASE . . .
NOTHING CAN HURT **THIS** SHIP—
—NOT EVEN A MUMMY'S CURSE!

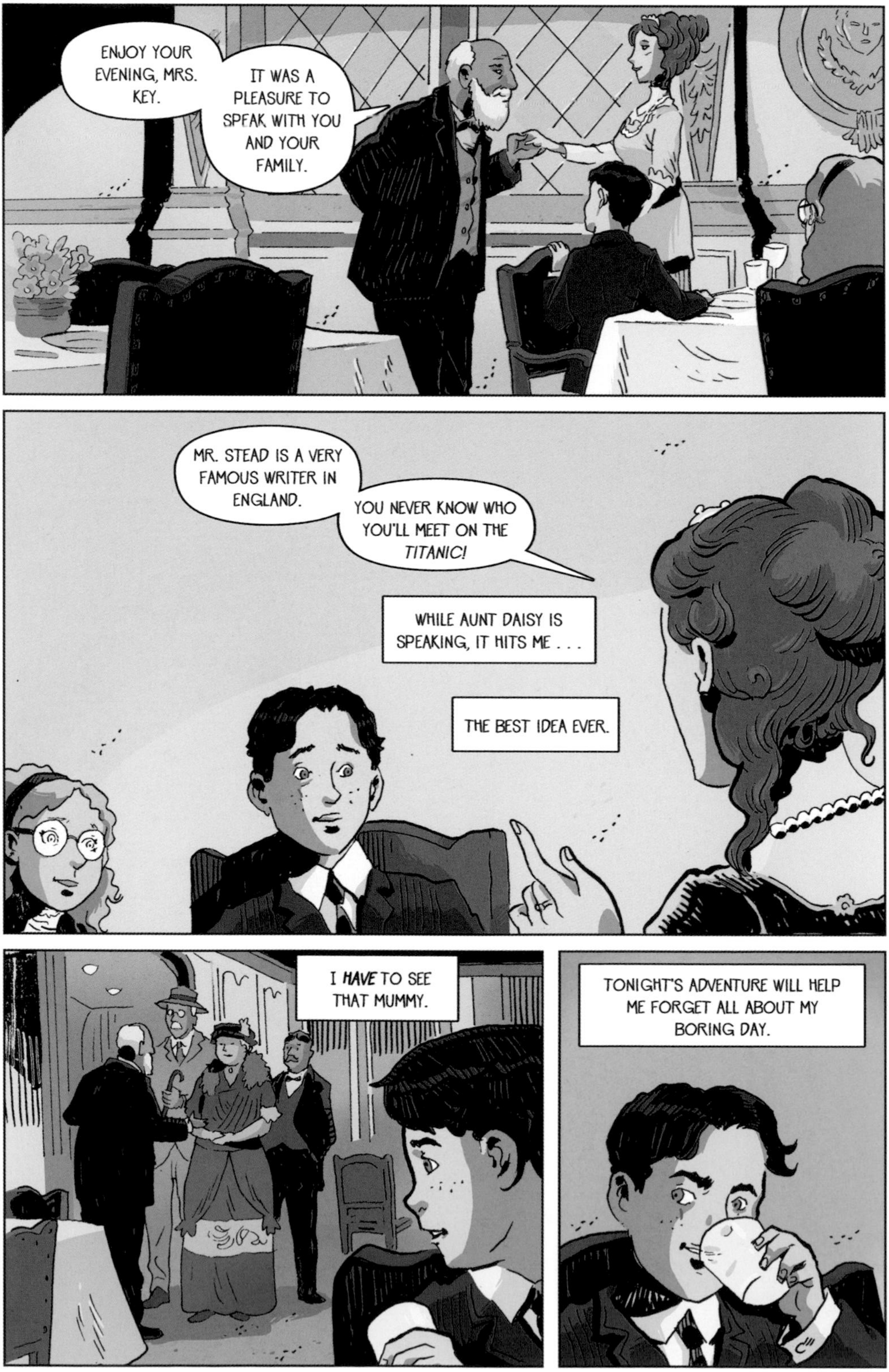
ENJOY YOUR EVENING, MRS. KEY.
IT WAS A PLEASURE TO SPEAK WITH YOU AND YOUR FAMILY.
MR. STEAD IS A VERY FAMOUS WRITER IN ENGLAND.
YOU NEVER KNOW WHO YOU'LL MEET ON THE *TITANIC!*
WHILE AUNT DAISY IS SPEAKING, IT HITS ME . . .
THE BEST IDEA EVER.
I ***HAVE*** TO SEE THAT MUMMY.
TONIGHT'S ADVENTURE WILL HELP ME FORGET ALL ABOUT MY BORING DAY.

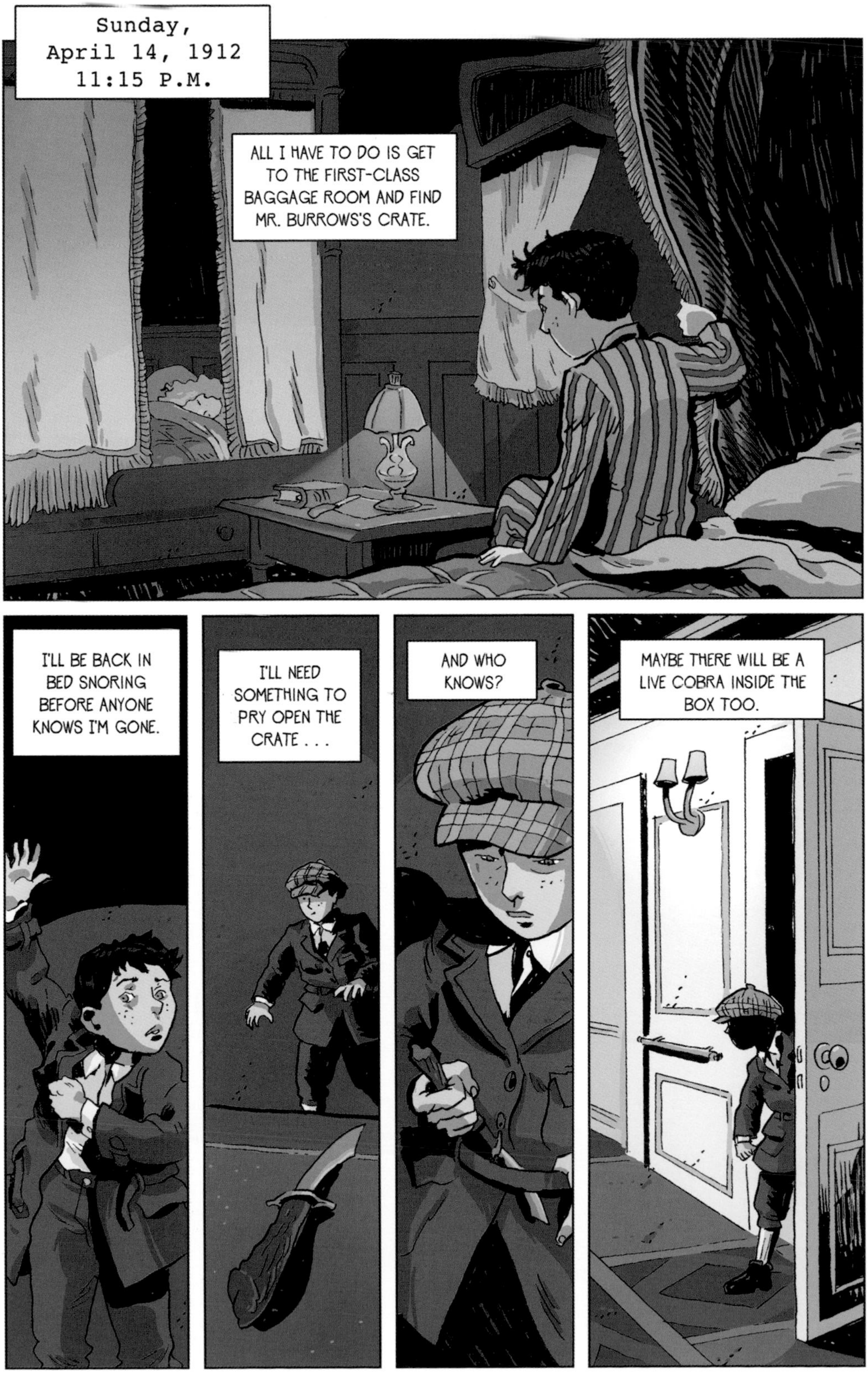
Sunday, April 14, 1912 11:15 P.M.
ALL I HAVE TO DO IS GET TO THE FIRST-CLASS BAGGAGE ROOM AND FIND MR. BURROWS'S CRATE.
I'LL BE BACK IN BED SNORING BEFORE ANYONE KNOWS I'M GONE.
I'LL NEED SOMETHING TO PRY OPEN THE CRATE . . .
AND WHO KNOWS?
MAYBE THERE WILL BE A LIVE COBRA INSIDE THE BOX TOO.

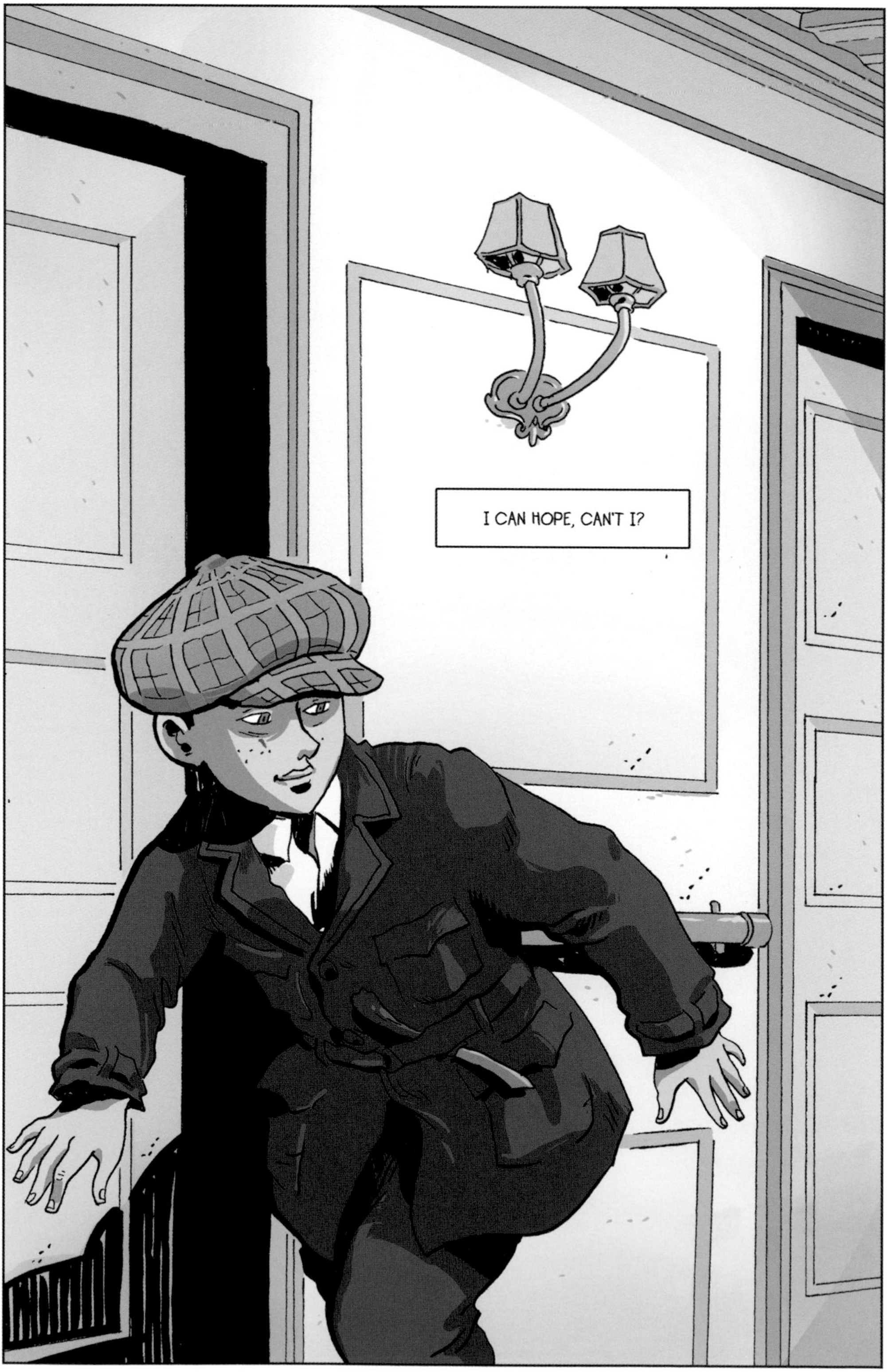
I CAN HOPE, CAN'T I?

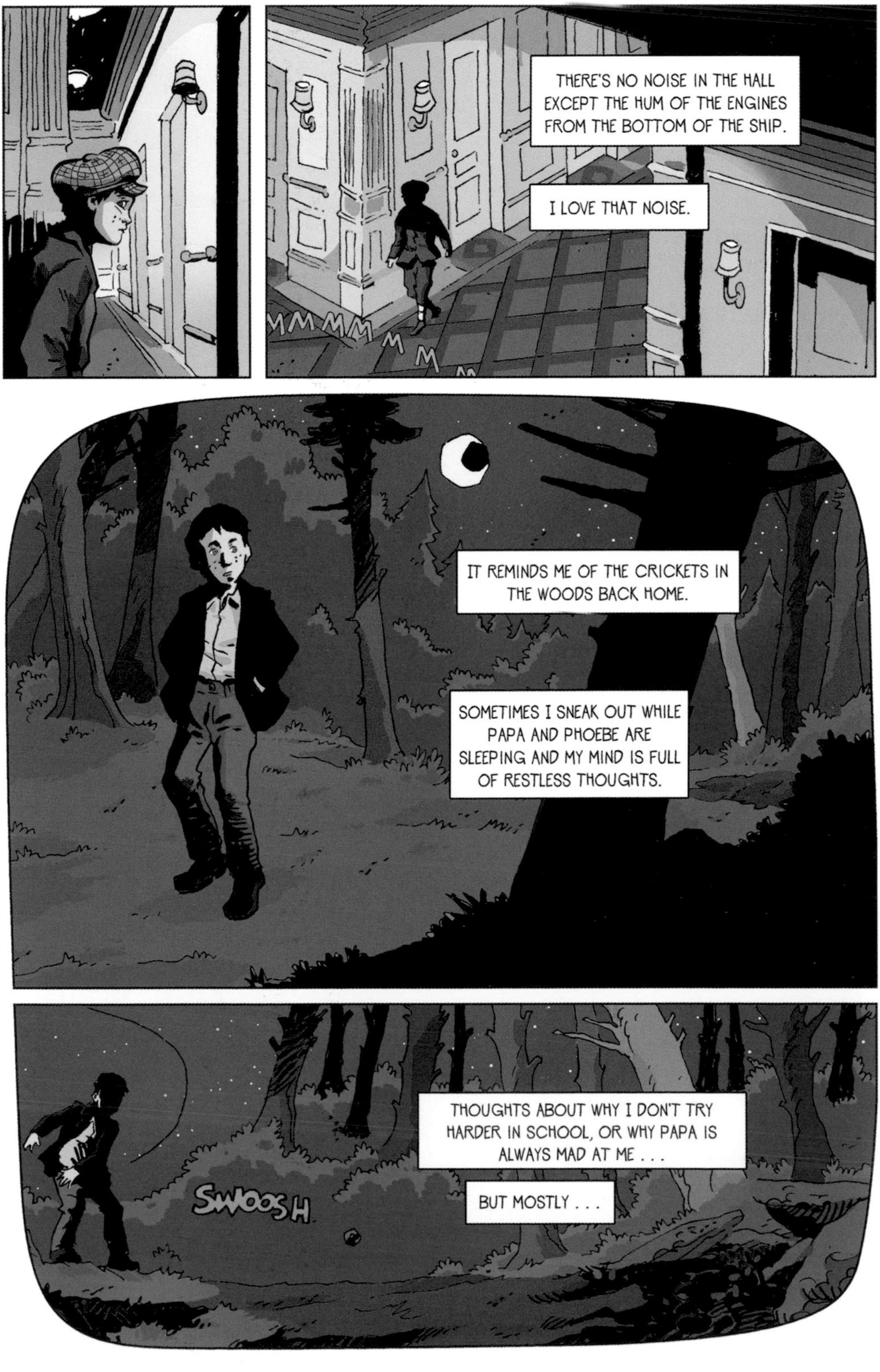
THERE'S NO NOISE IN THE HALL EXCEPT THE HUM OF THE ENGINES FROM THE BOTTOM OF THE SHIP.
I LOVE THAT NOISE.
MMMMM
M M
IT REMINDS ME OF THE CRICKETS IN THE WOODS BACK HOME.
SOMETIMES I SNEAK OUT WHILE PAPA AND PHOEBE ARE SLEEPING AND MY MIND IS FULL OF RESTLESS THOUGHTS.
THOUGHTS ABOUT WHY I DON'T TRY HARDER IN SCHOOL, OR WHY PAPA IS ALWAYS MAD AT ME . . .
BUT MOSTLY . . .
SWOOSH

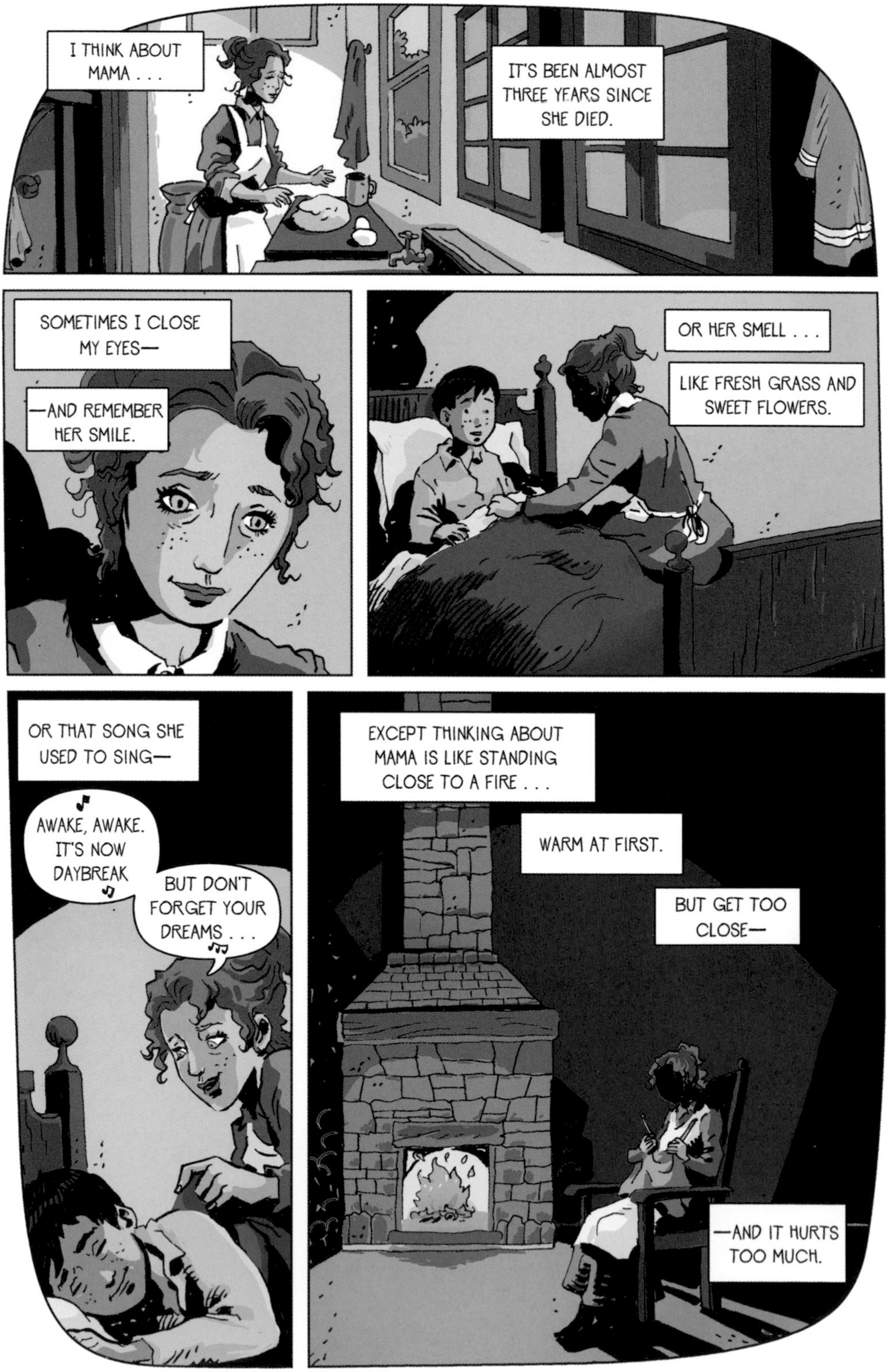
I THINK ABOUT MAMA . . .
IT'S BEEN ALMOST THREE YEARS SINCE SHE DIED.
SOMETIMES I CLOSE MY EYES—
—AND REMEMBER HER SMILE.
OR HER SMELL . . .
LIKE FRESH GRASS AND SWEET FLOWERS.
OR THAT SONG SHE USED TO SING—
AWAKE, AWAKE. IT'S NOW DAYBREAK
BUT DON'T FORGET YOUR DREAMS . . .
EXCEPT THINKING ABOUT MAMA IS LIKE STANDING CLOSE TO A FIRE . . .
WARM AT FIRST.
BUT GET TOO CLOSE—
—AND IT HURTS TOO MUCH.

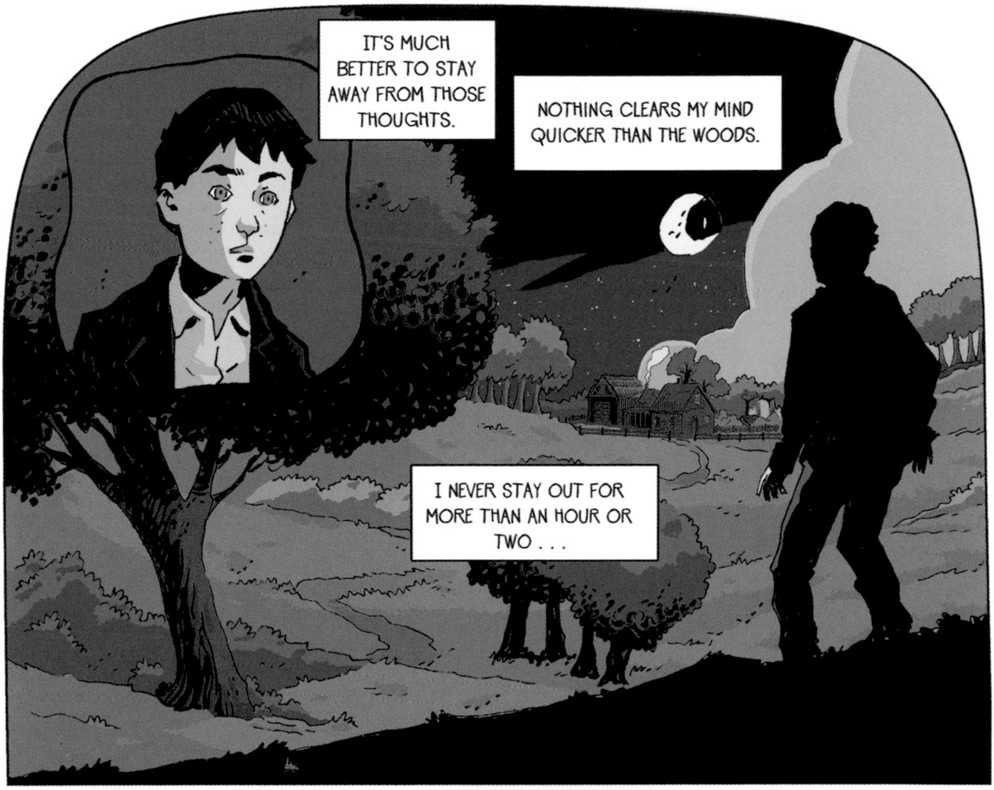
IT'S MUCH BETTER TO STAY AWAY FROM THOSE THOUGHTS.
NOTHING CLEARS MY MIND QUICKER THAN THE WOODS.
I NEVER STAY OUT FOR MORE THAN AN HOUR OR TWO . . .

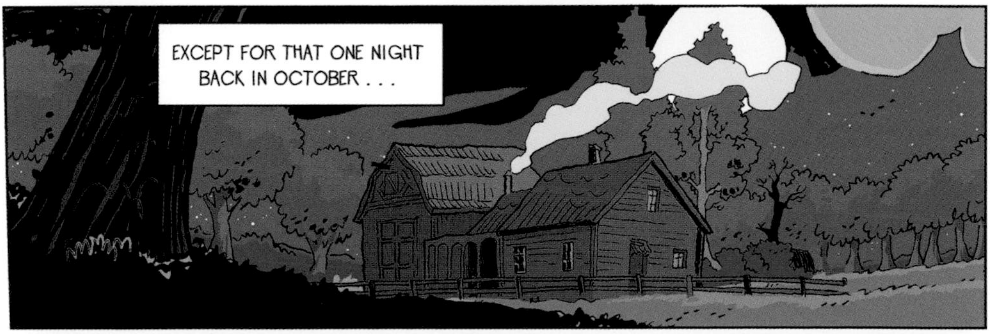
EXCEPT FOR THAT ONE NIGHT BACK IN OCTOBER . . .

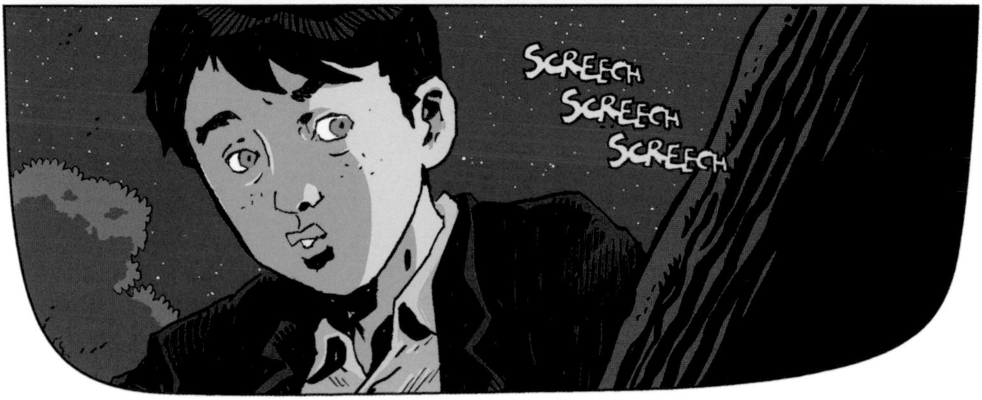
SCREECH
SCREECH
SCREECH

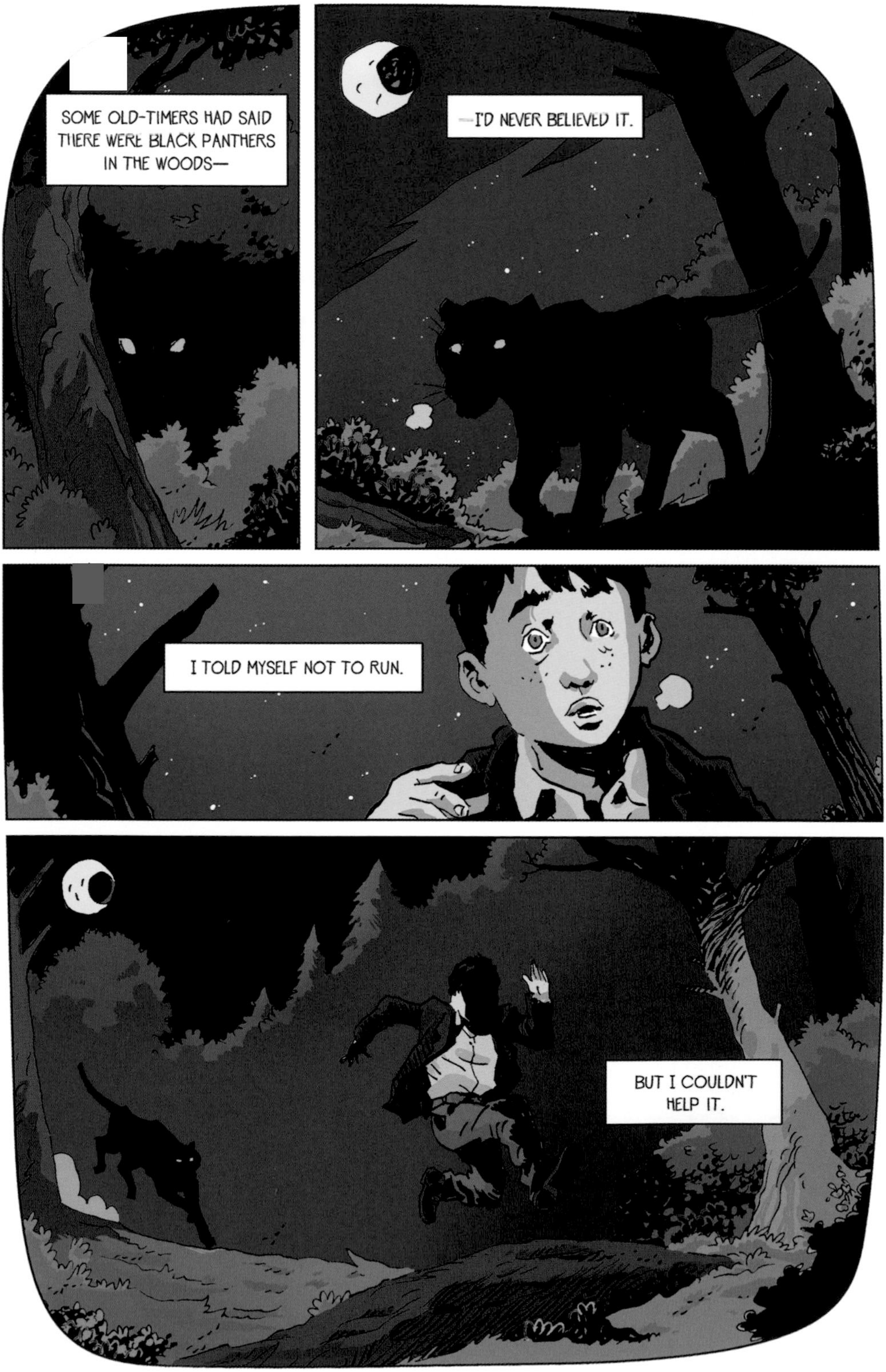
SOME OLD-TIMERS HAD SAID THERE WERE BLACK PANTHERS IN THE WOODS—
—I'D NEVER BELIEVED IT.
I TOLD MYSELF NOT TO RUN.
BUT I COULDN'T HELP IT.

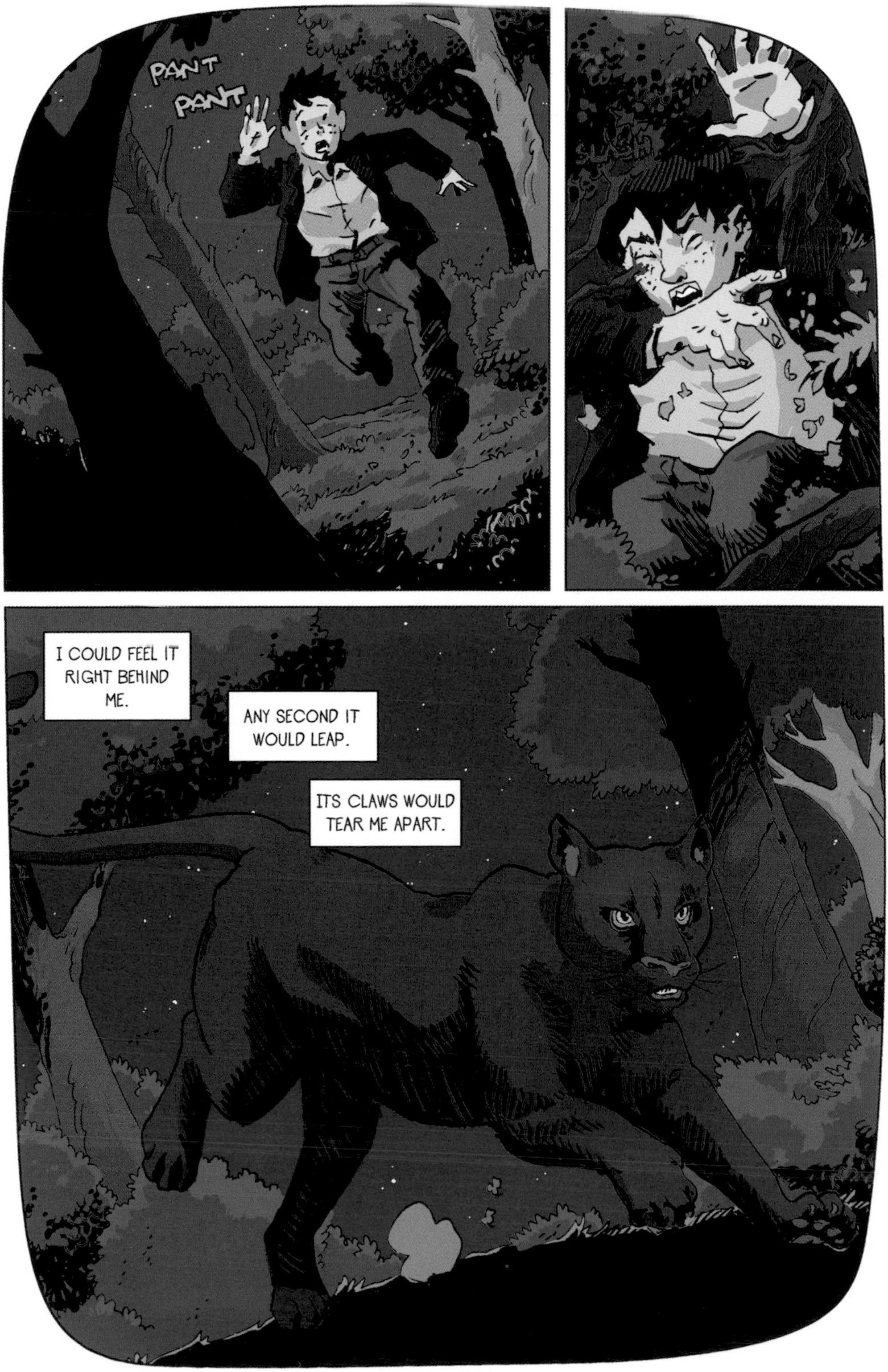
PANT
PANT
I COULD FEEL IT RIGHT BEHIND ME.
ANY SECOND IT WOULD LEAP.
ITS CLAWS WOULD TEAR ME APART.

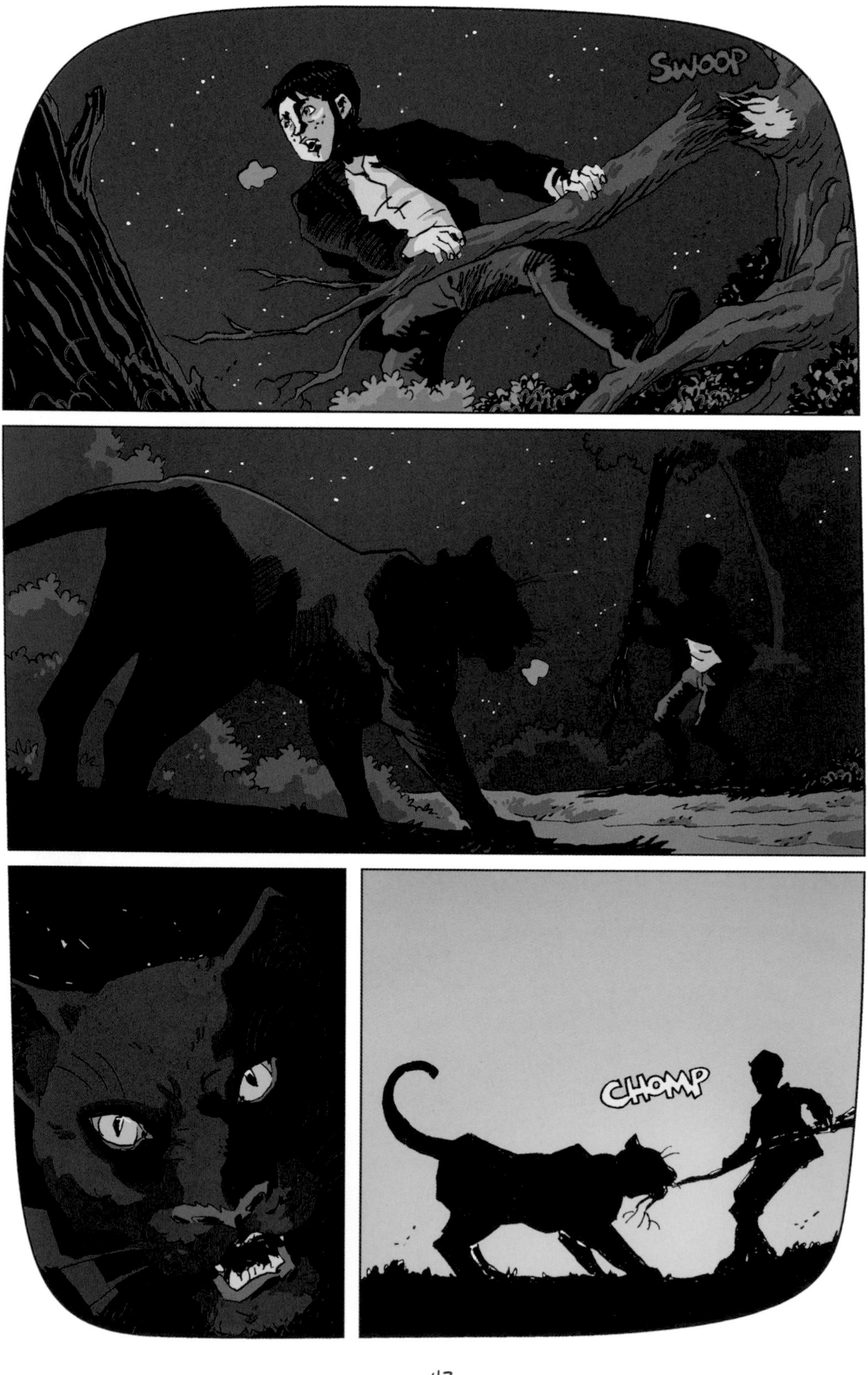
SWOOP
CHOMP

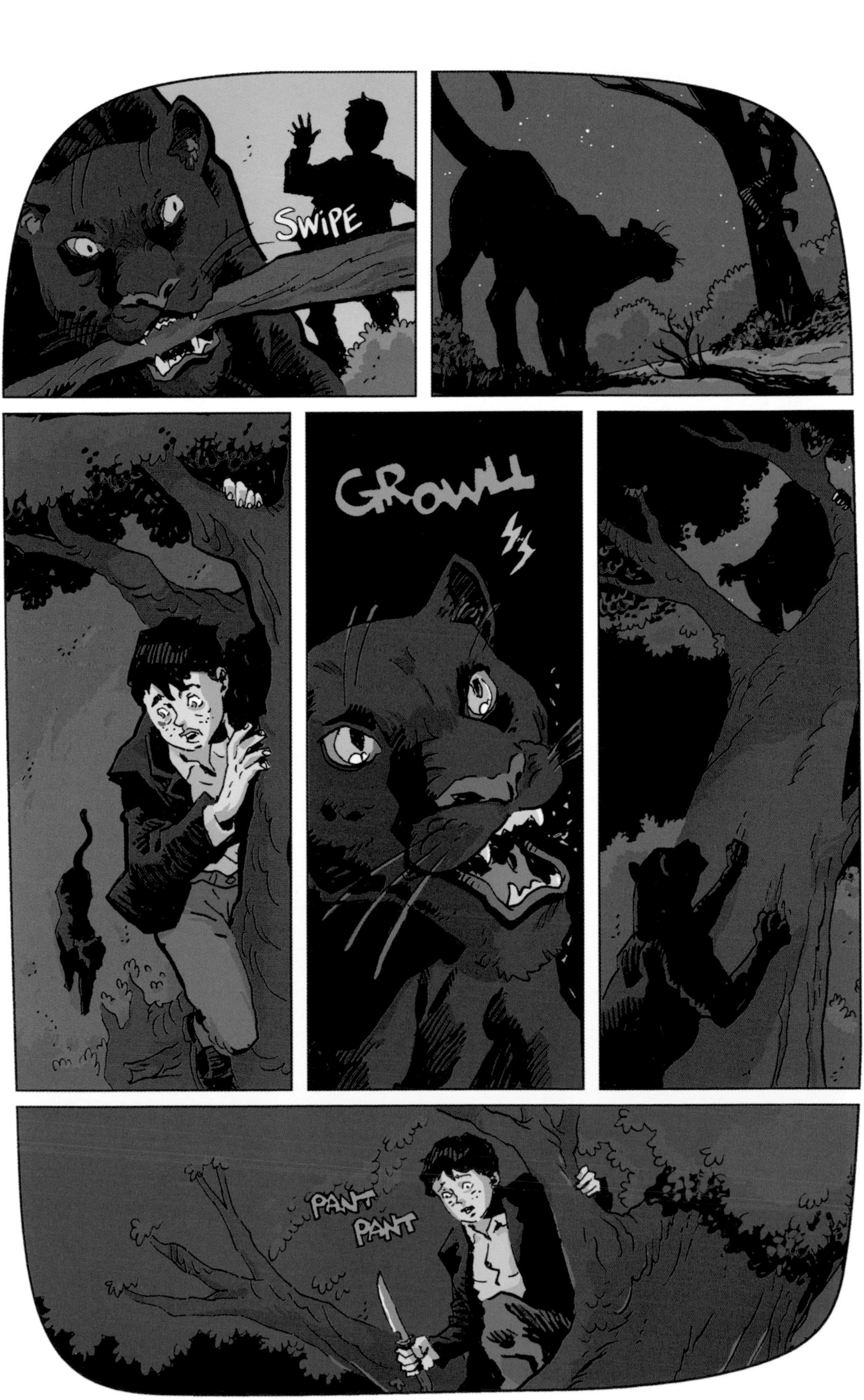
SWIPE
GROWL
PANT
PANT

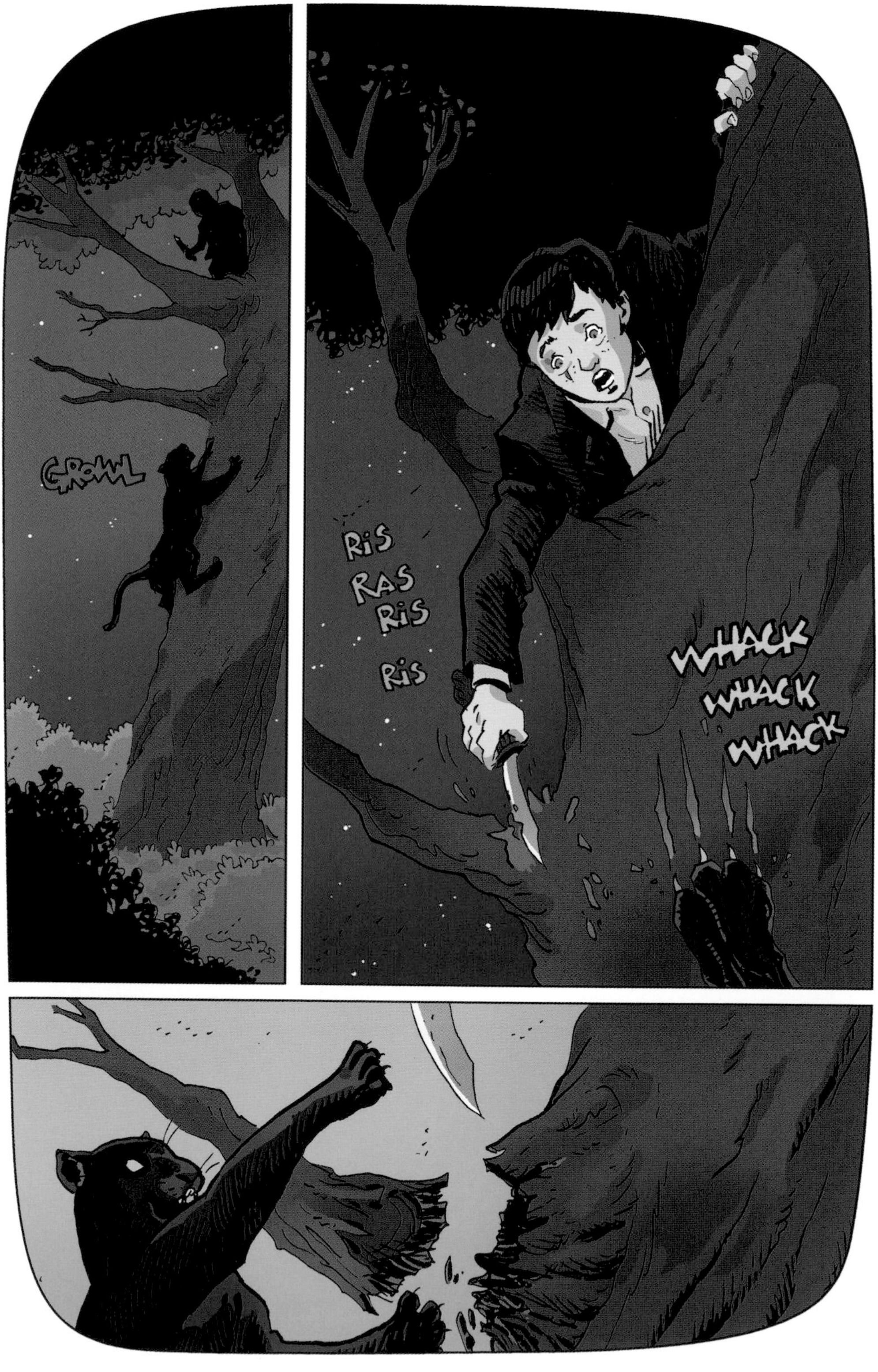
GROWL
RIS
RAS
RIS
RIS
WHACK
WHACK
WHACK

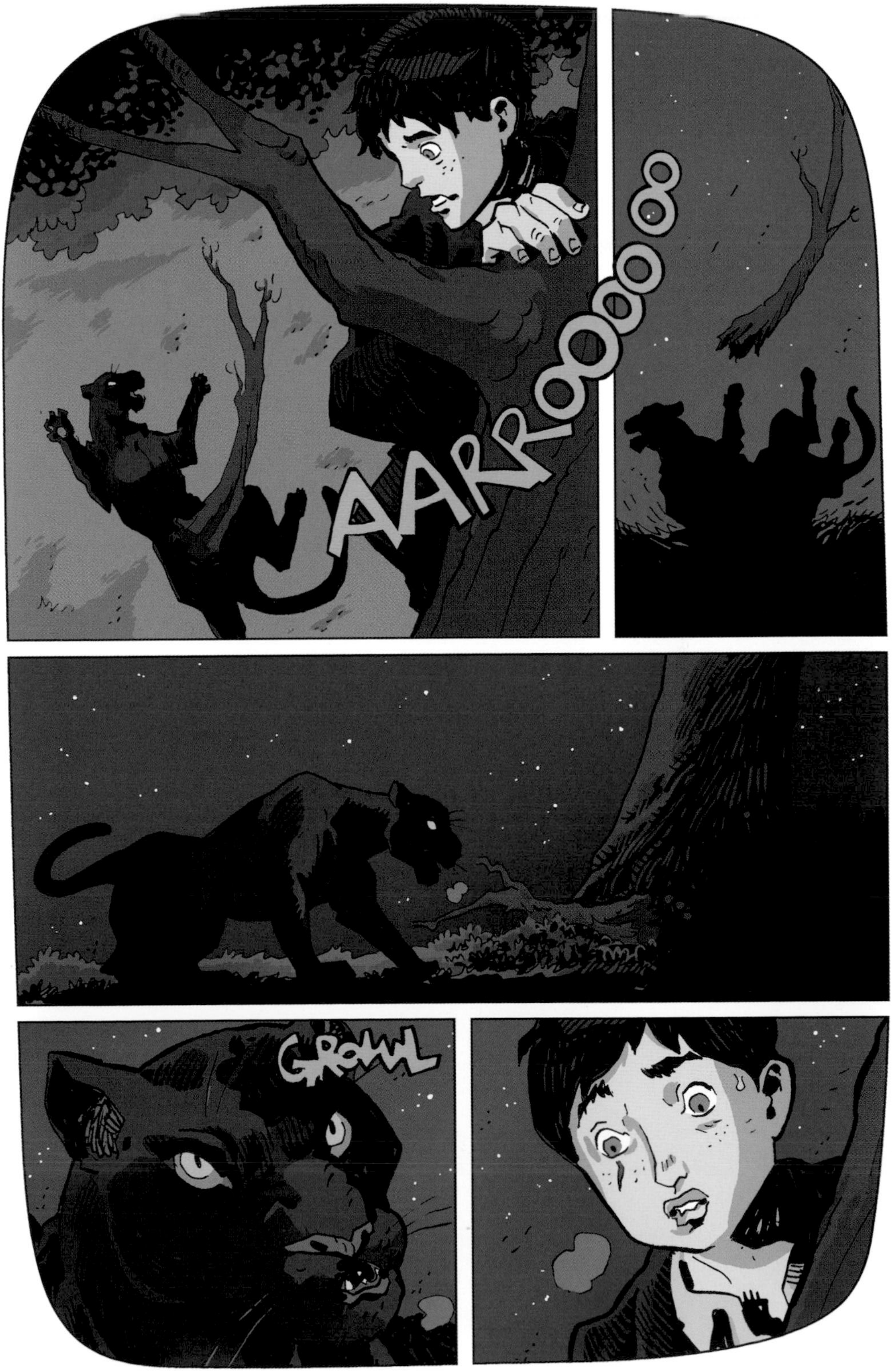
AARROOOOO
GROWL

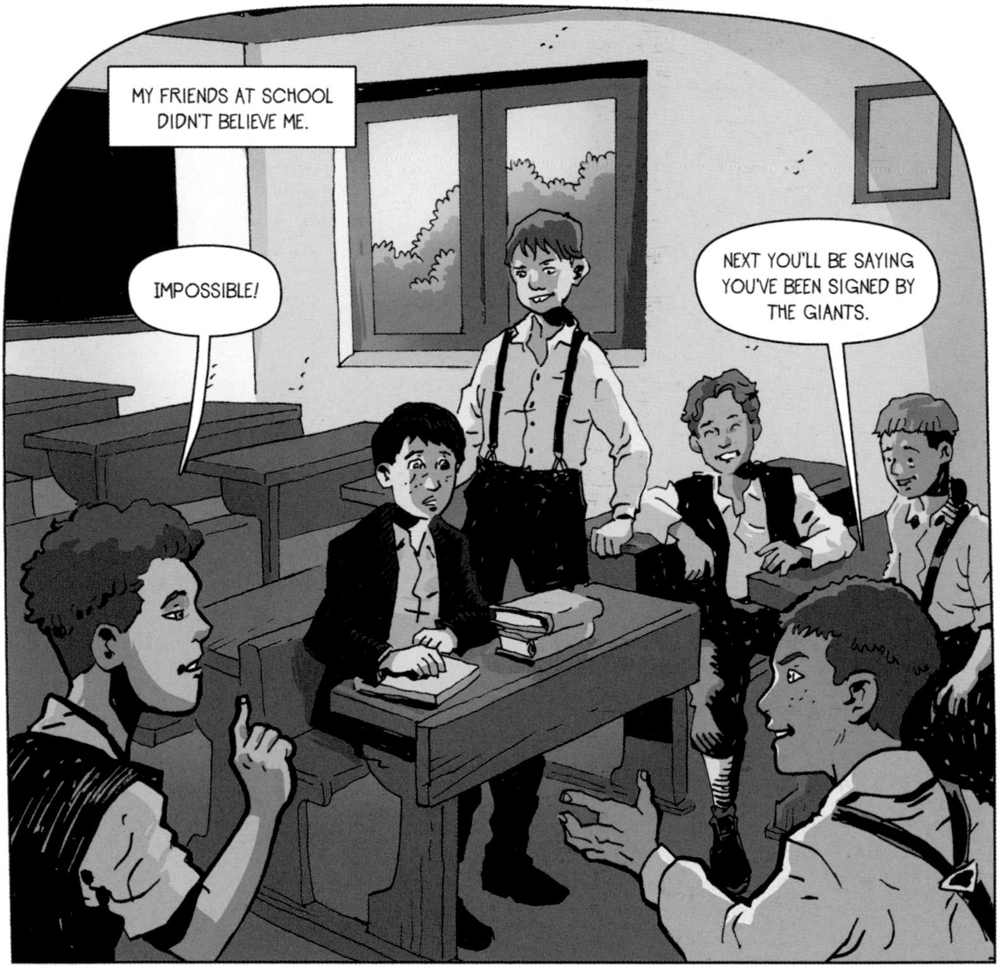
MY FRIENDS AT SCHOOL DIDN'T BELIEVE ME.
IMPOSSIBLE!
NEXT YOU'LL BE SAYING YOU'VE BEEN SIGNED BY THE GIANTS.

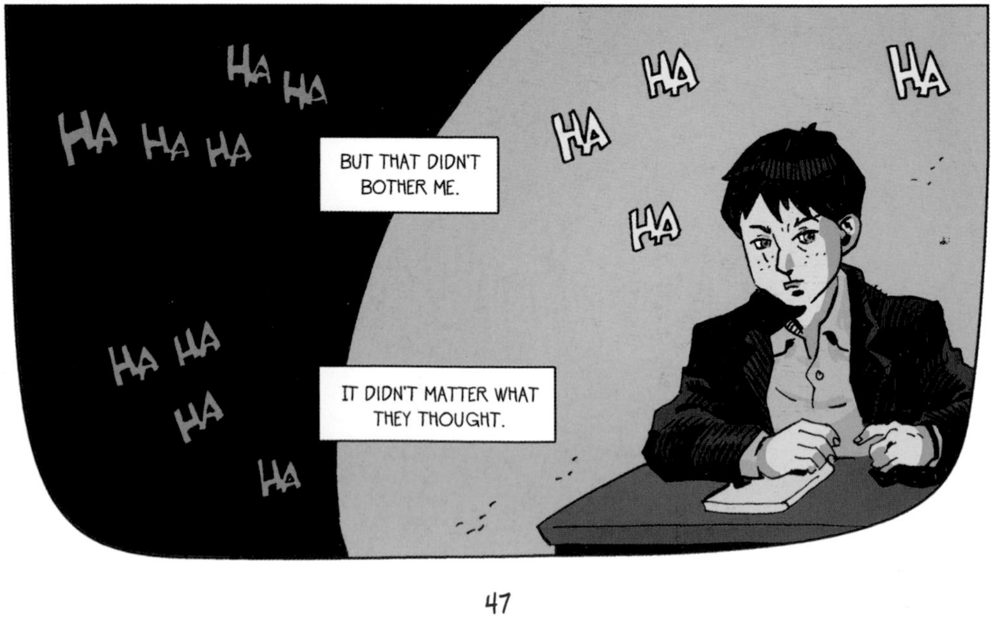
HA HA
HA HA HA
HA
HA
HA
HA
BUT THAT DIDN'T BOTHER ME.
HA
HA HA
HA
IT DIDN'T MATTER WHAT THEY THOUGHT.
HA

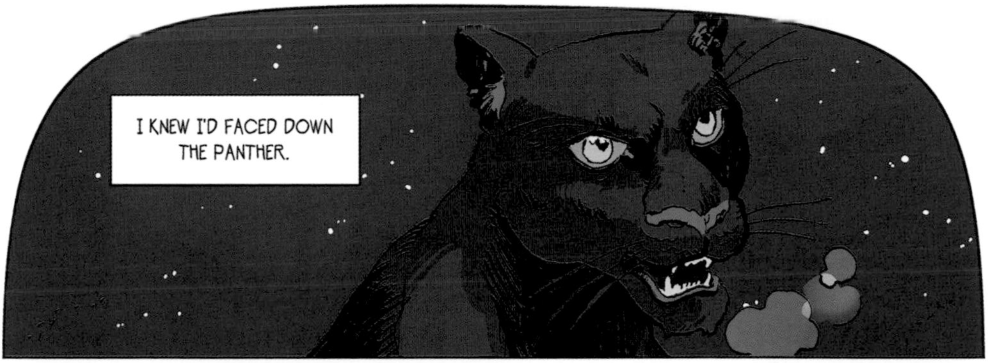
I KNEW I'D FACED DOWN THE PANTHER.
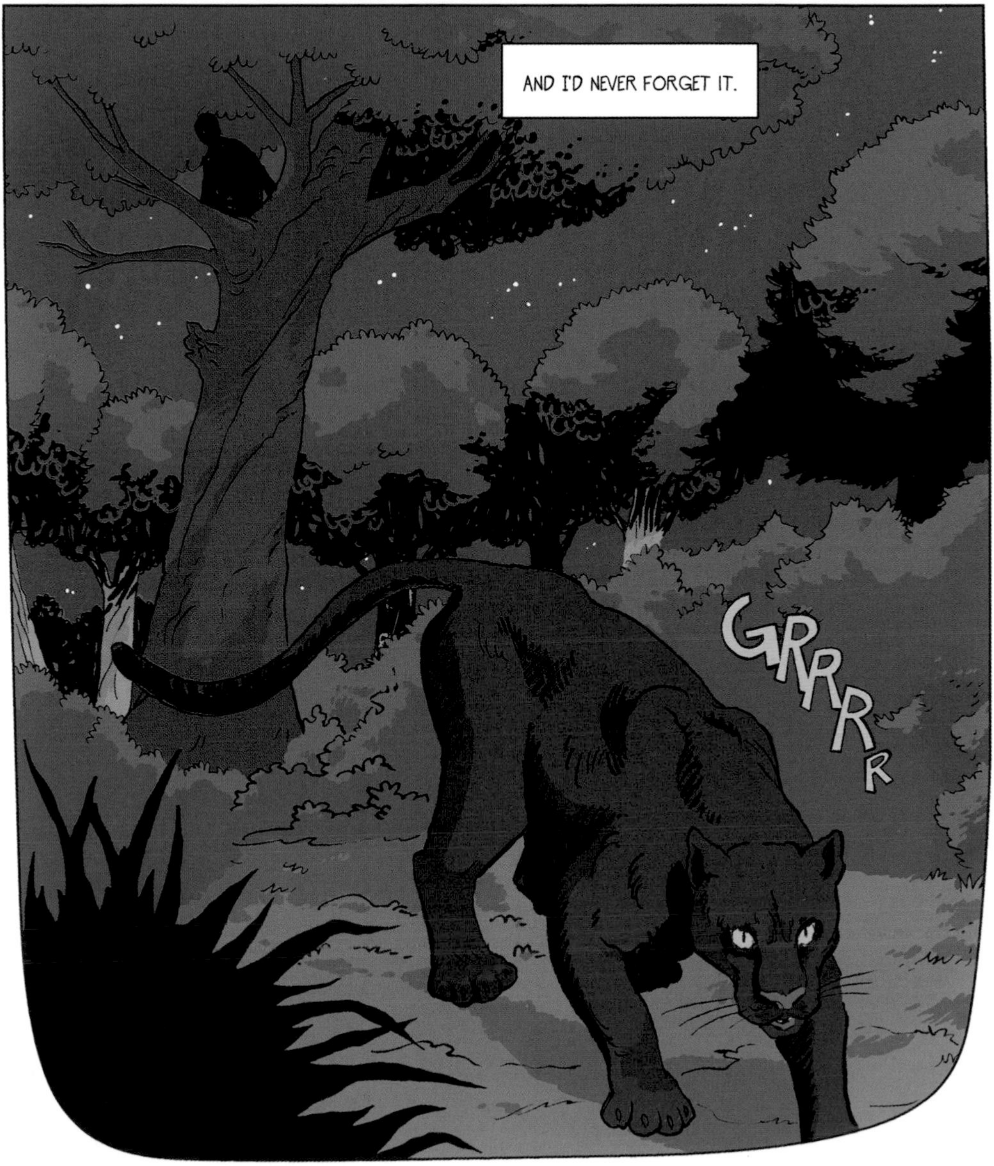
AND I'D NEVER FORGET IT.
GRRRRR

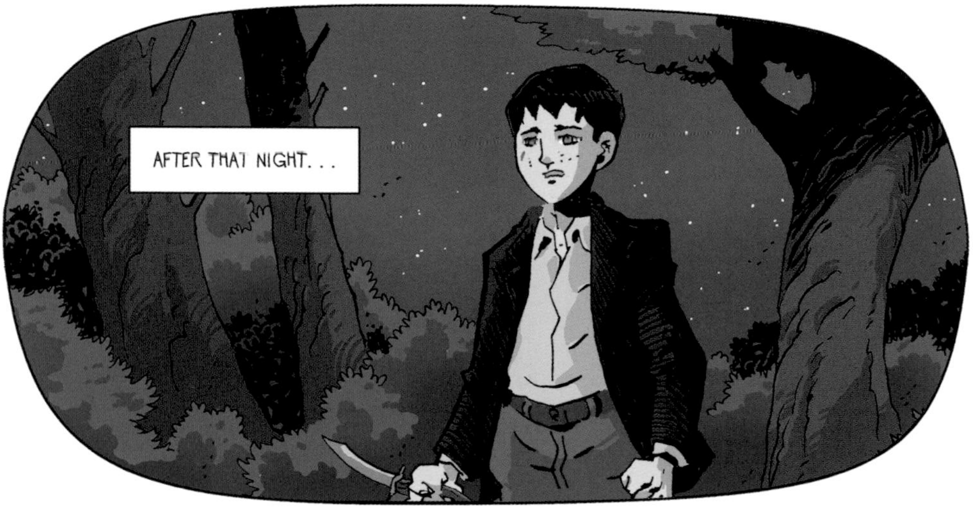
AFTER THAT NIGHT. . .

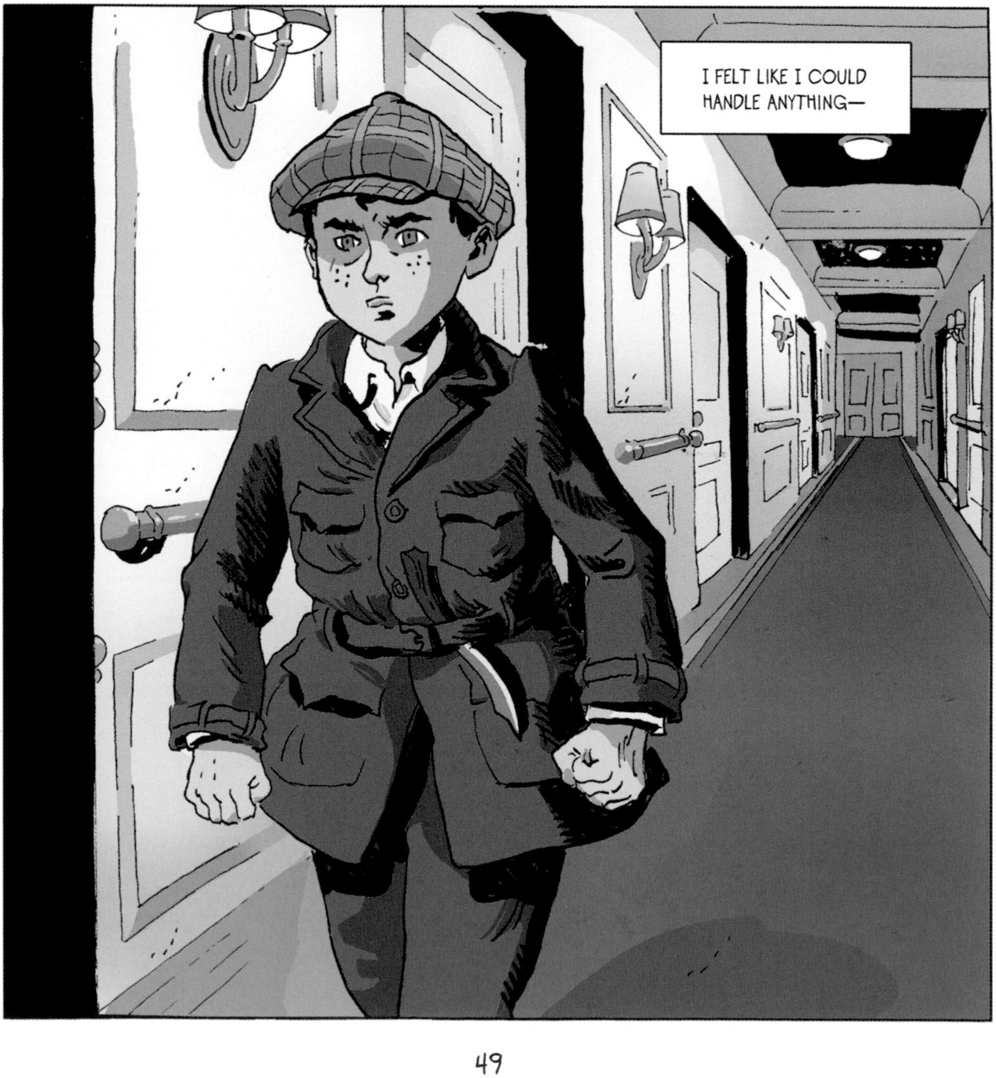
I FELT LIKE I COULD HANDLE ANYTHING—

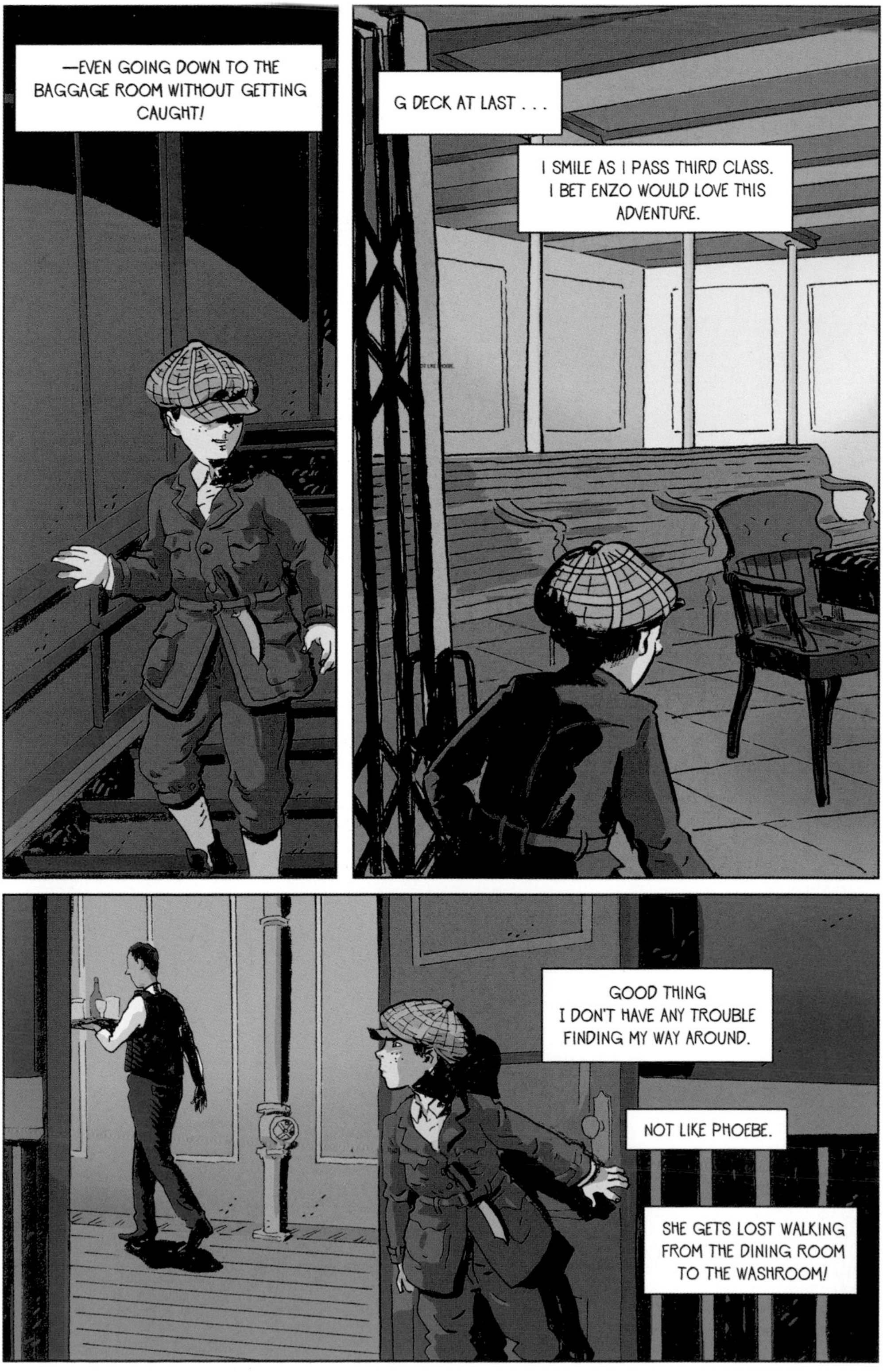
—EVEN GOING DOWN TO THE BAGGAGE ROOM WITHOUT GETTING CAUGHT!
G DECK AT LAST . . .
I SMILE AS I PASS THIRD CLASS. I BET ENZO WOULD LOVE THIS ADVENTURE.
GOOD THING I DON'T HAVE ANY TROUBLE FINDING MY WAY AROUND.
NOT LIKE PHOEBE.
SHE GETS LOST WALKING FROM THE DINING ROOM TO THE WASHROOM!

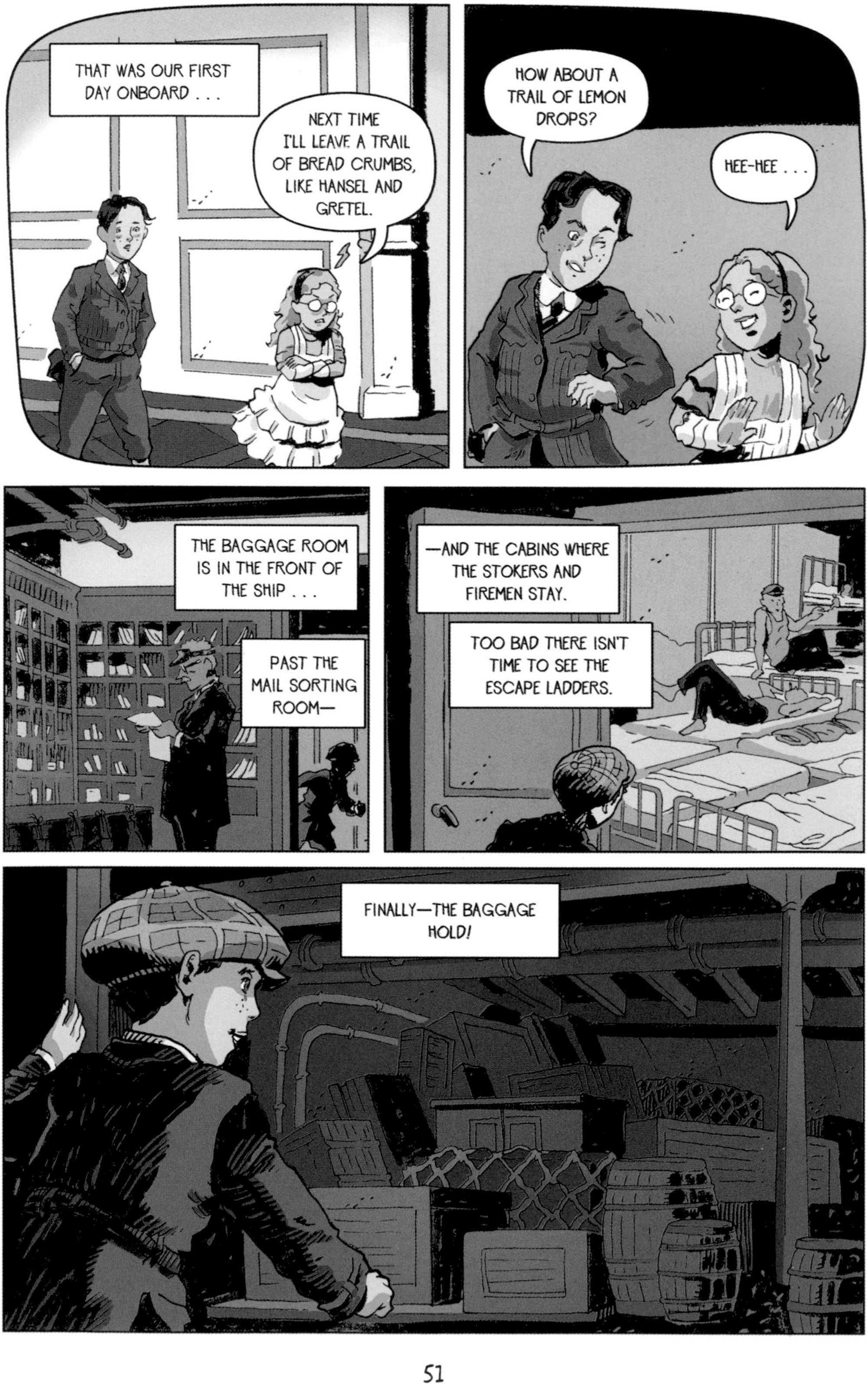
THAT WAS OUR FIRST DAY ONBOARD . . .
NEXT TIME I'LL LEAVE A TRAIL OF BREAD CRUMBS, LIKE HANSEL AND GRETEL.
HOW ABOUT A TRAIL OF LEMON DROPS?
HEE-HEE . . .
THE BAGGAGE ROOM IS IN THE FRONT OF THE SHIP . . .
PAST THE MAIL SORTING ROOM—
—AND THE CABINS WHERE THE STOKERS AND FIREMEN STAY.
TOO BAD THERE ISN'T TIME TO SEE THE ESCAPE LADDERS.
FINALLY—THE BAGGAGE HOLD!

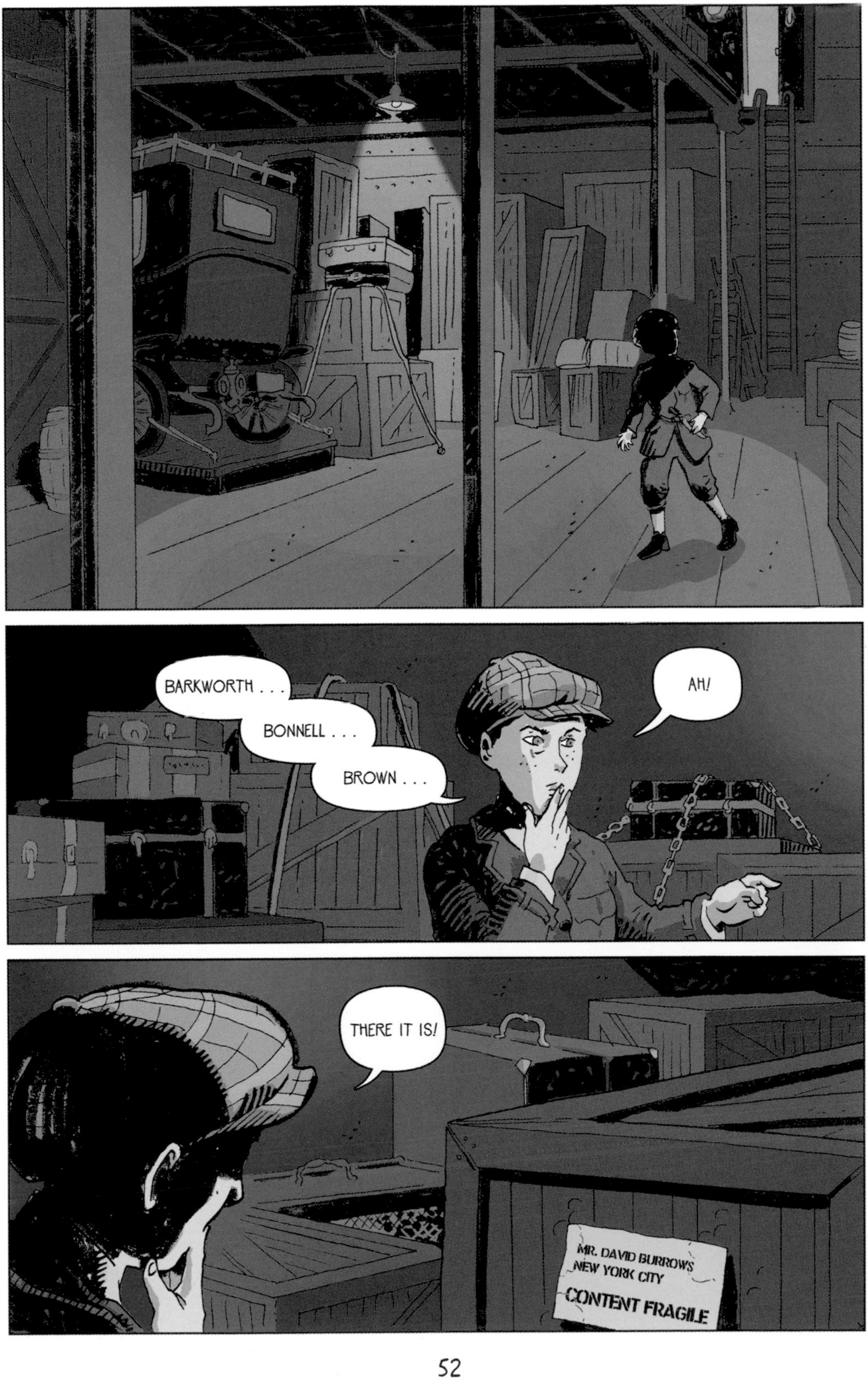
BARKWORTH . . .
BONNELL . . .
BROWN . . .
AH!
THERE IT IS!
MR. DAVID BURROWS
NEW YORK CITY
CONTENT FRAGILE

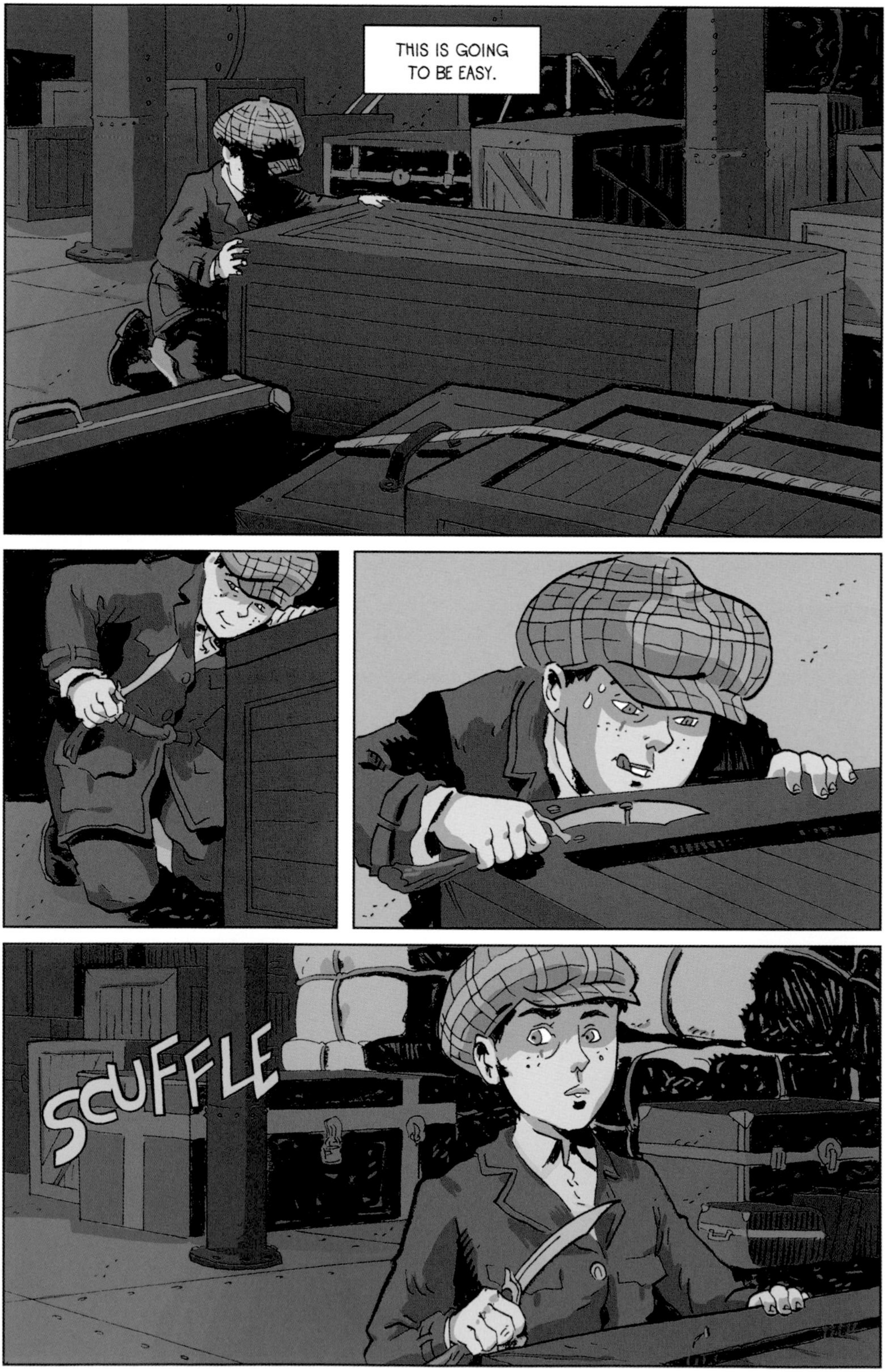
THIS IS GOING
TO BE EASY.
SCUFFLE

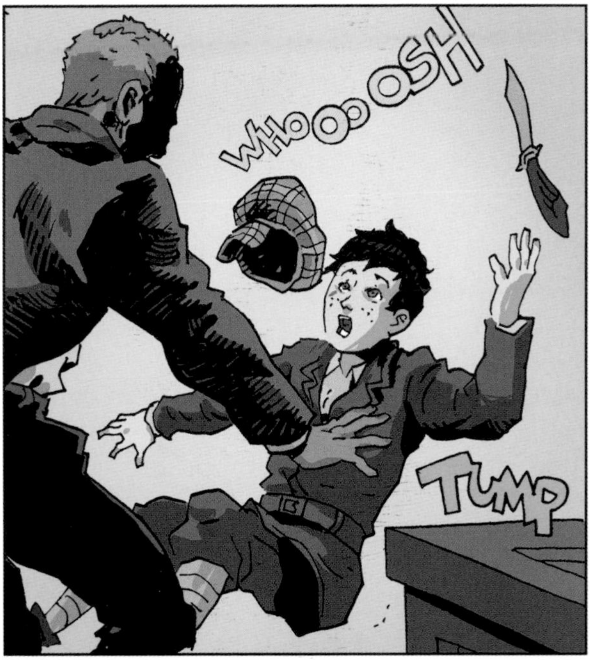
WHOOOOSH
TUMP
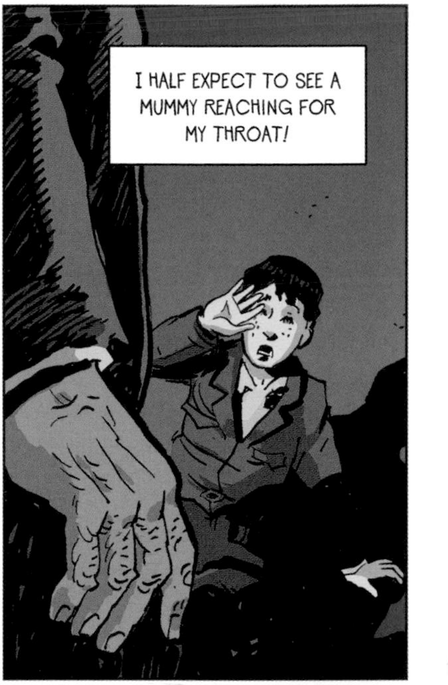
I HALF EXPECT TO SEE A MUMMY REACHING FOR MY THROAT!
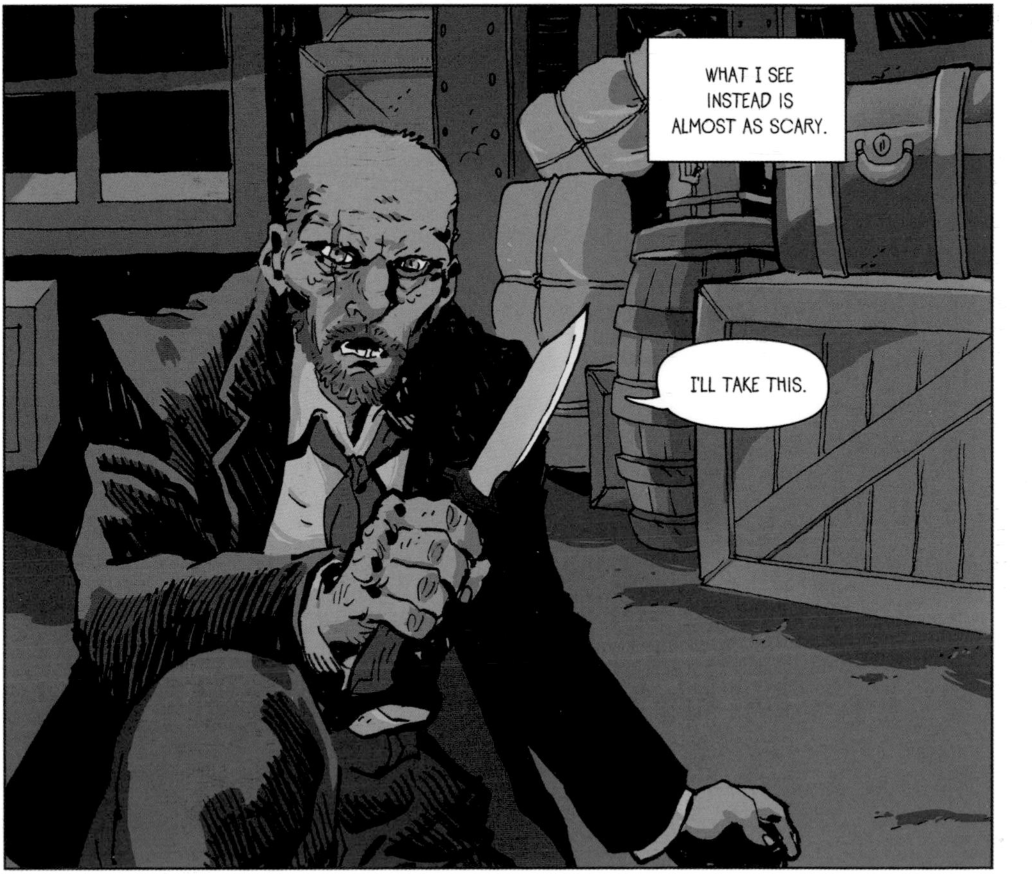
WHAT I SEE INSTEAD IS ALMOST AS SCARY.
I'LL TAKE THIS.

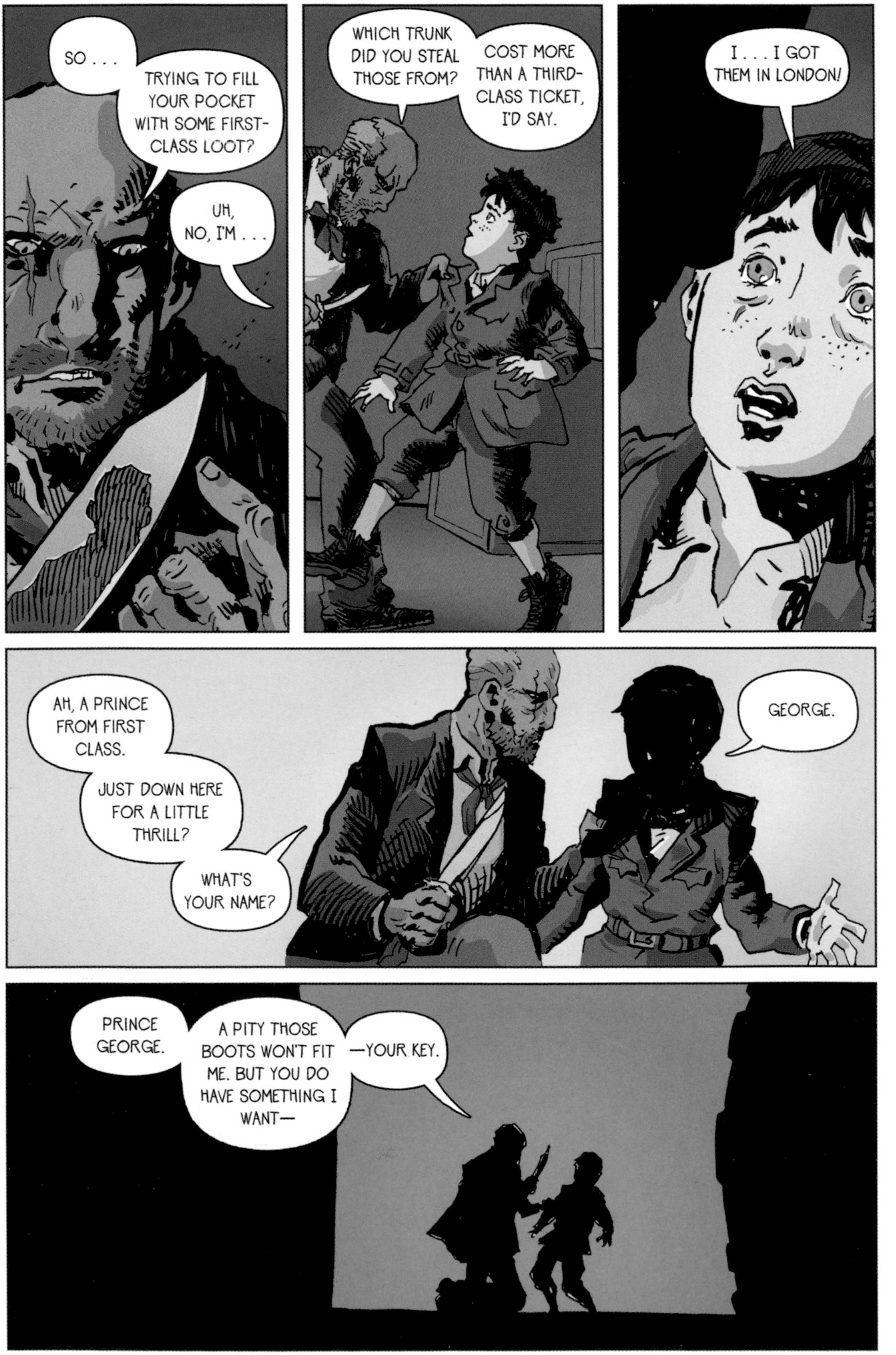
SO . . .
TRYING TO FILL YOUR POCKET WITH SOME FIRST-CLASS LOOT?
UH, NO, I'M . . .
WHICH TRUNK DID YOU STEAL THOSE FROM?
COST MORE THAN A THIRD-CLASS TICKET, I'D SAY.
I . . . I GOT THEM IN LONDON!
AH, A PRINCE FROM FIRST CLASS.
JUST DOWN HERE FOR A LITTLE THRILL?
WHAT'S YOUR NAME?
GEORGE.
PRINCE GEORGE.
A PITY THOSE BOOTS WON'T FIT ME. BUT YOU DO HAVE SOMETHING I WANT—
—YOUR KEY.

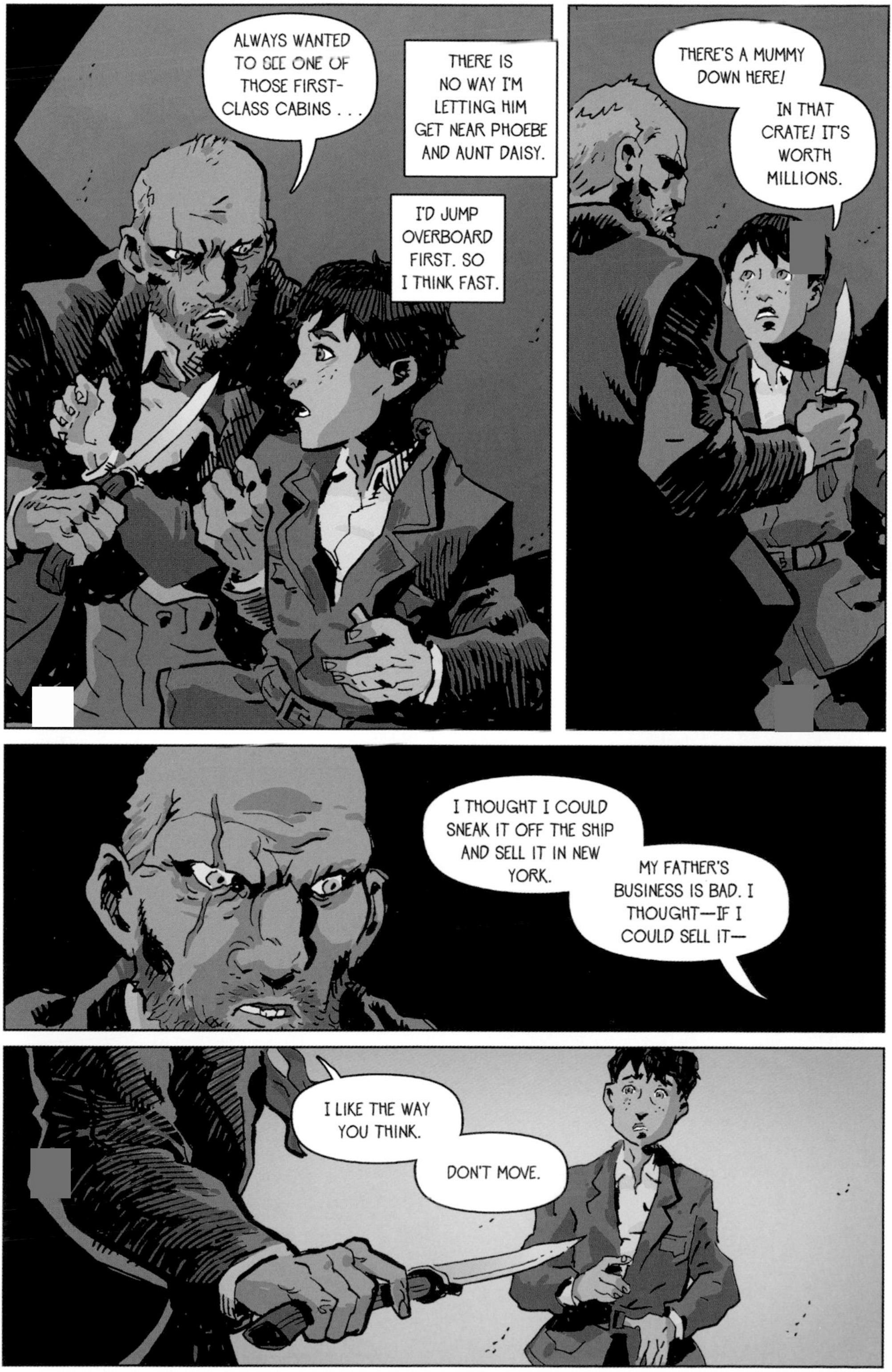
ALWAYS WANTED TO SEE ONE OF THOSE FIRST-CLASS CABINS . . .
THERE IS NO WAY I'M LETTING HIM GET NEAR PHOEBE AND AUNT DAISY.
I'D JUMP OVERBOARD FIRST. SO I THINK FAST.
THERE'S A MUMMY DOWN HERE!
IN THAT CRATE! IT'S WORTH MILLIONS.
I THOUGHT I COULD SNEAK IT OFF THE SHIP AND SELL IT IN NEW YORK.
MY FATHER'S BUSINESS IS BAD. I THOUGHT—IF I COULD SELL IT—
I LIKE THE WAY YOU THINK.
DON'T MOVE.

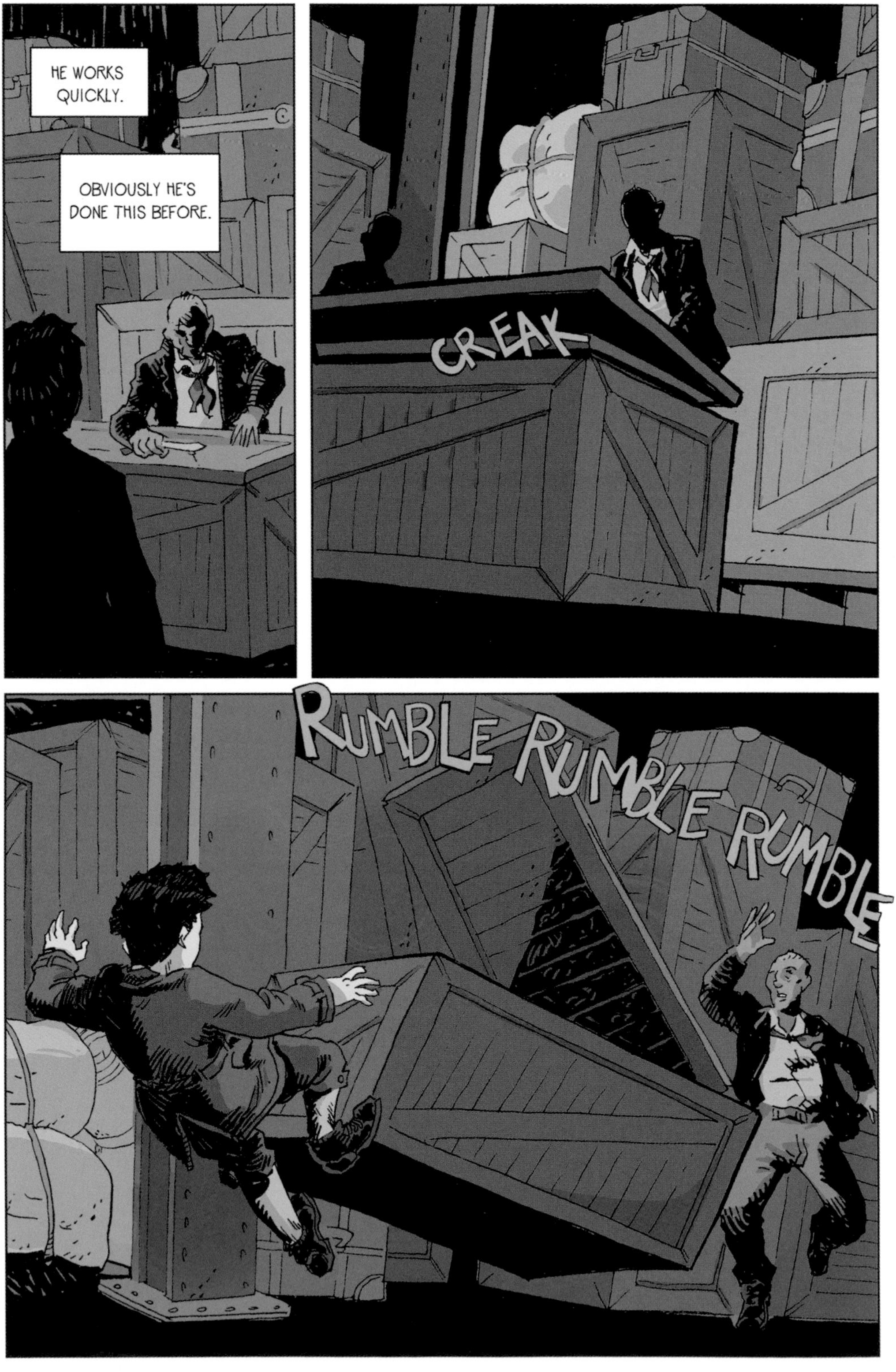
HE WORKS QUICKLY.
OBVIOUSLY HE'S DONE THIS BEFORE.
CREAK
RUMBLE RUMBLE RUMBLE

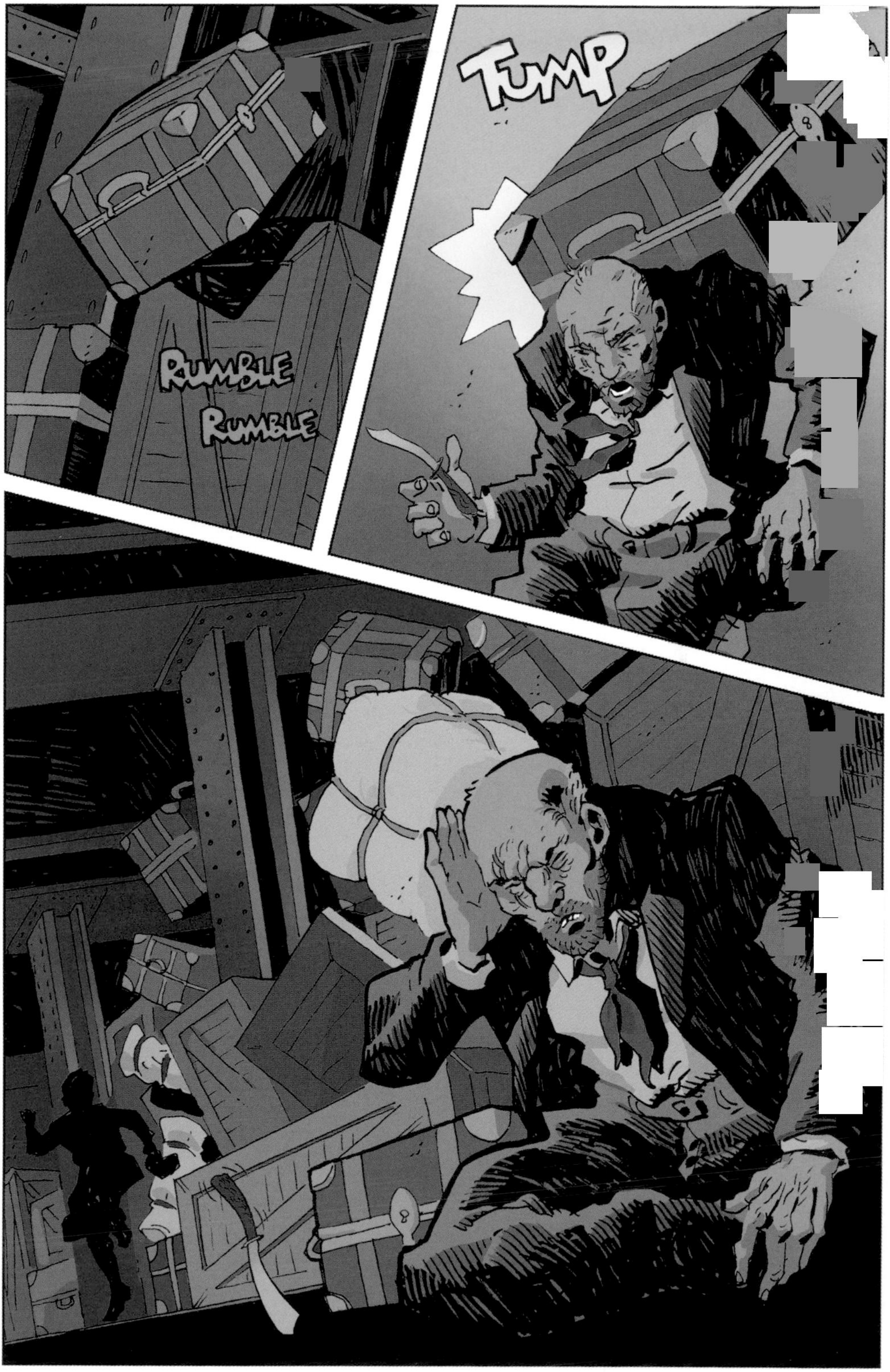
RUMBLE
RUMBLE
TUMP

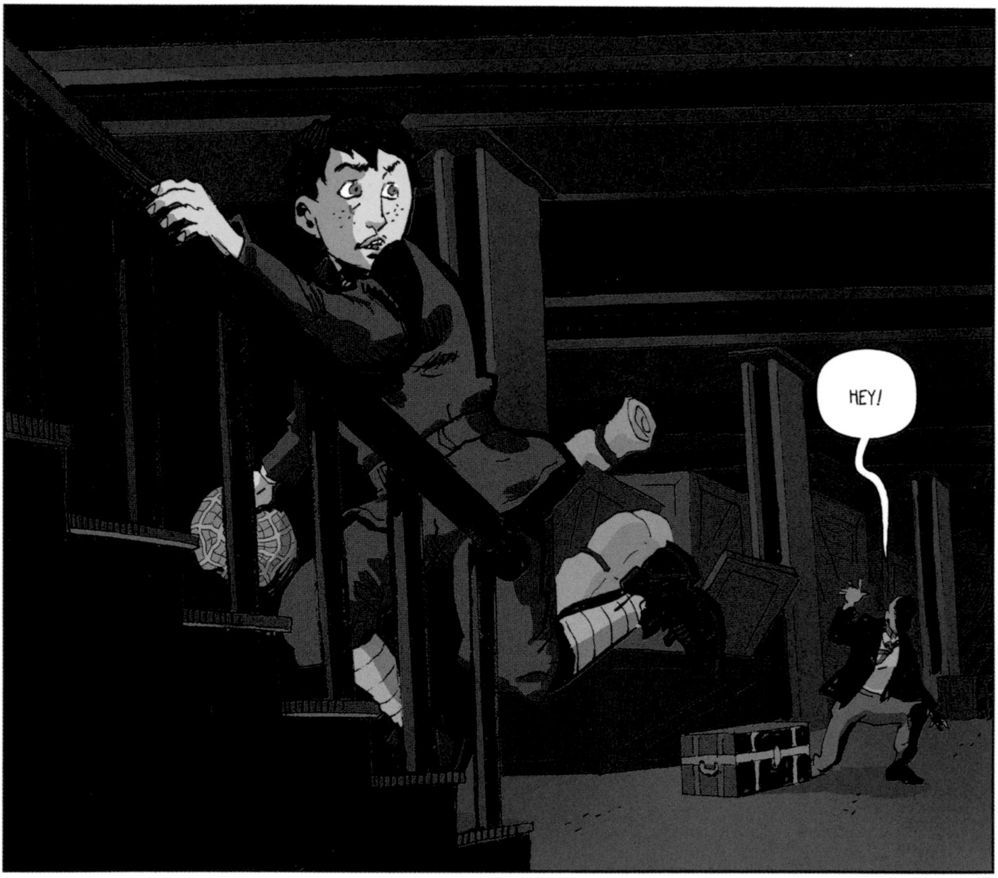
HEY!

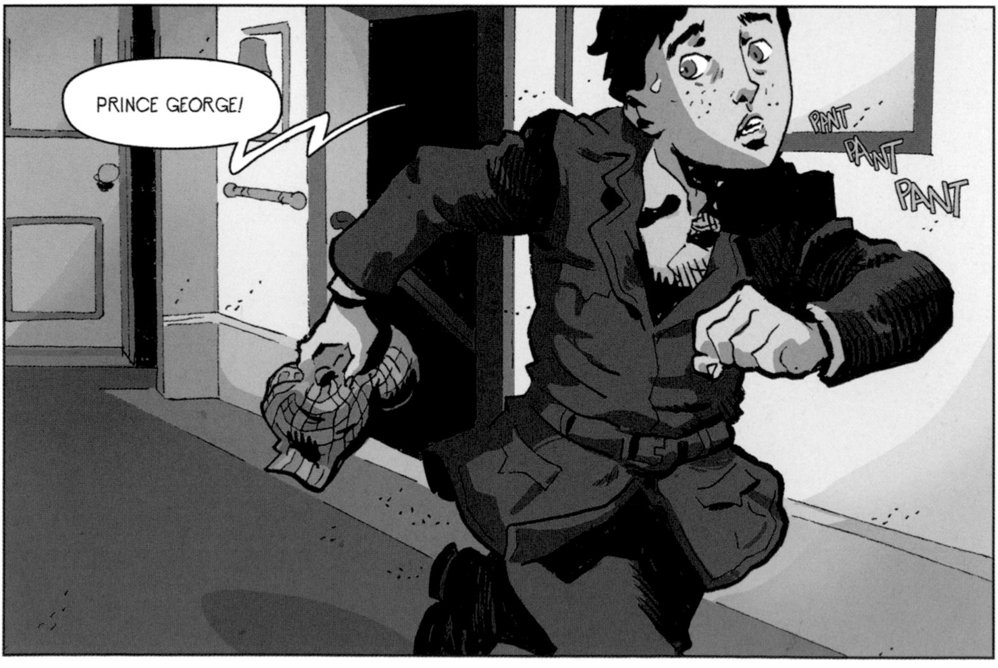
PRINCE GEORGE!
PANT PANT PANT

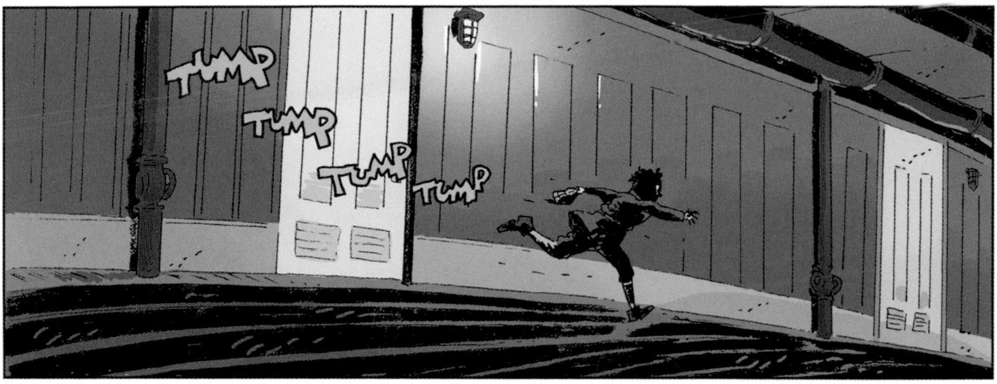
TUMP
TUMP
TUMP
TUMP

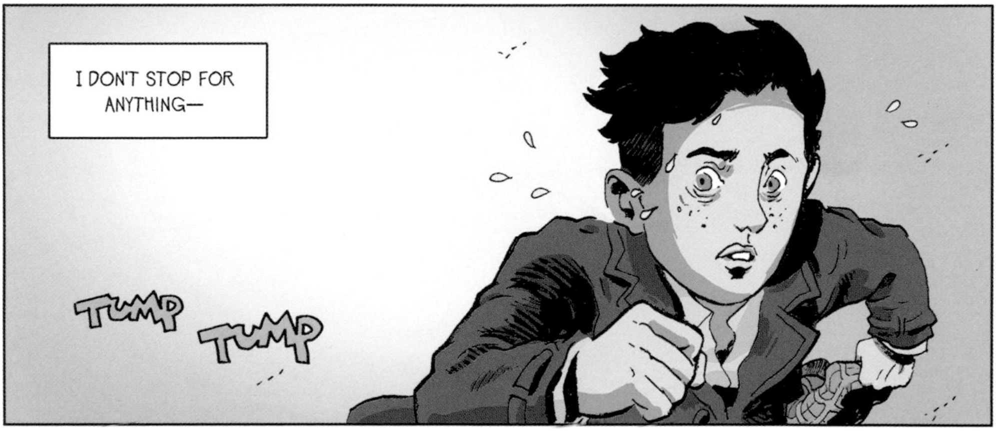
I DON'T STOP FOR ANYTHING—
TUMP
TUMP

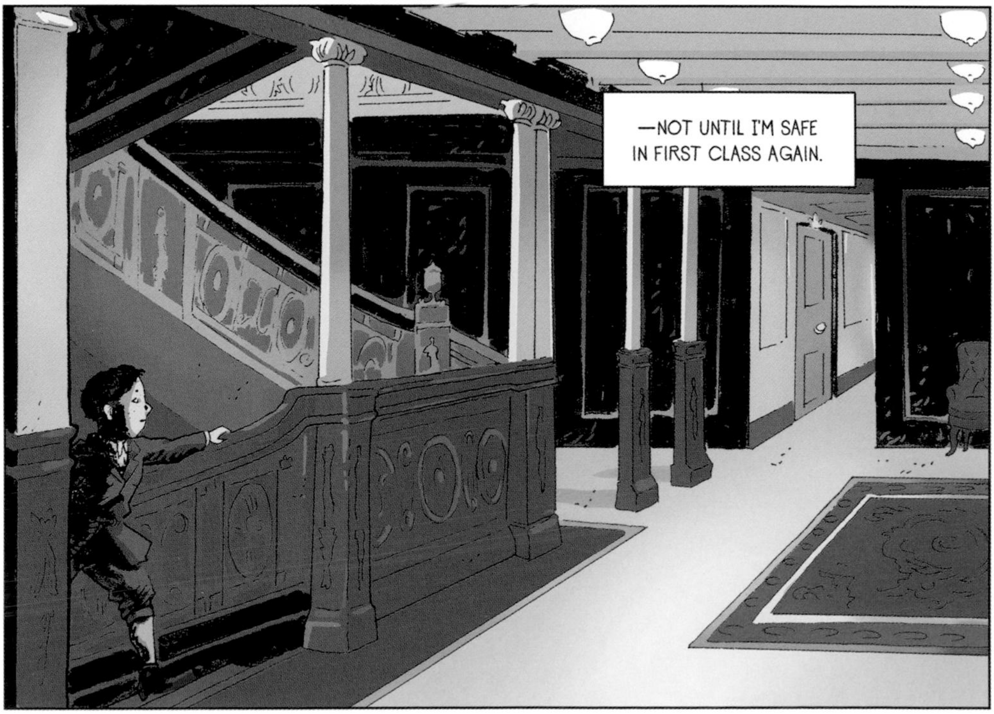
—NOT UNTIL I'M SAFE IN FIRST CLASS AGAIN.

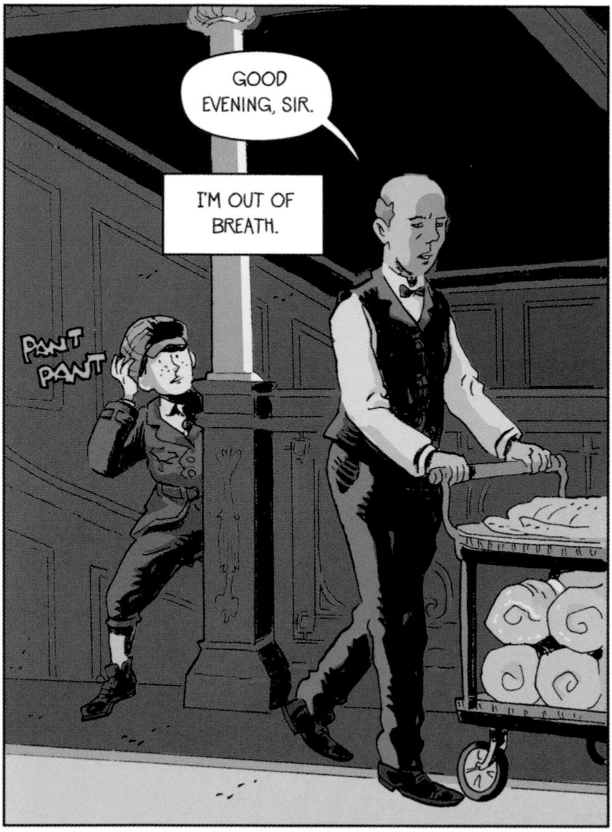
GOOD EVENING, SIR.
I'M OUT OF BREATH.
PANT PANT

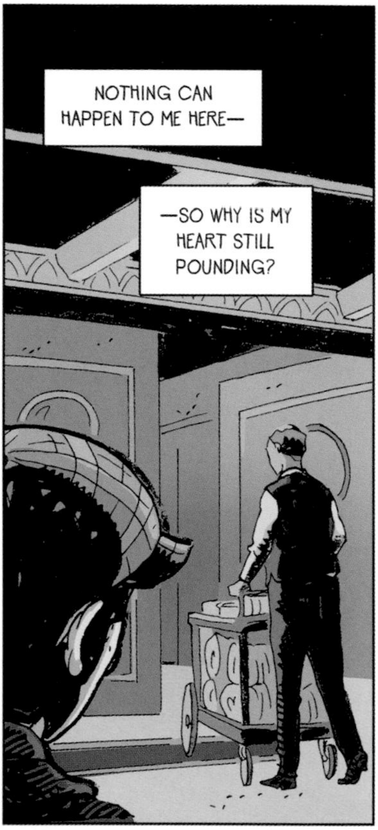
NOTHING CAN HAPPEN TO ME HERE—
—SO WHY IS MY HEART STILL POUNDING?

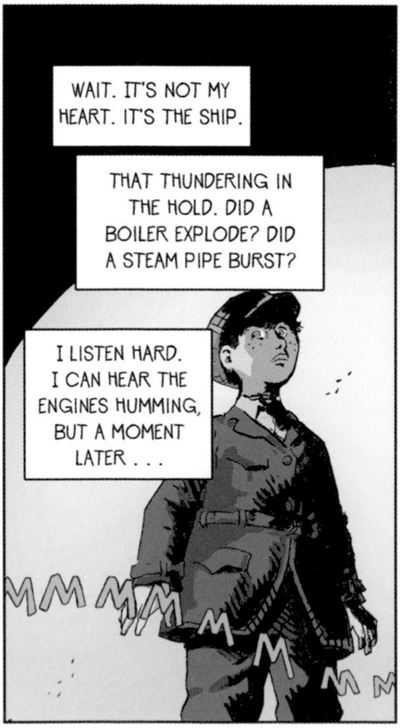
WAIT. IT'S NOT MY HEART. IT'S THE SHIP.
THAT THUNDERING IN THE HOLD. DID A BOILER EXPLODE? DID A STEAM PIPE BURST?
I LISTEN HARD. I CAN HEAR THE ENGINES HUMMING, BUT A MOMENT LATER . . .
MMMMMMMMMM

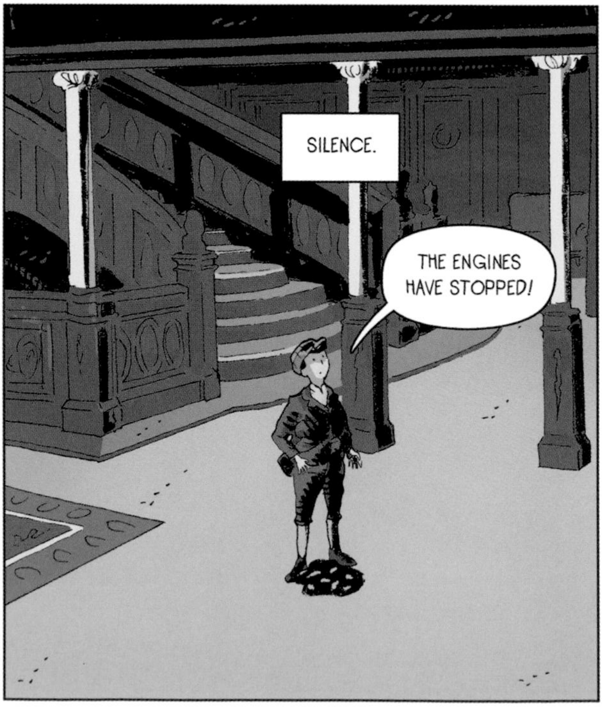
SILENCE.
THE ENGINES HAVE STOPPED!

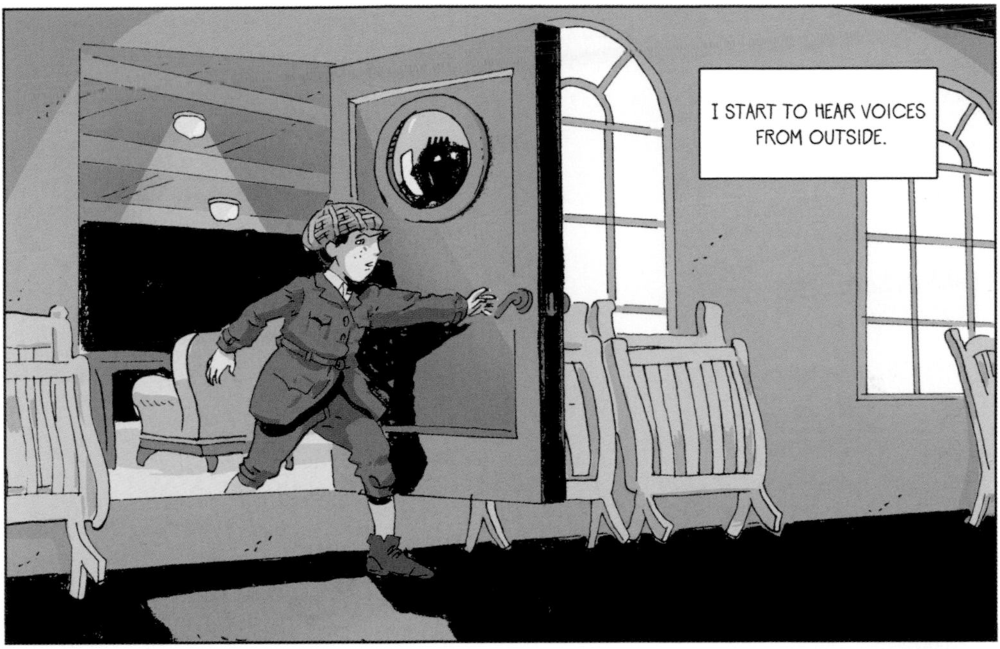
I START TO HEAR VOICES FROM OUTSIDE.

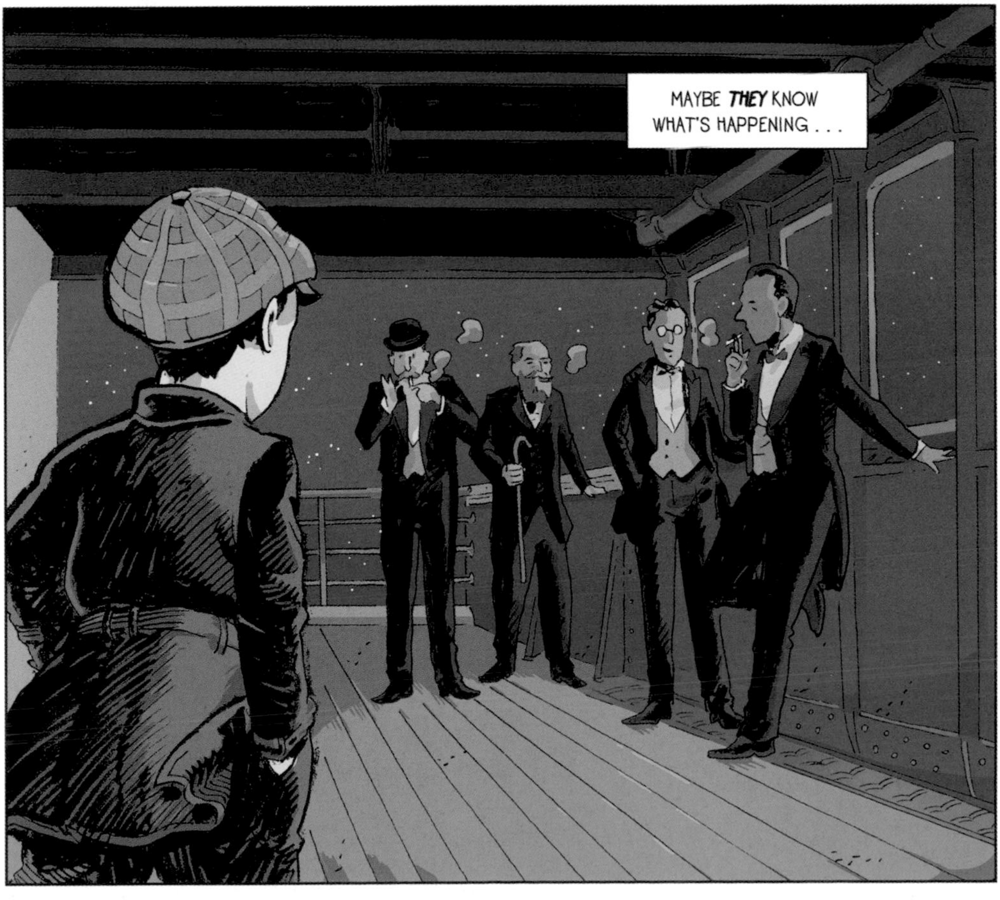
MAYBE **THEY** KNOW WHAT'S HAPPENING . . .

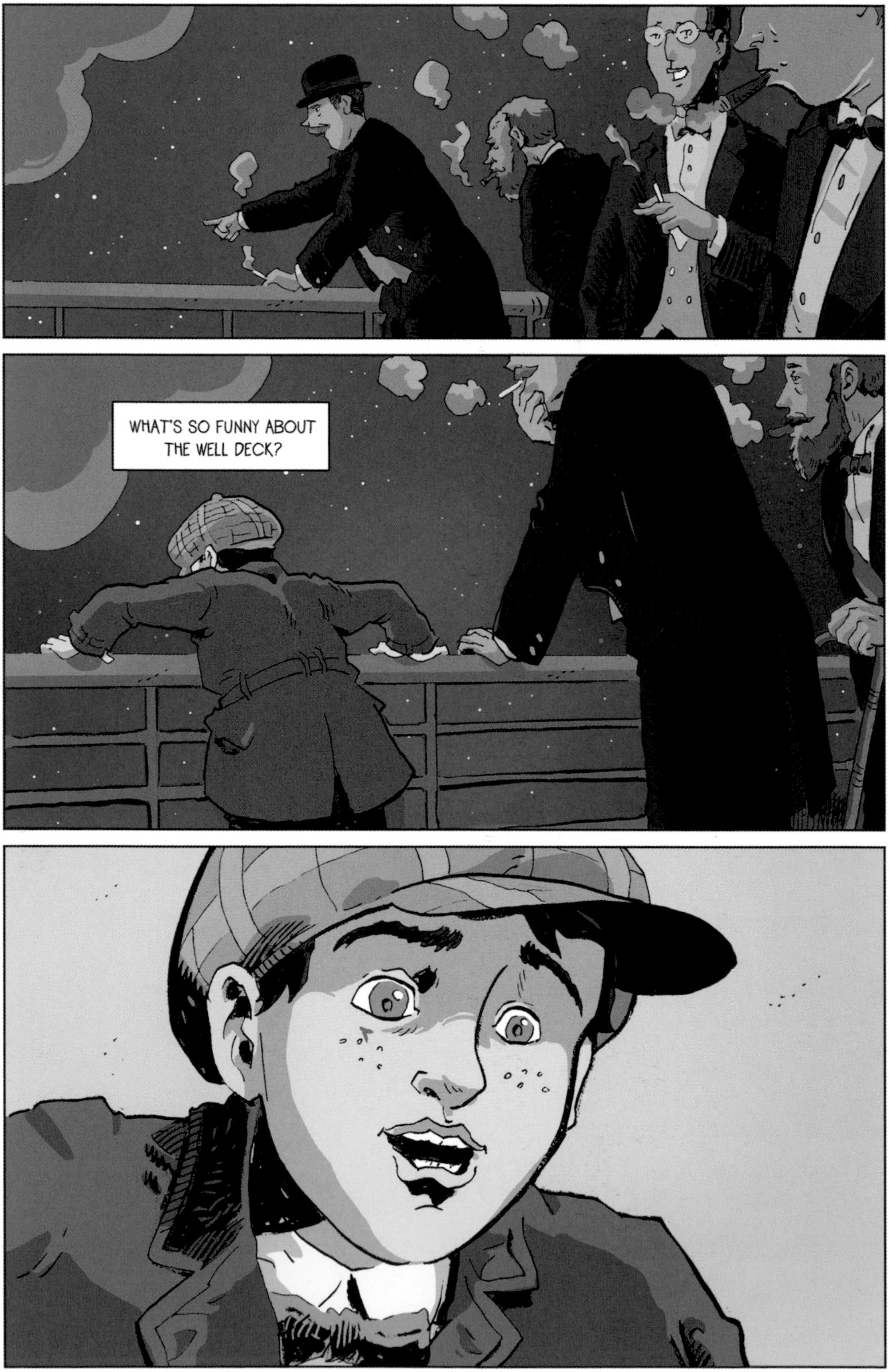
WHAT'S SO FUNNY ABOUT THE WELL DECK?

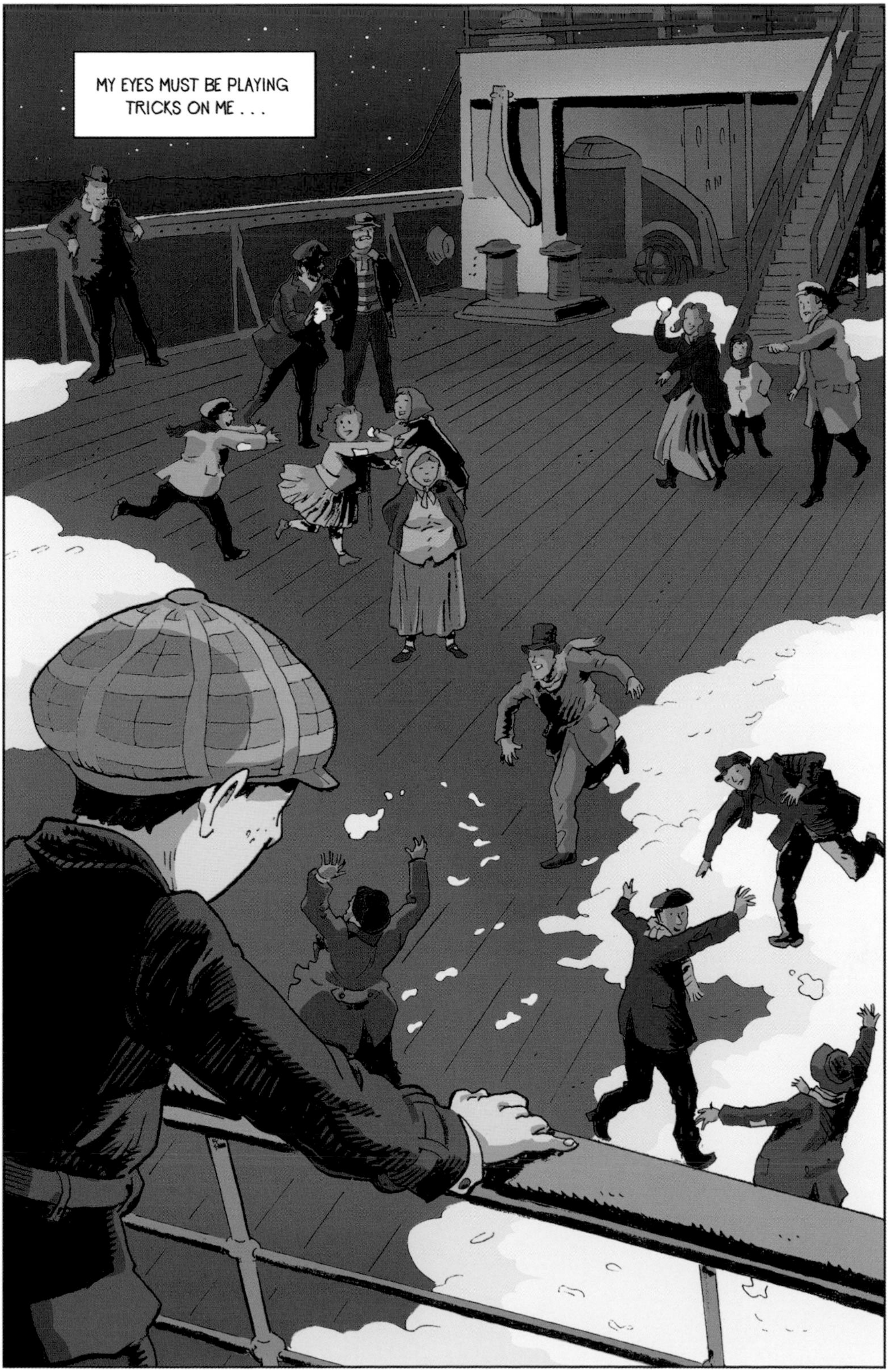
MY EYES MUST BE PLAYING TRICKS ON ME . . .

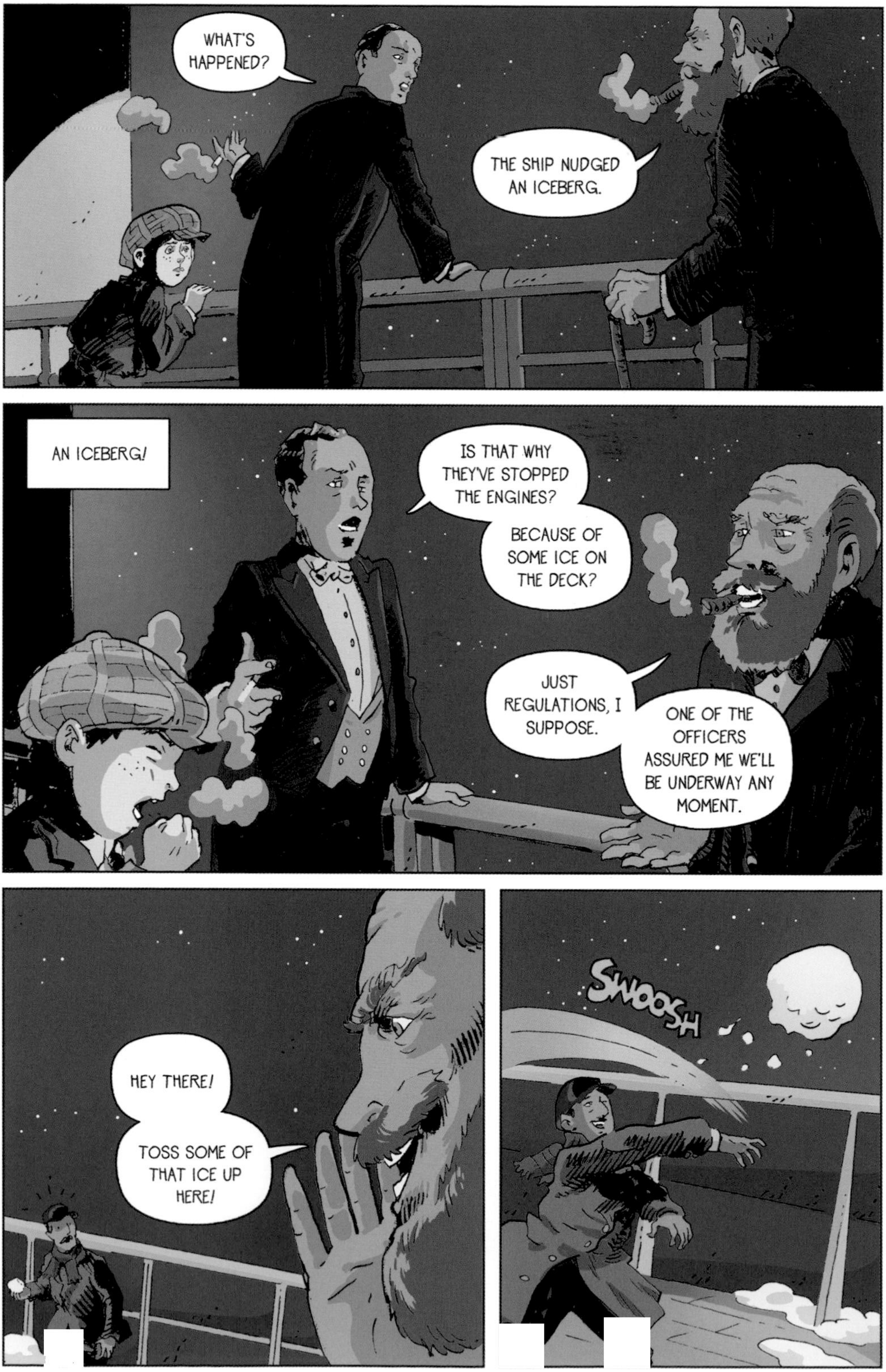
WHAT'S HAPPENED?
THE SHIP NUDGED AN ICEBERG.
AN ICEBERG!
IS THAT WHY THEY'VE STOPPED THE ENGINES?
BECAUSE OF SOME ICE ON THE DECK?
JUST REGULATIONS, I SUPPOSE.
ONE OF THE OFFICERS ASSURED ME WE'LL BE UNDERWAY ANY MOMENT.
HEY THERE!
TOSS SOME OF THAT ICE UP HERE!
SWOOSH

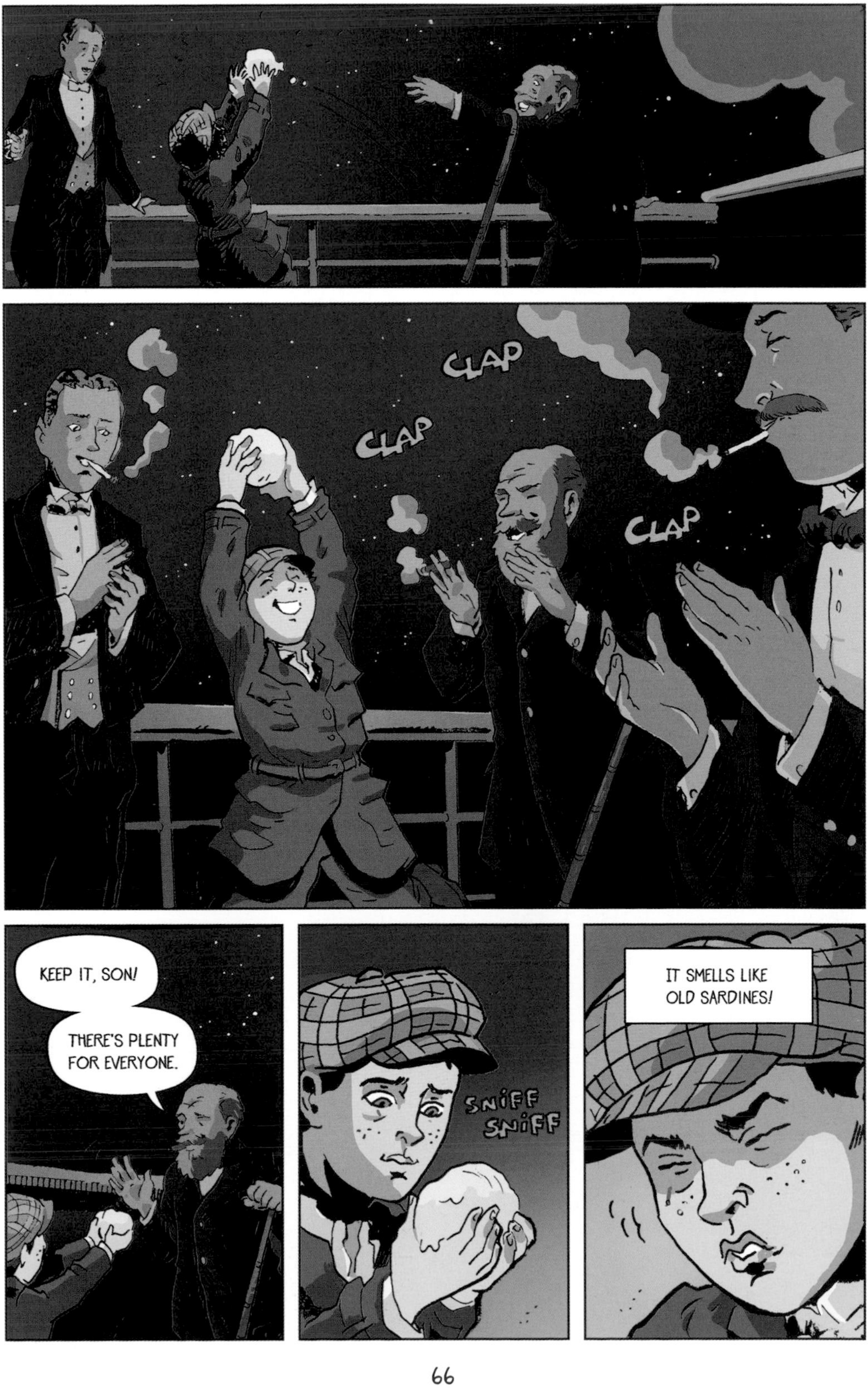
CLAP
CLAP
CLAP
KEEP IT, SON!
THERE'S PLENTY FOR EVERYONE.
SNIFF SNIFF
IT SMELLS LIKE OLD SARDINES!

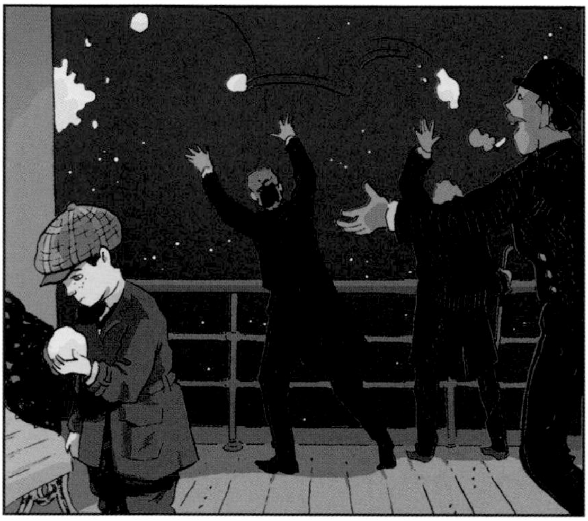
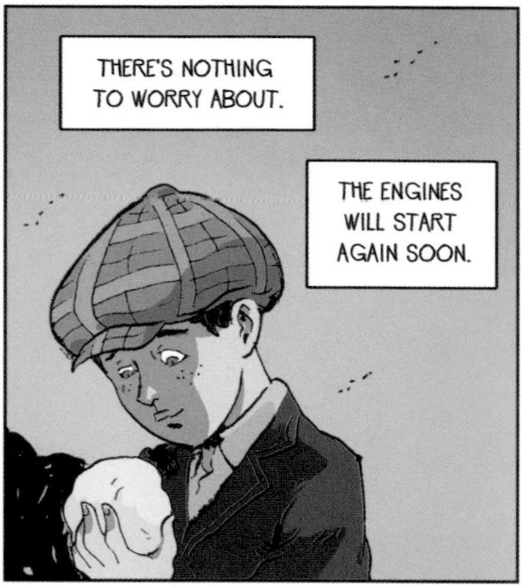
THERE'S NOTHING TO WORRY ABOUT.
THE ENGINES WILL START AGAIN SOON.
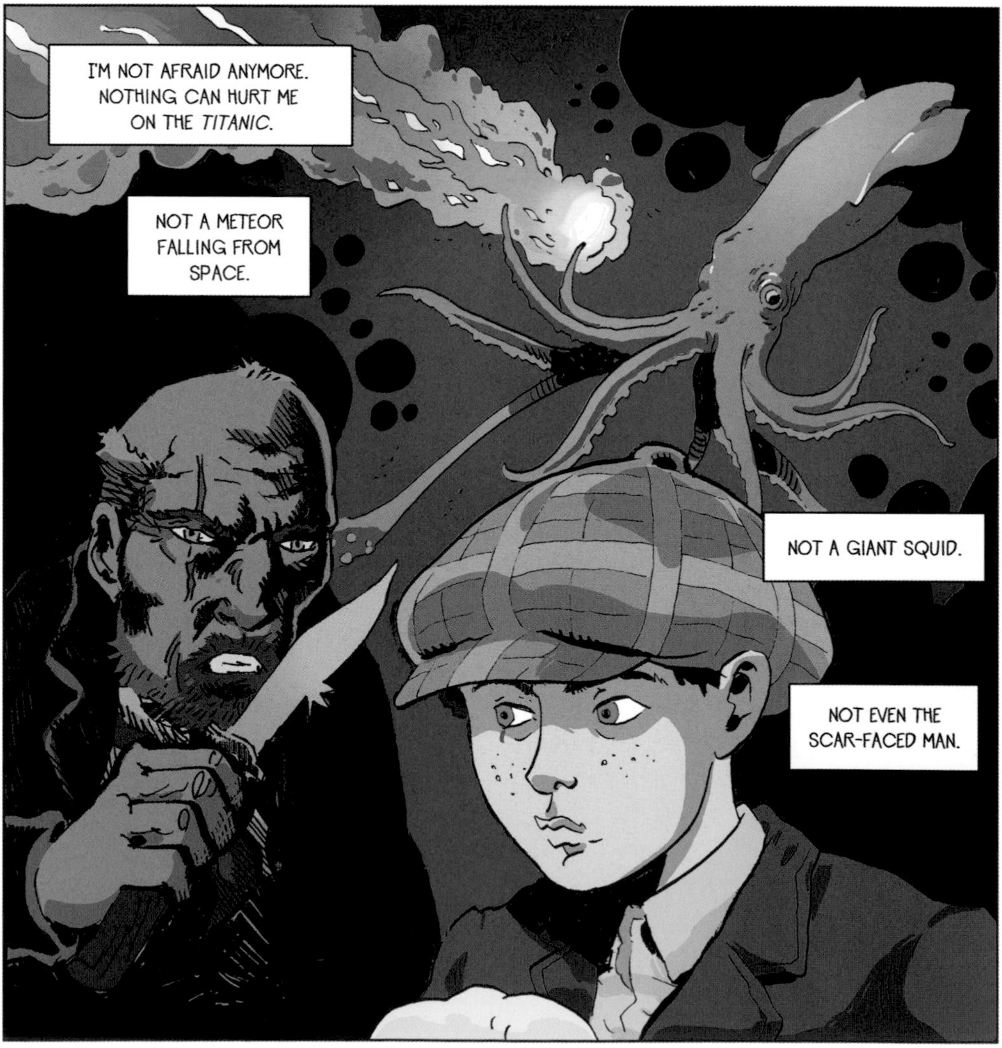
I'M NOT AFRAID ANYMORE. NOTHING CAN HURT ME ON THE *TITANIC*.
NOT A METEOR FALLING FROM SPACE.
NOT A GIANT SQUID.
NOT EVEN THE SCAR-FACED MAN.

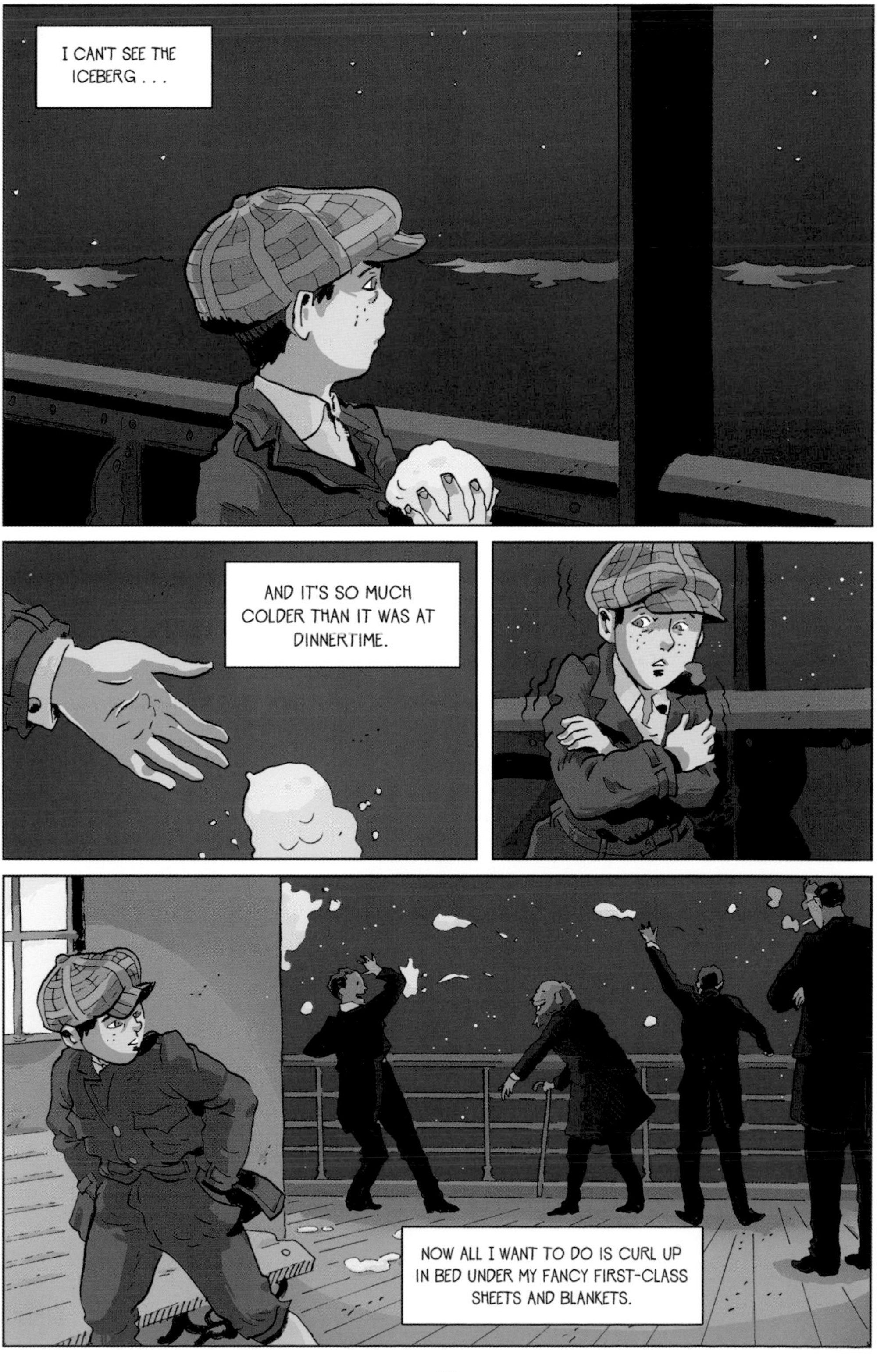
I CAN'T SEE THE ICEBERG . . .
AND IT'S SO MUCH COLDER THAN IT WAS AT DINNERTIME.
NOW ALL I WANT TO DO IS CURL UP IN BED UNDER MY FANCY FIRST-CLASS SHEETS AND BLANKETS.

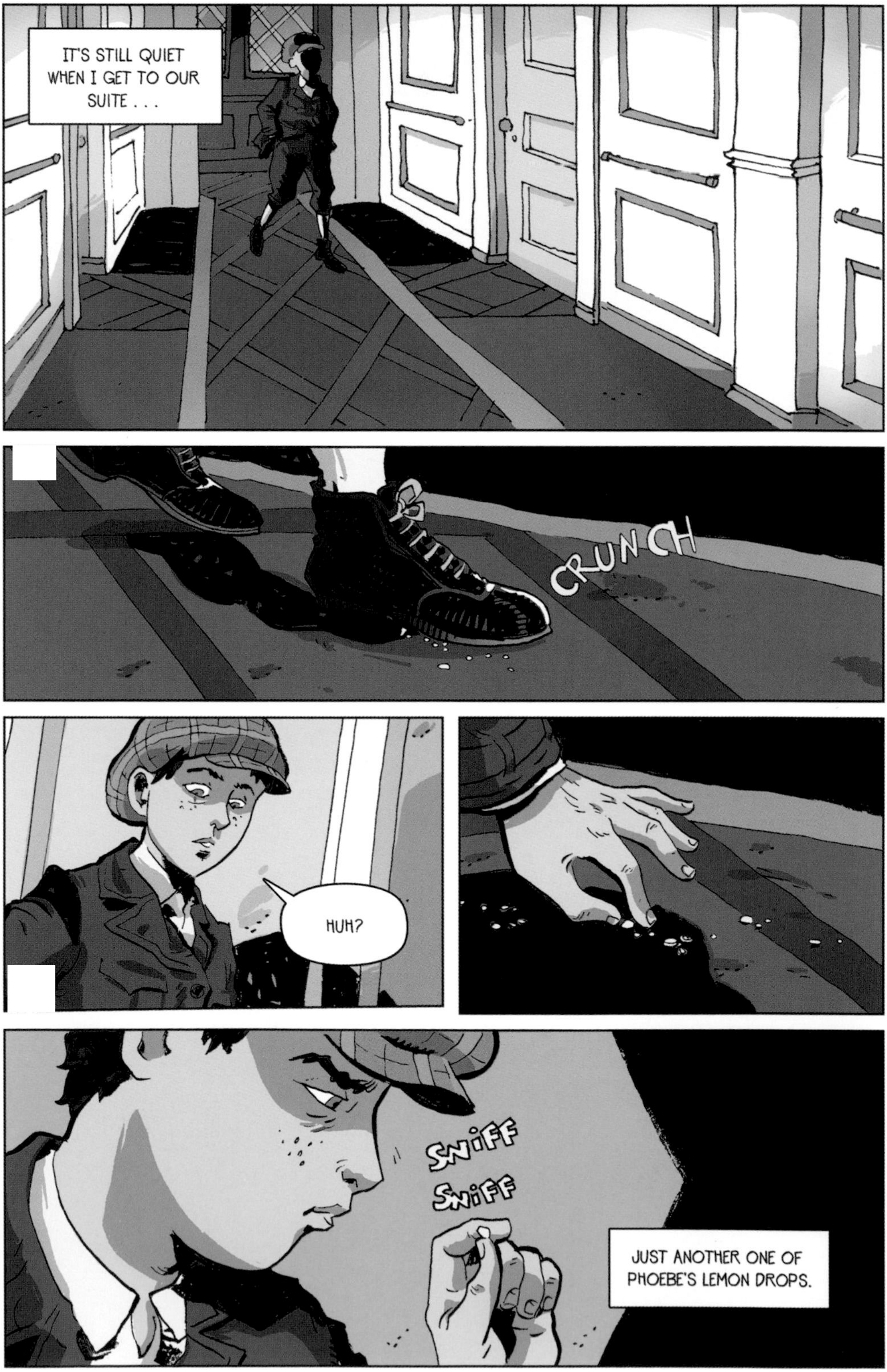
IT'S STILL QUIET WHEN I GET TO OUR SUITE . . .
CRUNCH
HUH?
SNIFF
SNIFF
JUST ANOTHER ONE OF PHOEBE'S LEMON DROPS.

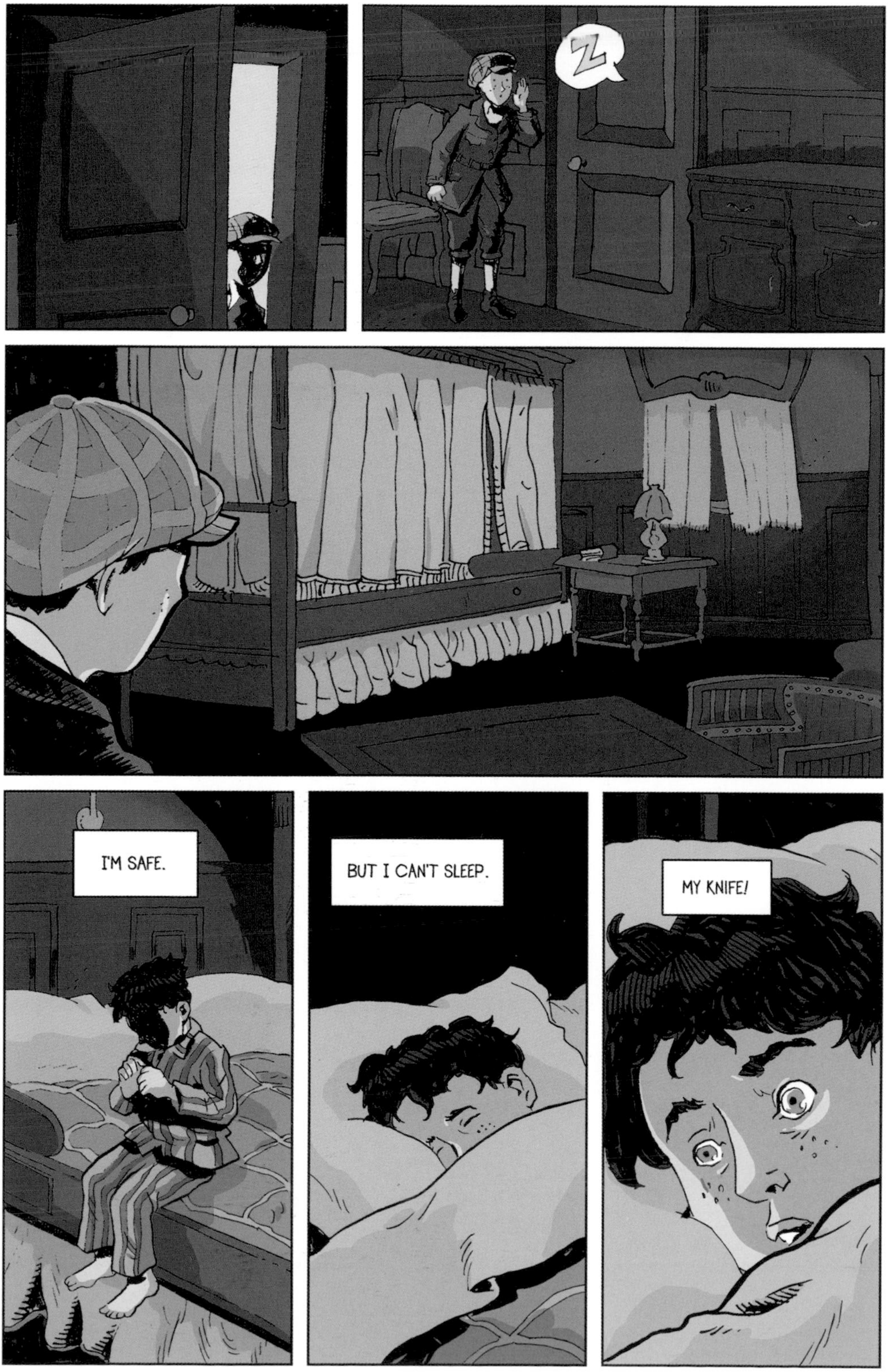
Z
I'M SAFE.
BUT I CAN'T SLEEP.
MY KNIFE!

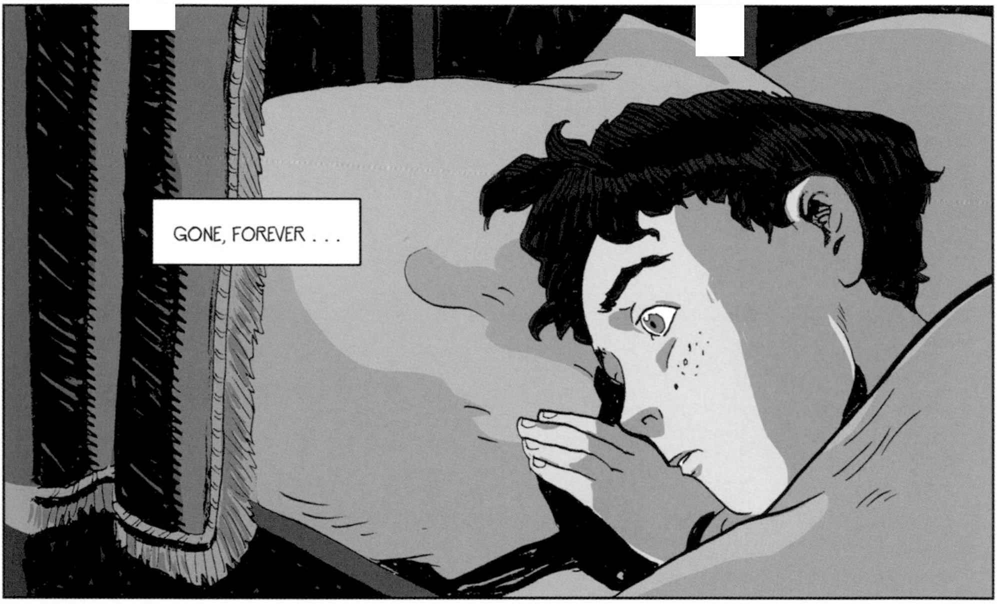
GONE, FOREVER . . .

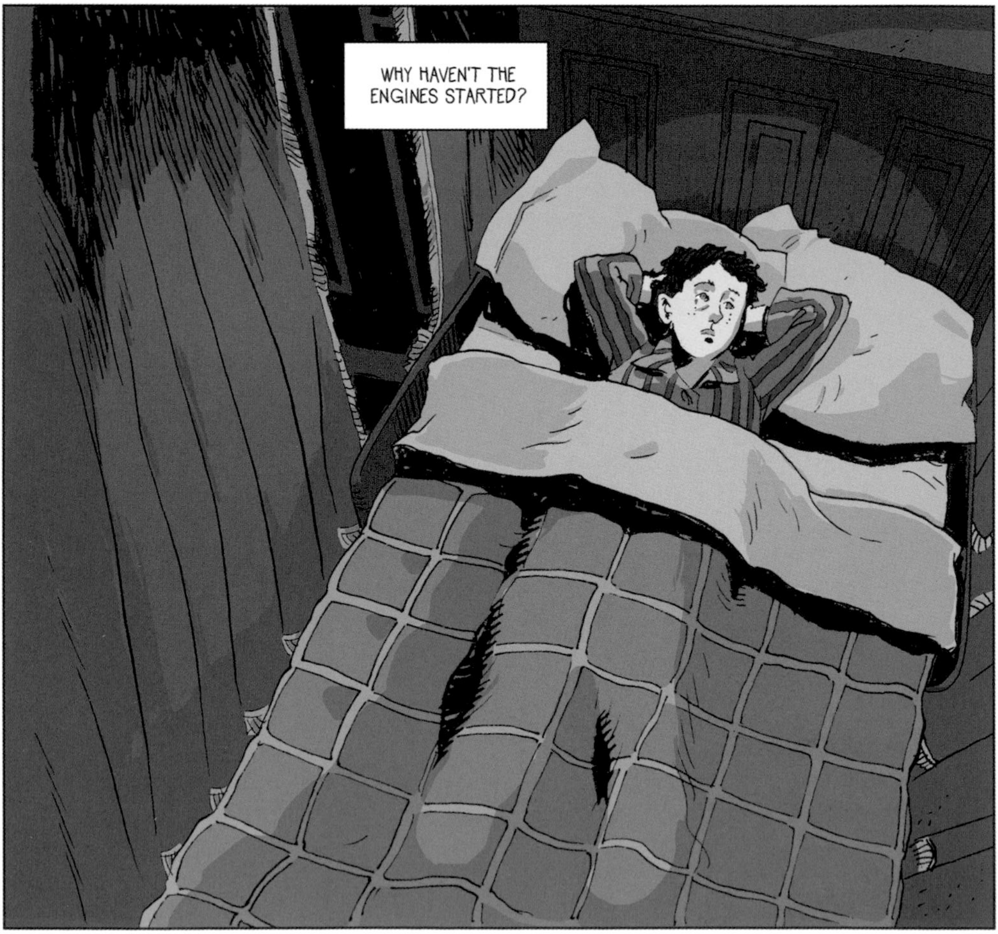
WHY HAVEN'T THE ENGINES STARTED?

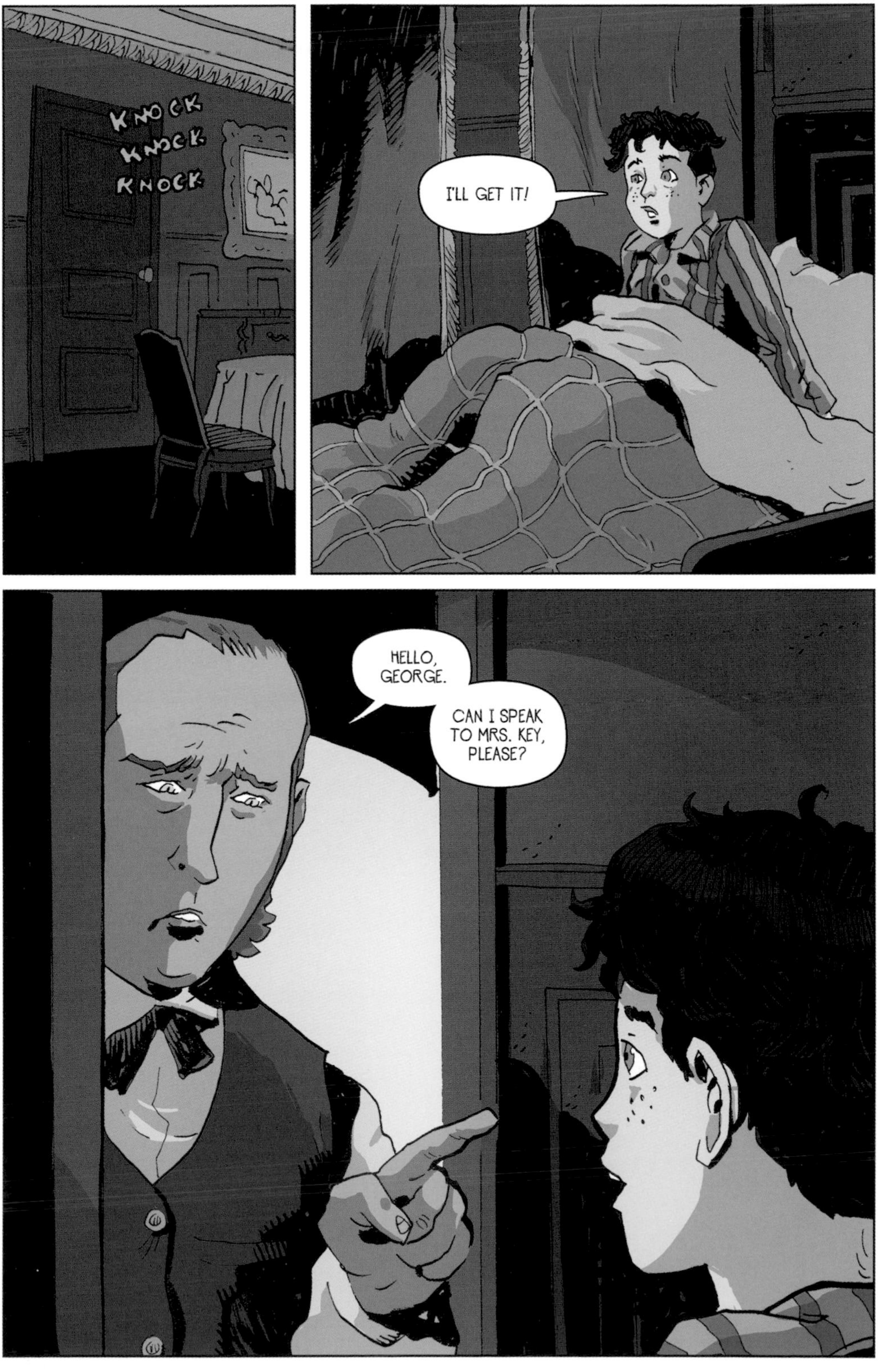
KNOCK
KNOCK
KNOCK
I'LL GET IT!
HELLO, GEORGE.
CAN I SPEAK TO MRS. KEY, PLEASE?

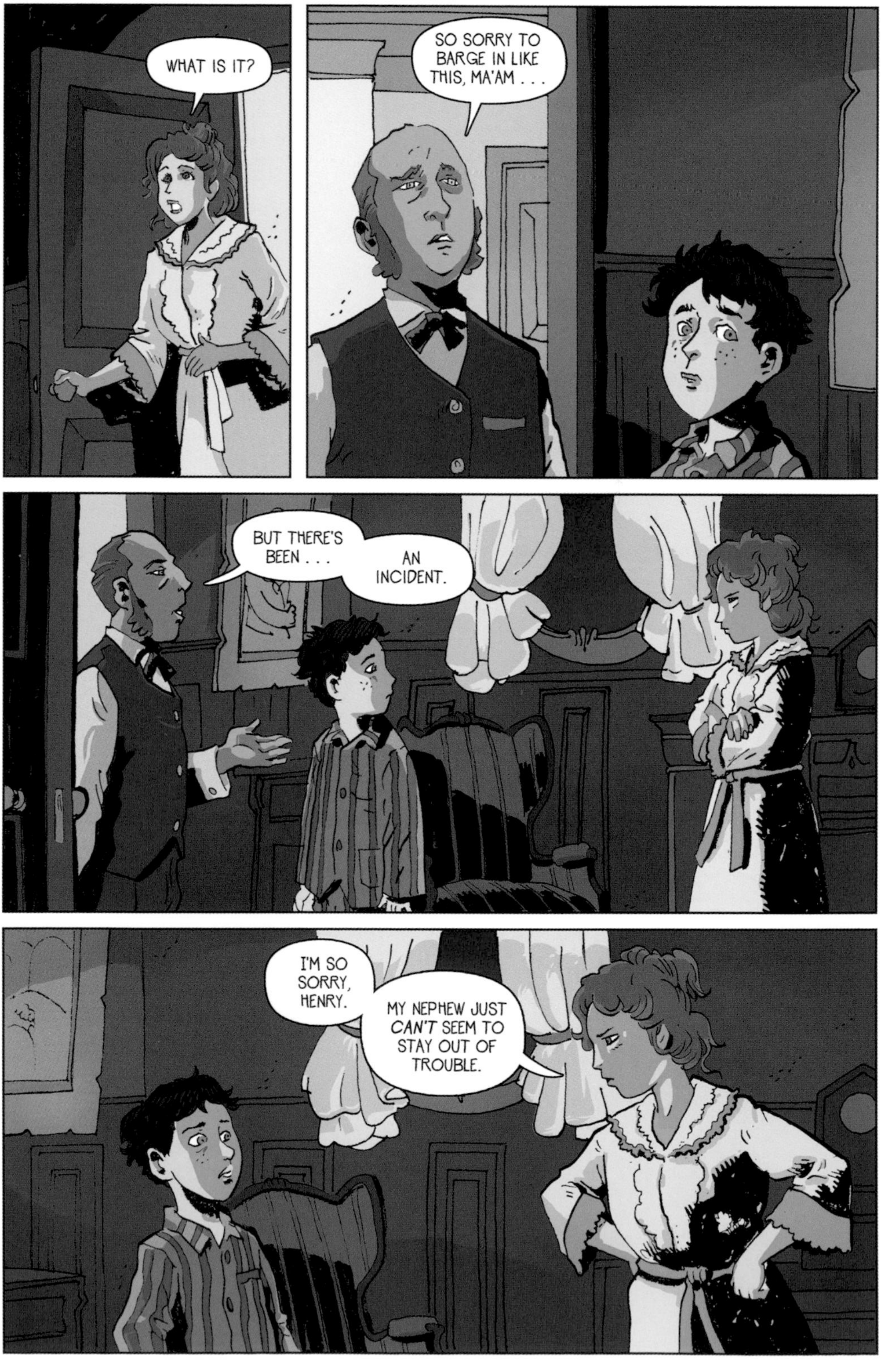
WHAT IS IT?
SO SORRY TO BARGE IN LIKE THIS, MA'AM . . .
BUT THERE'S BEEN . . .
AN INCIDENT.
I'M SO SORRY, HENRY.
MY NEPHEW JUST *CAN'T* SEEM TO STAY OUT OF TROUBLE.

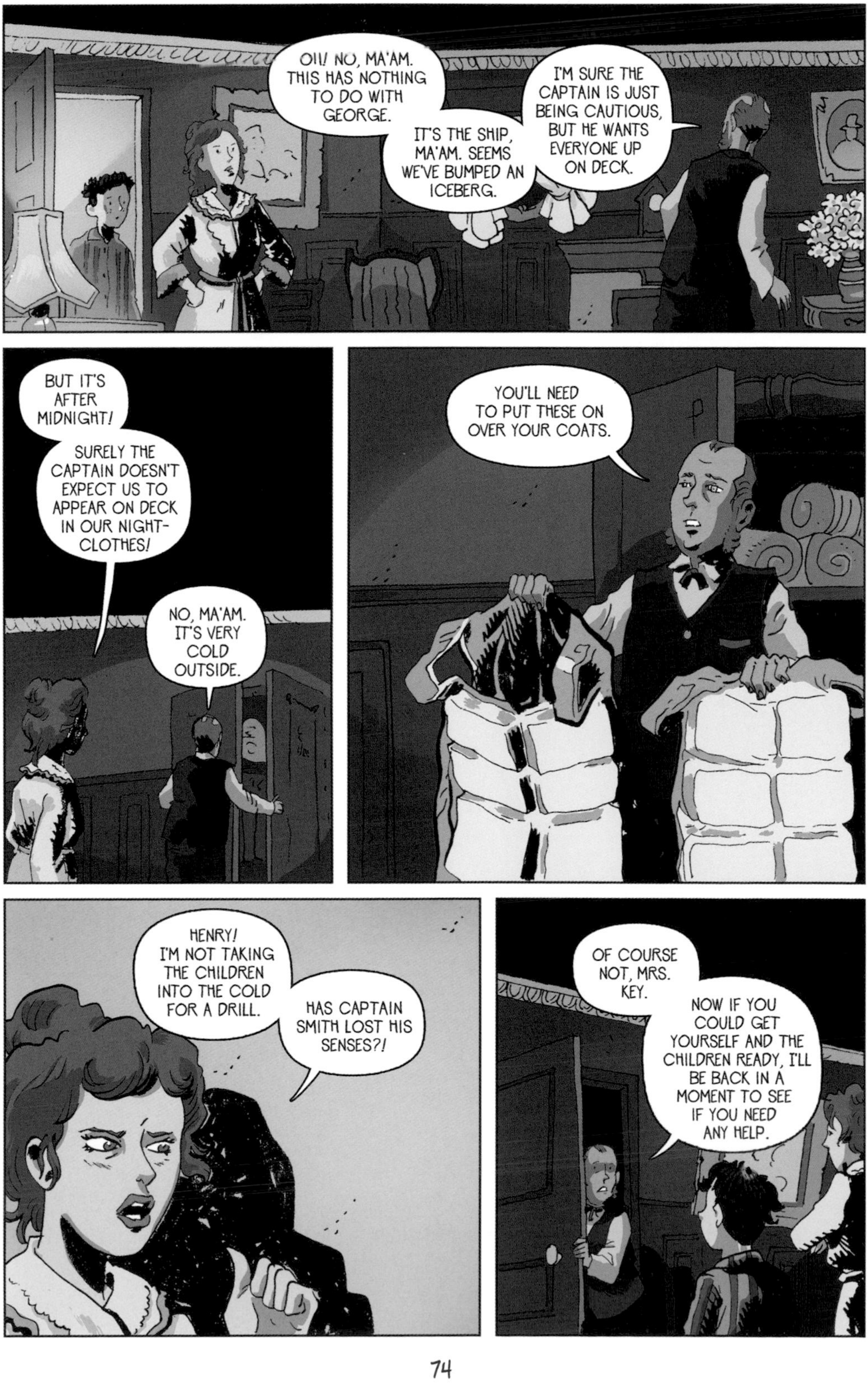
OH! NO, MA'AM. THIS HAS NOTHING TO DO WITH GEORGE.
IT'S THE SHIP, MA'AM. SEEMS WE'VE BUMPED AN ICEBERG.
I'M SURE THE CAPTAIN IS JUST BEING CAUTIOUS, BUT HE WANTS EVERYONE UP ON DECK.
BUT IT'S AFTER MIDNIGHT!
SURELY THE CAPTAIN DOESN'T EXPECT US TO APPEAR ON DECK IN OUR NIGHT-CLOTHES!
NO, MA'AM. IT'S VERY COLD OUTSIDE.
YOU'LL NEED TO PUT THESE ON OVER YOUR COATS.
HENRY! I'M NOT TAKING THE CHILDREN INTO THE COLD FOR A DRILL.
HAS CAPTAIN SMITH LOST HIS SENSES?!
OF COURSE NOT, MRS. KEY.
NOW IF YOU COULD GET YOURSELF AND THE CHILDREN READY, I'LL BE BACK IN A MOMENT TO SEE IF YOU NEED ANY HELP.

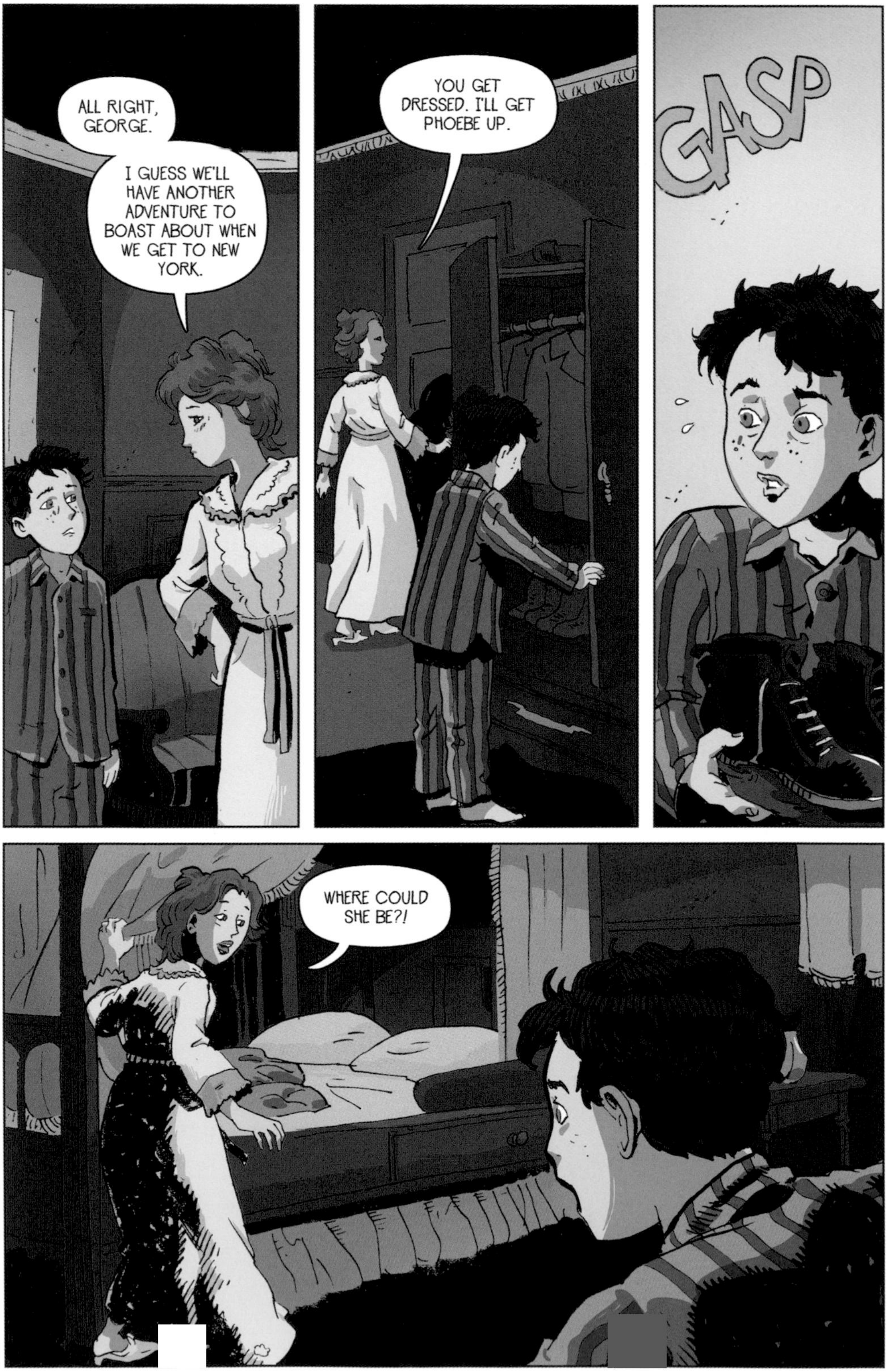
ALL RIGHT, GEORGE.
I GUESS WE'LL HAVE ANOTHER ADVENTURE TO BOAST ABOUT WHEN WE GET TO NEW YORK.
YOU GET DRESSED. I'LL GET PHOEBE UP.
GASP
WHERE COULD SHE BE?!

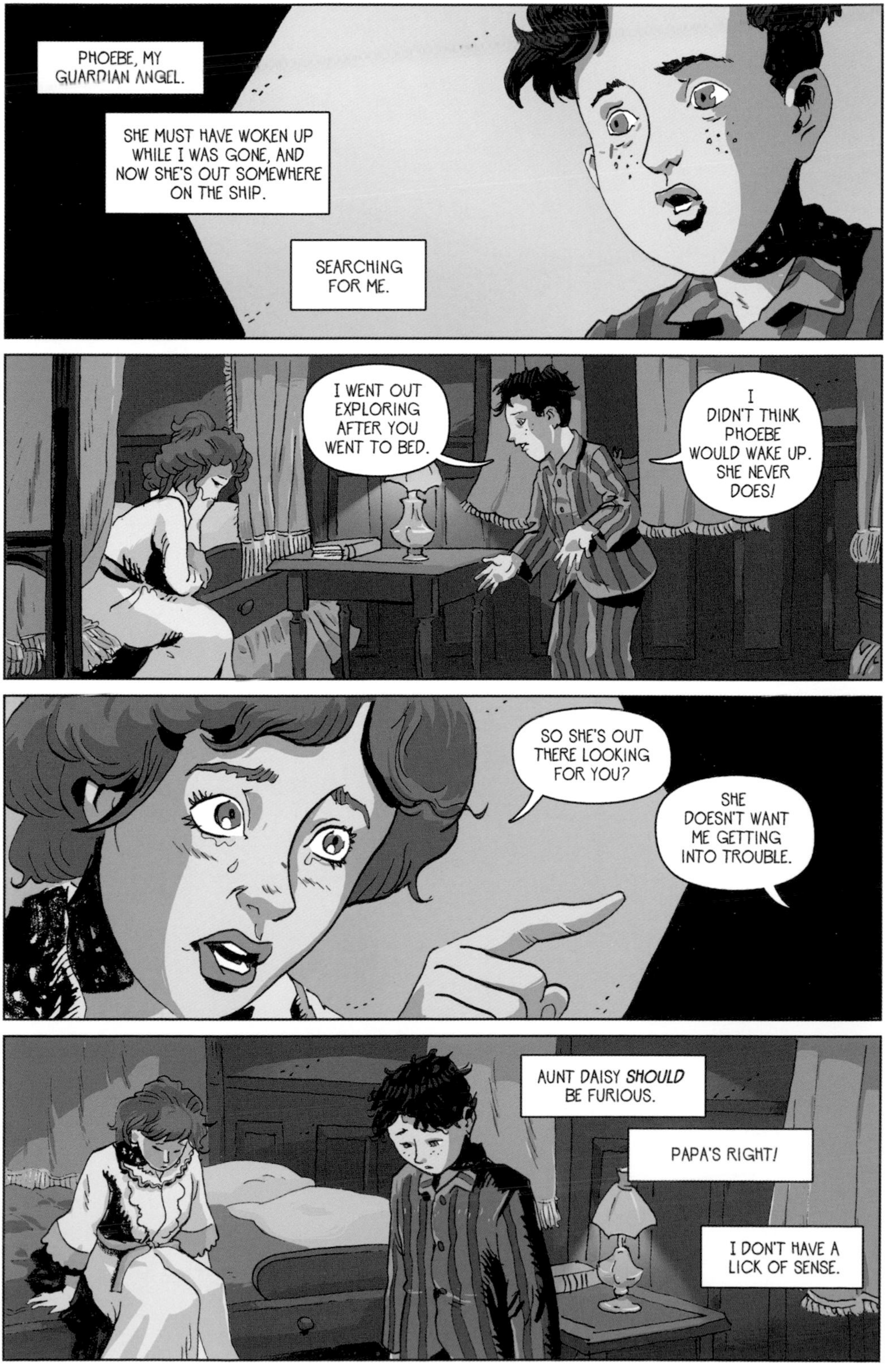
PHOEBE, MY GUARDIAN ANGEL.
SHE MUST HAVE WOKEN UP WHILE I WAS GONE, AND NOW SHE'S OUT SOMEWHERE ON THE SHIP.
SEARCHING FOR ME.
I WENT OUT EXPLORING AFTER YOU WENT TO BED.
I DIDN'T THINK PHOEBE WOULD WAKE UP. SHE NEVER DOES!
SO SHE'S OUT THERE LOOKING FOR YOU?
SHE DOESN'T WANT ME GETTING INTO TROUBLE.
AUNT DAISY *SHOULD* BE FURIOUS.
PAPA'S RIGHT!
I DON'T HAVE A LICK OF SENSE.

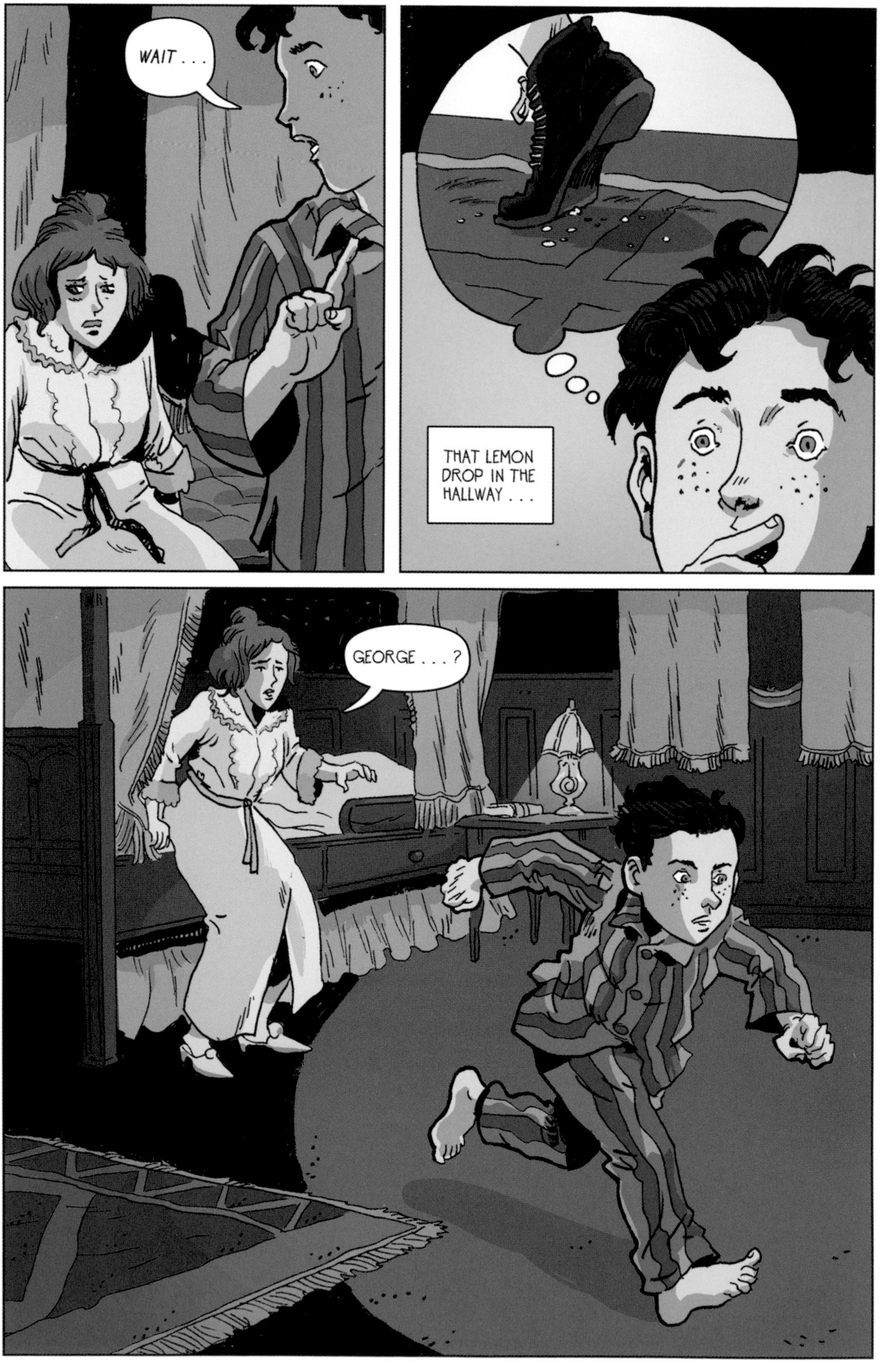
WAIT . . .
THAT LEMON DROP IN THE HALLWAY . . .
GEORGE . . . ?

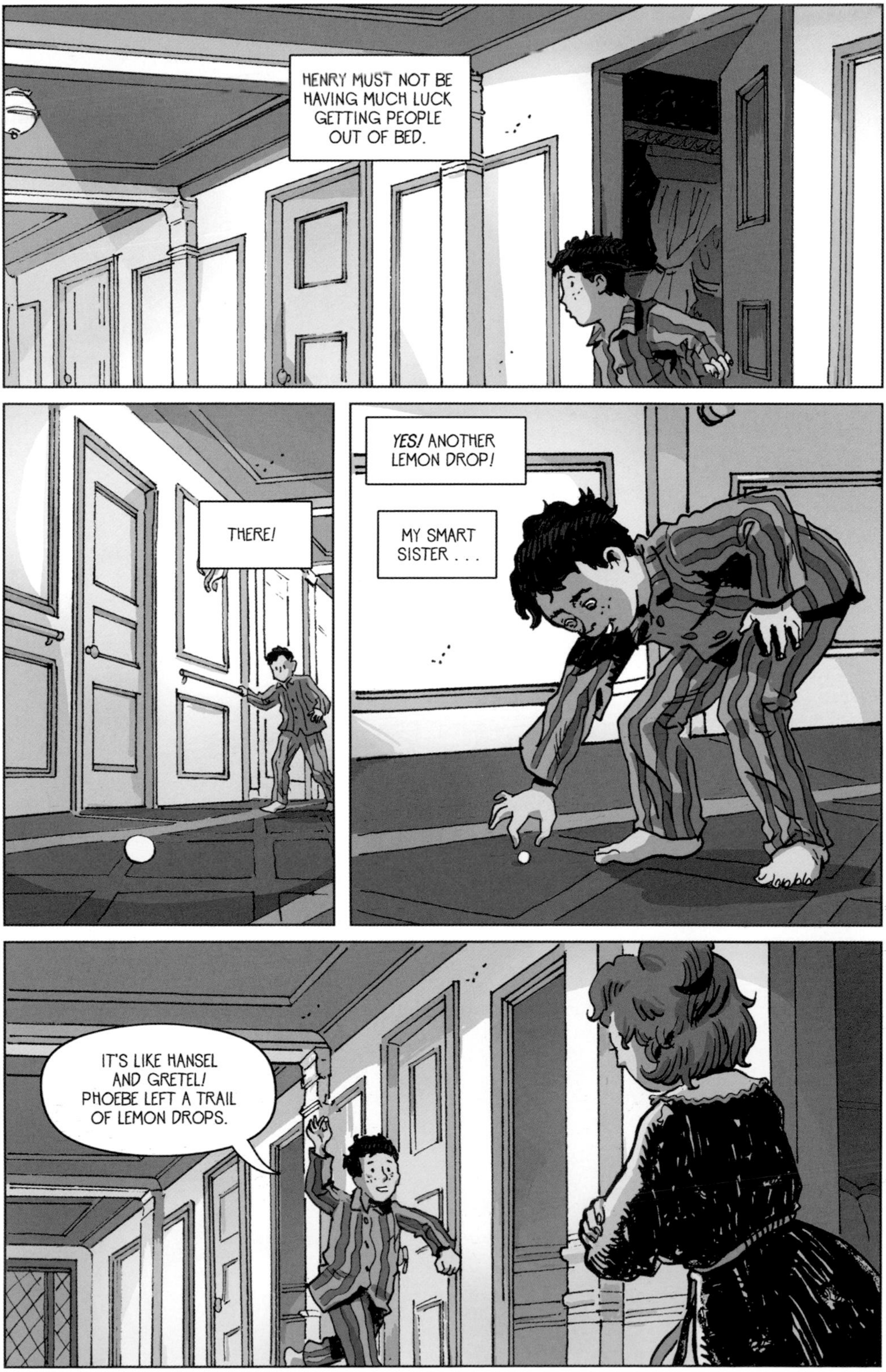
HENRY MUST NOT BE HAVING MUCH LUCK GETTING PEOPLE OUT OF BED.
THERE!
YES! ANOTHER LEMON DROP!
MY SMART SISTER . . .
IT'S LIKE HANSEL AND GRETEL! PHOEBE LEFT A TRAIL OF LEMON DROPS.

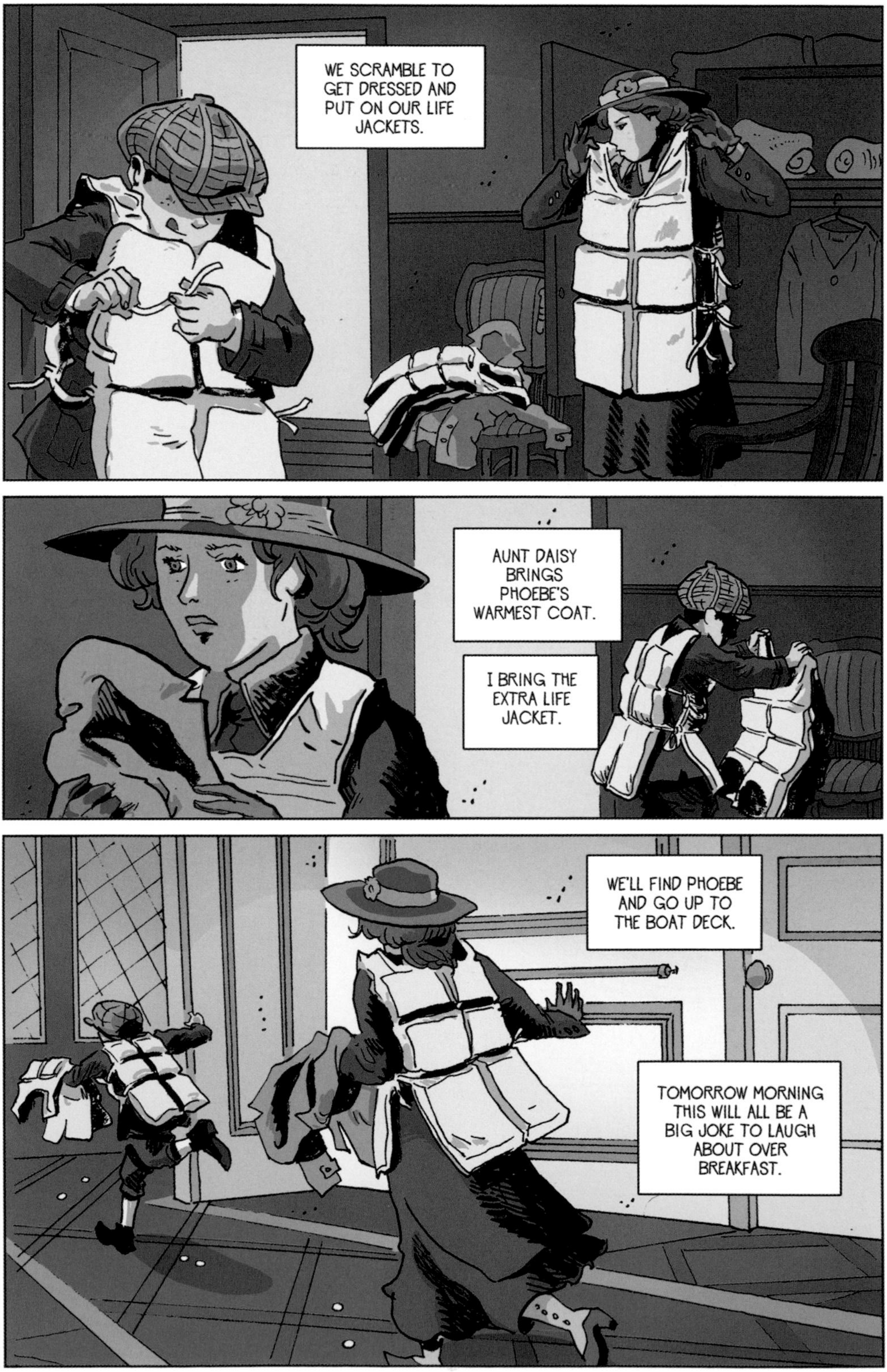
WE SCRAMBLE TO GET DRESSED AND PUT ON OUR LIFE JACKETS.
AUNT DAISY BRINGS PHOEBE'S WARMEST COAT.
I BRING THE EXTRA LIFE JACKET.
WE'LL FIND PHOEBE AND GO UP TO THE BOAT DECK.
TOMORROW MORNING THIS WILL ALL BE A BIG JOKE TO LAUGH ABOUT OVER BREAKFAST.

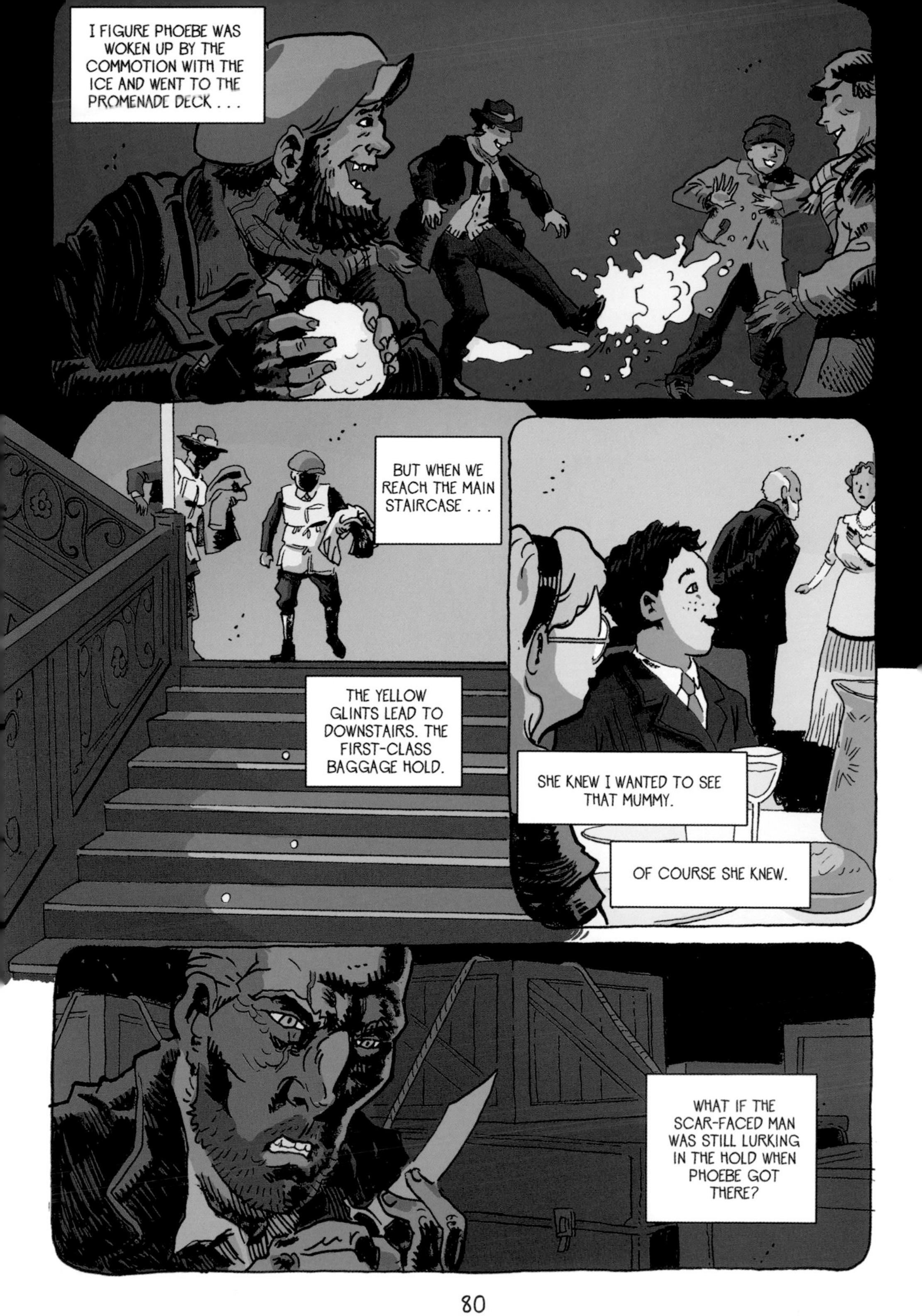
I FIGURE PHOEBE WAS WOKEN UP BY THE COMMOTION WITH THE ICE AND WENT TO THE PROMENADE DECK . . .
BUT WHEN WE REACH THE MAIN STAIRCASE . . .
THE YELLOW GLINTS LEAD TO DOWNSTAIRS. THE FIRST-CLASS BAGGAGE HOLD.
SHE KNEW I WANTED TO SEE THAT MUMMY.
OF COURSE SHE KNEW.
WHAT IF THE SCAR-FACED MAN WAS STILL LURKING IN THE HOLD WHEN PHOEBE GOT THERE?

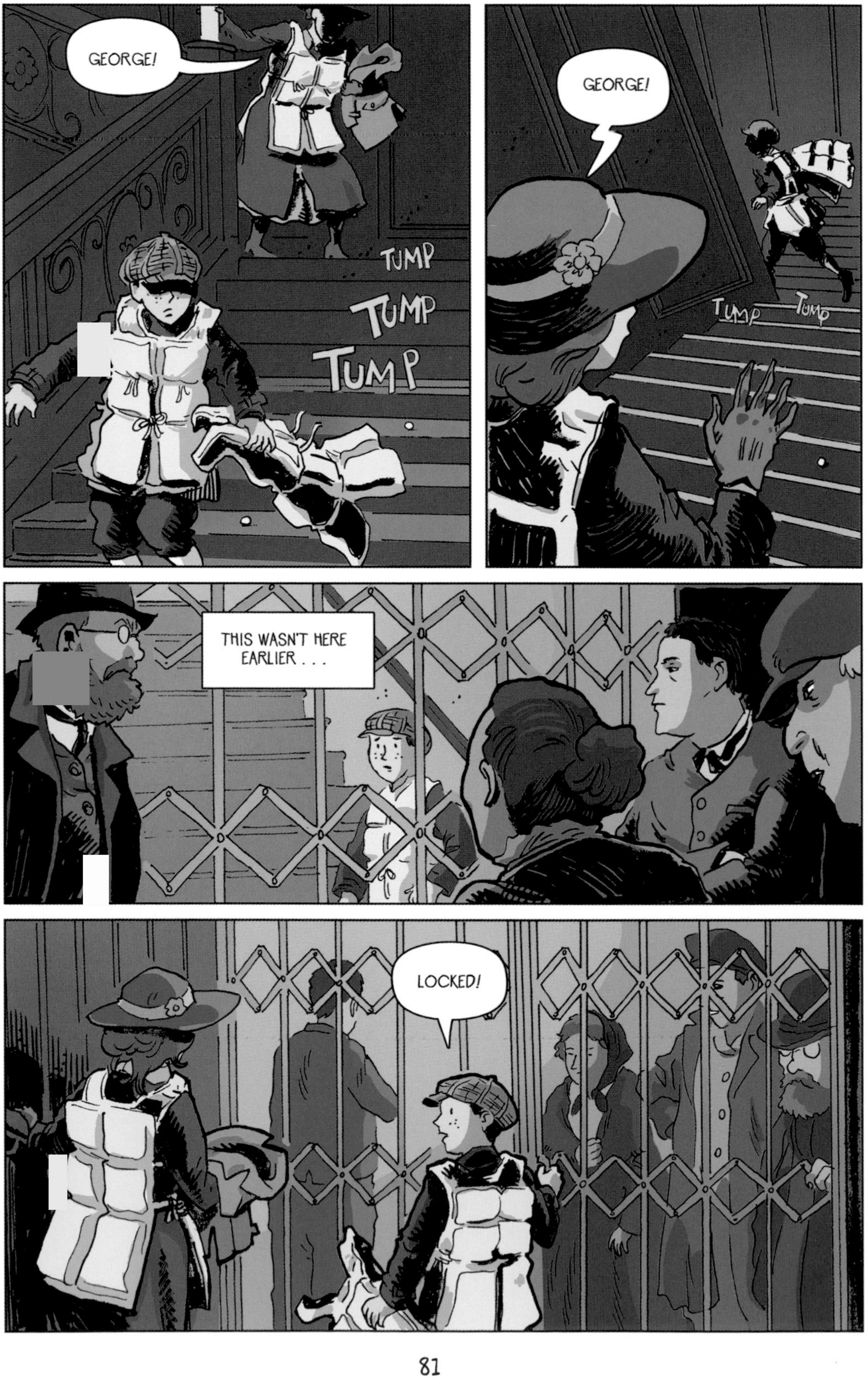
GEORGE!
TUMP
TUMP
TUMP
GEORGE!
TUMP
TUMP
THIS WASN'T HERE EARLIER . . .
LOCKED!

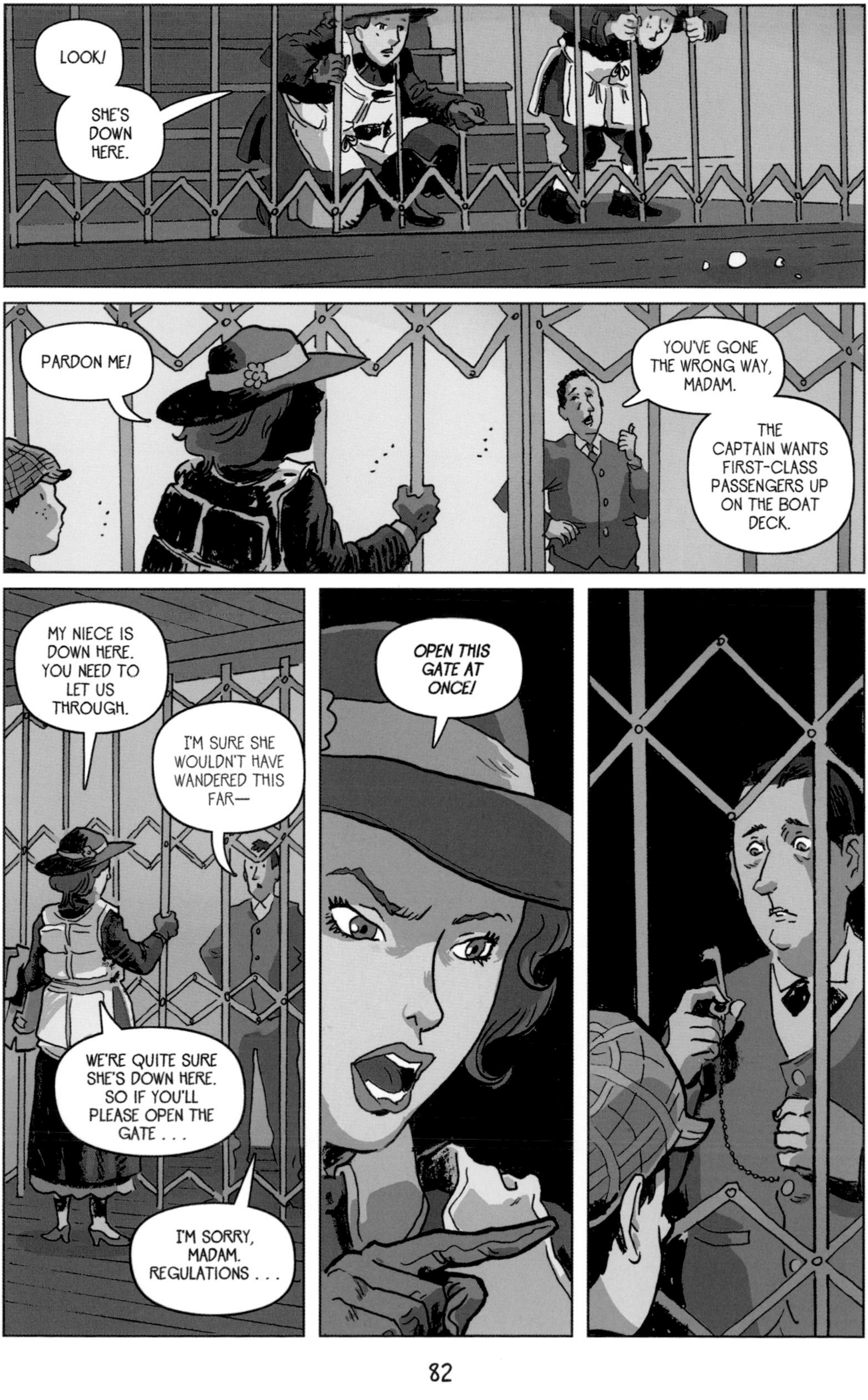
LOOK!
SHE'S DOWN HERE.
PARDON ME!
YOU'VE GONE THE WRONG WAY, MADAM.
THE CAPTAIN WANTS FIRST-CLASS PASSENGERS UP ON THE BOAT DECK.
MY NIECE IS DOWN HERE. YOU NEED TO LET US THROUGH.
I'M SURE SHE WOULDN'T HAVE WANDERED THIS FAR—
WE'RE QUITE SURE SHE'S DOWN HERE. SO IF YOU'LL PLEASE OPEN THE GATE . . .
I'M SORRY, MADAM. REGULATIONS . . .
OPEN THIS GATE AT ONCE!

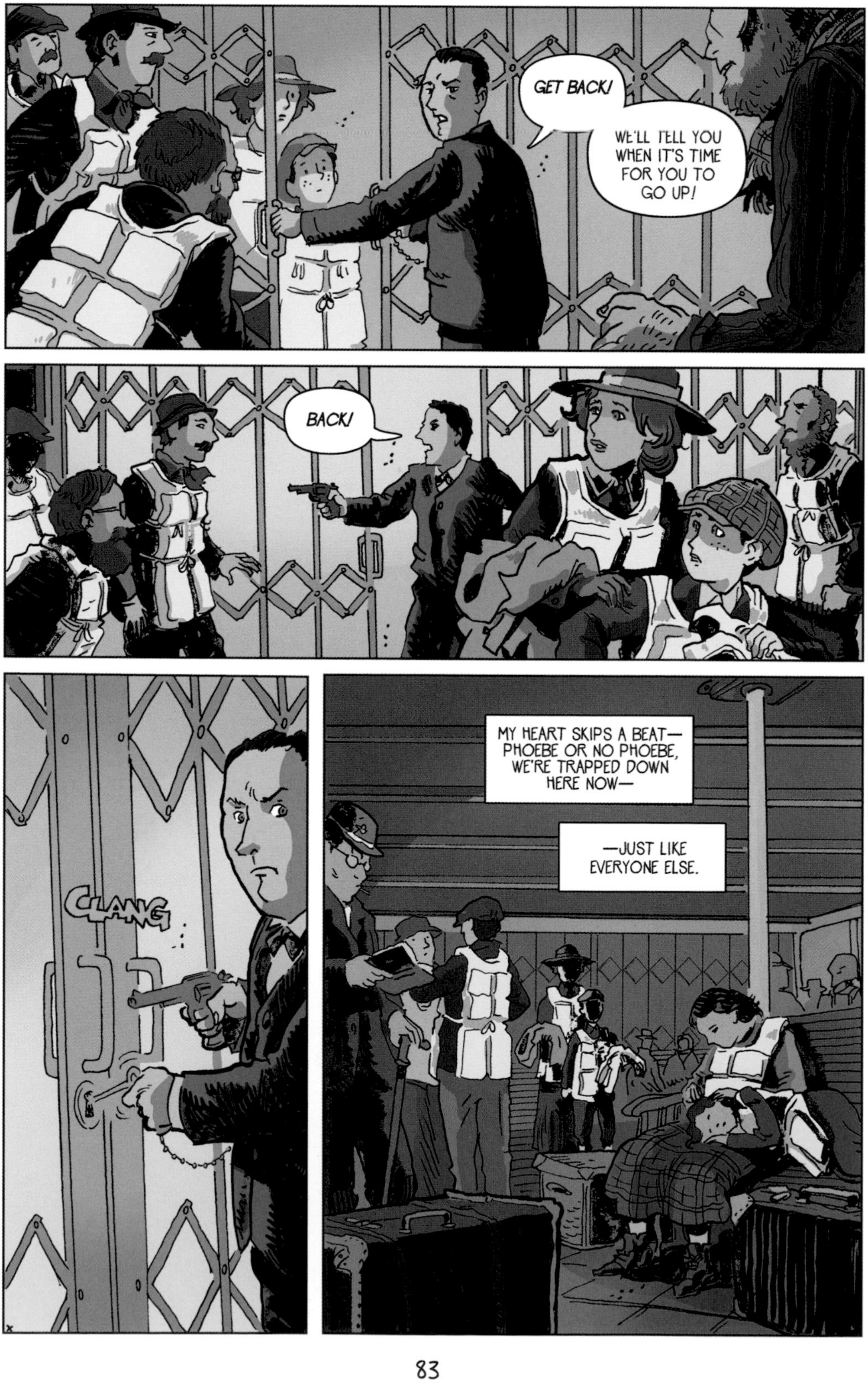
GET BACK!
WE'LL TELL YOU WHEN IT'S TIME FOR YOU TO GO UP!
BACK!
CLANG
MY HEART SKIPS A BEAT— PHOEBE OR NO PHOEBE, WE'RE TRAPPED DOWN HERE NOW—
—JUST LIKE EVERYONE ELSE.

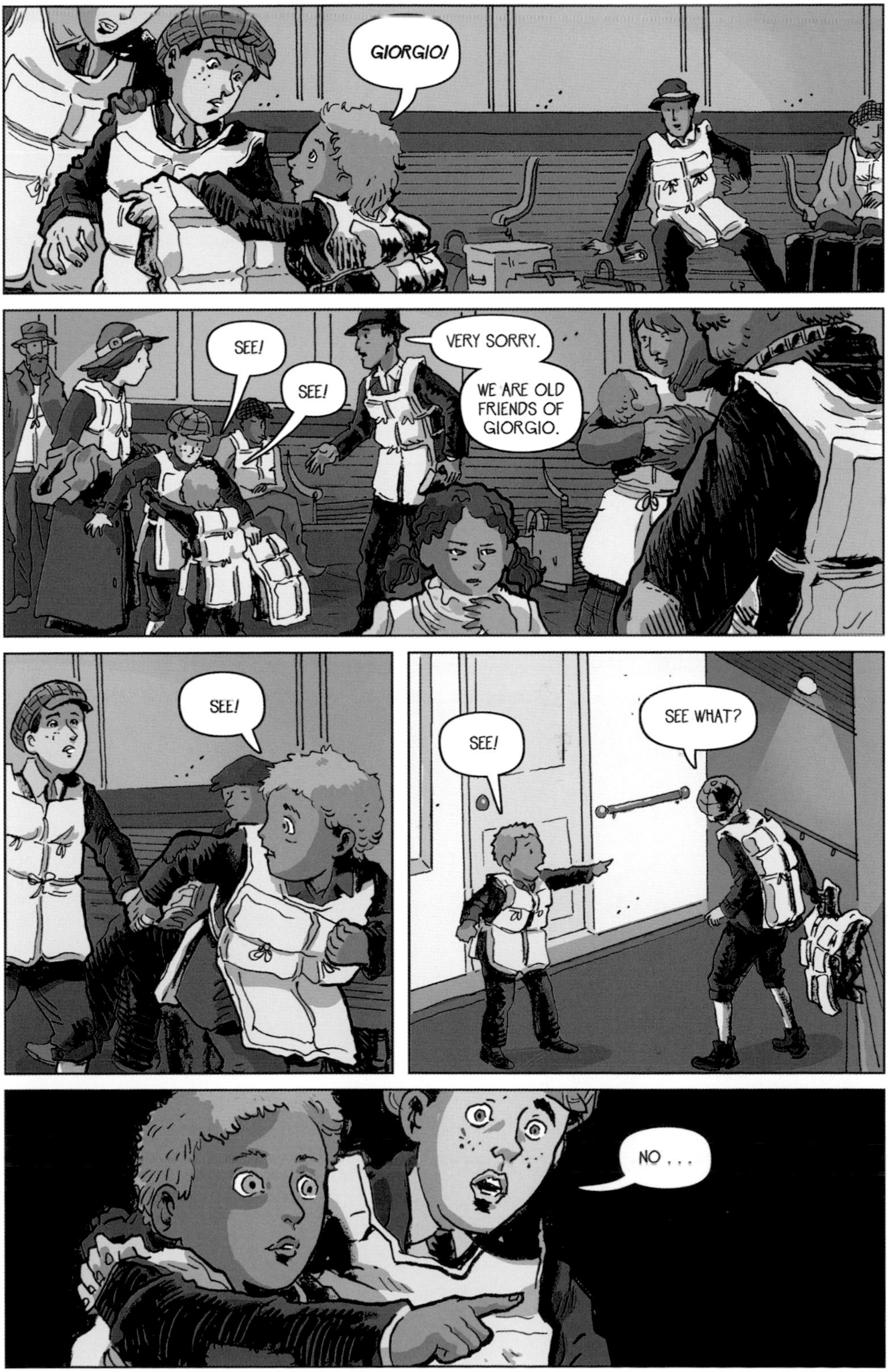
GIORGIO!
SEE!
SEE!
VERY SORRY.
WE ARE OLD FRIENDS OF GIORGIO.
SEE!
SEE!
SEE WHAT?
NO . . .

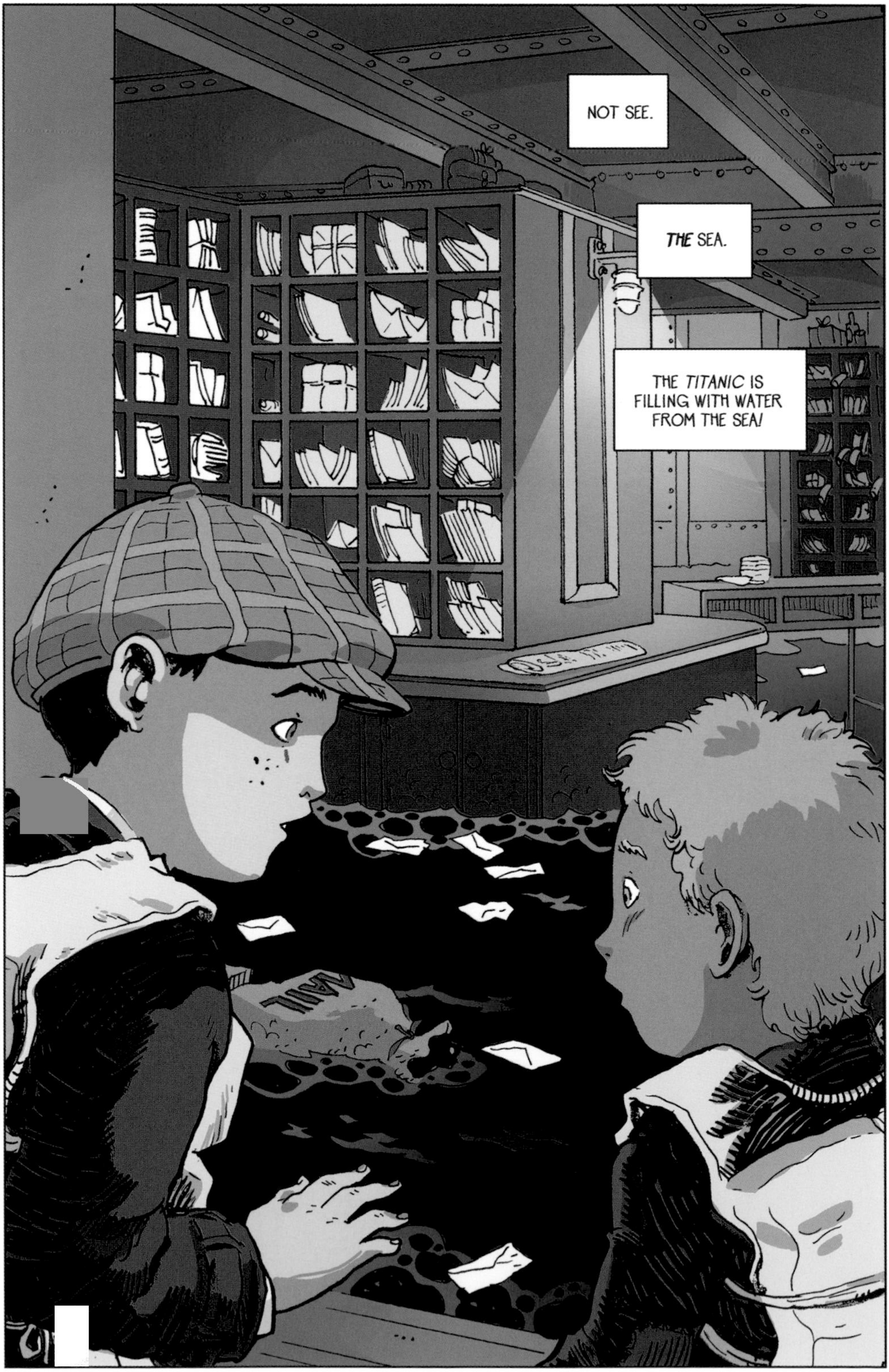
NOT SEE.
THE SEA.
THE *TITANIC* IS FILLING WITH WATER FROM THE SEA!
MAIL

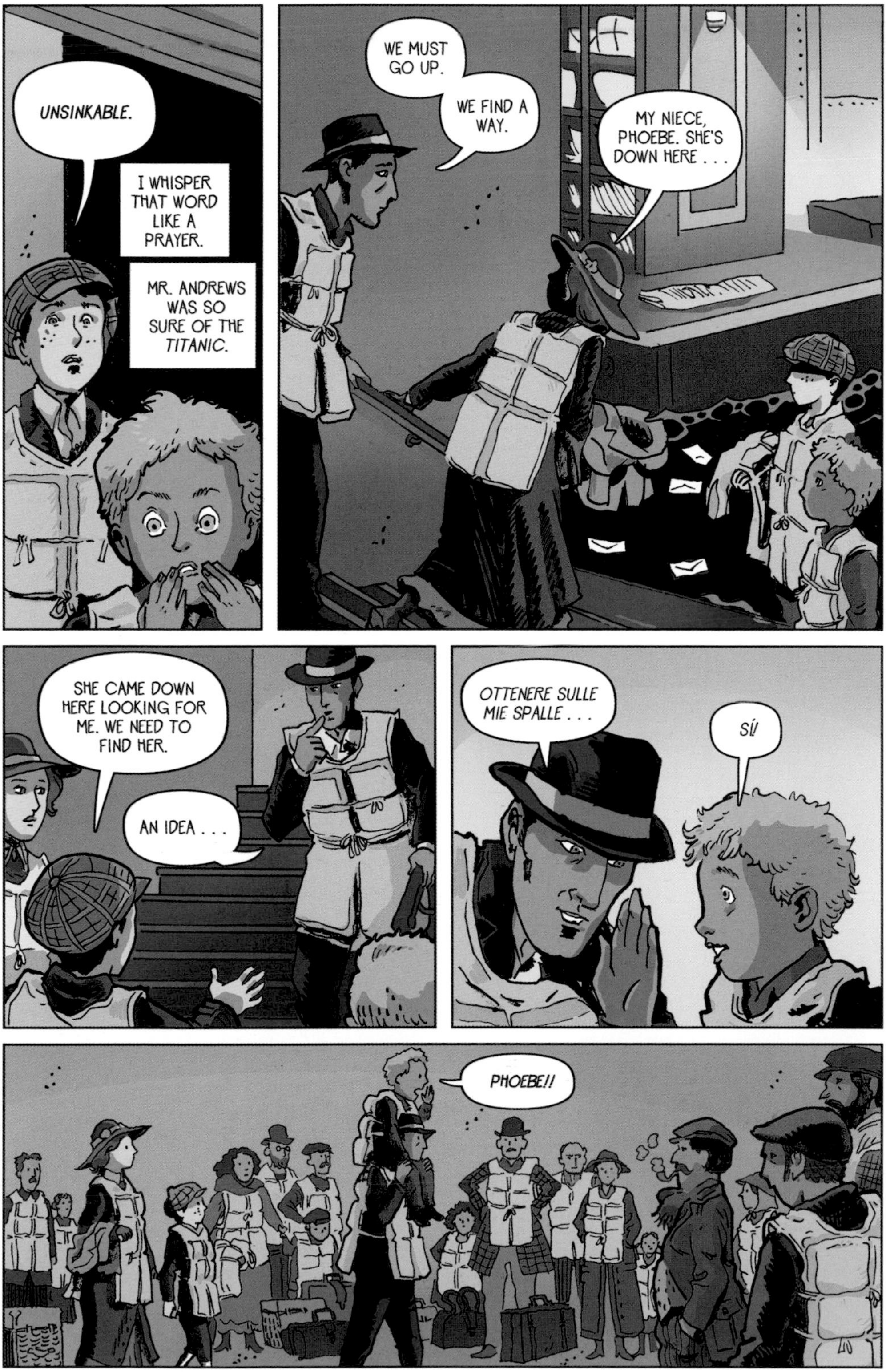
UNSINKABLE.
I WHISPER THAT WORD LIKE A PRAYER.
MR. ANDREWS WAS SO SURE OF THE *TITANIC*.
WE MUST GO UP.
WE FIND A WAY.
MY NIECE, PHOEBE. SHE'S DOWN HERE . . .
SHE CAME DOWN HERE LOOKING FOR ME. WE NEED TO FIND HER.
AN IDEA . . .
OTTENERE SULLE MIE SPALLE . . .
SÍ!
PHOEBE!!

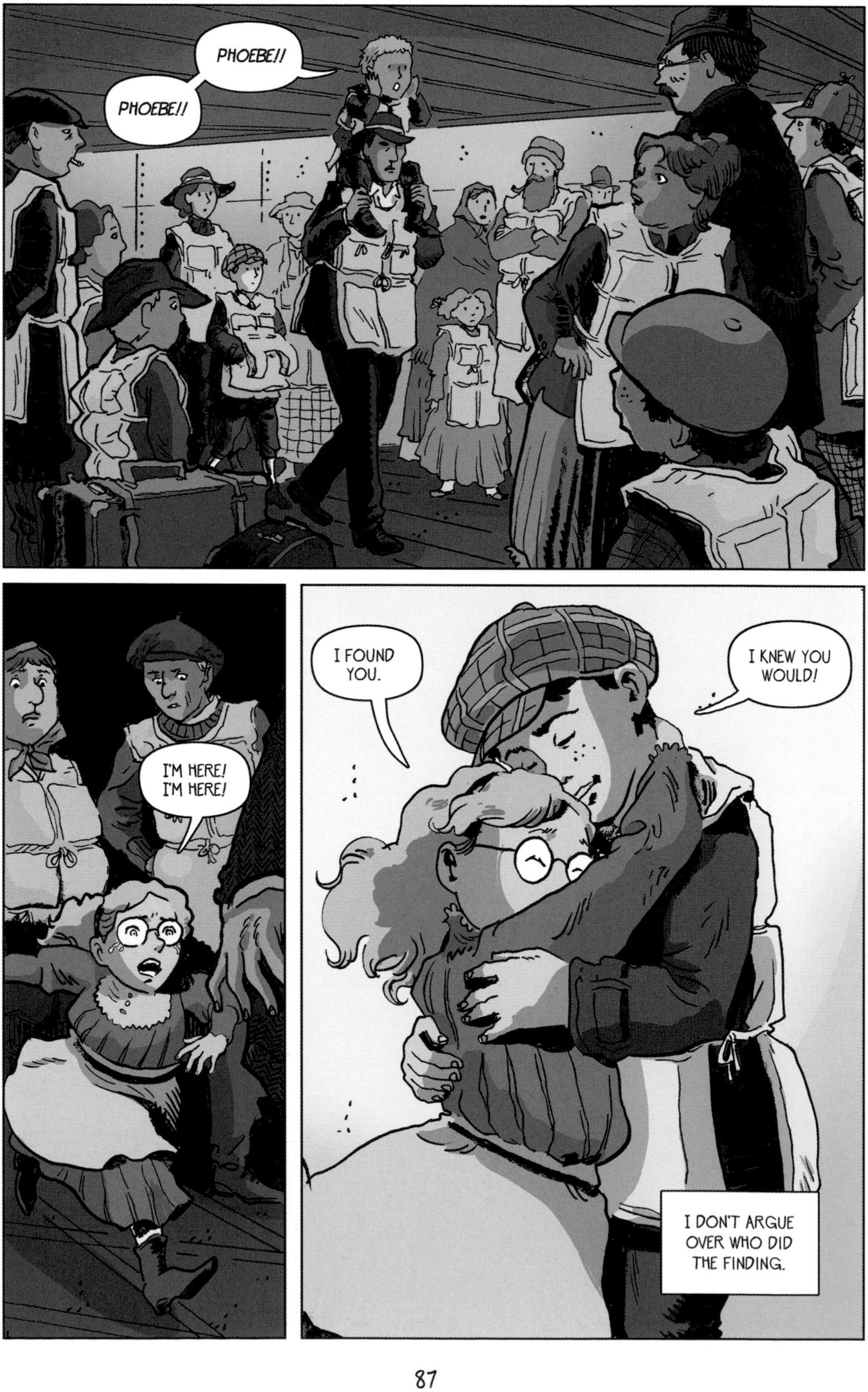
PHOEBE!!
PHOEBE!!
I'M HERE! I'M HERE!
I FOUND YOU.
I KNEW YOU WOULD!
I DON'T ARGUE OVER WHO DID THE FINDING.

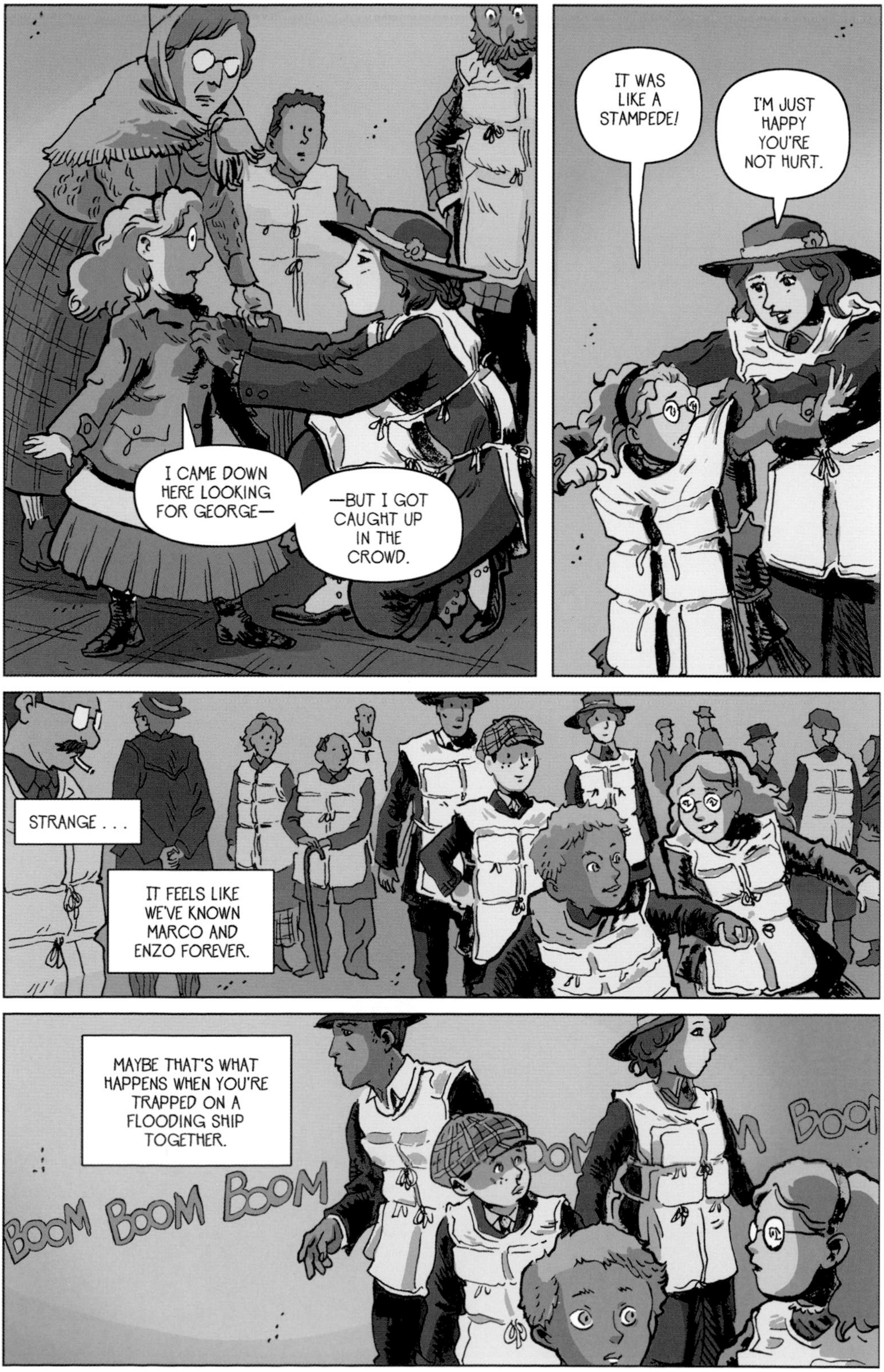
I CAME DOWN HERE LOOKING FOR GEORGE—
—BUT I GOT CAUGHT UP IN THE CROWD.
IT WAS LIKE A STAMPEDE!
I'M JUST HAPPY YOU'RE NOT HURT.
STRANGE . . .
IT FEELS LIKE WE'VE KNOWN MARCO AND ENZO FOREVER.
MAYBE THAT'S WHAT HAPPENS WHEN YOU'RE TRAPPED ON A FLOODING SHIP TOGETHER.
BOOM BOOM BOOM
BOOM

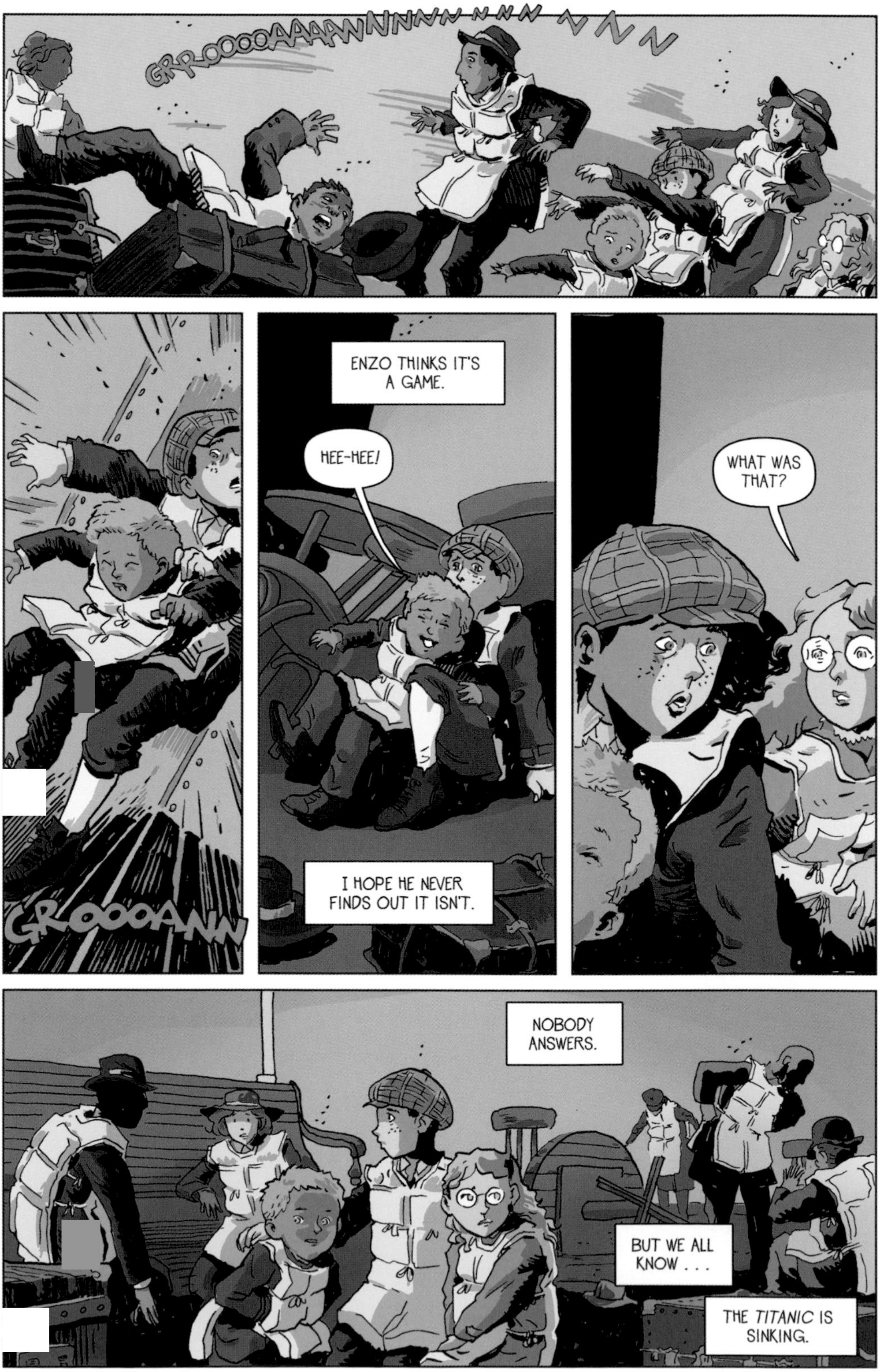
GRROOOOAAAANNNNNNNNNNN NNN
GROOOANN
ENZO THINKS IT'S A GAME.
HEE-HEE!
I HOPE HE NEVER FINDS OUT IT ISN'T.
WHAT WAS THAT?
NOBODY ANSWERS.
BUT WE ALL KNOW . . .
THE *TITANIC* IS SINKING.

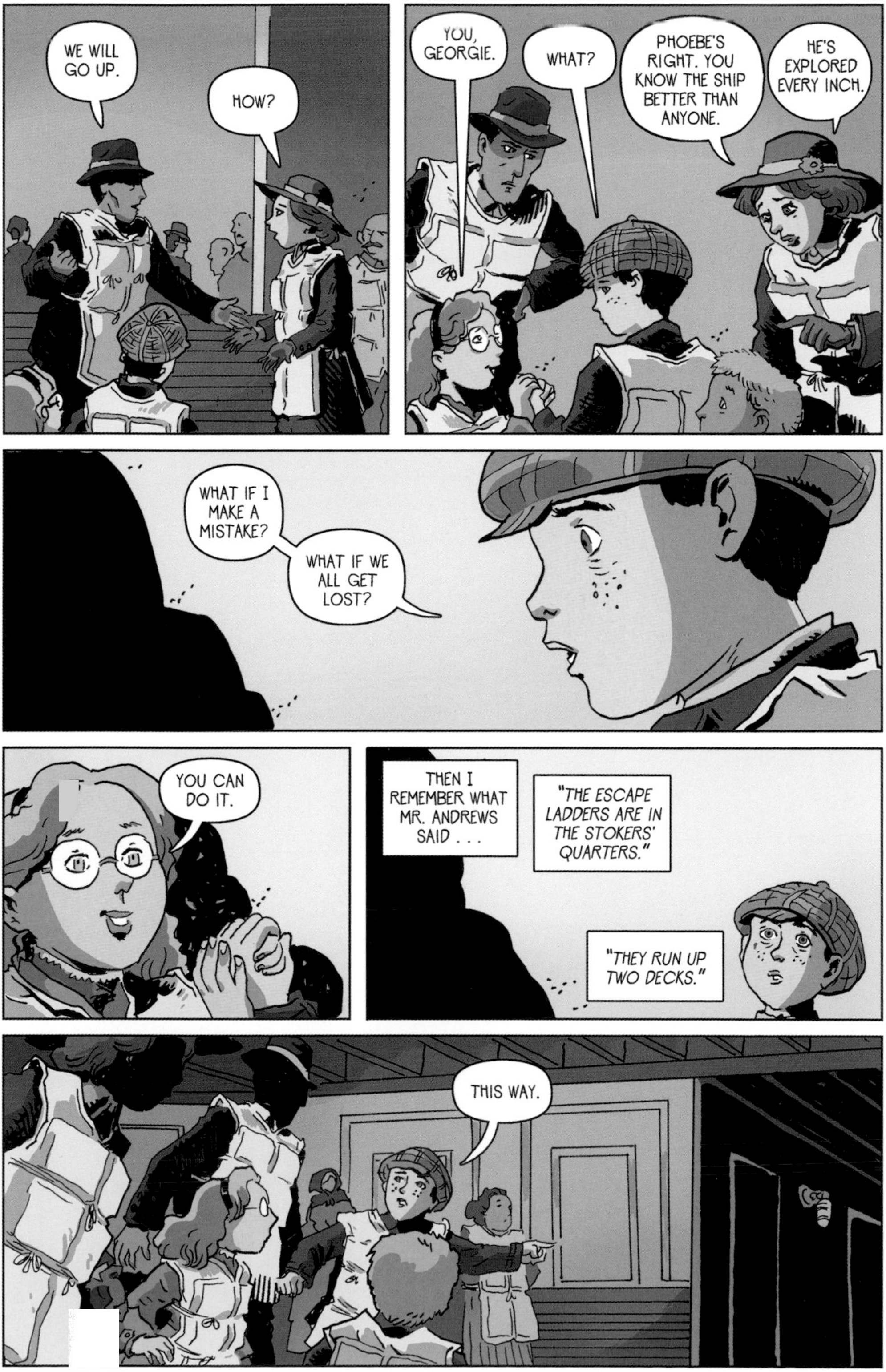
WE WILL GO UP.
HOW?
YOU, GEORGIE.
WHAT?
PHOEBE'S RIGHT. YOU KNOW THE SHIP BETTER THAN ANYONE.
HE'S EXPLORED EVERY INCH.
WHAT IF I MAKE A MISTAKE?
WHAT IF WE ALL GET LOST?
YOU CAN DO IT.
THEN I REMEMBER WHAT MR. ANDREWS SAID . . .
"THE ESCAPE LADDERS ARE IN THE STOKERS' QUARTERS."
"THEY RUN UP TWO DECKS."
THIS WAY.

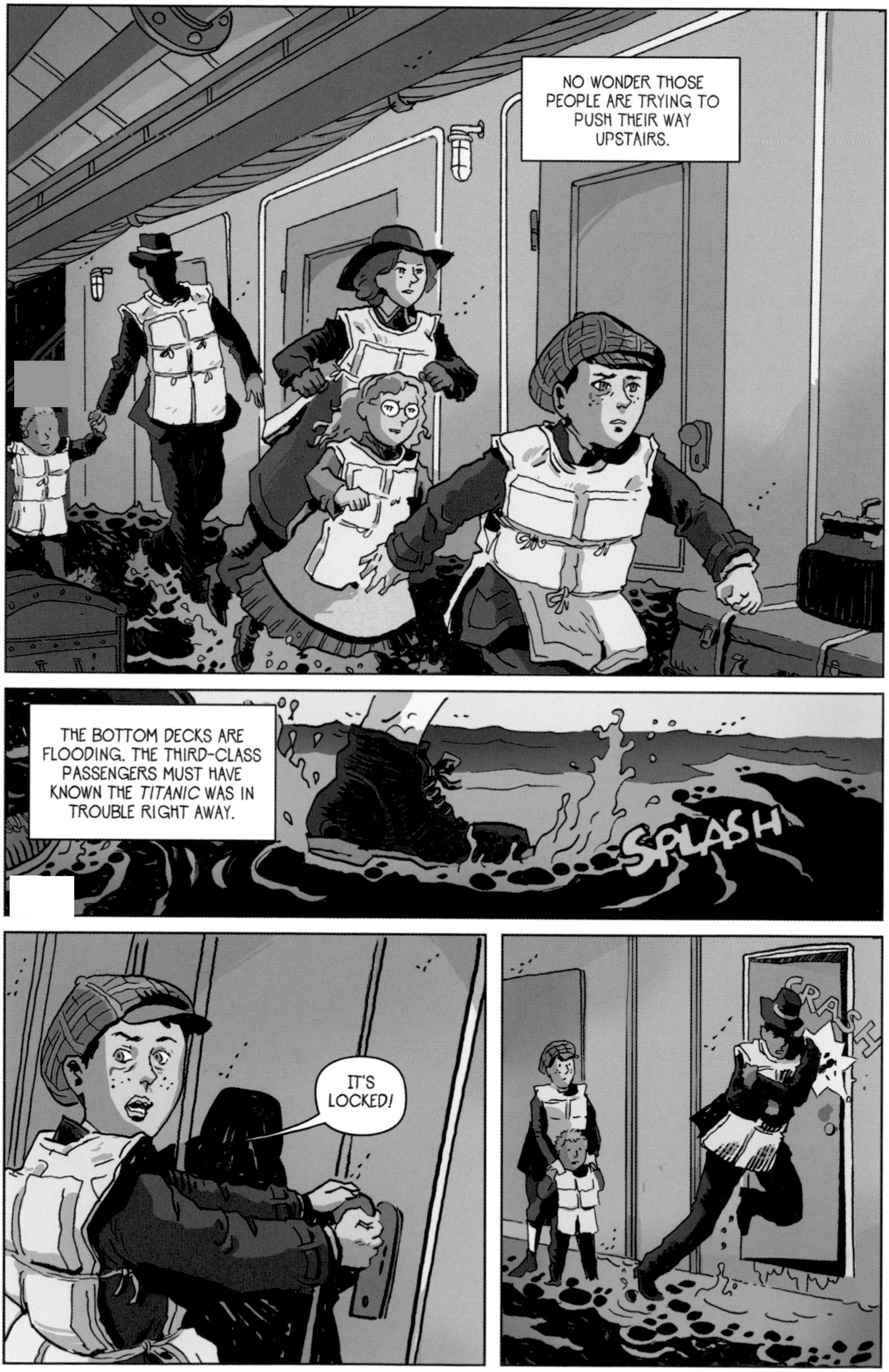
NO WONDER THOSE PEOPLE ARE TRYING TO PUSH THEIR WAY UPSTAIRS.
THE BOTTOM DECKS ARE FLOODING. THE THIRD-CLASS PASSENGERS MUST HAVE KNOWN THE *TITANIC* WAS IN TROUBLE RIGHT AWAY.
SPLASH
IT'S LOCKED!
CRASH

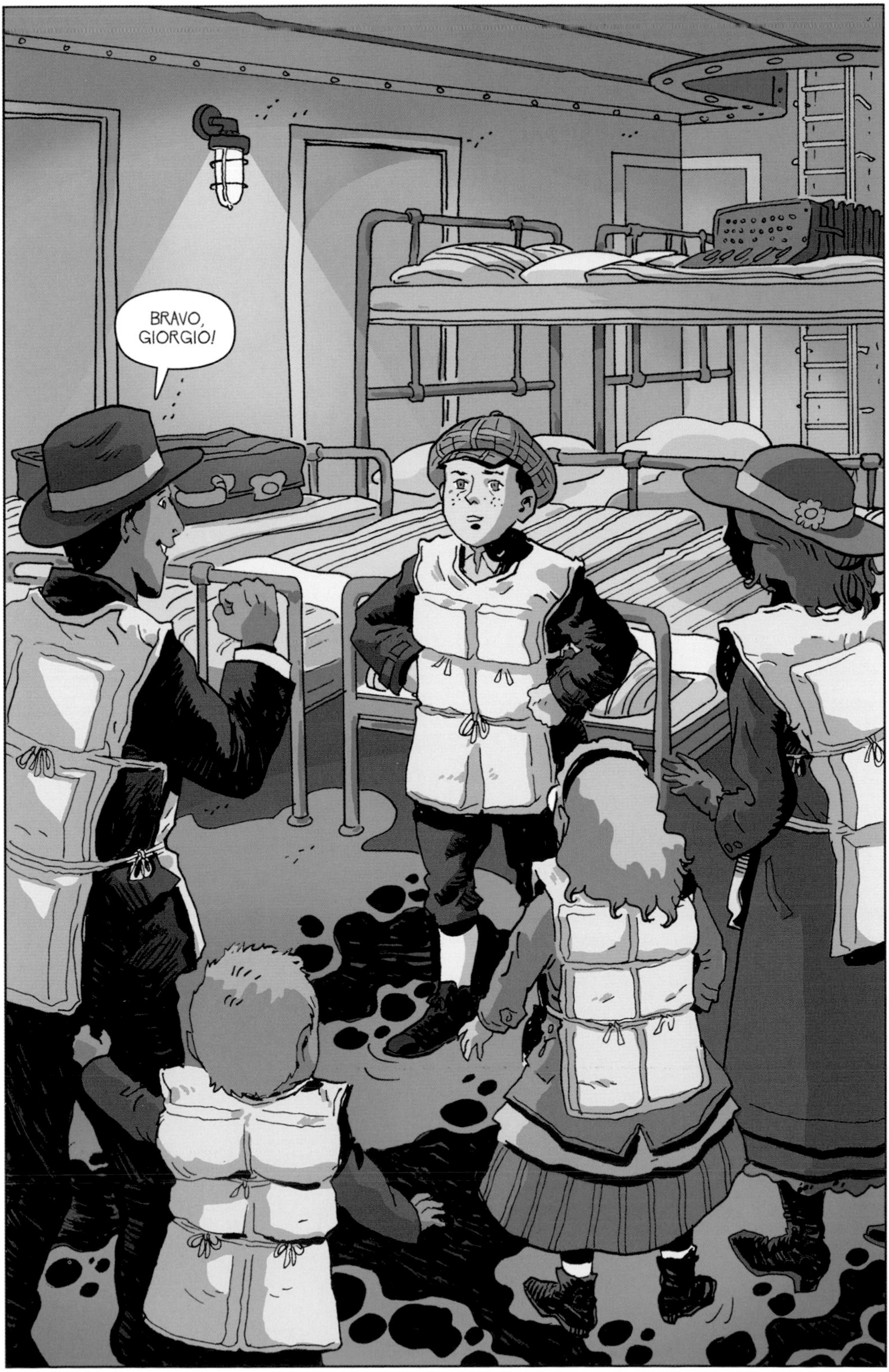
BRAVO, GIORGIO!

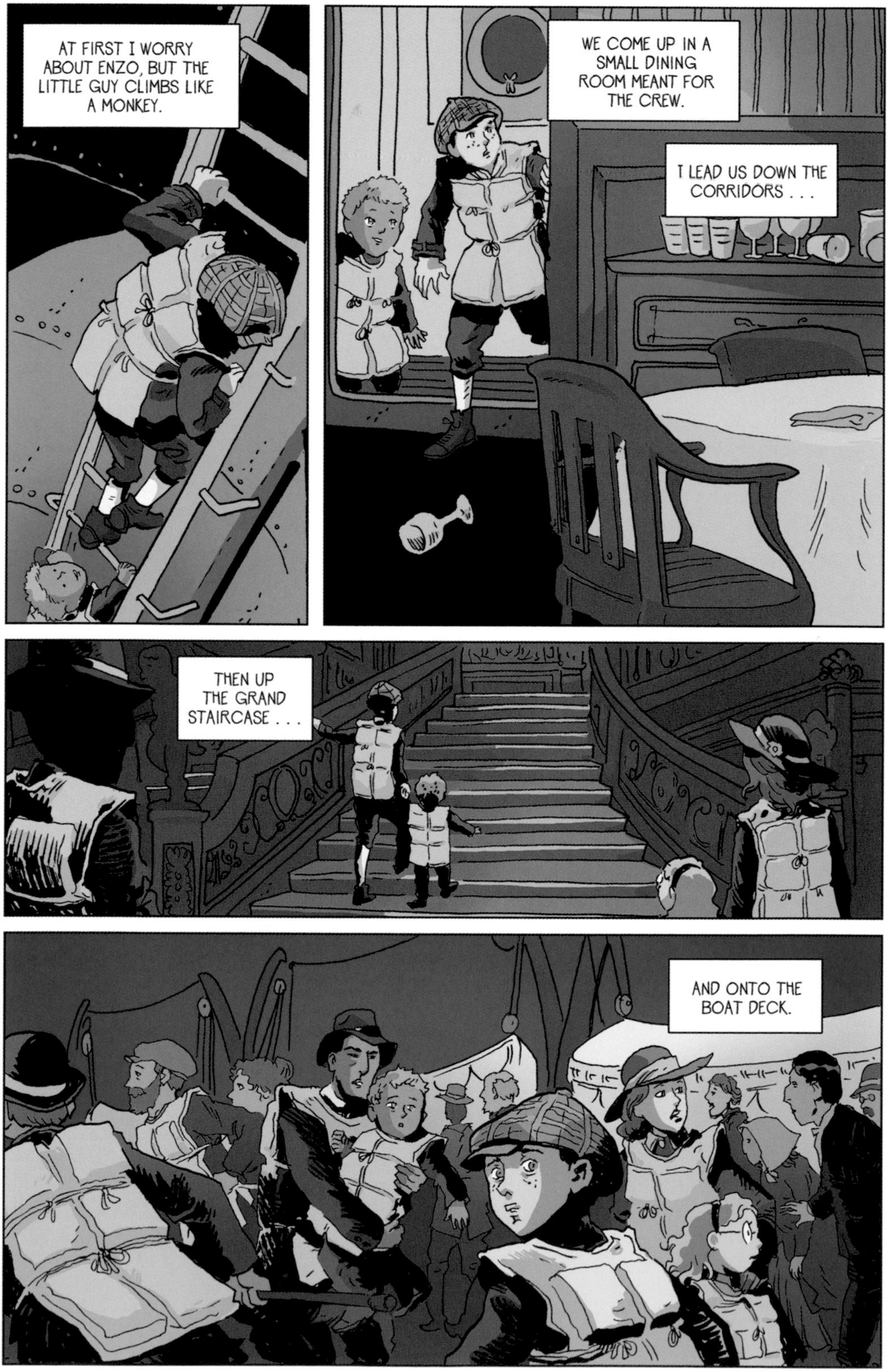
AT FIRST I WORRY ABOUT ENZO, BUT THE LITTLE GUY CLIMBS LIKE A MONKEY.
WE COME UP IN A SMALL DINING ROOM MEANT FOR THE CREW.
I LEAD US DOWN THE CORRIDORS . . .
THEN UP THE GRAND STAIRCASE . . .
AND ONTO THE BOAT DECK.

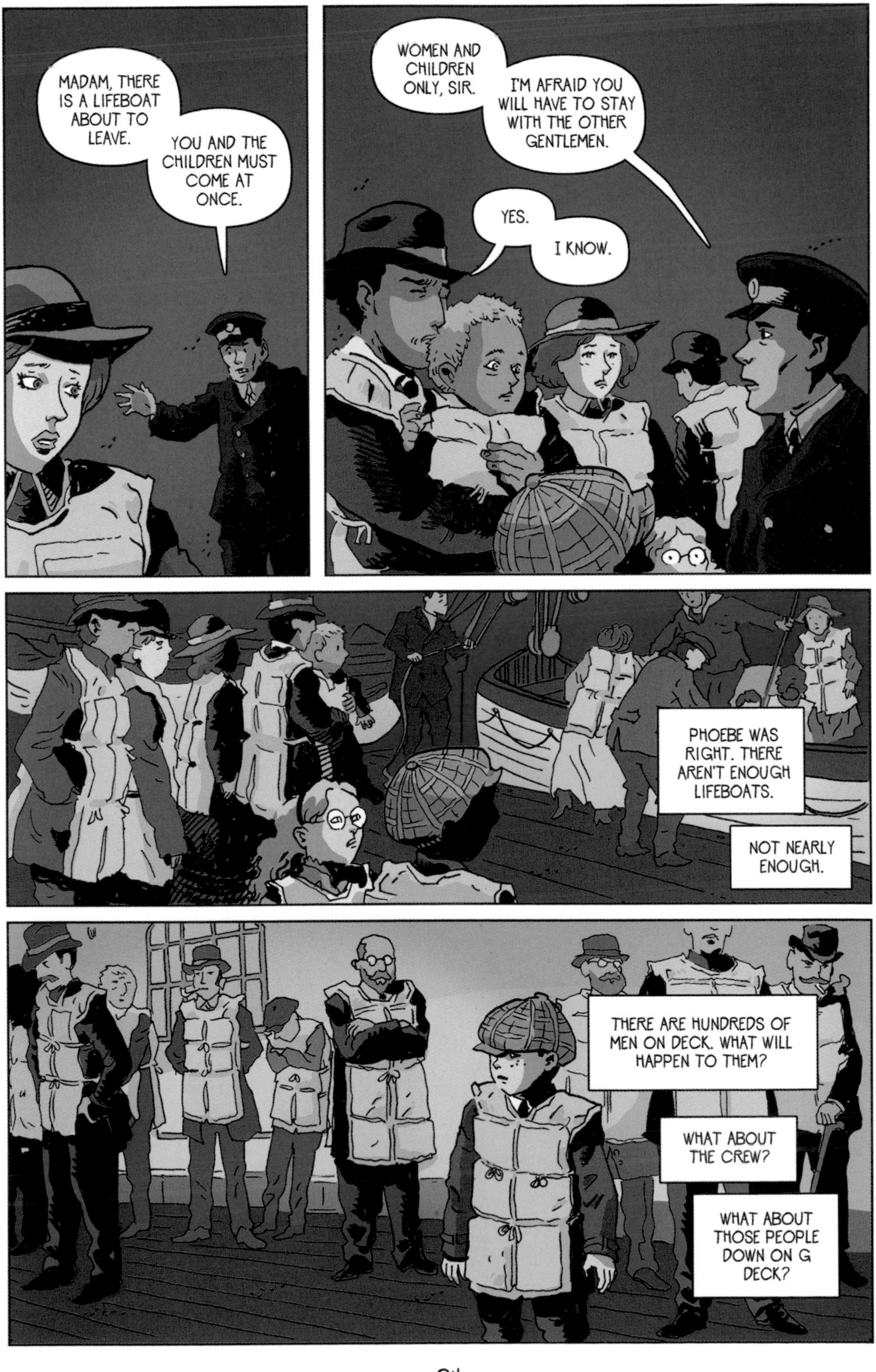
MADAM, THERE IS A LIFEBOAT ABOUT TO LEAVE.
YOU AND THE CHILDREN MUST COME AT ONCE.
WOMEN AND CHILDREN ONLY, SIR.
I'M AFRAID YOU WILL HAVE TO STAY WITH THE OTHER GENTLEMEN.
YES.
I KNOW.
PHOEBE WAS RIGHT. THERE AREN'T ENOUGH LIFEBOATS.
NOT NEARLY ENOUGH.
THERE ARE HUNDREDS OF MEN ON DECK. WHAT WILL HAPPEN TO THEM?
WHAT ABOUT THE CREW?
WHAT ABOUT THOSE PEOPLE DOWN ON G DECK?

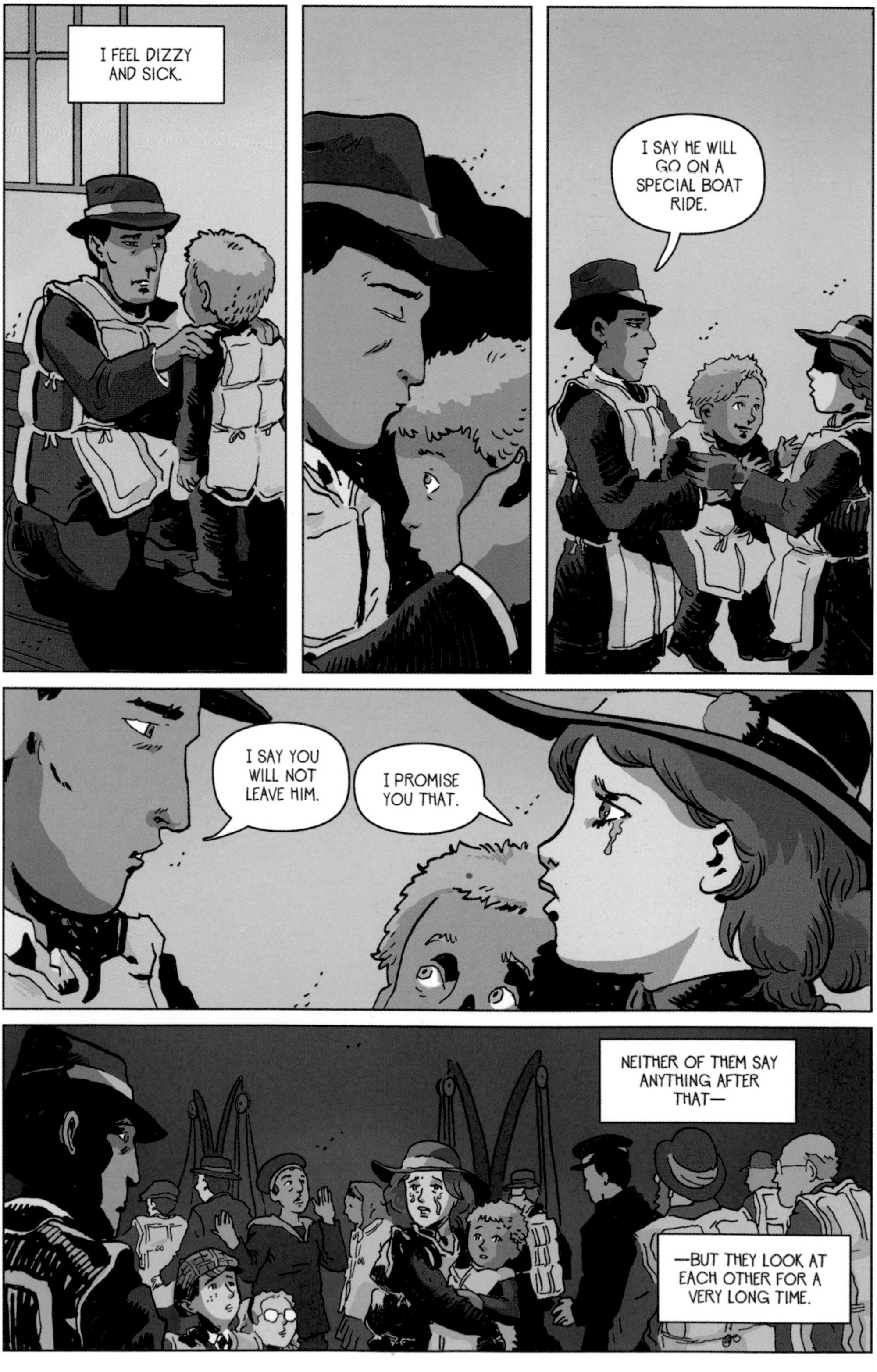
I FEEL DIZZY AND SICK.
I SAY HE WILL GO ON A SPECIAL BOAT RIDE.
I SAY YOU WILL NOT LEAVE HIM.
I PROMISE YOU THAT.
NEITHER OF THEM SAY ANYTHING AFTER THAT—
—BUT THEY LOOK AT EACH OTHER FOR A VERY LONG TIME.

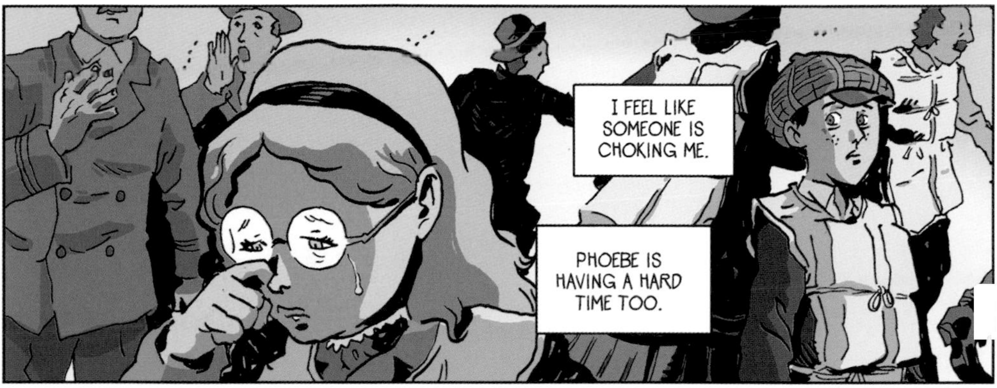
I FEEL LIKE SOMEONE IS CHOKING ME.
PHOEBE IS HAVING A HARD TIME TOO.

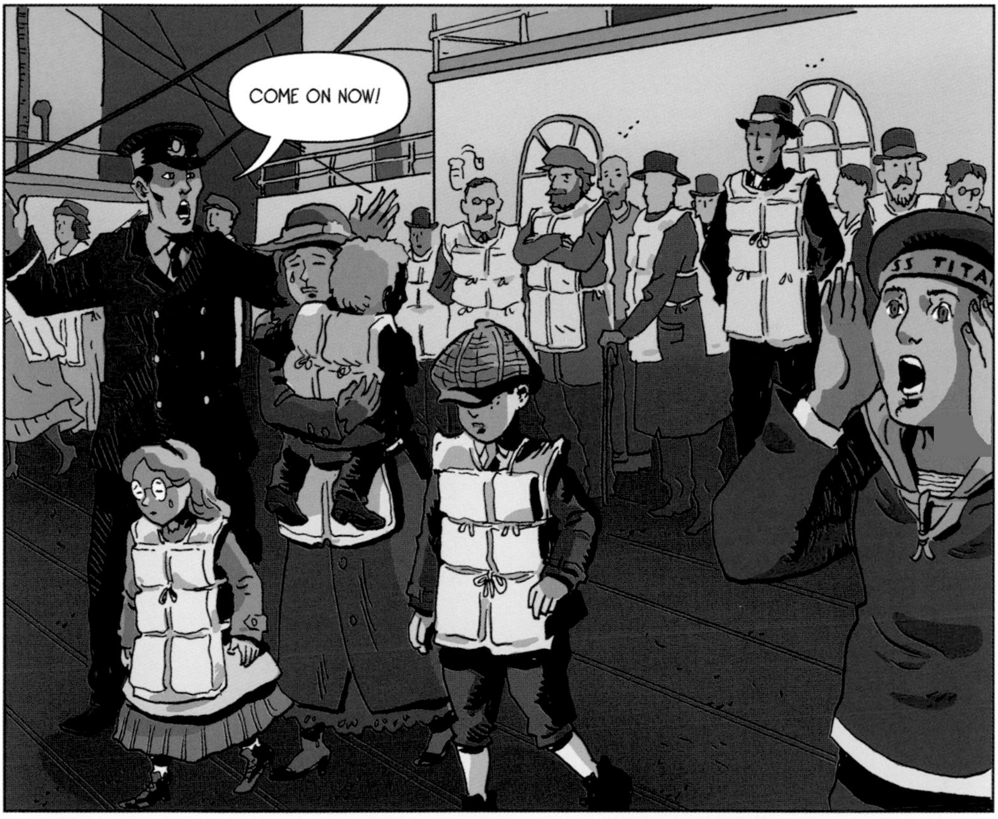
COME ON NOW!

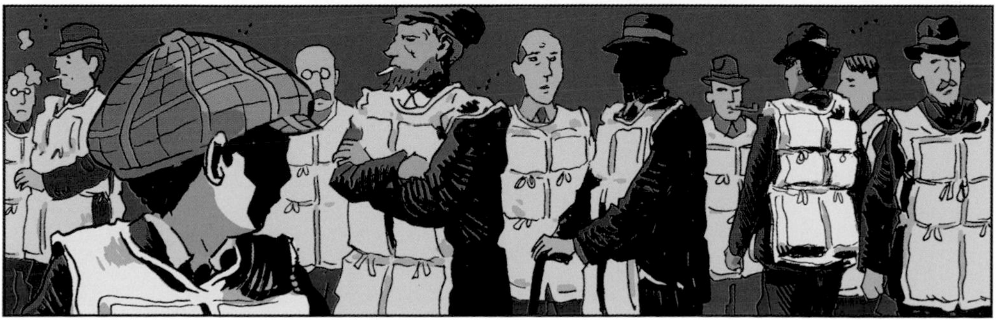

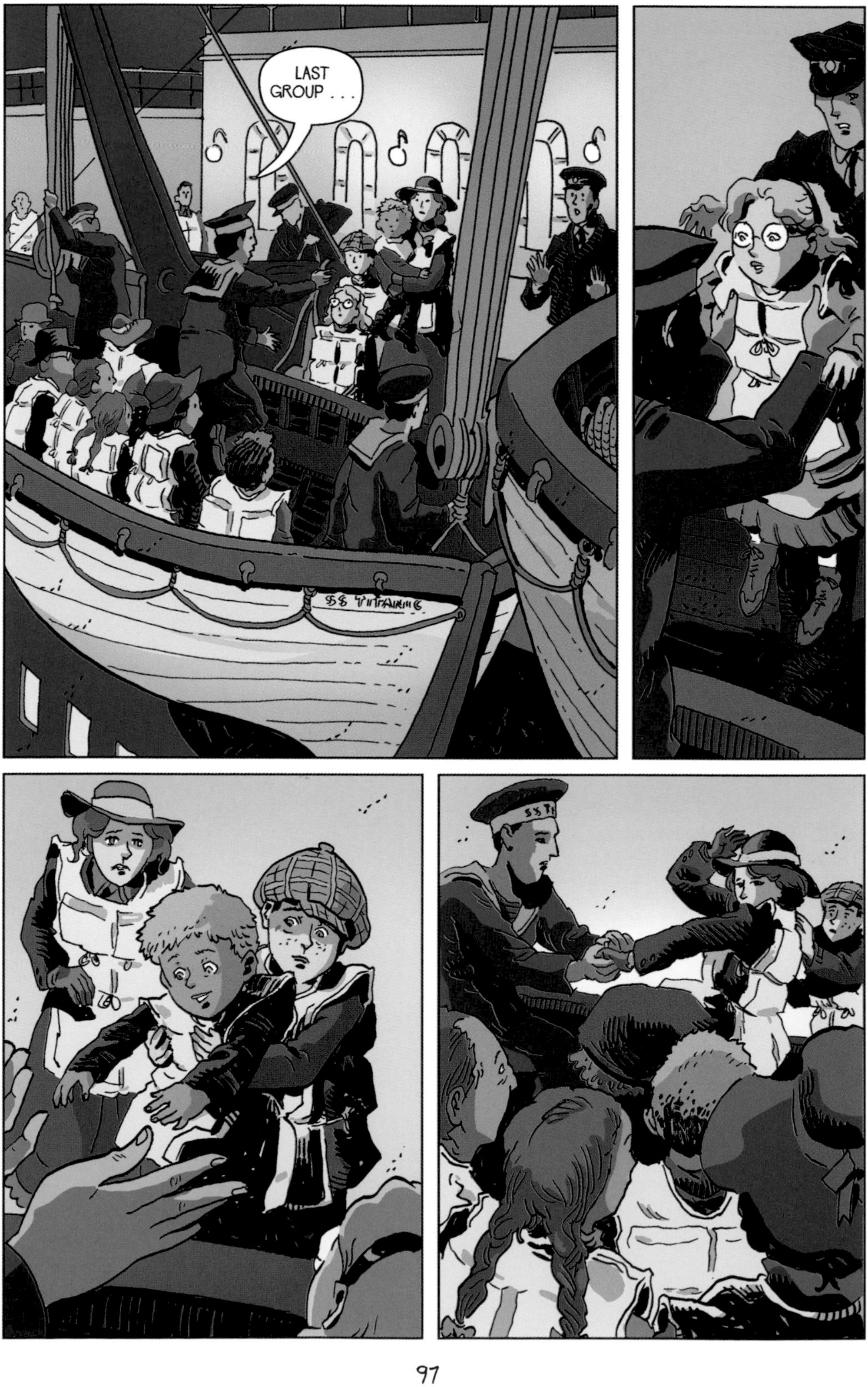
LAST GROUP . . .

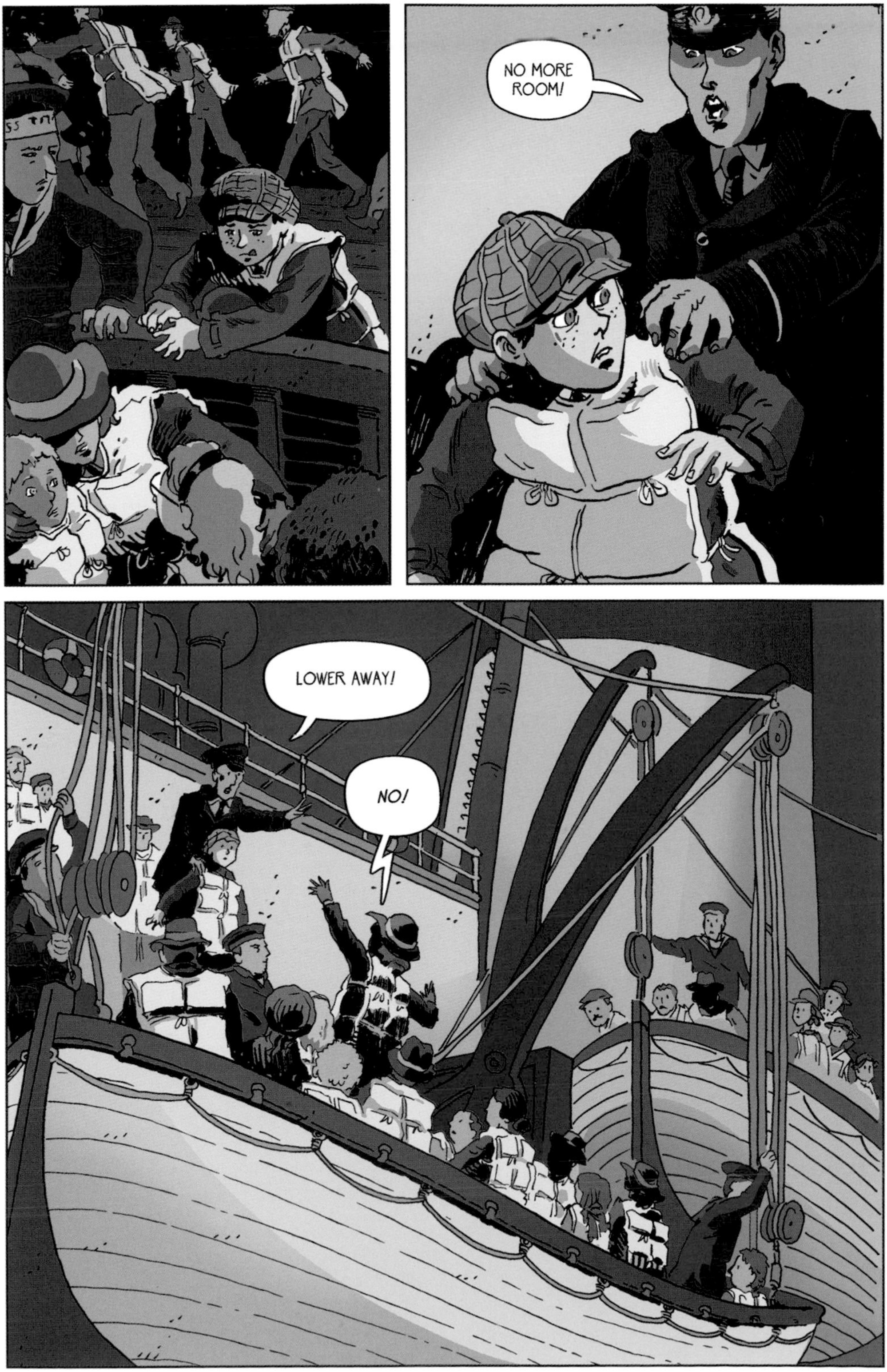
NO MORE ROOM!
LOWER AWAY!
NO!

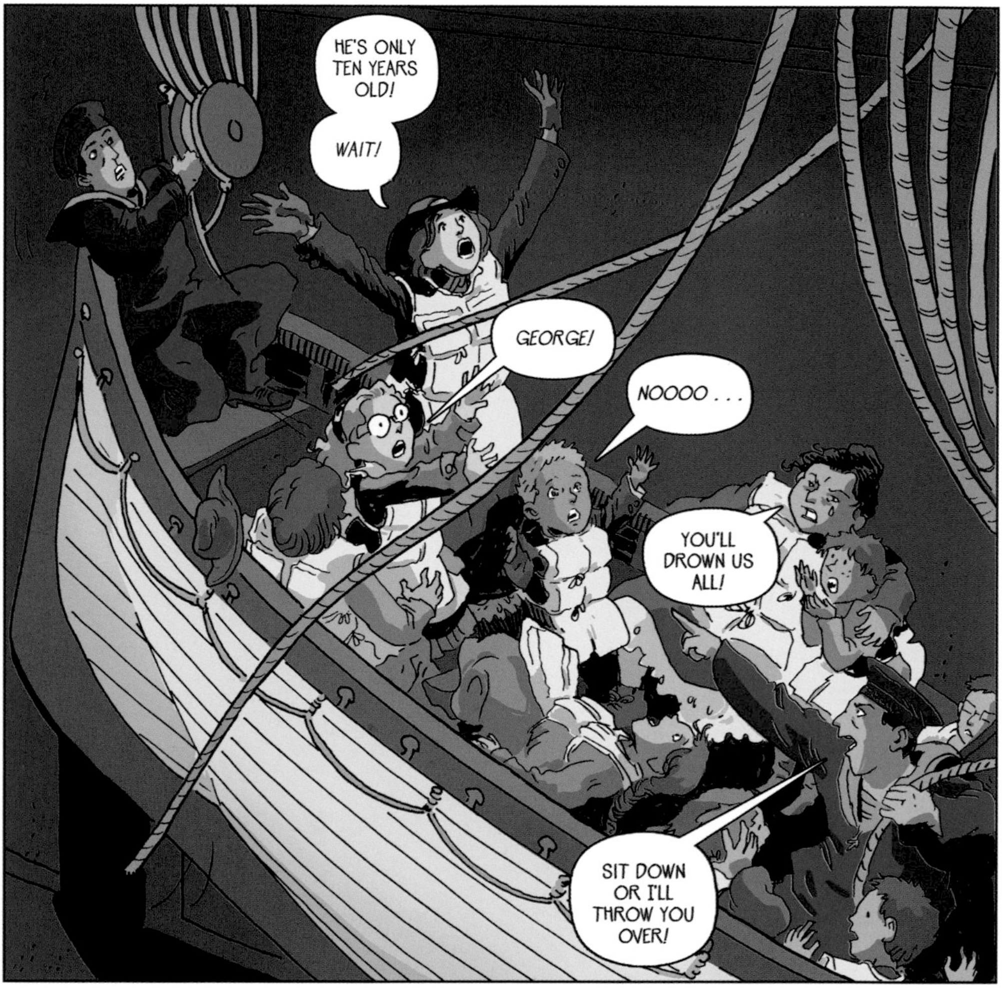
HE'S ONLY TEN YEARS OLD!
WAIT!
GEORGE!
NOOOO . . .
YOU'LL DROWN US ALL!
SIT DOWN OR I'LL THROW YOU OVER!

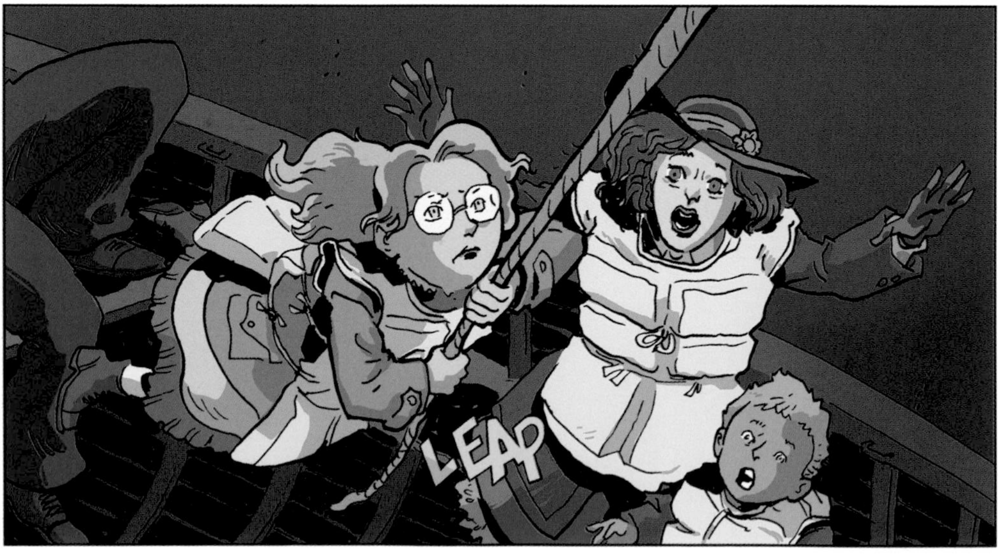
LEAP

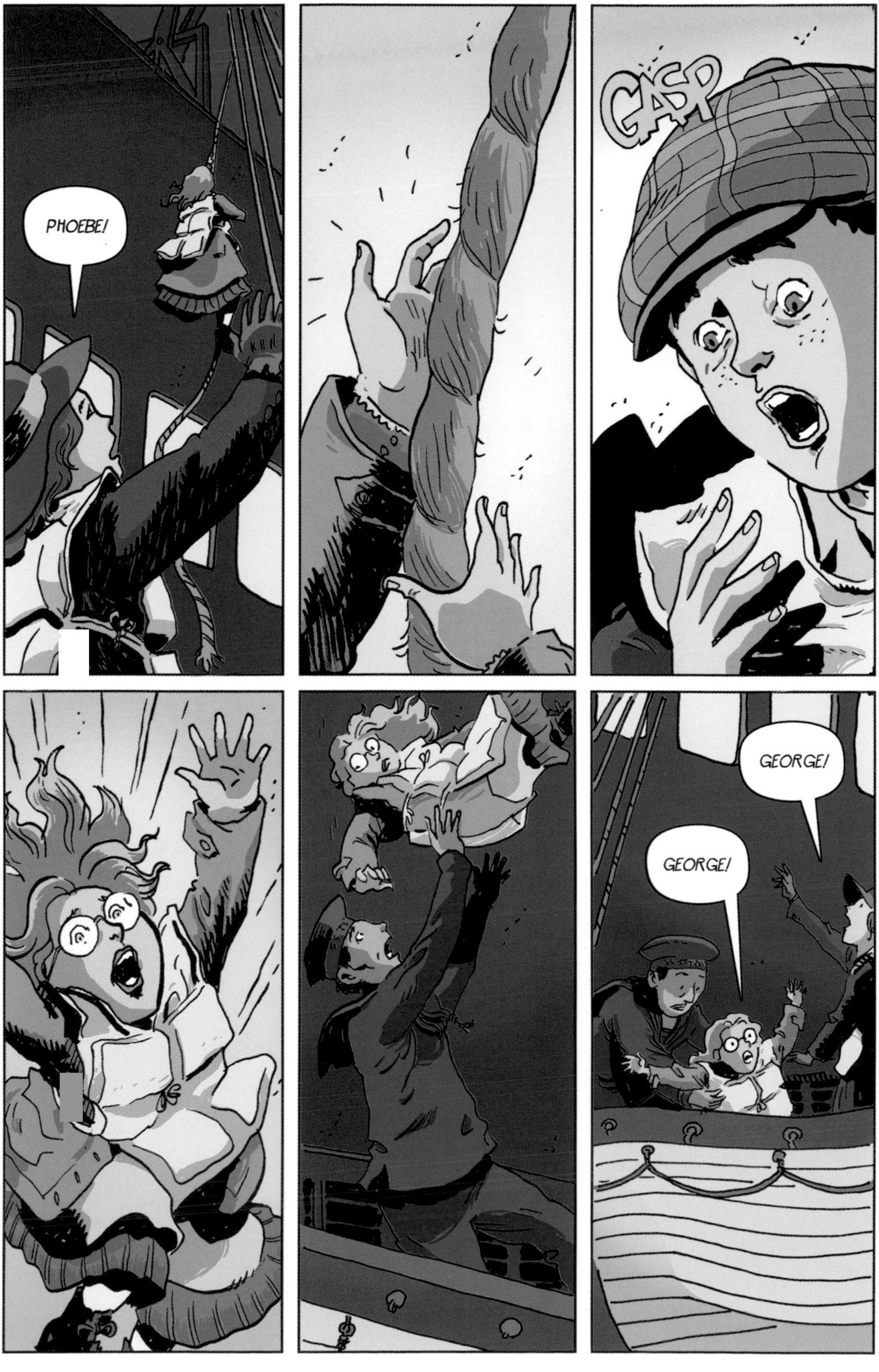
PHOEBE!
GASP
GEORGE!
GEORGE!

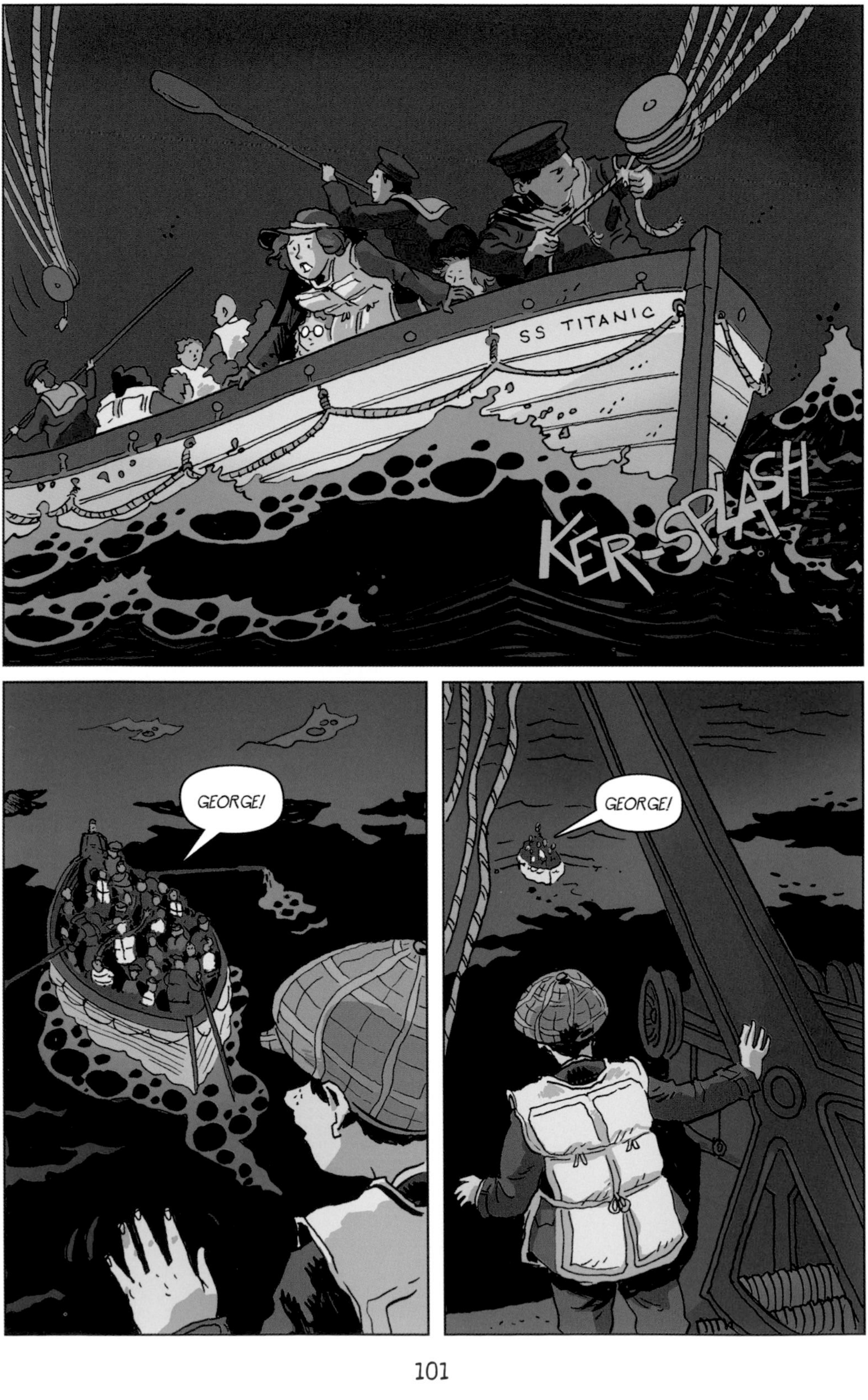
SS TITANIC
KER-SPLASH
GEORGE!
GEORGE!

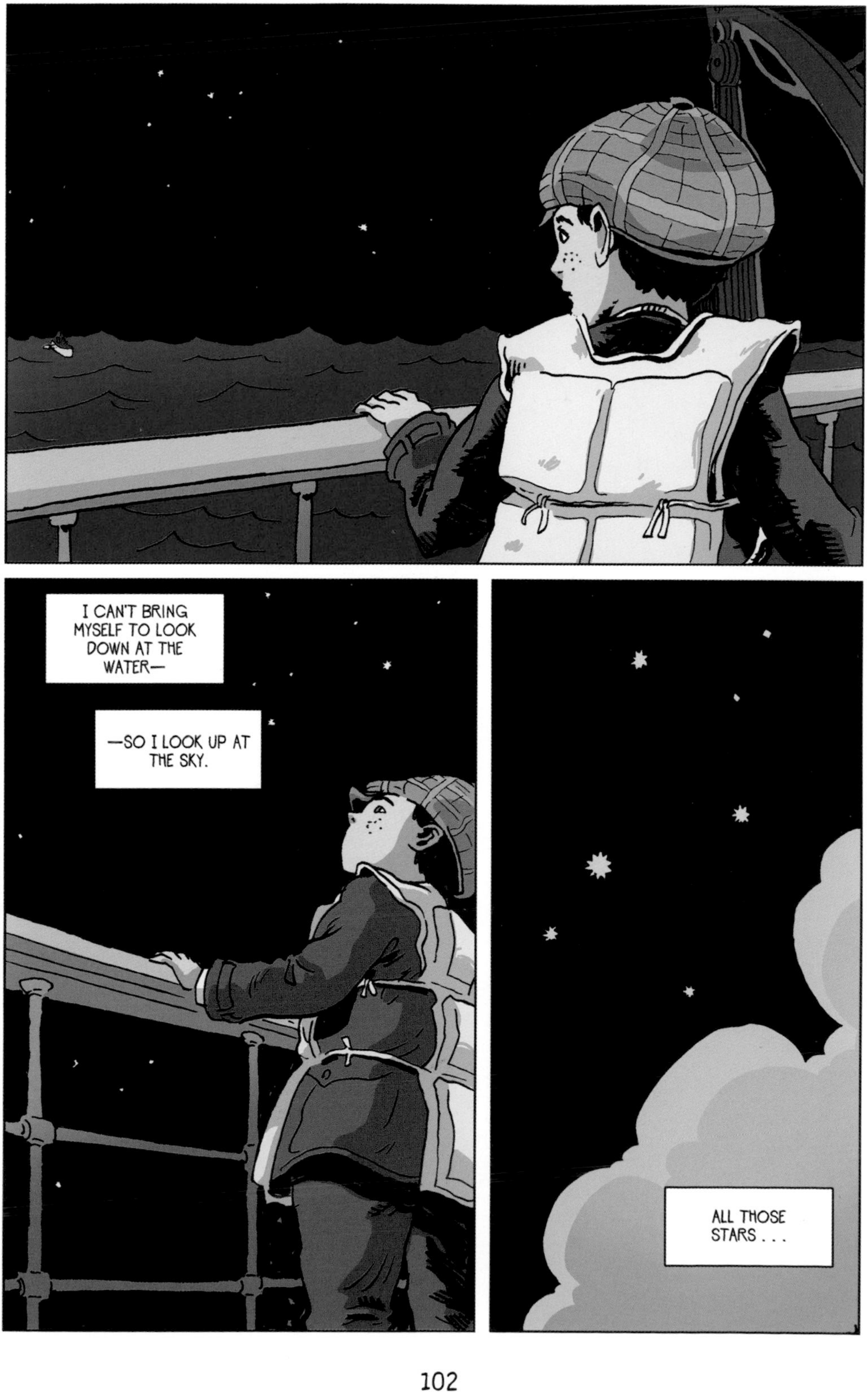
I CAN'T BRING MYSELF TO LOOK DOWN AT THE WATER—
—SO I LOOK UP AT THE SKY.
ALL THOSE STARS . . .

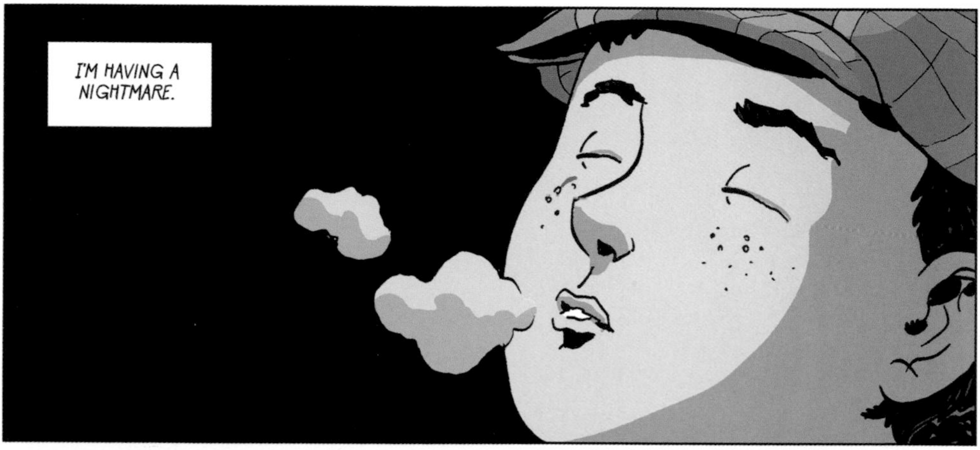
I'M HAVING A NIGHTMARE.

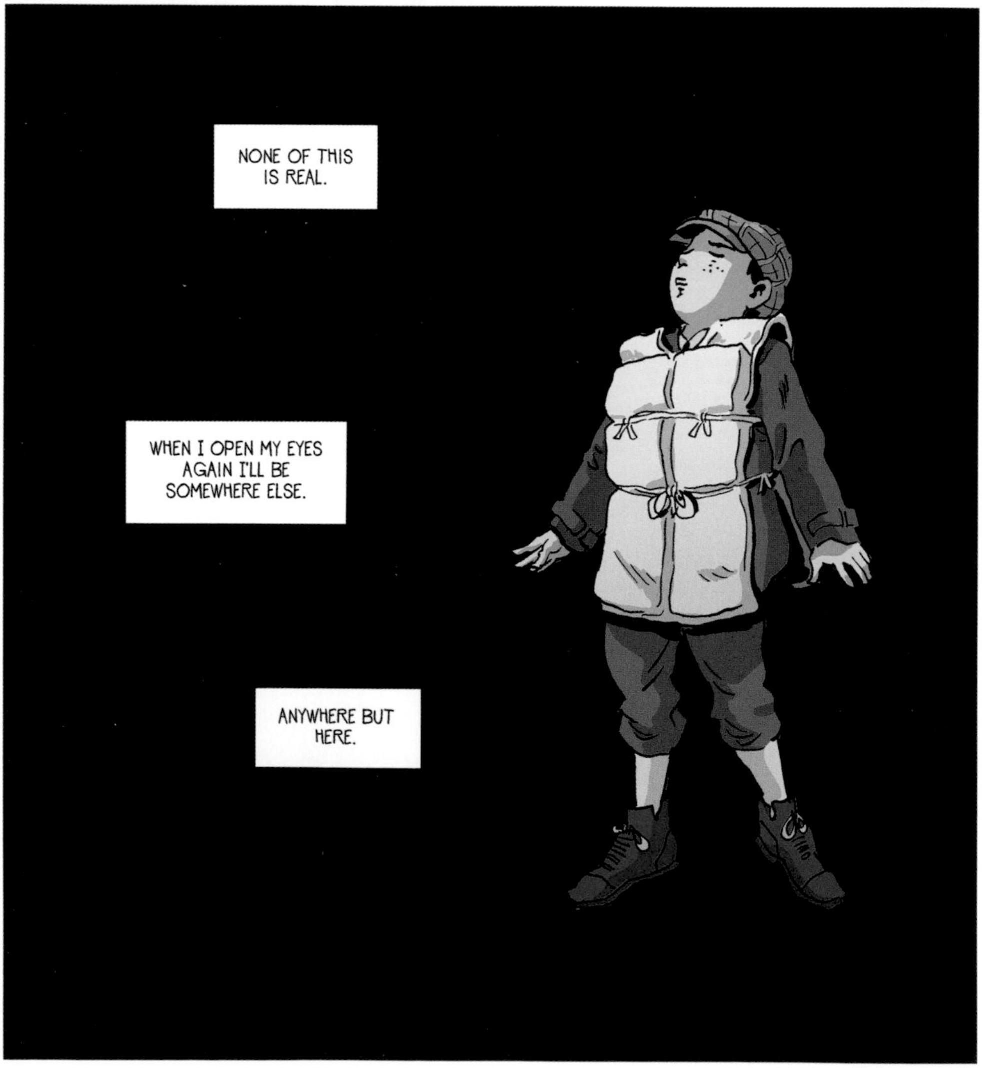
NONE OF THIS IS REAL.
WHEN I OPEN MY EYES AGAIN I'LL BE SOMEWHERE ELSE.
ANYWHERE BUT HERE.

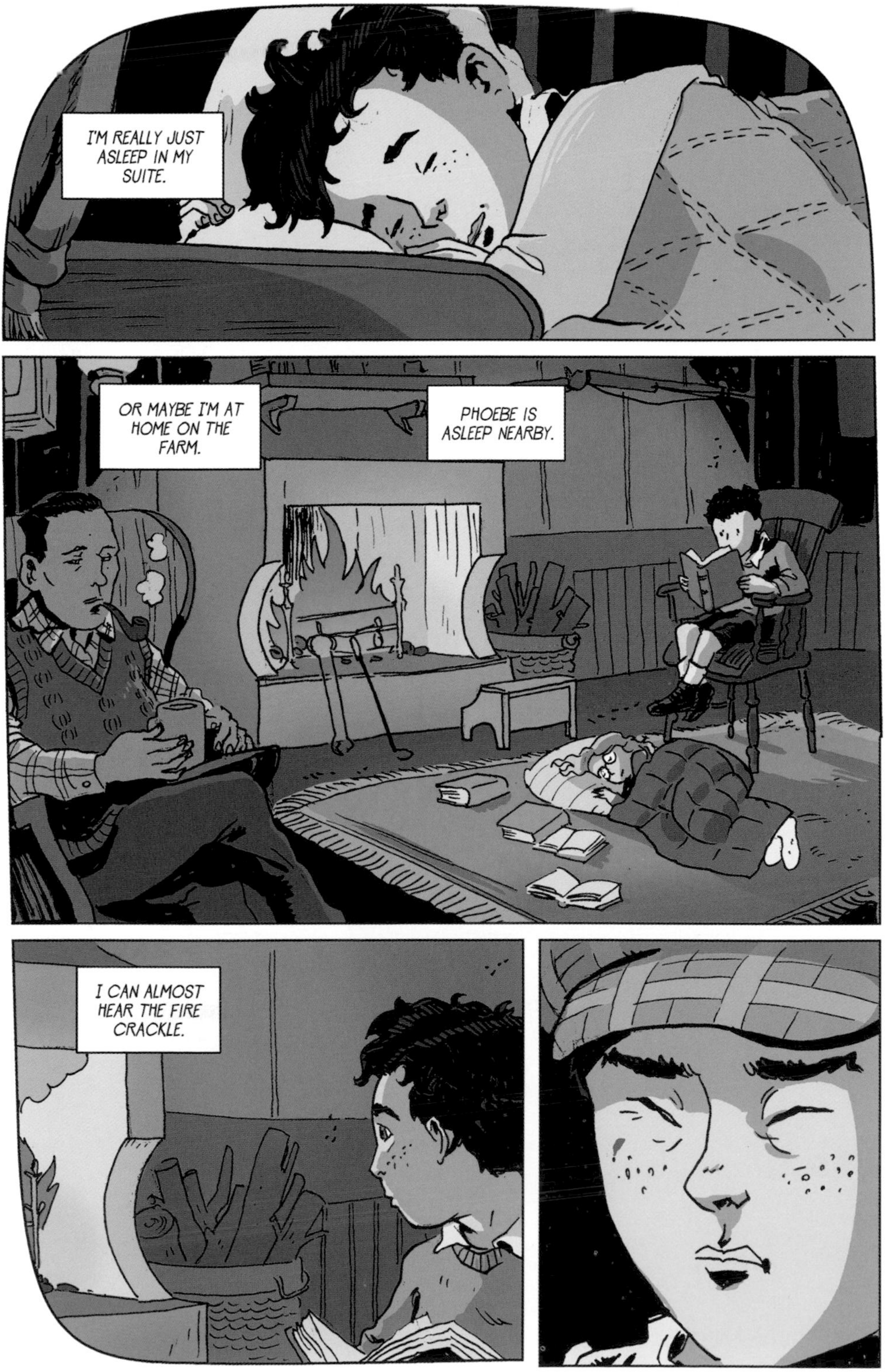
I'M REALLY JUST ASLEEP IN MY SUITE.
OR MAYBE I'M AT HOME ON THE FARM.
PHOEBE IS ASLEEP NEARBY.
I CAN ALMOST HEAR THE FIRE CRACKLE.

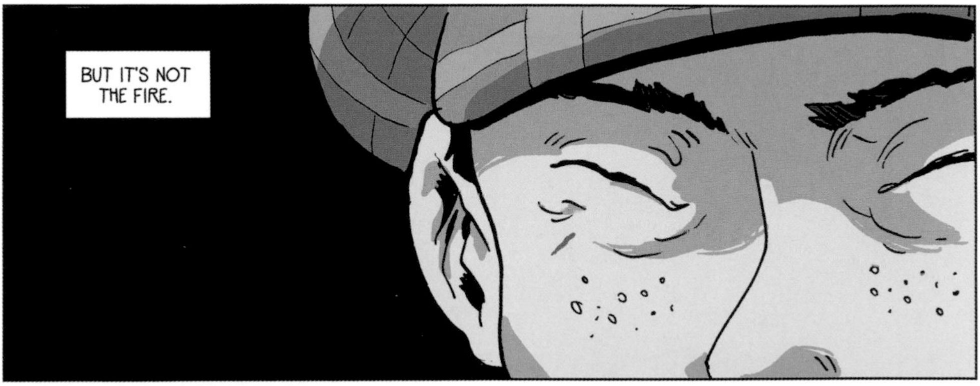
BUT IT'S NOT THE FIRE.

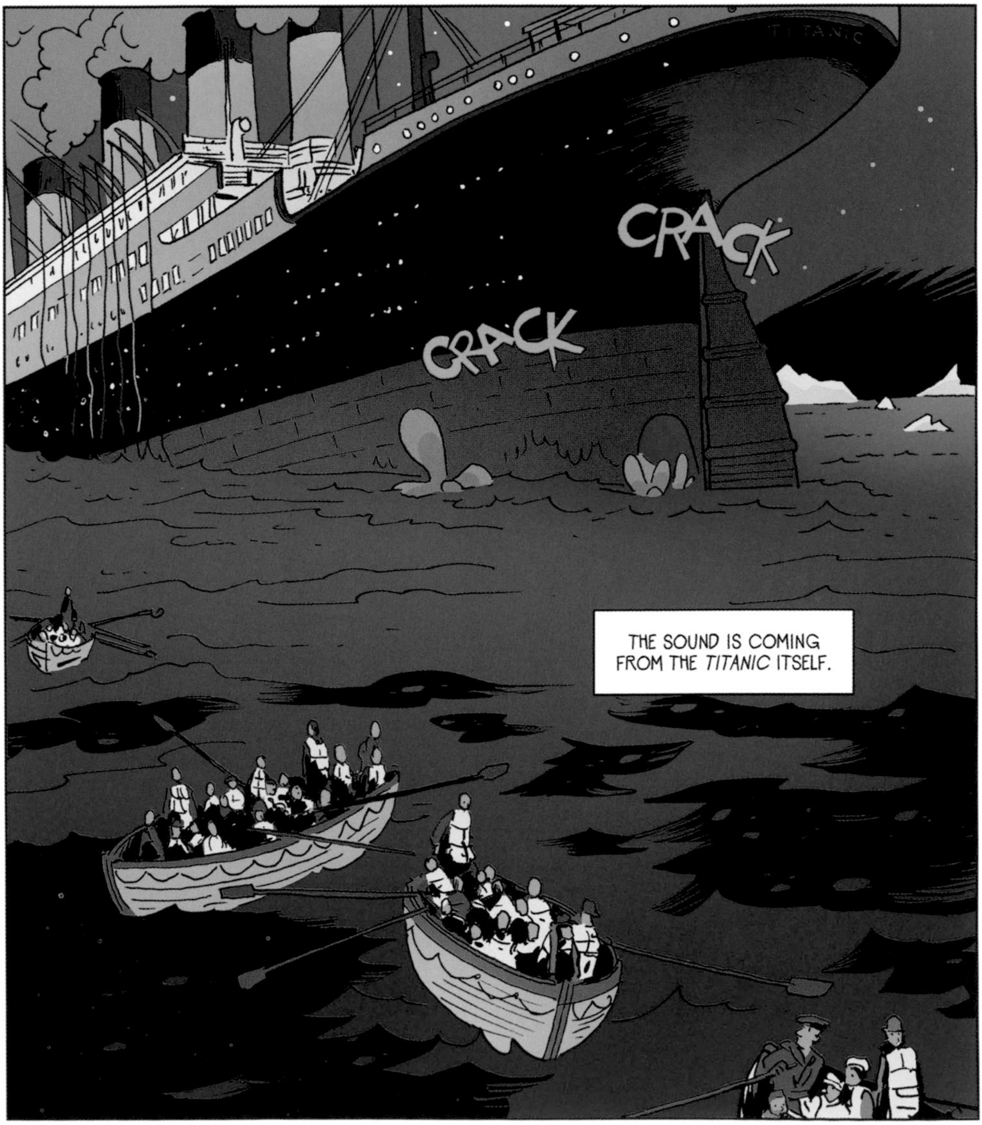
CRACK
CRACK
THE SOUND IS COMING FROM THE *TITANIC* ITSELF.

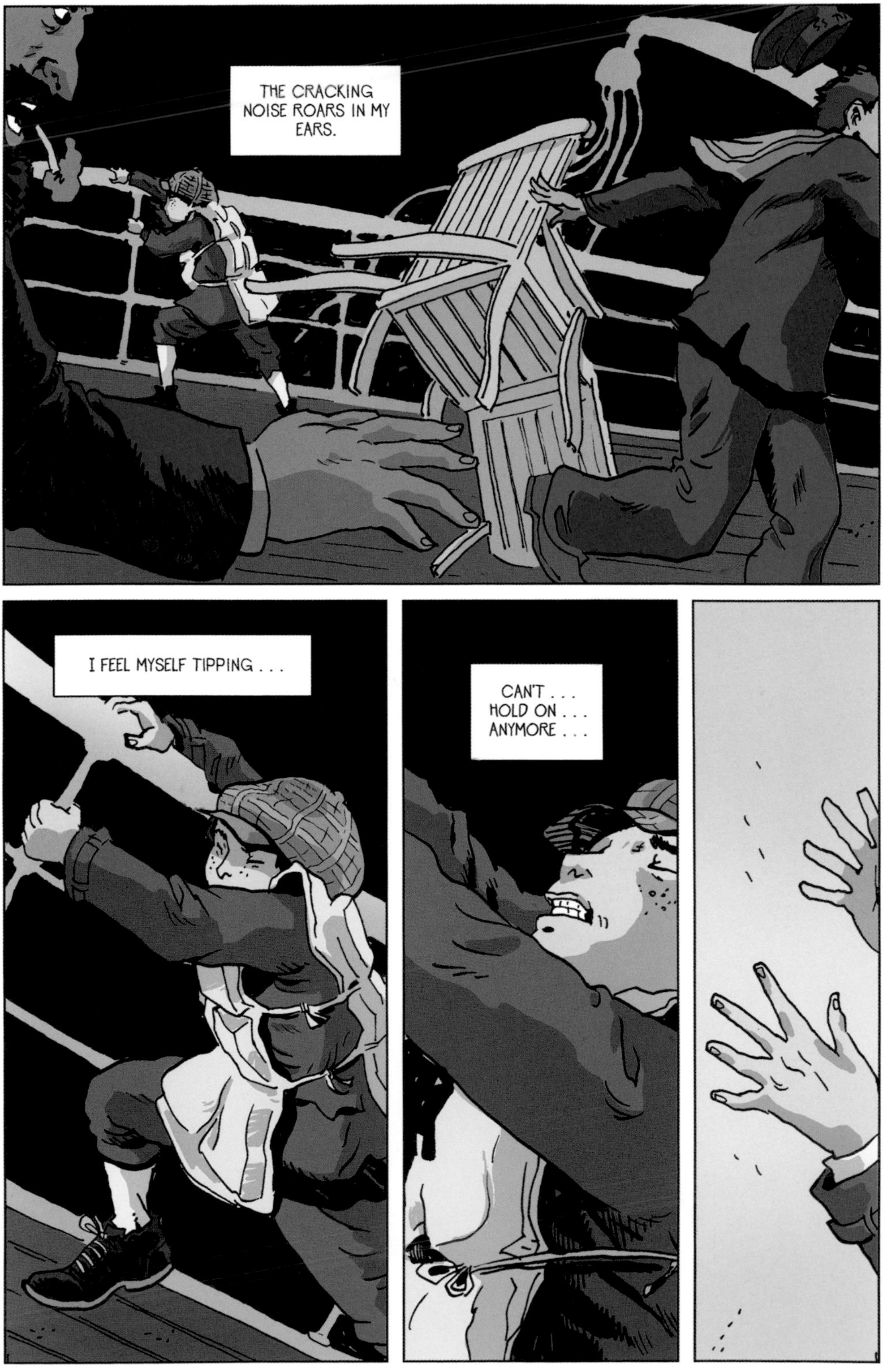
THE CRACKING NOISE ROARS IN MY EARS.
I FEEL MYSELF TIPPING . . .
CAN'T . . . HOLD ON . . . ANYMORE . . .

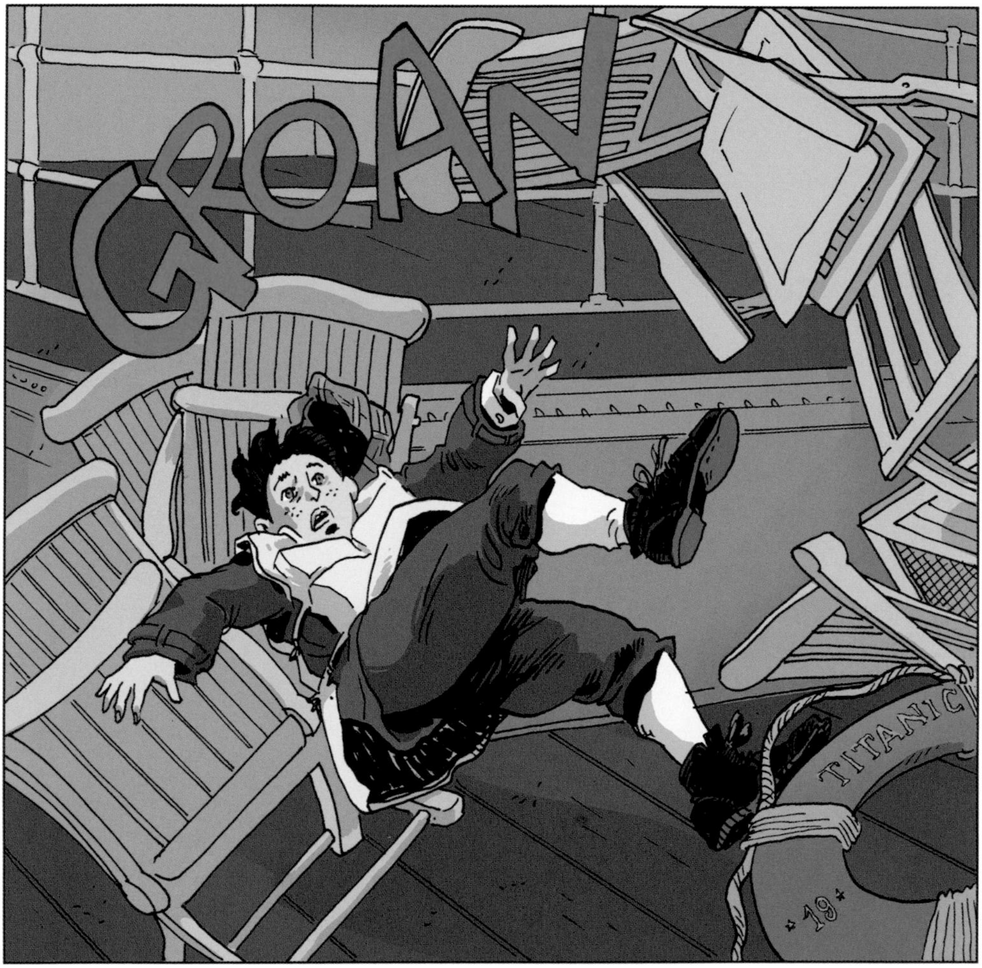
GROAN
TITANIC
19
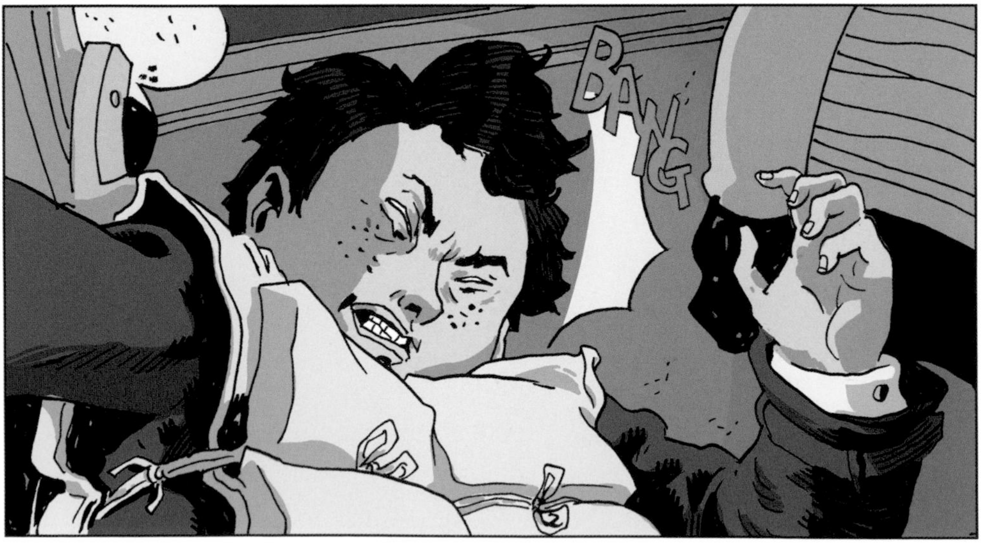
BANG

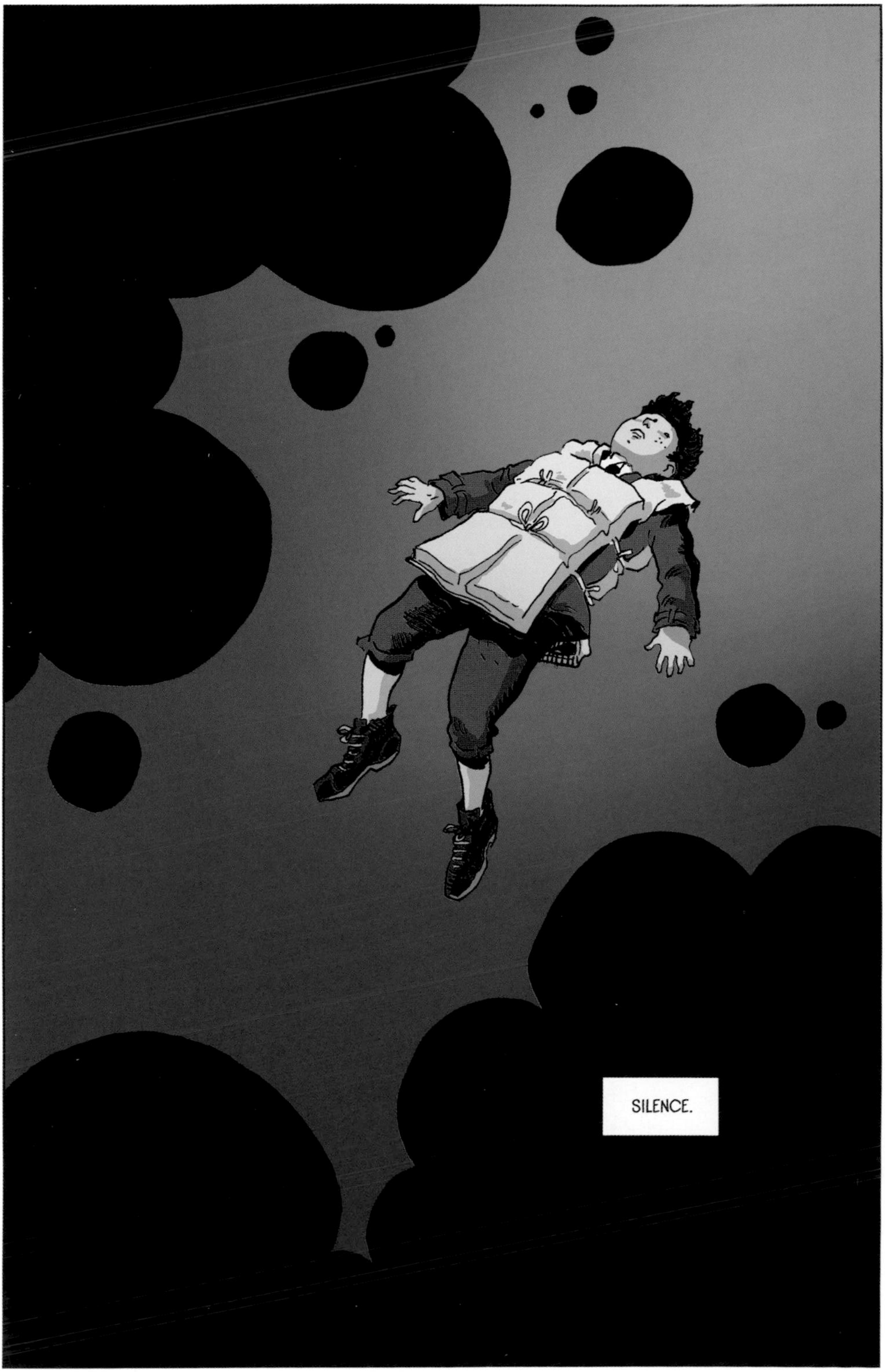
SILENCE.

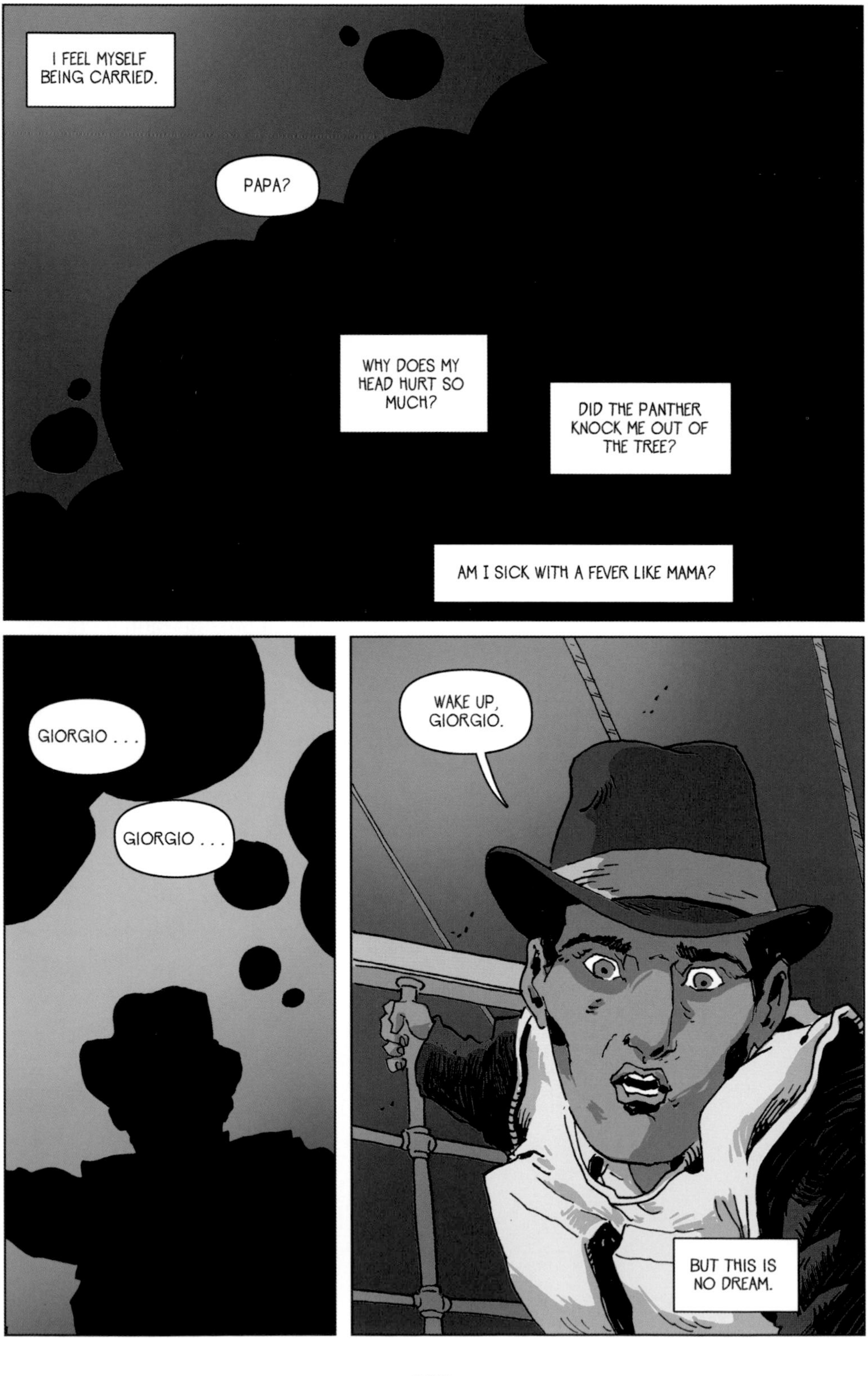
I FEEL MYSELF BEING CARRIED.
PAPA?
WHY DOES MY HEAD HURT SO MUCH?
DID THE PANTHER KNOCK ME OUT OF THE TREE?
AM I SICK WITH A FEVER LIKE MAMA?
GIORGIO . . .
GIORGIO . . .
WAKE UP, GIORGIO.
BUT THIS IS NO DREAM.

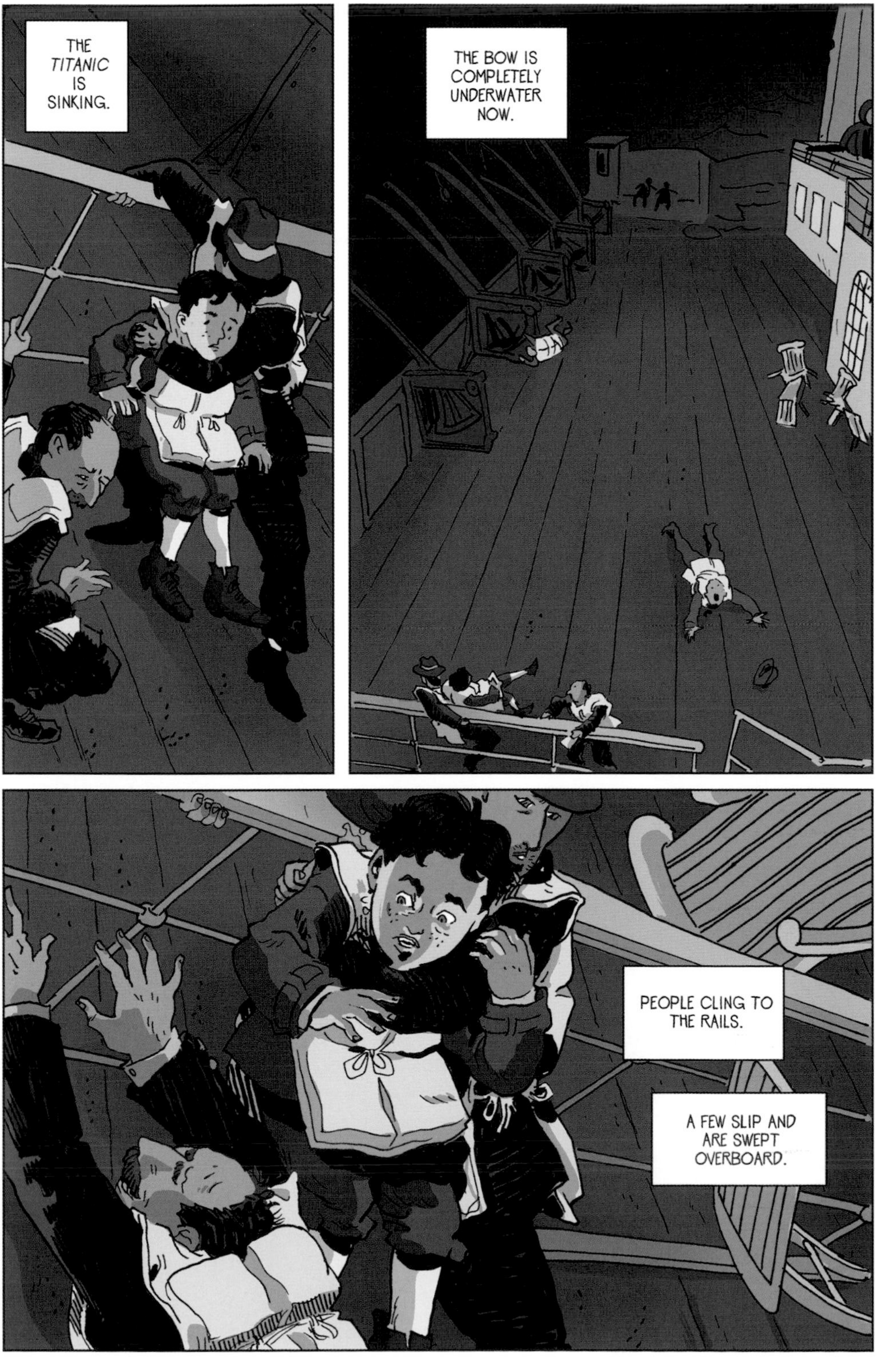
THE *TITANIC* IS SINKING.
THE BOW IS COMPLETELY UNDERWATER NOW.
PEOPLE CLING TO THE RAILS.
A FEW SLIP AND ARE SWEPT OVERBOARD.

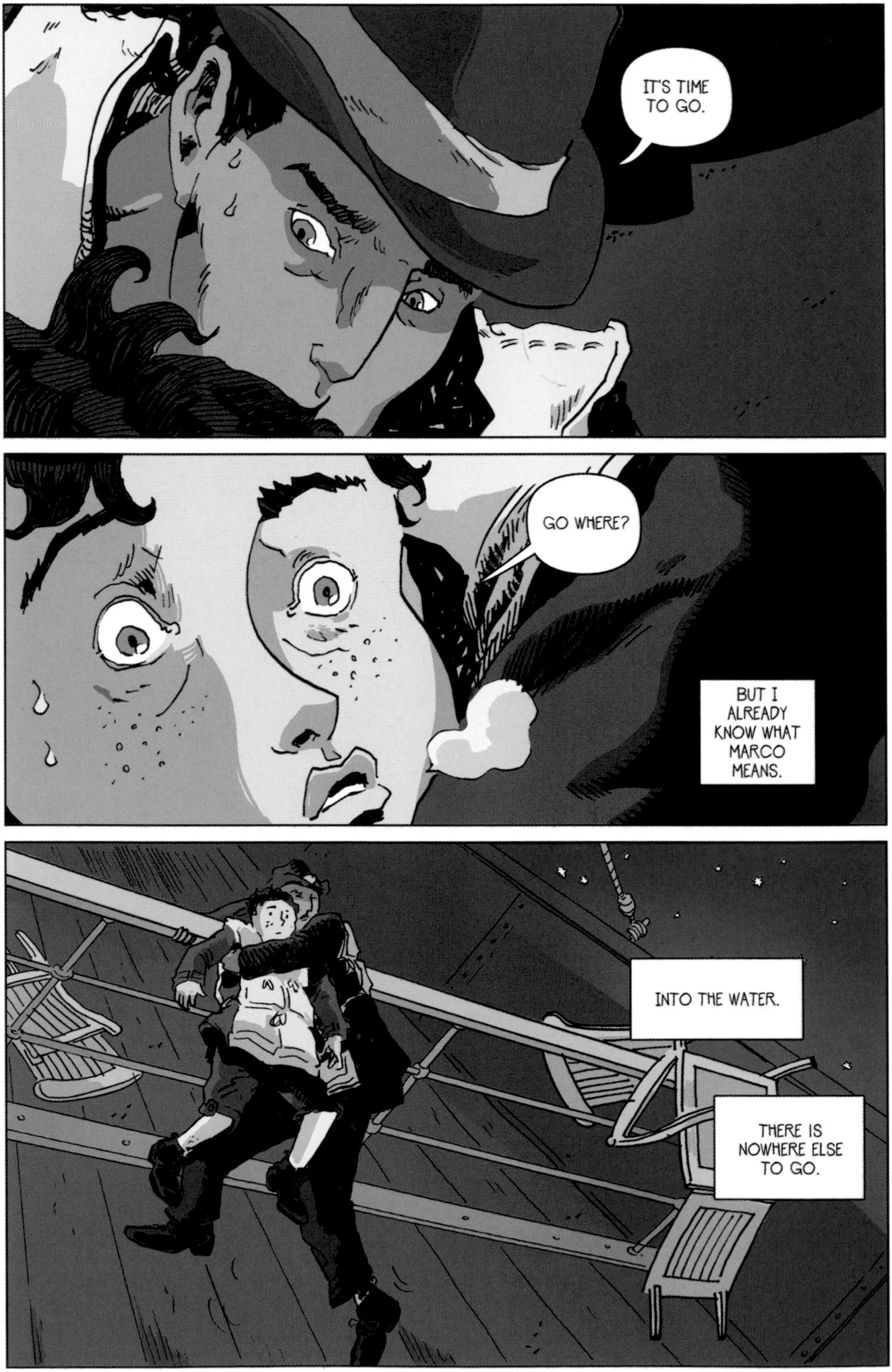
IT'S TIME TO GO.
GO WHERE?
BUT I ALREADY KNOW WHAT MARCO MEANS.
INTO THE WATER.
THERE IS NOWHERE ELSE TO GO.

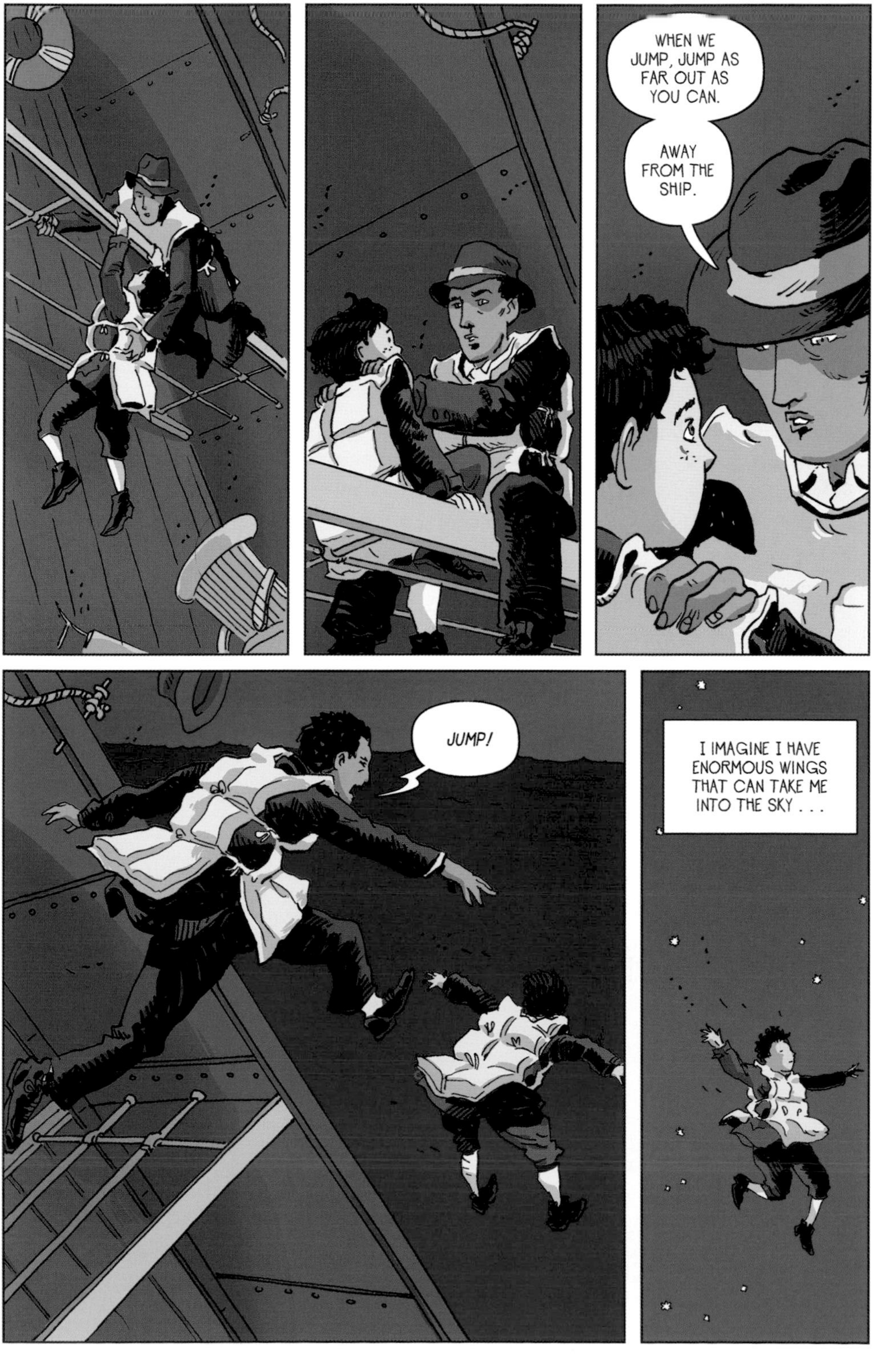
WHEN WE JUMP, JUMP AS FAR OUT AS YOU CAN.
AWAY FROM THE SHIP.
JUMP!
I IMAGINE I HAVE ENORMOUS WINGS THAT CAN TAKE ME INTO THE SKY . . .

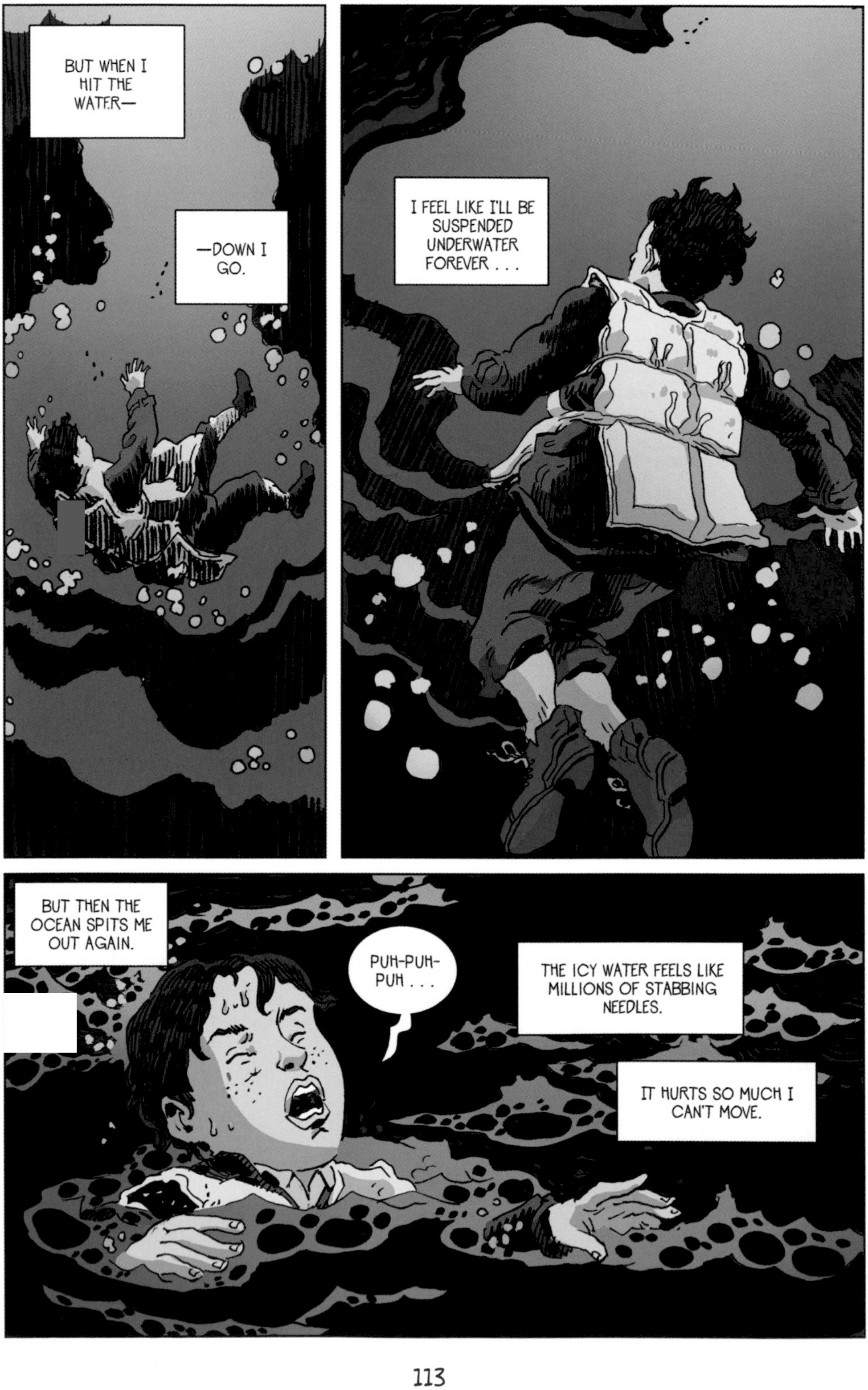
BUT WHEN I HIT THE WATER—
—DOWN I GO.
I FEEL LIKE I'LL BE SUSPENDED UNDERWATER FOREVER . . .
BUT THEN THE OCEAN SPITS ME OUT AGAIN.
PUH-PUH-PUH . . .
THE ICY WATER FEELS LIKE MILLIONS OF STABBING NEEDLES.
IT HURTS SO MUCH I CAN'T MOVE.

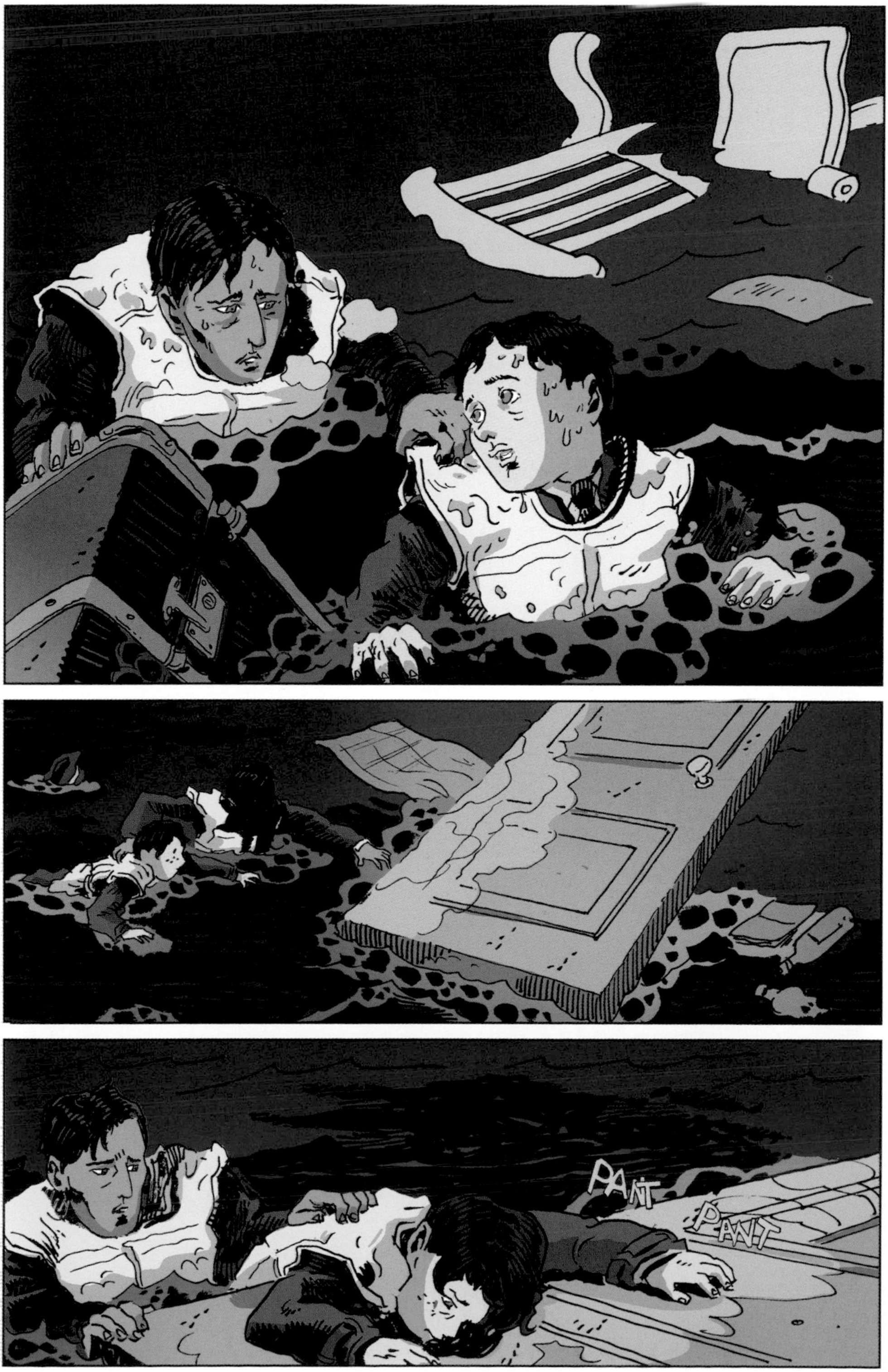
PANT
PANT

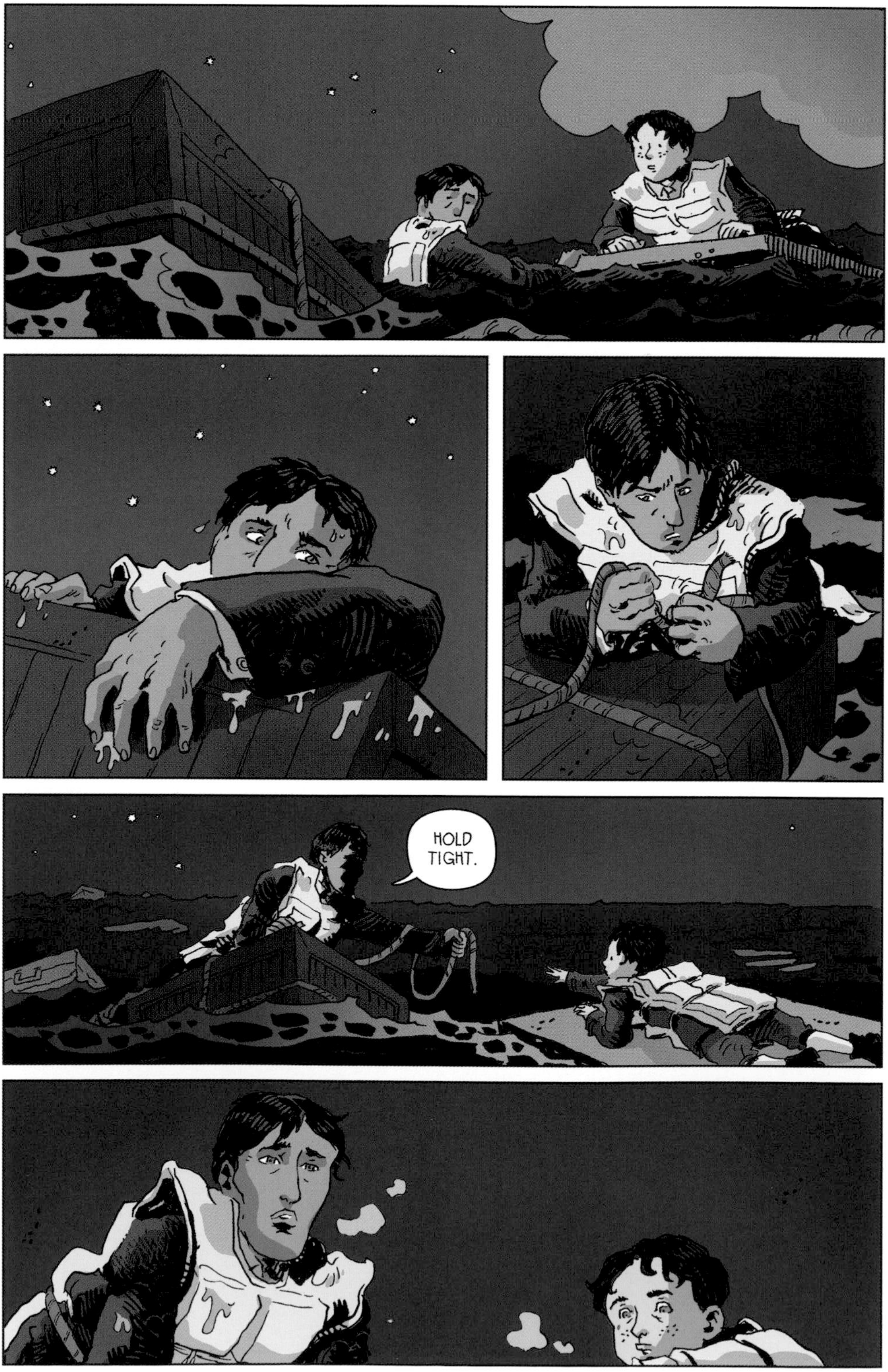
HOLD
TIGHT.

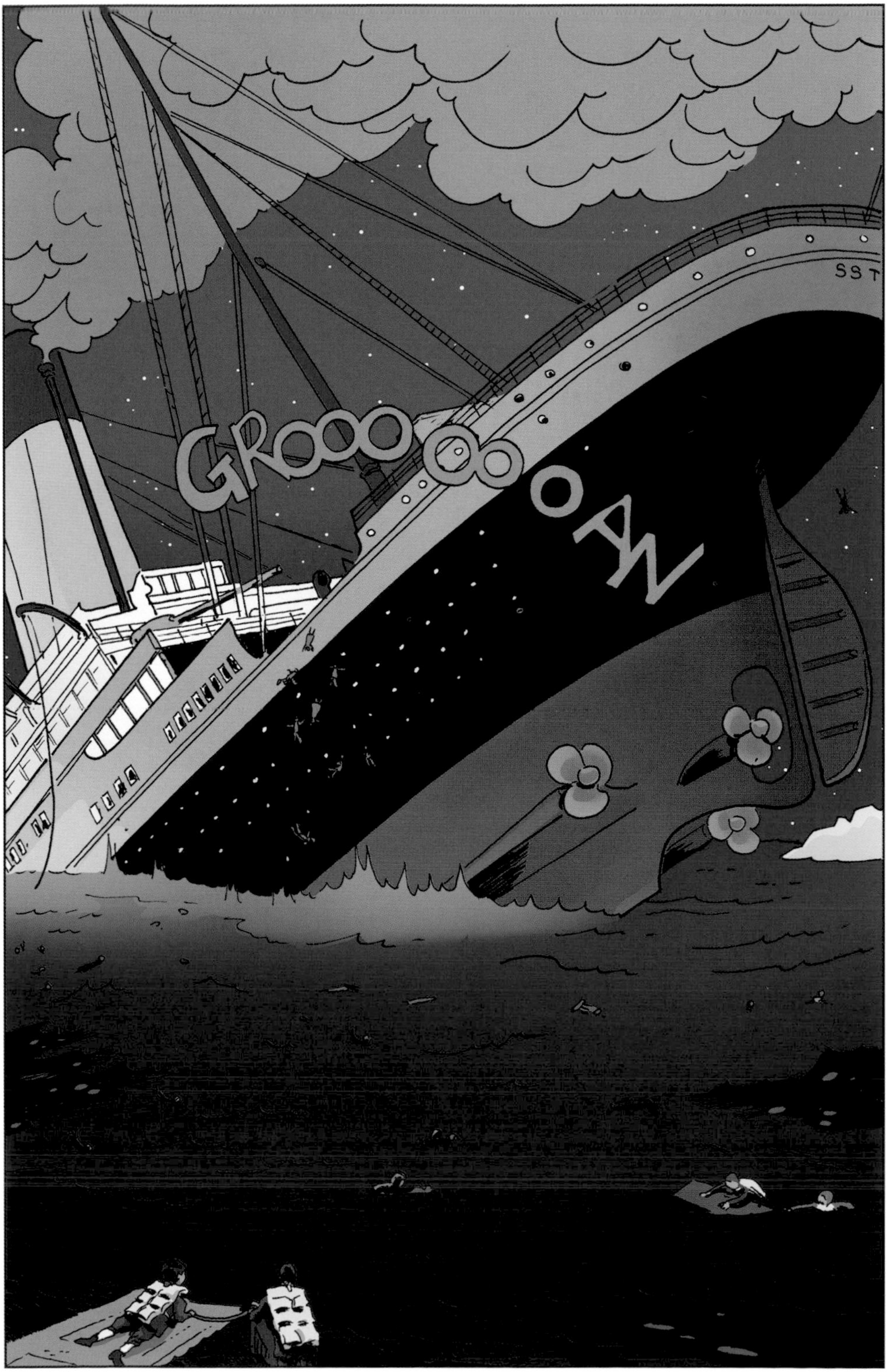
GROOOOOOAN
SST

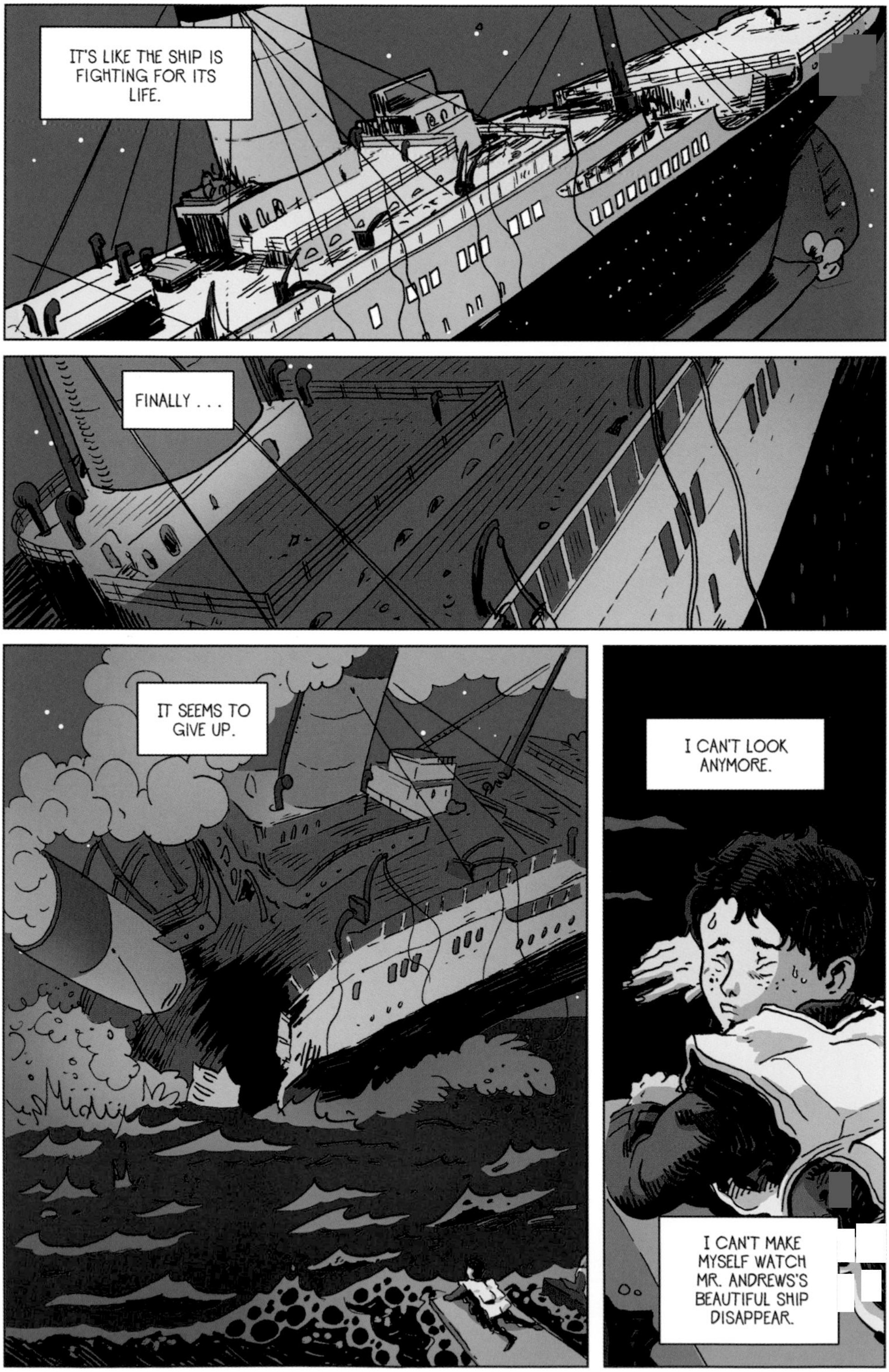
IT'S LIKE THE SHIP IS FIGHTING FOR ITS LIFE.
FINALLY . . .
IT SEEMS TO GIVE UP.
I CAN'T LOOK ANYMORE.
I CAN'T MAKE MYSELF WATCH MR. ANDREWS'S BEAUTIFUL SHIP DISAPPEAR.

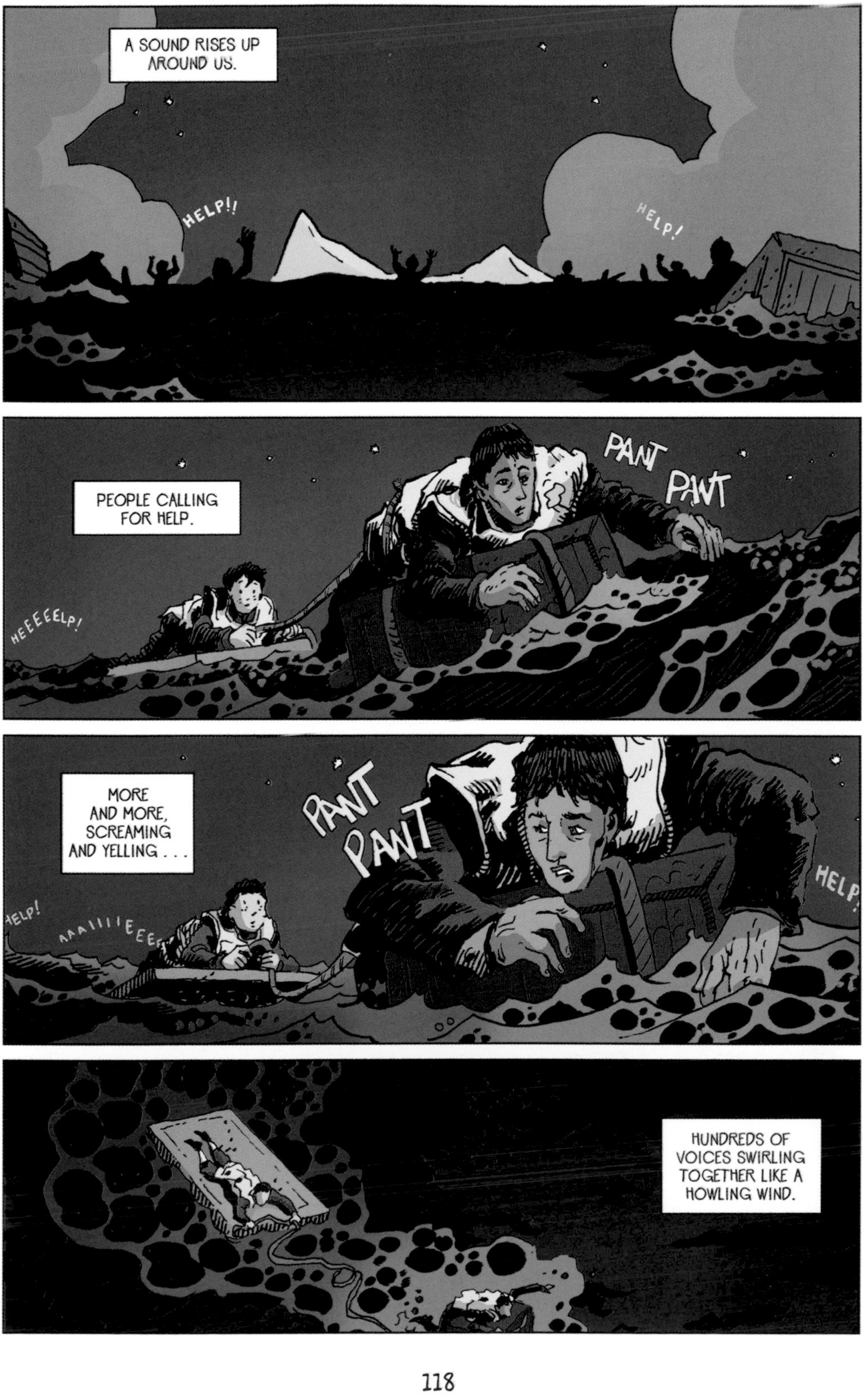
A SOUND RISES UP AROUND US.
HELP!!
HELP!
PEOPLE CALLING FOR HELP.
PANT PANT
HEEEEELP!
MORE AND MORE, SCREAMING AND YELLING . . .
PANT PANT
HELP!
HELP!
AAAIIIIEEE
HUNDREDS OF VOICES SWIRLING TOGETHER LIKE A HOWLING WIND.

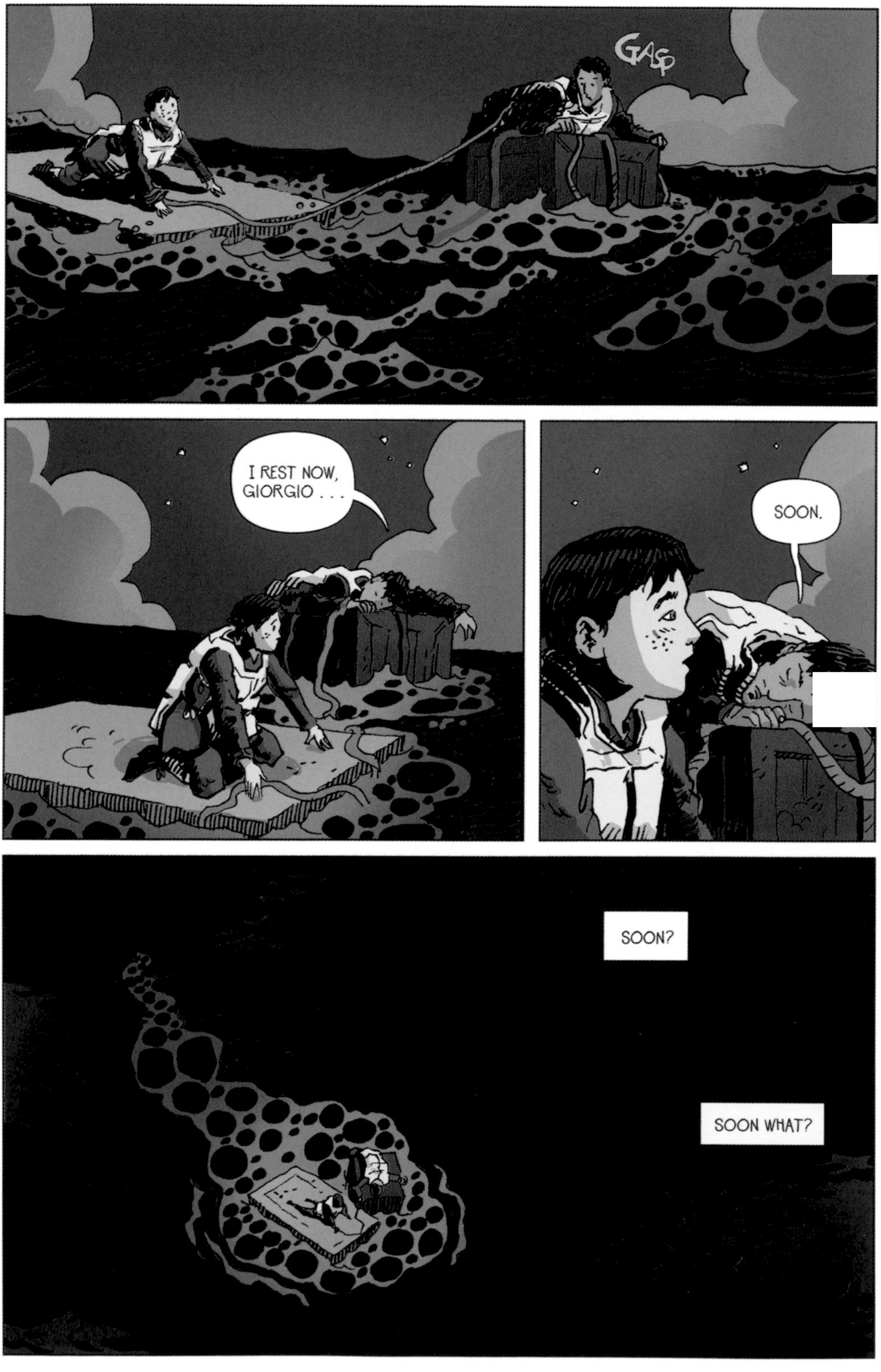
GASP
I REST NOW, GIORGIO . . .
SOON.
SOON?
SOON WHAT?

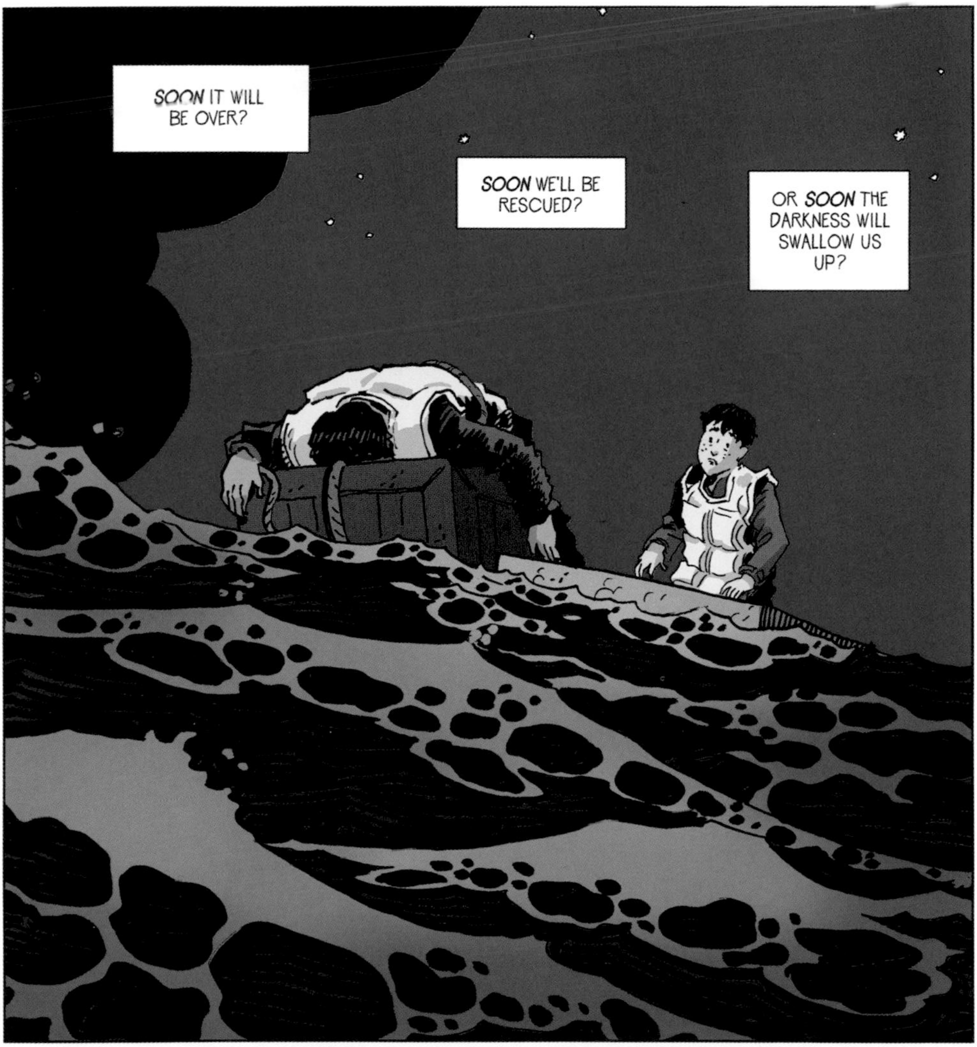
SOON IT WILL BE OVER?
SOON WE'LL BE RESCUED?
OR SOON THE DARKNESS WILL SWALLOW US UP?

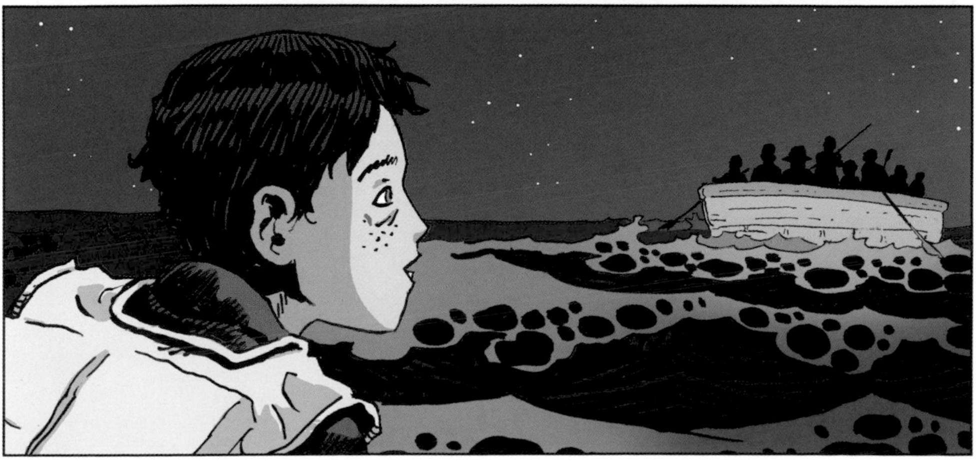

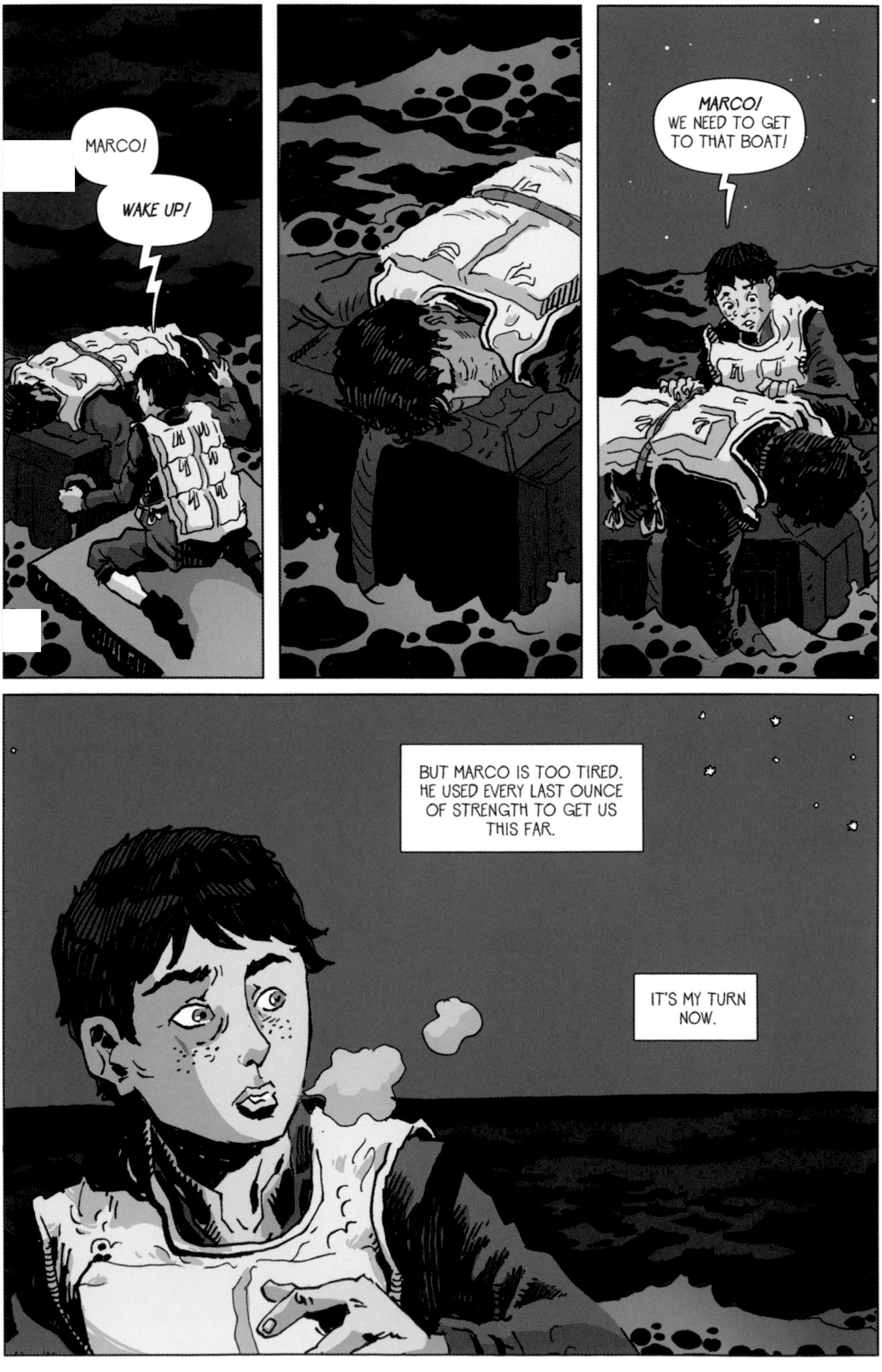
MARCO!
WAKE UP!
MARCO!
WE NEED TO GET
TO THAT BOAT!
BUT MARCO IS TOO TIRED.
HE USED EVERY LAST OUNCE
OF STRENGTH TO GET US
THIS FAR.
IT'S MY TURN
NOW.

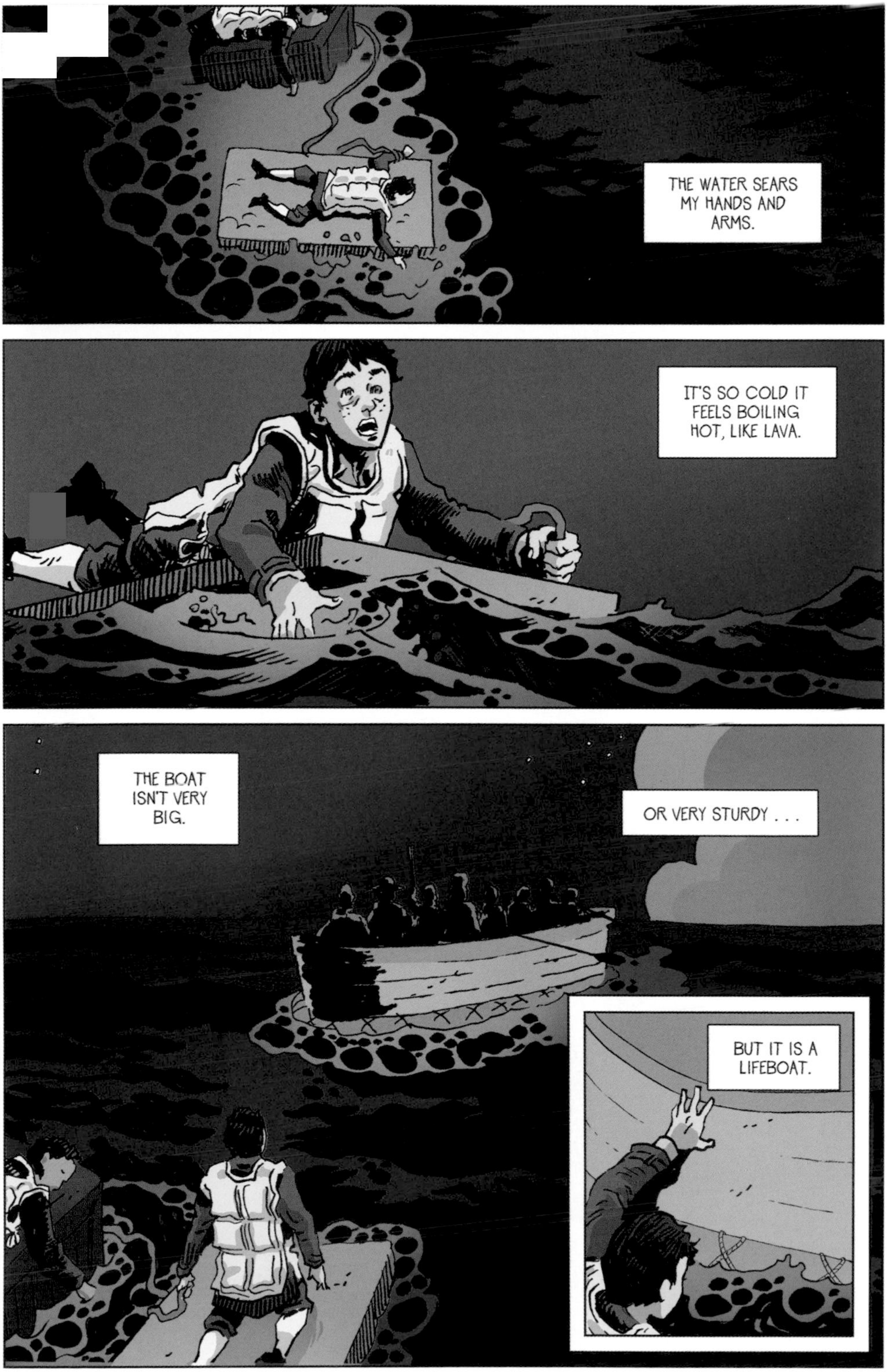
THE WATER SEARS MY HANDS AND ARMS.
IT'S SO COLD IT FEELS BOILING HOT, LIKE LAVA.
THE BOAT ISN'T VERY BIG.
OR VERY STURDY . . .
BUT IT IS A LIFEBOAT.

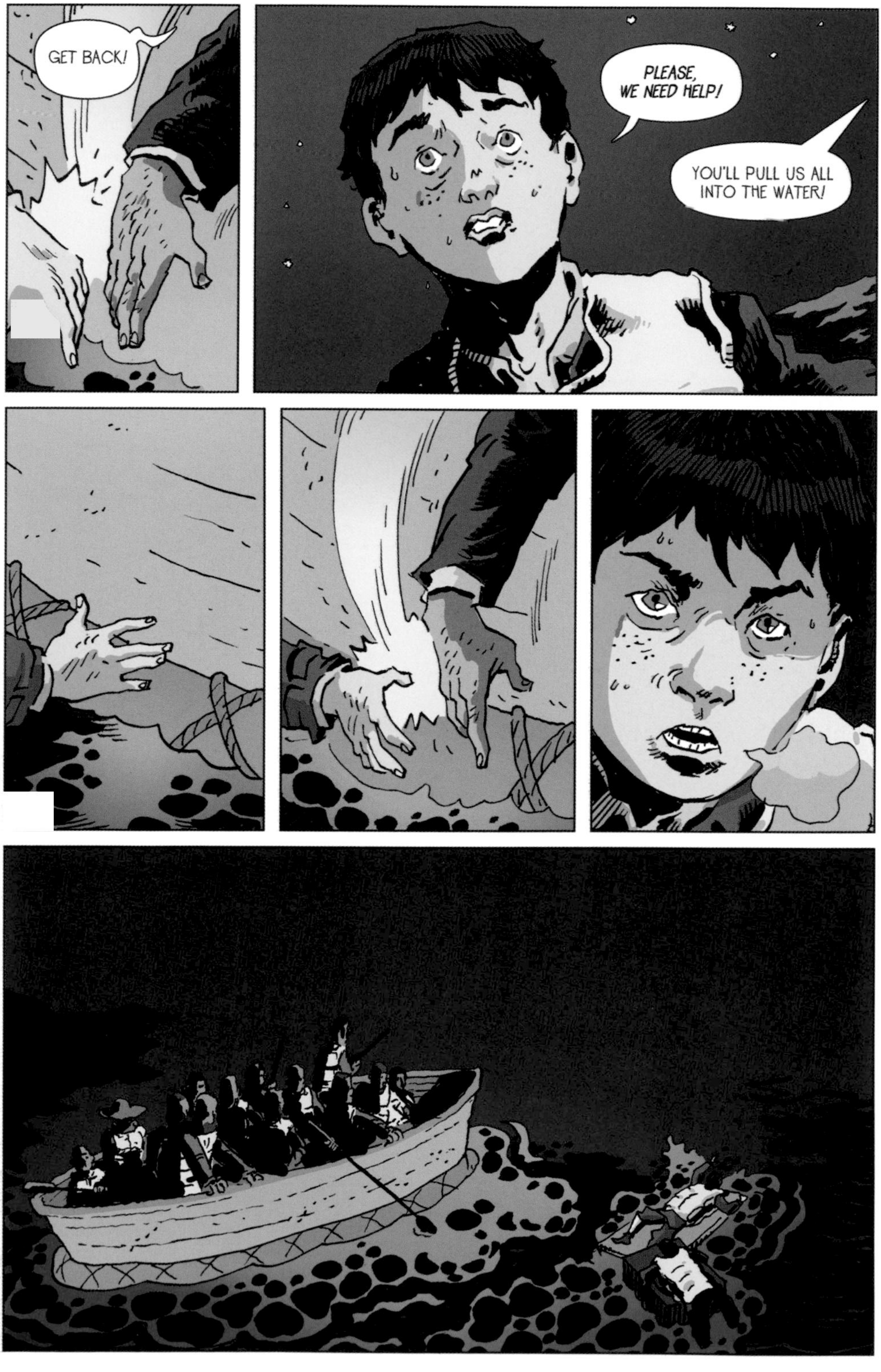
GET BACK!
PLEASE, WE NEED HELP!
YOU'LL PULL US ALL INTO THE WATER!

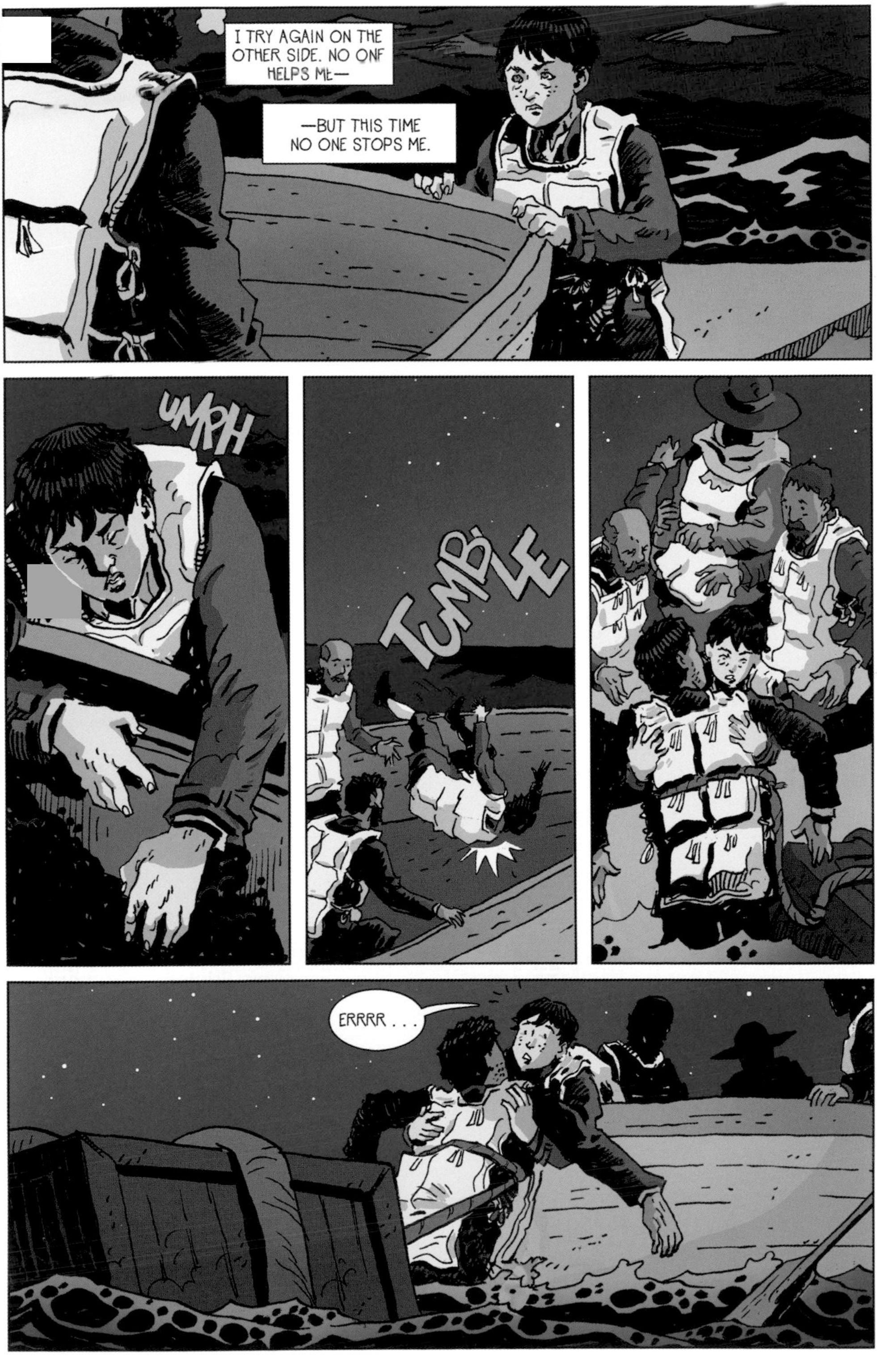
I TRY AGAIN ON THE OTHER SIDE. NO ONE HELPS ME—
—BUT THIS TIME NO ONE STOPS ME.
UMPH
TUMBLE
ERRRR . . .

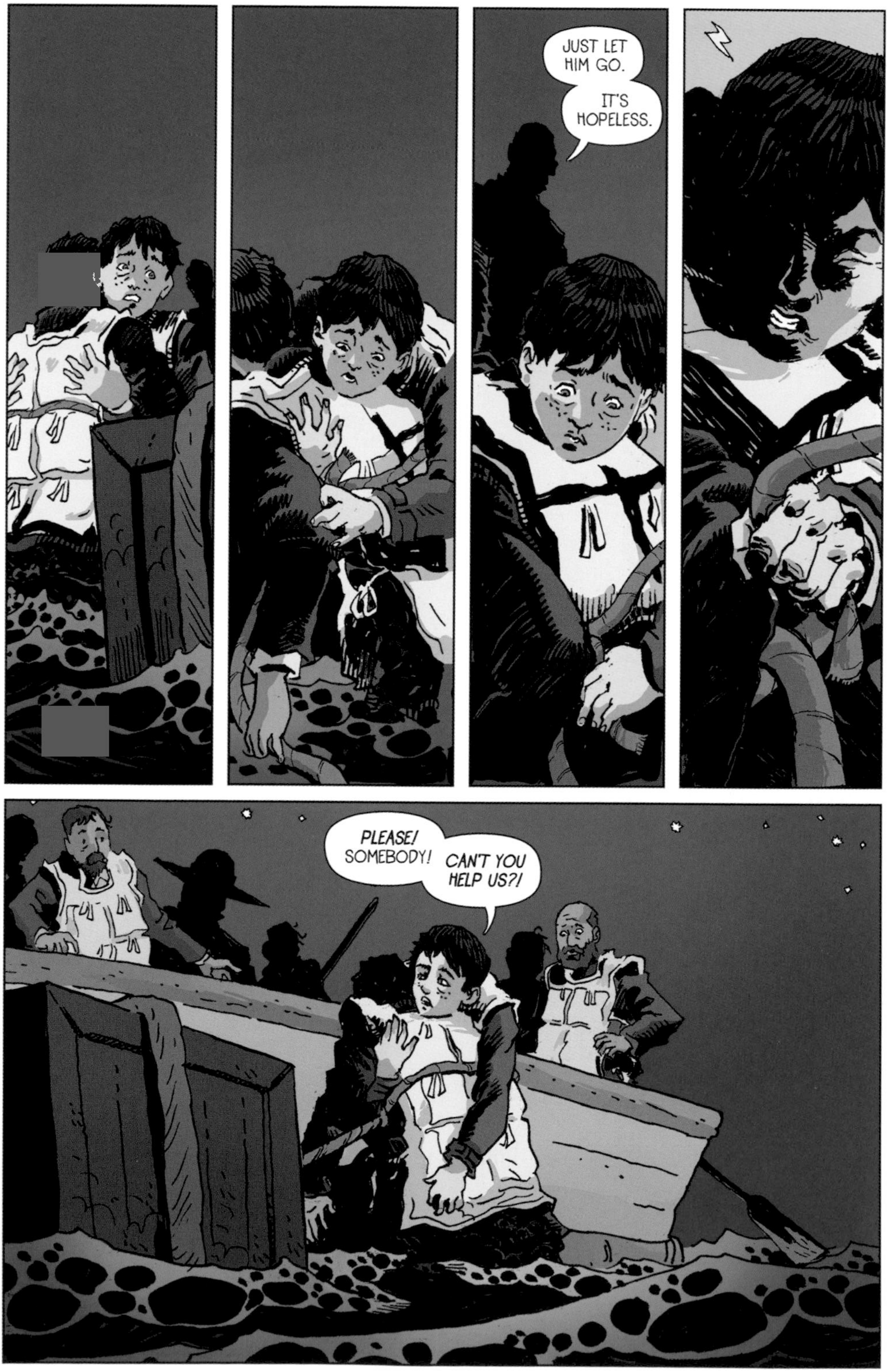
JUST LET HIM GO.
IT'S HOPELESS.
PLEASE! SOMEBODY!
CAN'T YOU HELP US?!

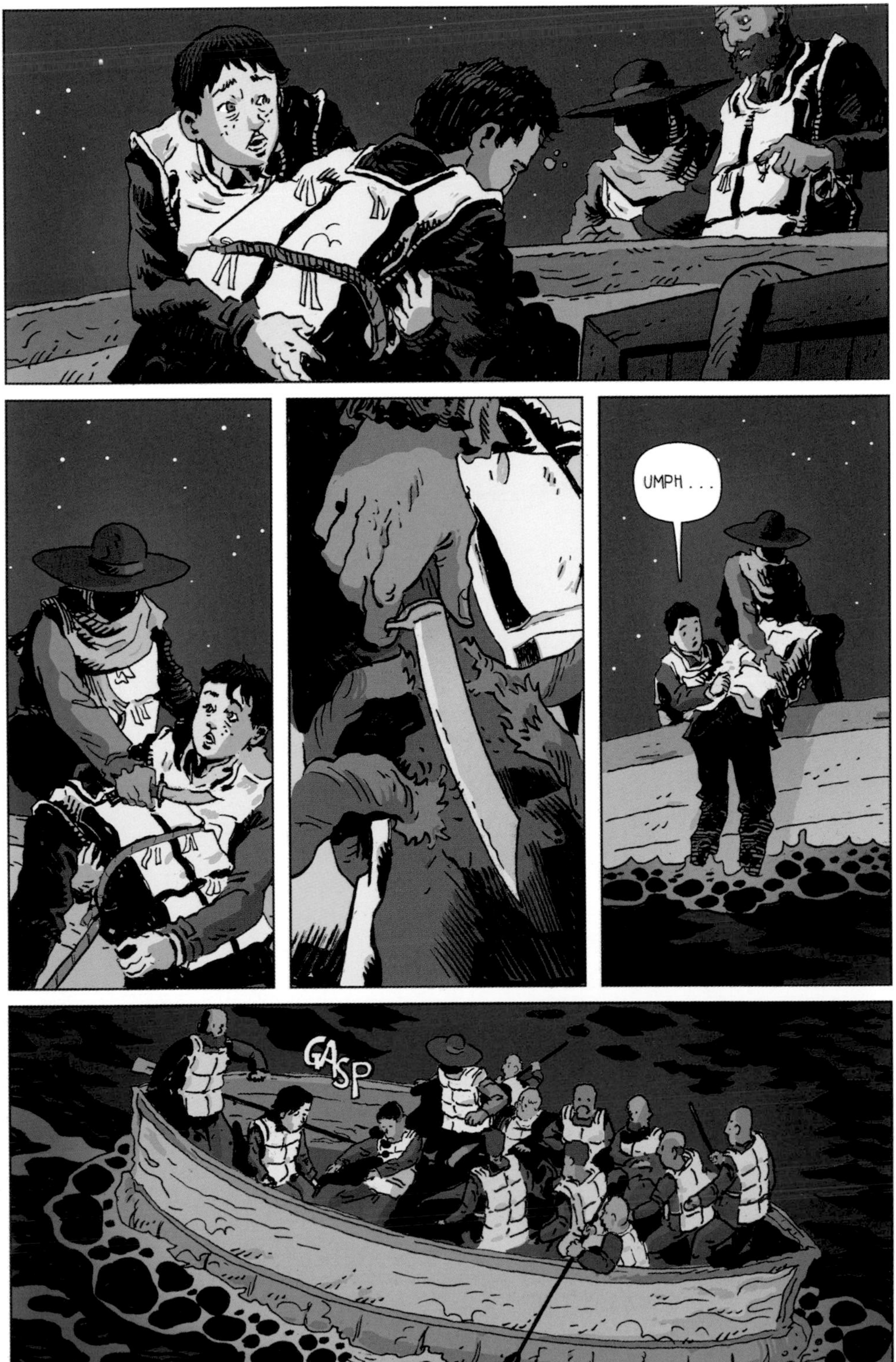
UMPH . . .
GASP

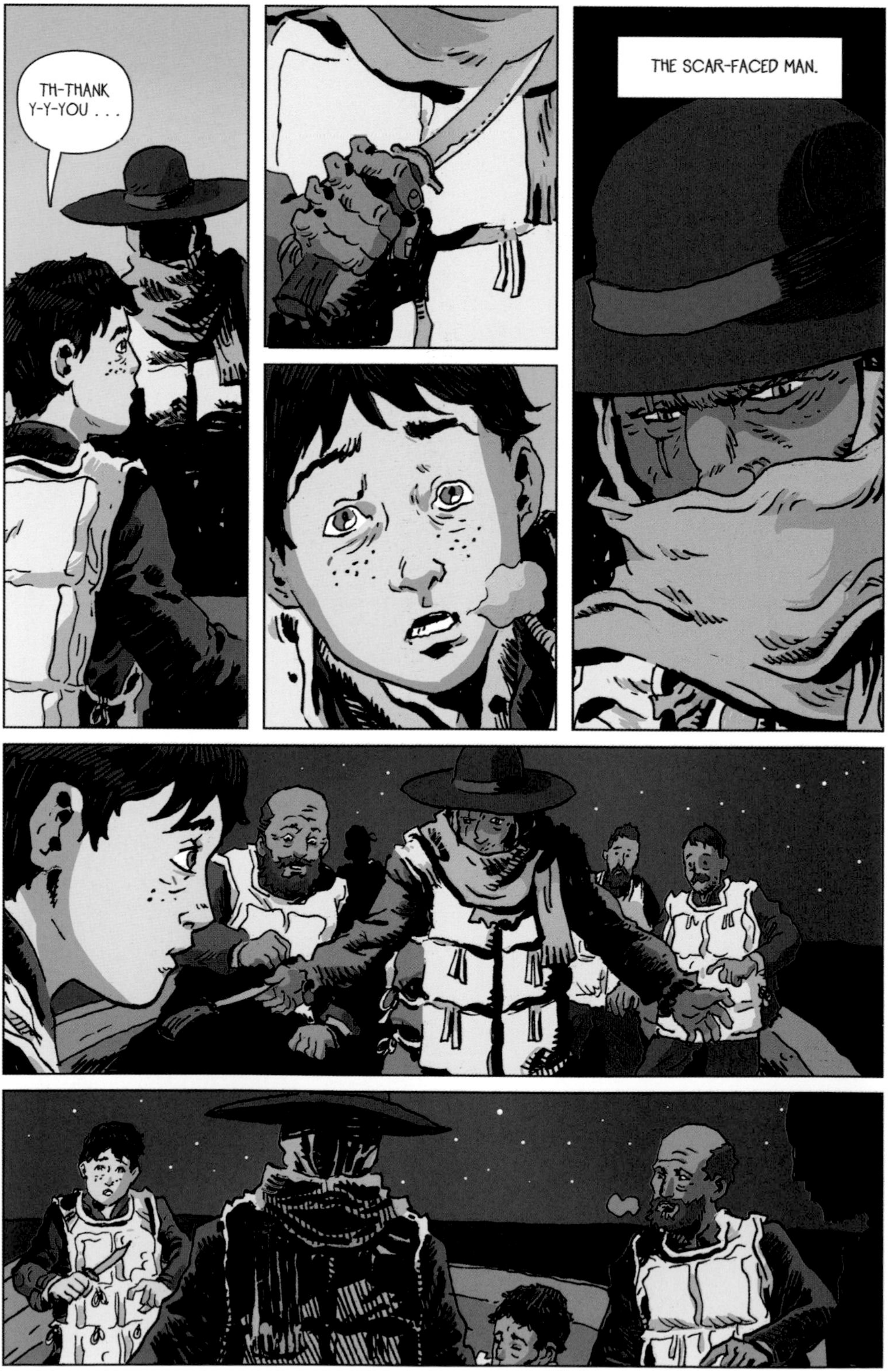
TH-THANK Y-Y-YOU . . .
THE SCAR-FACED MAN.

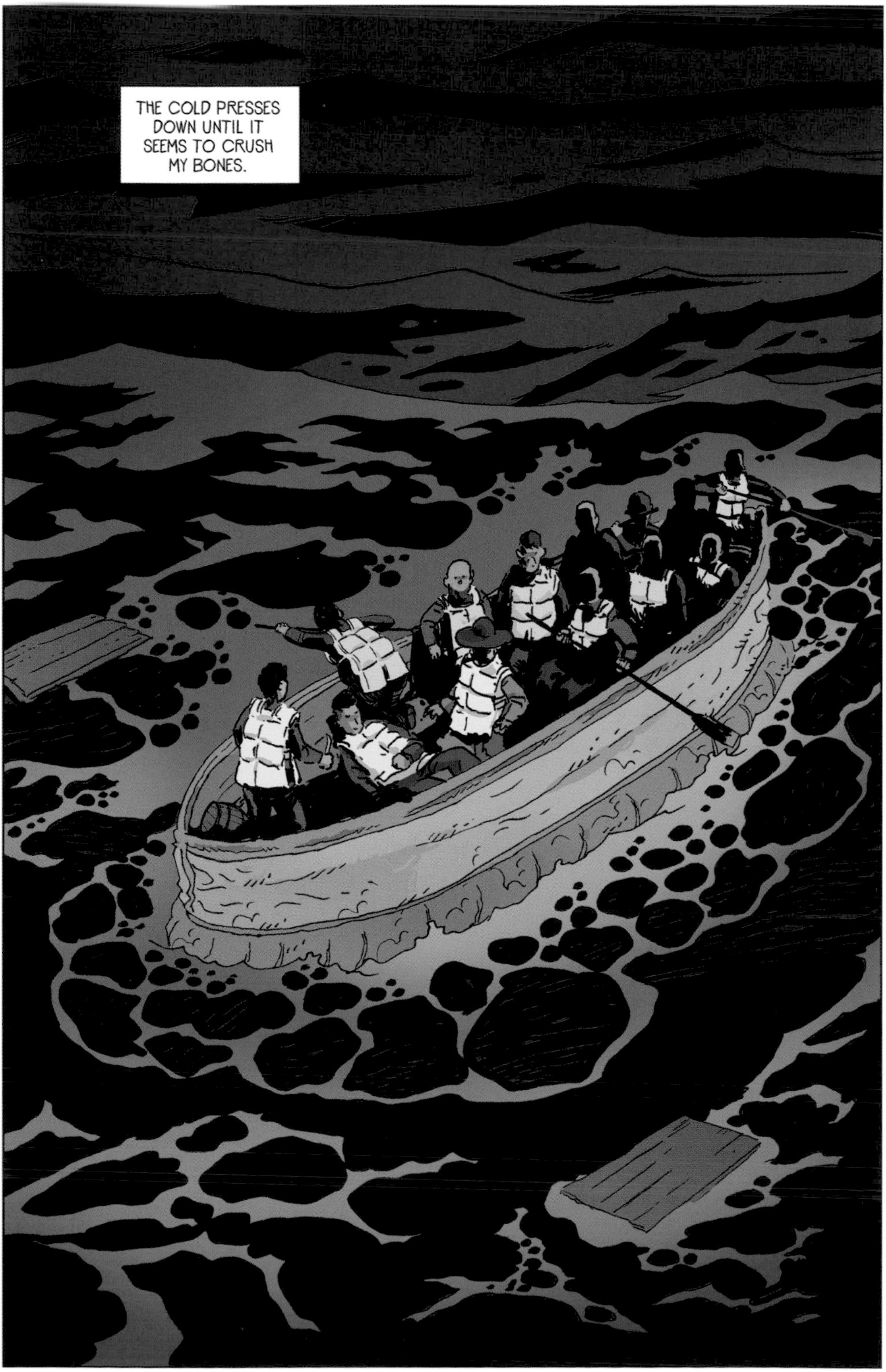
THE COLD PRESSES DOWN UNTIL IT SEEMS TO CRUSH MY BONES.

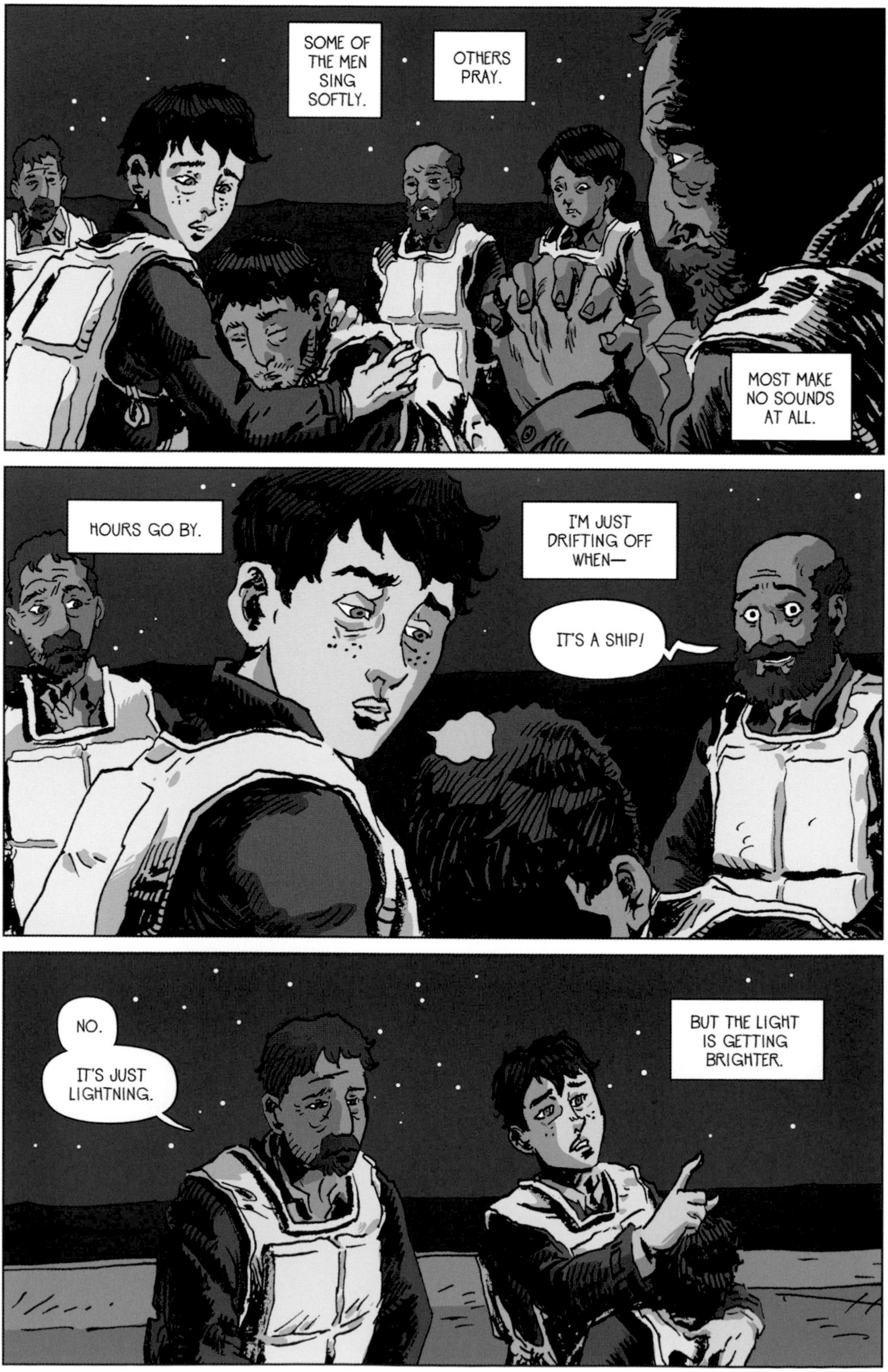
SOME OF THE MEN SING SOFTLY.
OTHERS PRAY.
MOST MAKE NO SOUNDS AT ALL.
HOURS GO BY.
I'M JUST DRIFTING OFF WHEN—
IT'S A SHIP!
NO.
IT'S JUST LIGHTNING.
BUT THE LIGHT IS GETTING BRIGHTER.

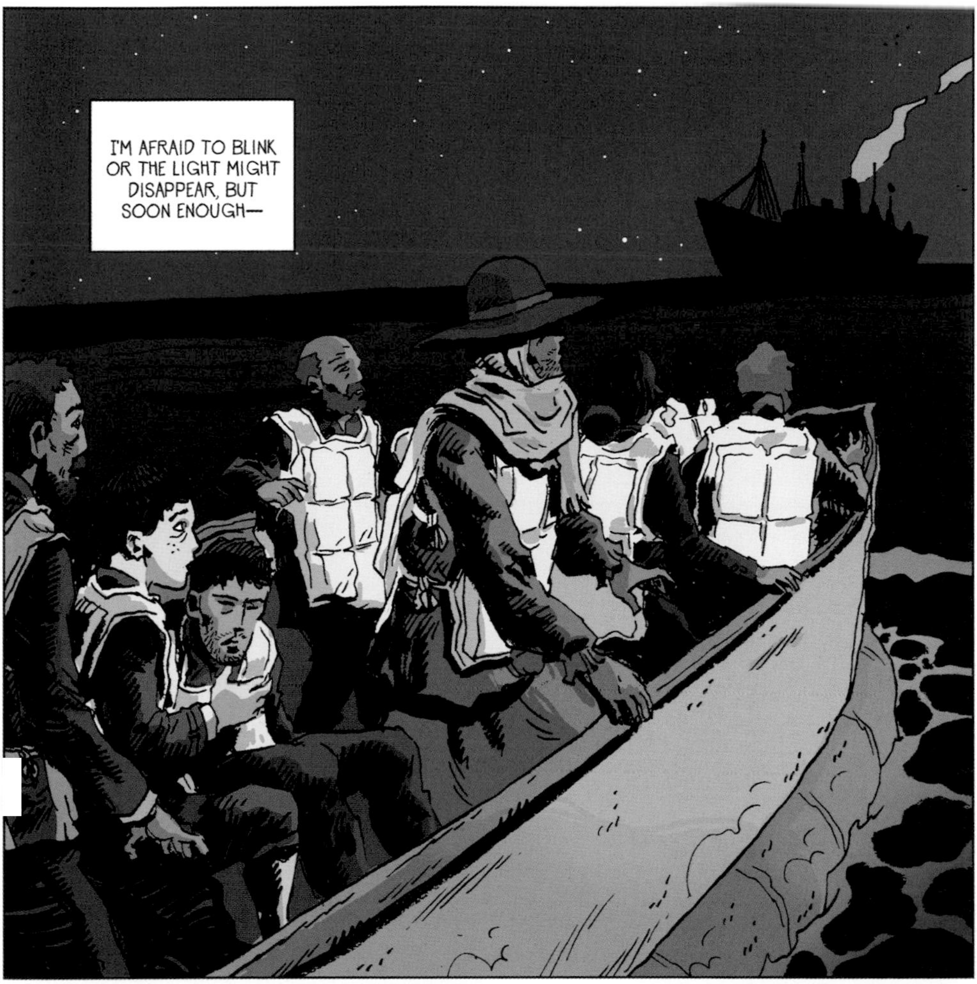
I'M AFRAID TO BLINK OR THE LIGHT MIGHT DISAPPEAR, BUT SOON ENOUGH—

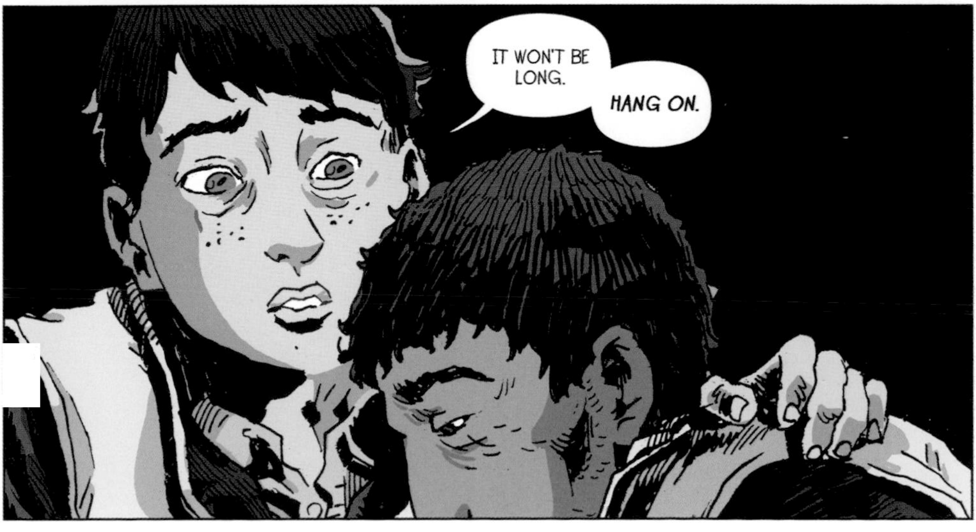
IT WON'T BE LONG.
HANG ON.

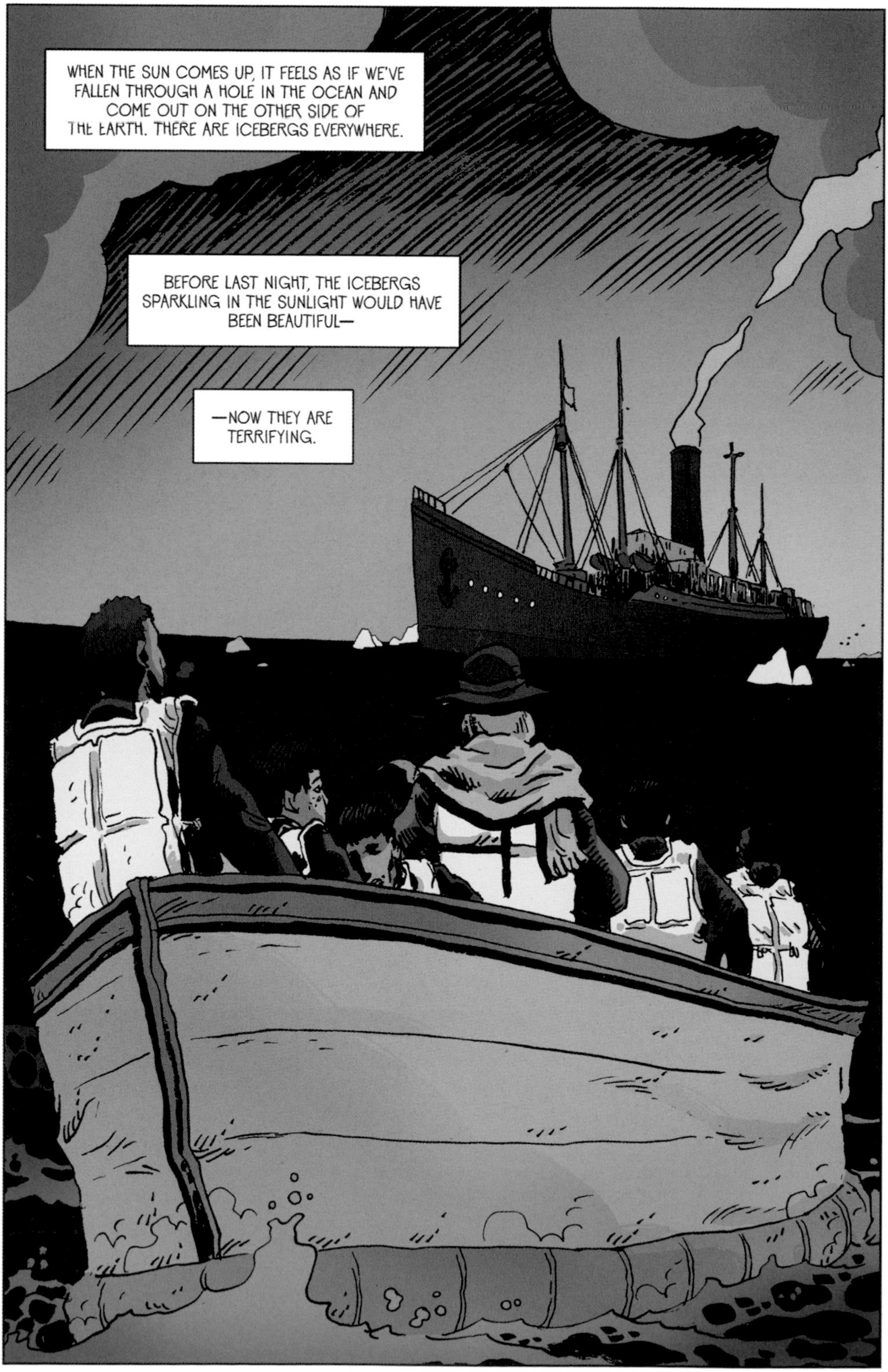
WHEN THE SUN COMES UP, IT FEELS AS IF WE'VE FALLEN THROUGH A HOLE IN THE OCEAN AND COME OUT ON THE OTHER SIDE OF THE EARTH. THERE ARE ICEBERGS EVERYWHERE.
BEFORE LAST NIGHT, THE ICEBERGS SPARKLING IN THE SUNLIGHT WOULD HAVE BEEN BEAUTIFUL—
—NOW THEY ARE TERRIFYING.

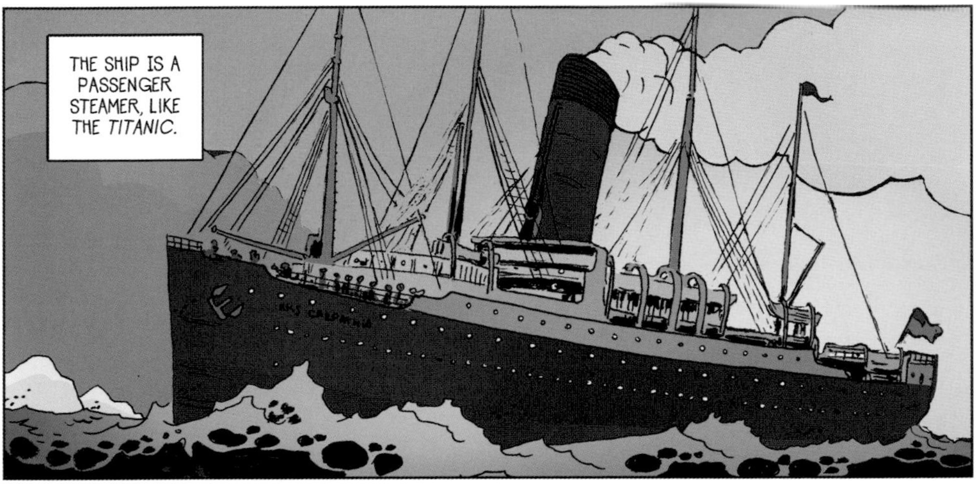
THE SHIP IS A PASSENGER STEAMER, LIKE THE *TITANIC*.

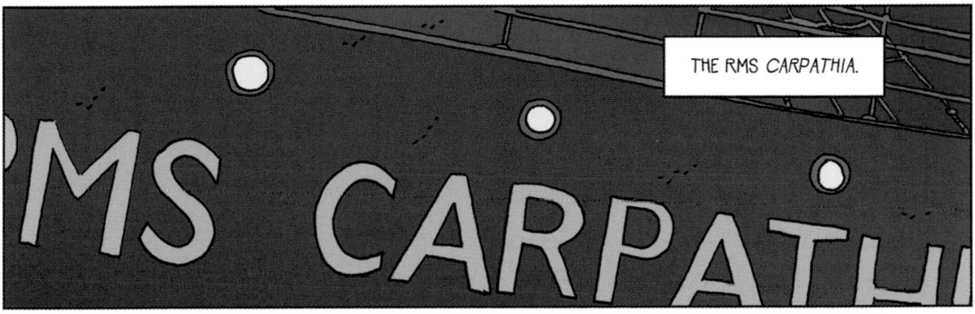
THE RMS *CARPATHIA*.

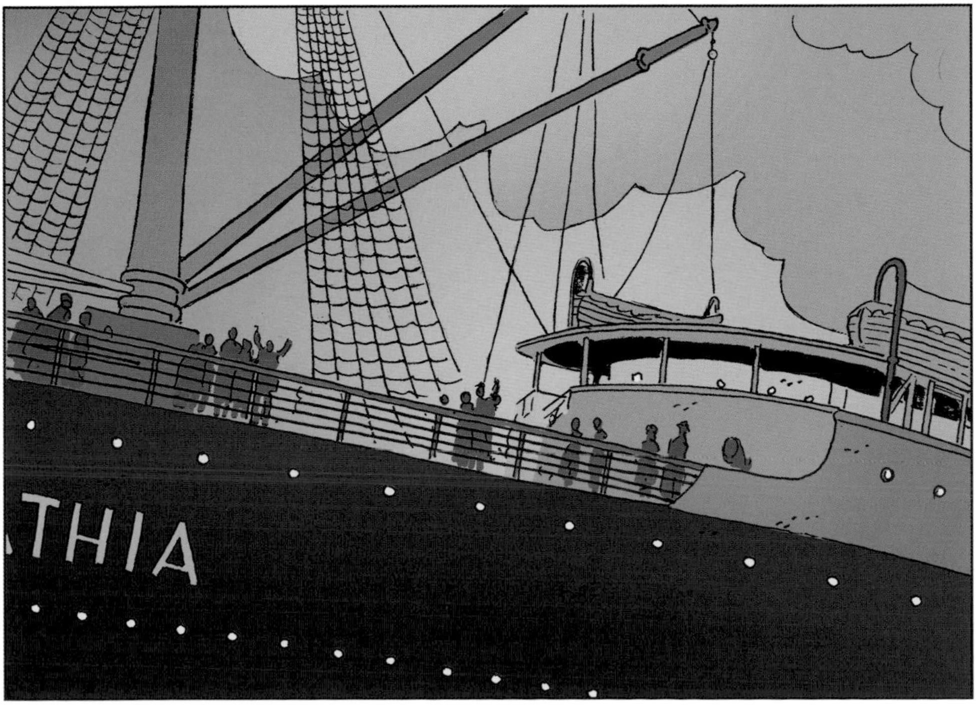

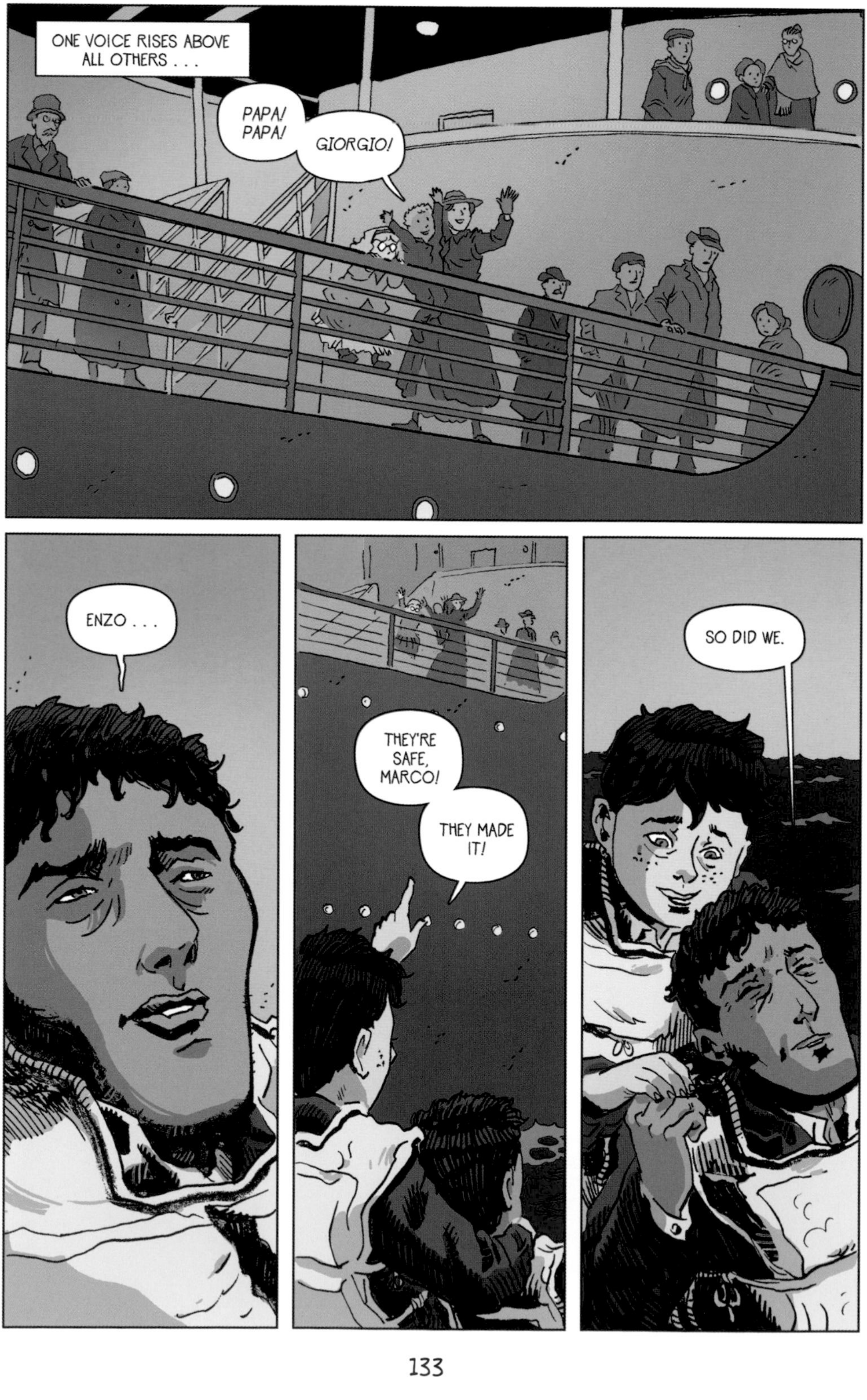
ONE VOICE RISES ABOVE ALL OTHERS . . .
PAPA! PAPA!
GIORGIO!
ENZO . . .
THEY'RE SAFE, MARCO!
THEY MADE IT!
SO DID WE.

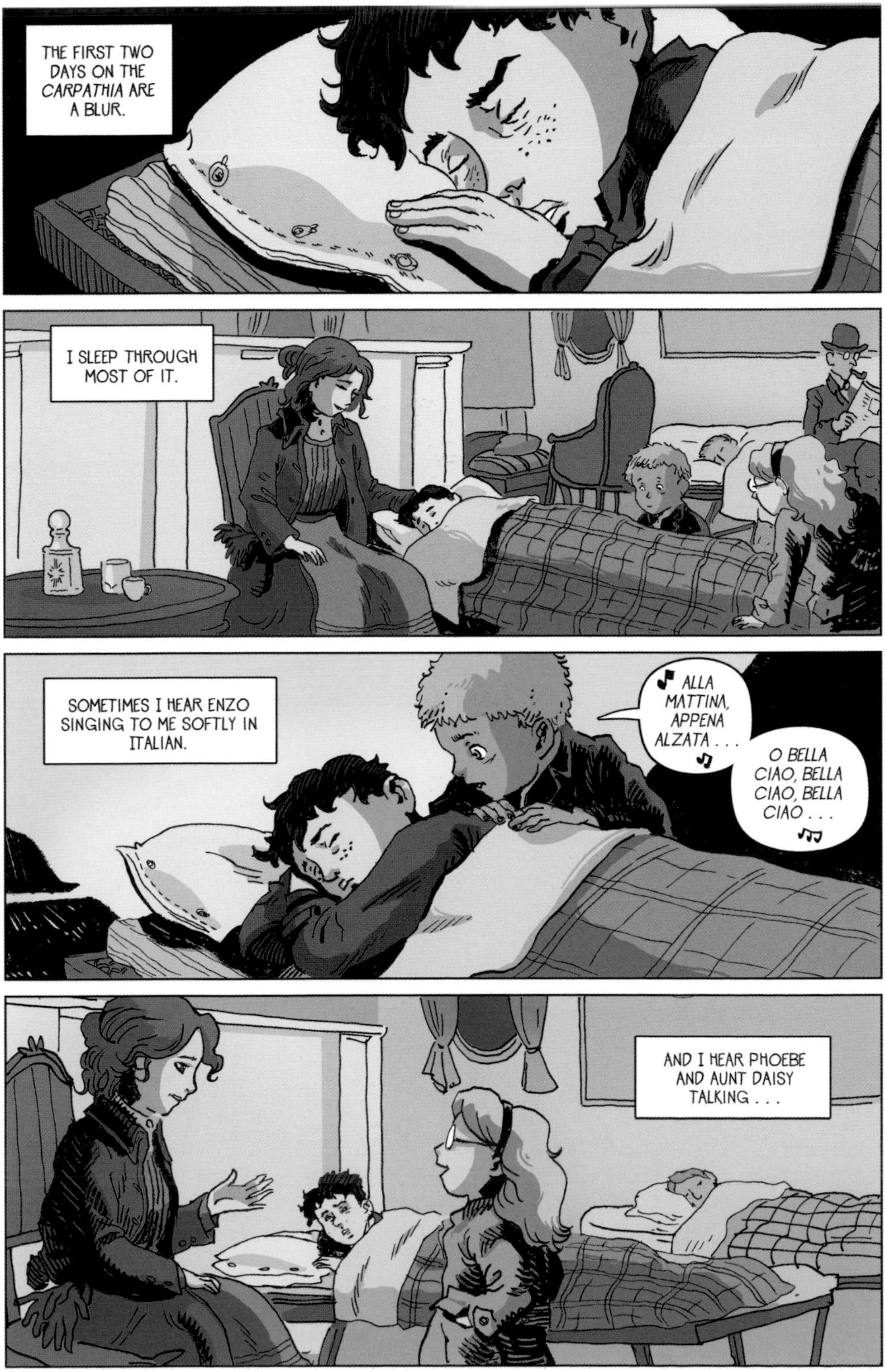
THE FIRST TWO DAYS ON THE *CARPATHIA* ARE A BLUR.
I SLEEP THROUGH MOST OF IT.
SOMETIMES I HEAR ENZO SINGING TO ME SOFTLY IN ITALIAN.
♪ ALLA MATTINA, APPENA ALZATA . . . ♫
O BELLA CIAO, BELLA CIAO, BELLA CIAO . . . ♫
AND I HEAR PHOEBE AND AUNT DAISY TALKING . . .

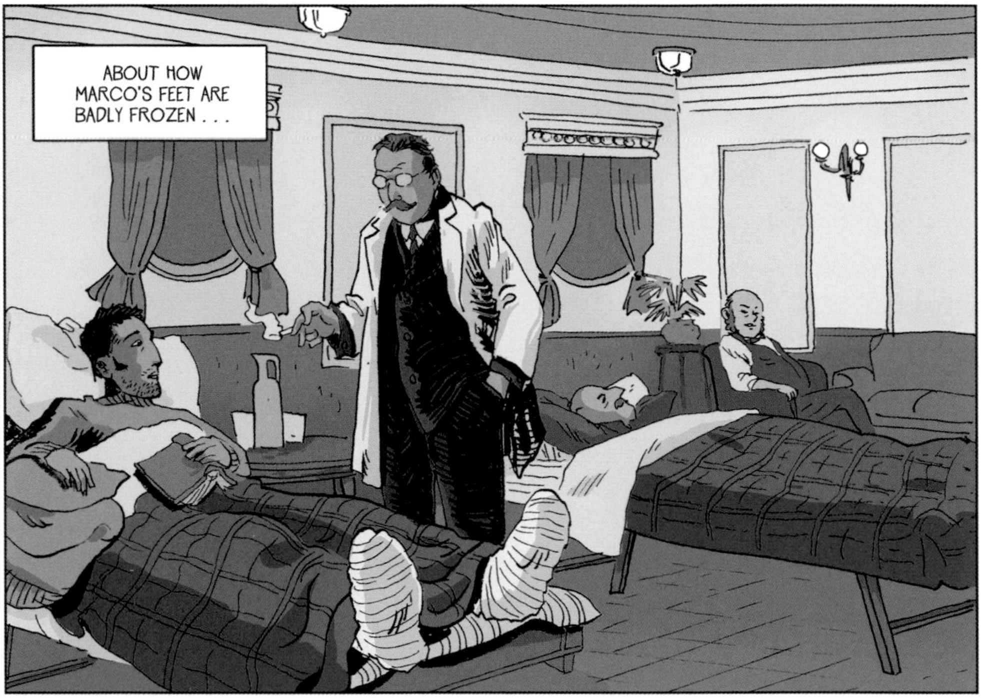
ABOUT HOW MARCO'S FEET ARE BADLY FROZEN . . .

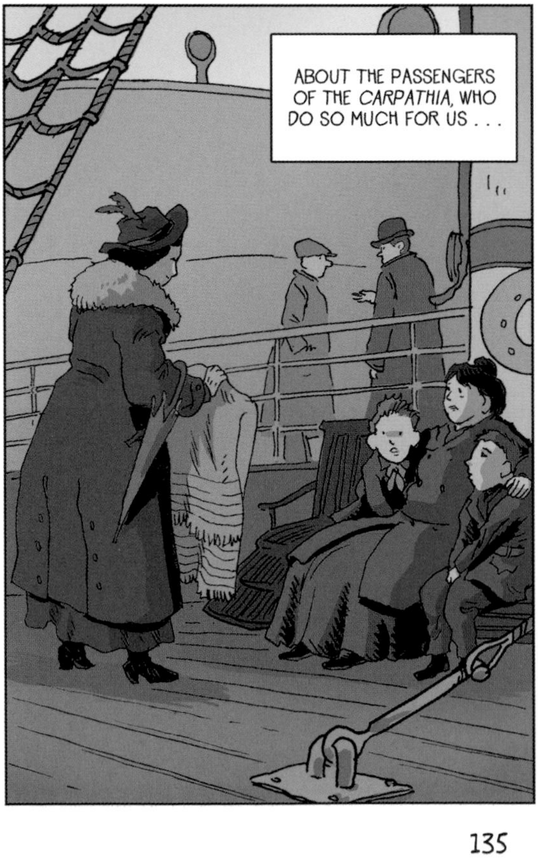
ABOUT THE PASSENGERS OF THE *CARPATHIA*, WHO DO SO MUCH FOR US . . .

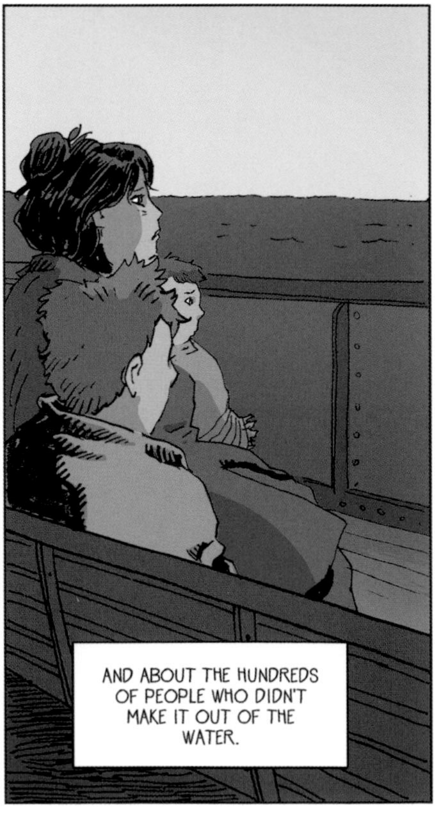
AND ABOUT THE HUNDREDS OF PEOPLE WHO DIDN'T MAKE IT OUT OF THE WATER.

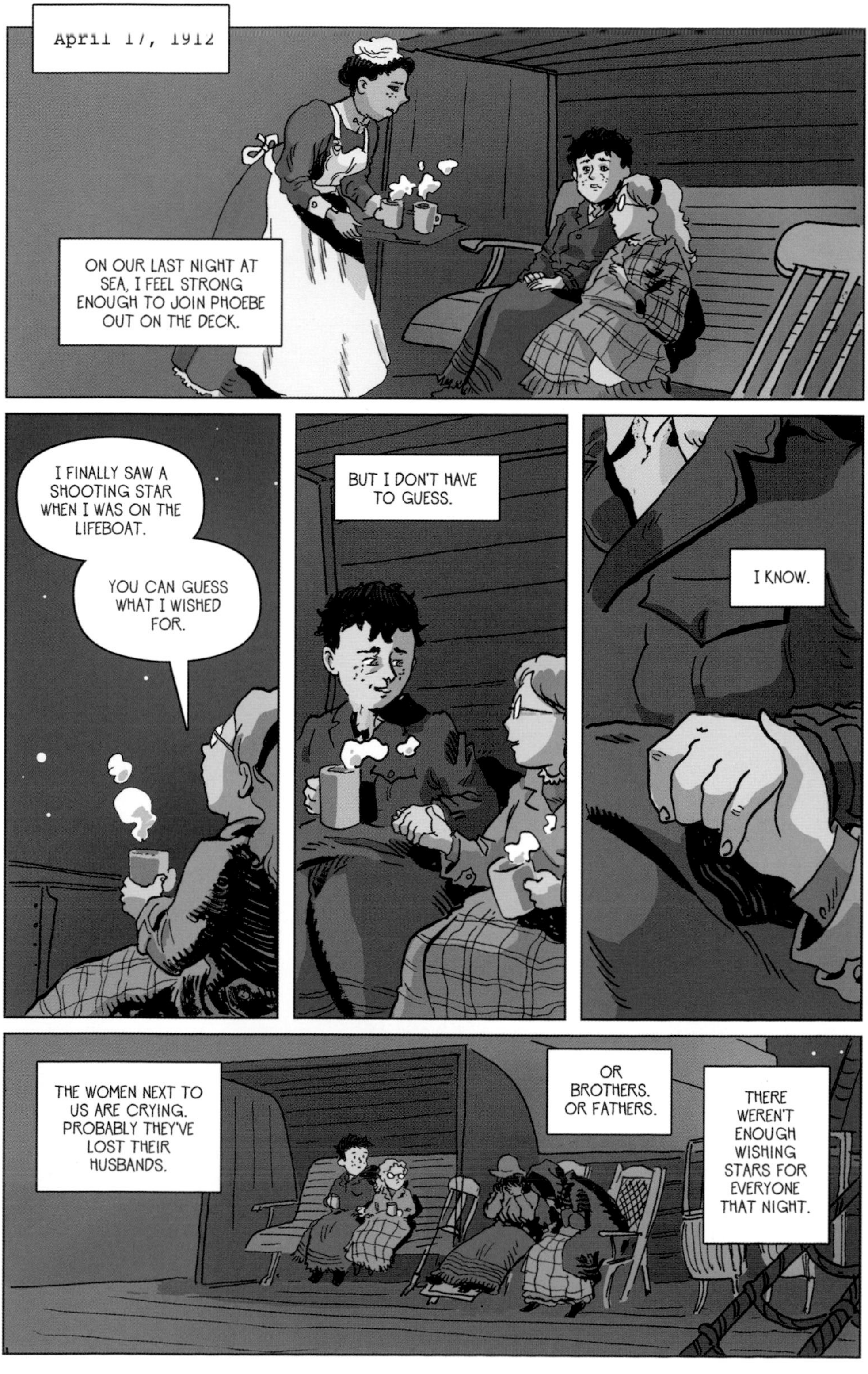
April 17, 1912
ON OUR LAST NIGHT AT SEA, I FEEL STRONG ENOUGH TO JOIN PHOEBE OUT ON THE DECK.
I FINALLY SAW A SHOOTING STAR WHEN I WAS ON THE LIFEBOAT.
YOU CAN GUESS WHAT I WISHED FOR.
BUT I DON'T HAVE TO GUESS.
I KNOW.
THE WOMEN NEXT TO US ARE CRYING. PROBABLY THEY'VE LOST THEIR HUSBANDS.
OR BROTHERS. OR FATHERS.
THERE WEREN'T ENOUGH WISHING STARS FOR EVERYONE THAT NIGHT.

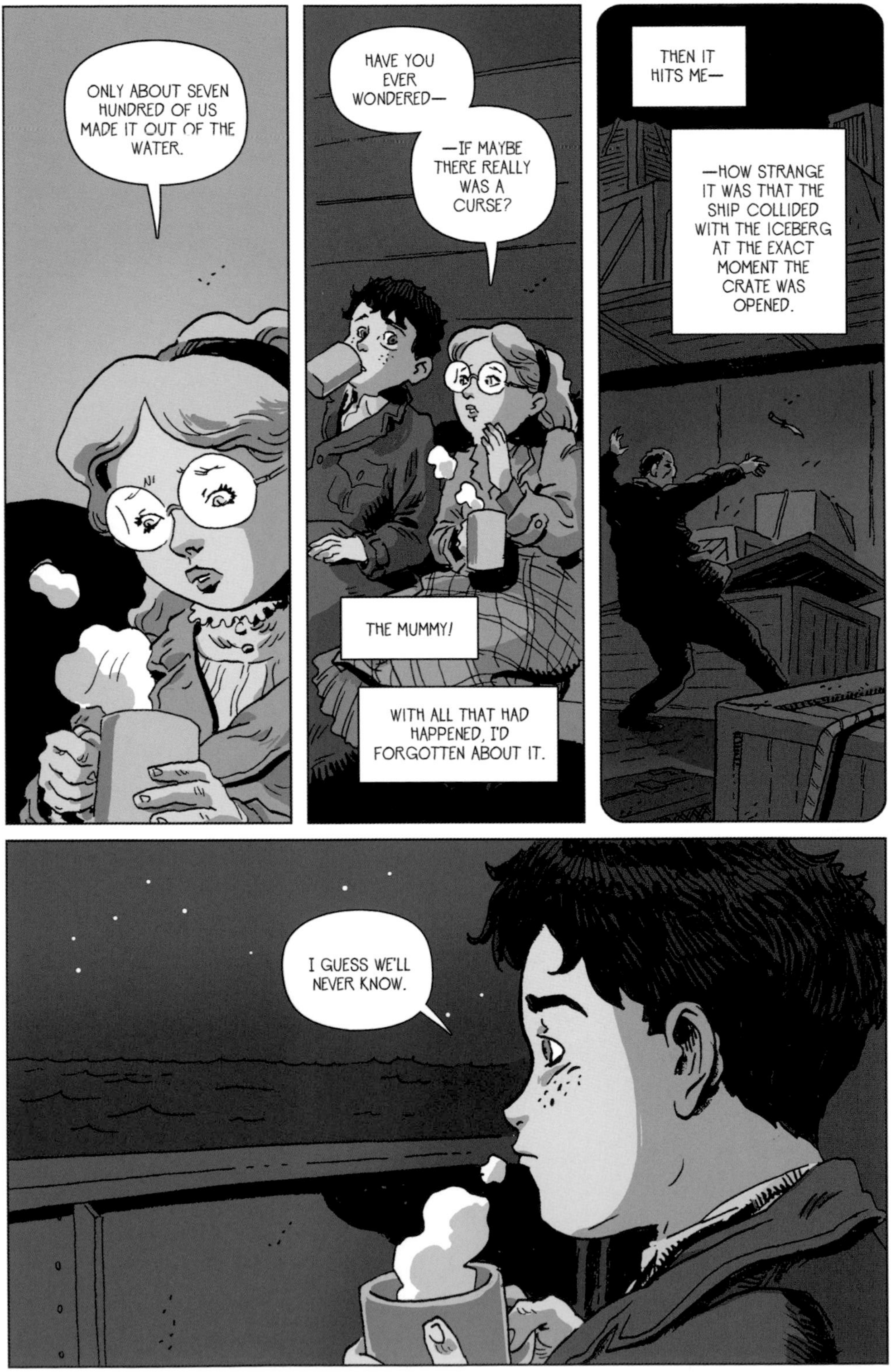
ONLY ABOUT SEVEN HUNDRED OF US MADE IT OUT OF THE WATER.
HAVE YOU EVER WONDERED—
—IF MAYBE THERE REALLY WAS A CURSE?
THE MUMMY!
WITH ALL THAT HAD HAPPENED, I'D FORGOTTEN ABOUT IT.
THEN IT HITS ME—
—HOW STRANGE IT WAS THAT THE SHIP COLLIDED WITH THE ICEBERG AT THE EXACT MOMENT THE CRATE WAS OPENED.
I GUESS WE'LL NEVER KNOW.

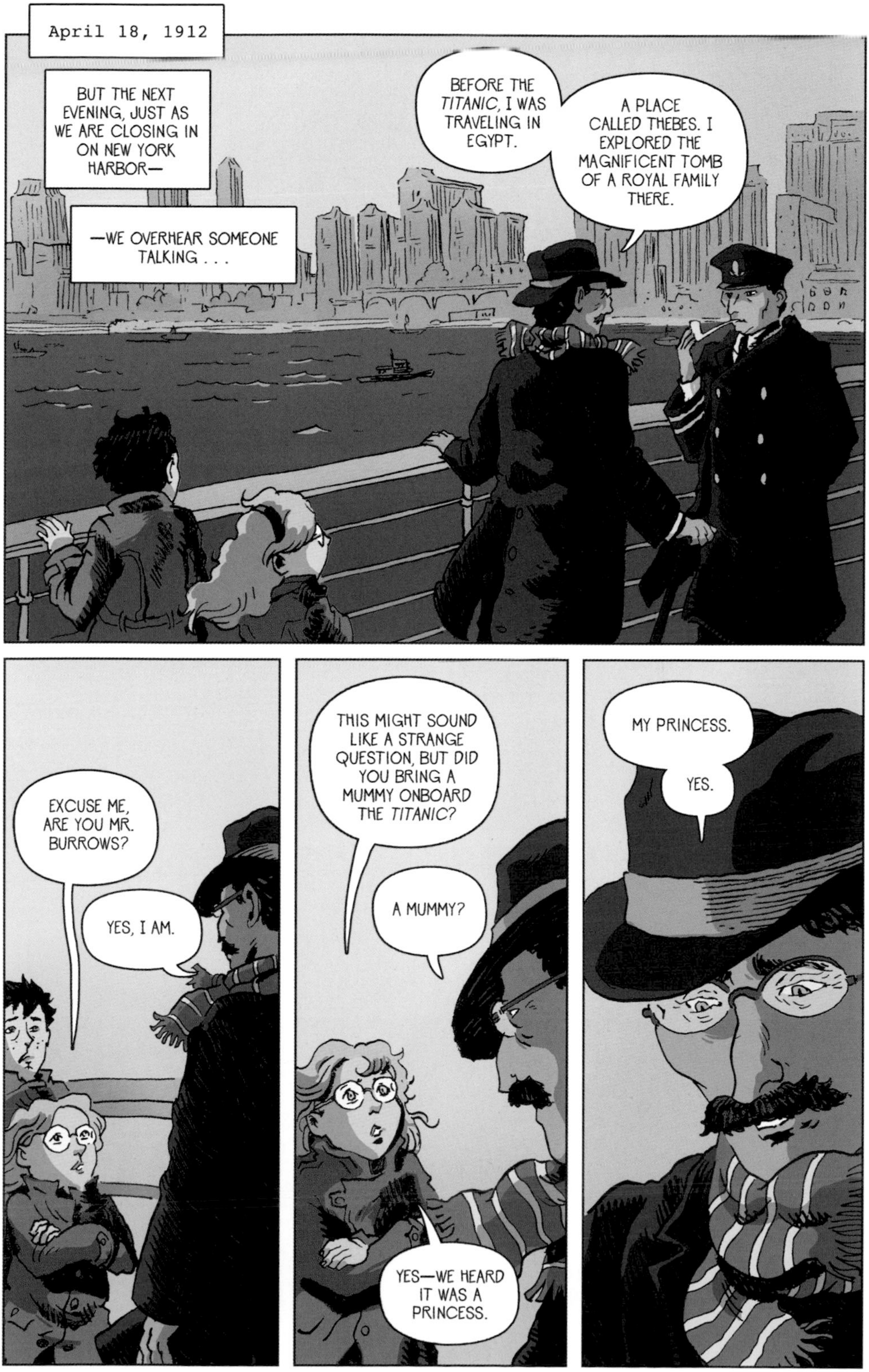
April 18, 1912
BUT THE NEXT EVENING, JUST AS WE ARE CLOSING IN ON NEW YORK HARBOR—
—WE OVERHEAR SOMEONE TALKING . . .
BEFORE THE *TITANIC*, I WAS TRAVELING IN EGYPT.
A PLACE CALLED THEBES. I EXPLORED THE MAGNIFICENT TOMB OF A ROYAL FAMILY THERE.
EXCUSE ME, ARE YOU MR. BURROWS?
YES, I AM.
THIS MIGHT SOUND LIKE A STRANGE QUESTION, BUT DID YOU BRING A MUMMY ONBOARD THE *TITANIC*?
A MUMMY?
YES—WE HEARD IT WAS A PRINCESS.
MY PRINCESS.
YES.

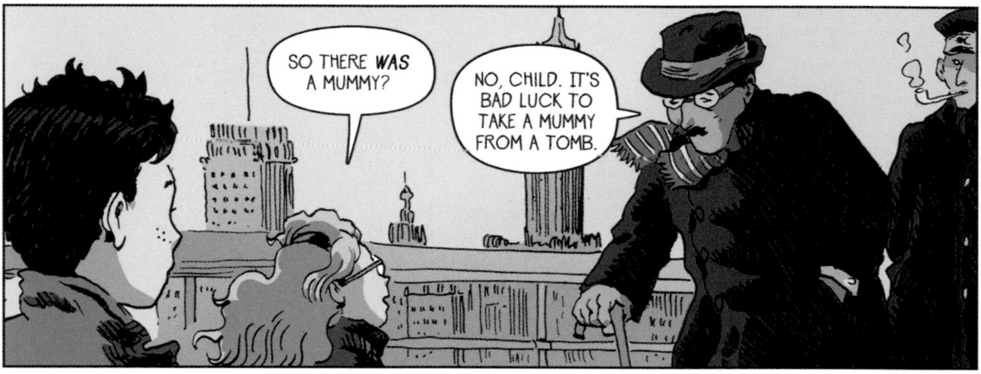
SO THERE WAS A MUMMY?
NO, CHILD. IT'S BAD LUCK TO TAKE A MUMMY FROM A TOMB.
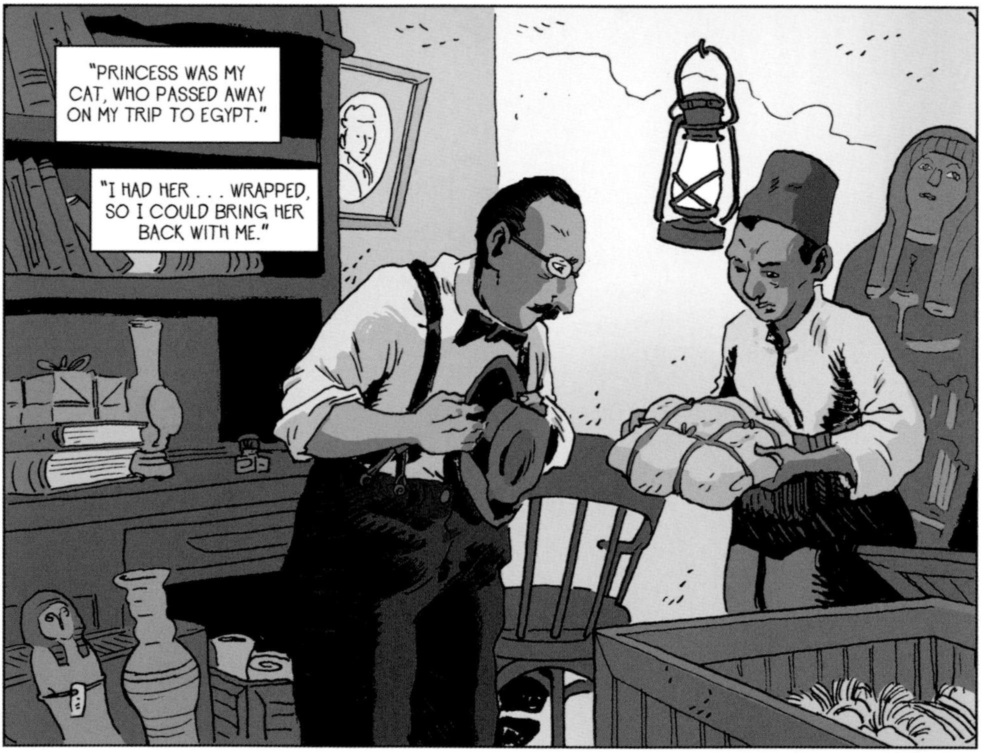
"PRINCESS WAS MY CAT, WHO PASSED AWAY ON MY TRIP TO EGYPT."
"I HAD HER . . . WRAPPED, SO I COULD BRING HER BACK WITH ME."
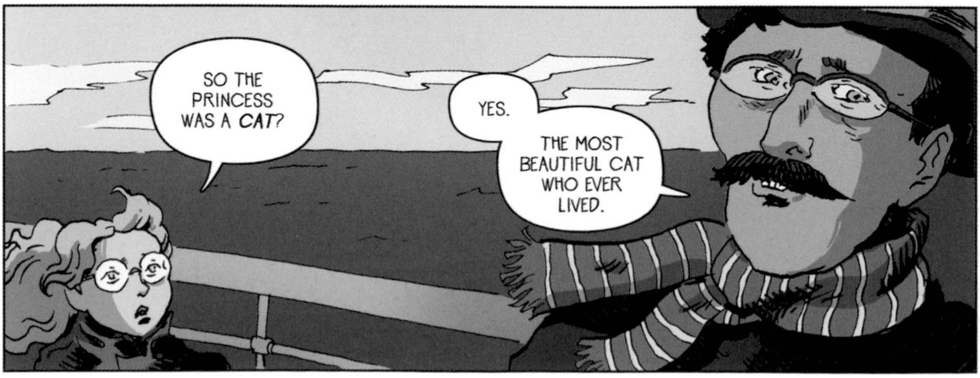
SO THE PRINCESS WAS A CAT?
YES.
THE MOST BEAUTIFUL CAT WHO EVER LIVED.

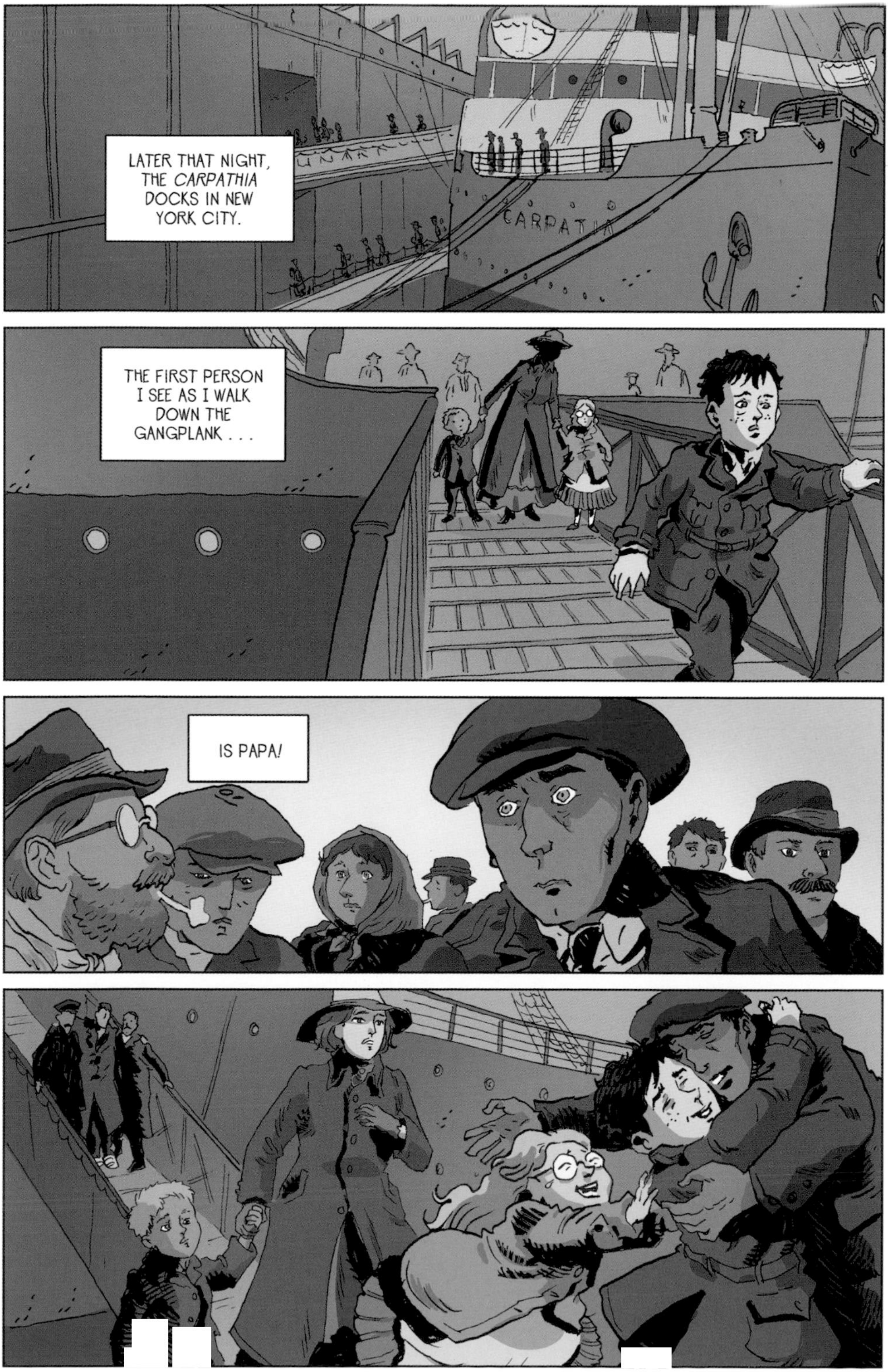
LATER THAT NIGHT, THE *CARPATHIA* DOCKS IN NEW YORK CITY.
THE FIRST PERSON I SEE AS I WALK DOWN THE GANGPLANK . . .
IS PAPA!

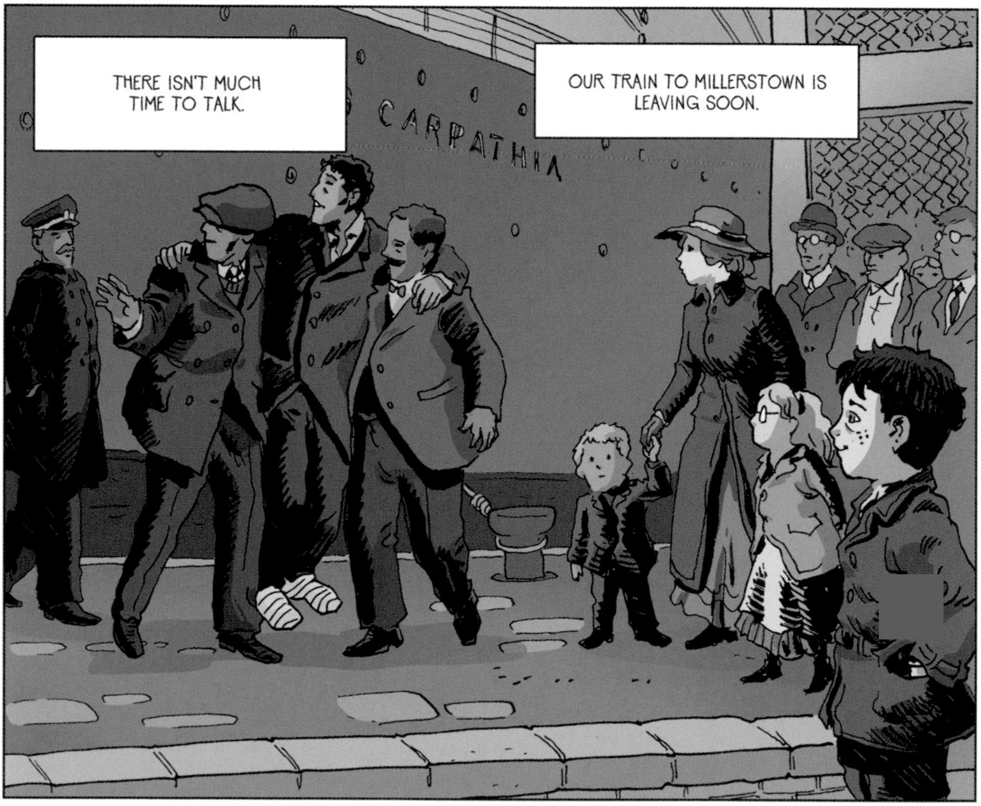
THERE ISN'T MUCH TIME TO TALK.
OUR TRAIN TO MILLERSTOWN IS LEAVING SOON.
CARPATHIA

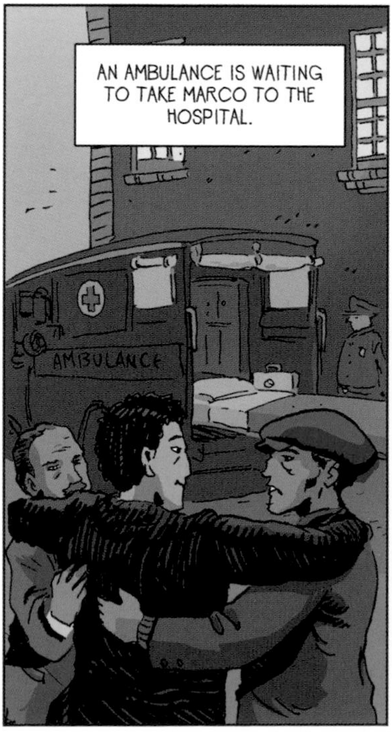
AN AMBULANCE IS WAITING TO TAKE MARCO TO THE HOSPITAL.
AMBULANCE

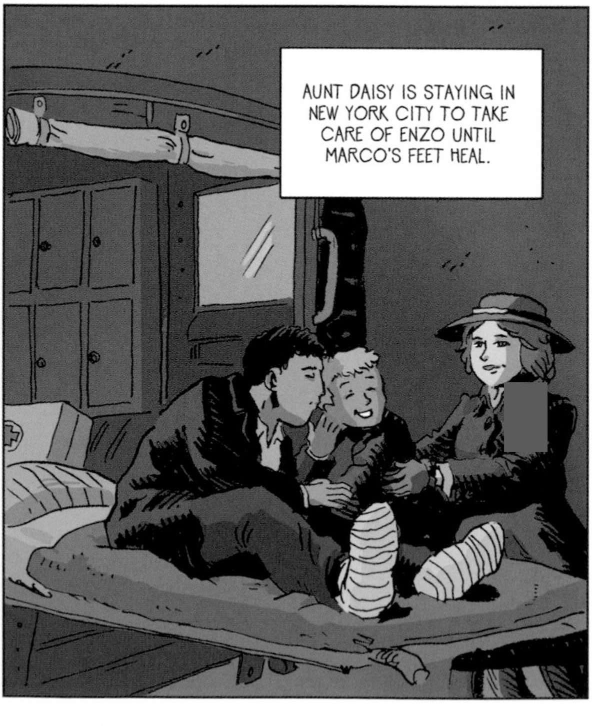
AUNT DAISY IS STAYING IN NEW YORK CITY TO TAKE CARE OF ENZO UNTIL MARCO'S FEET HEAL.

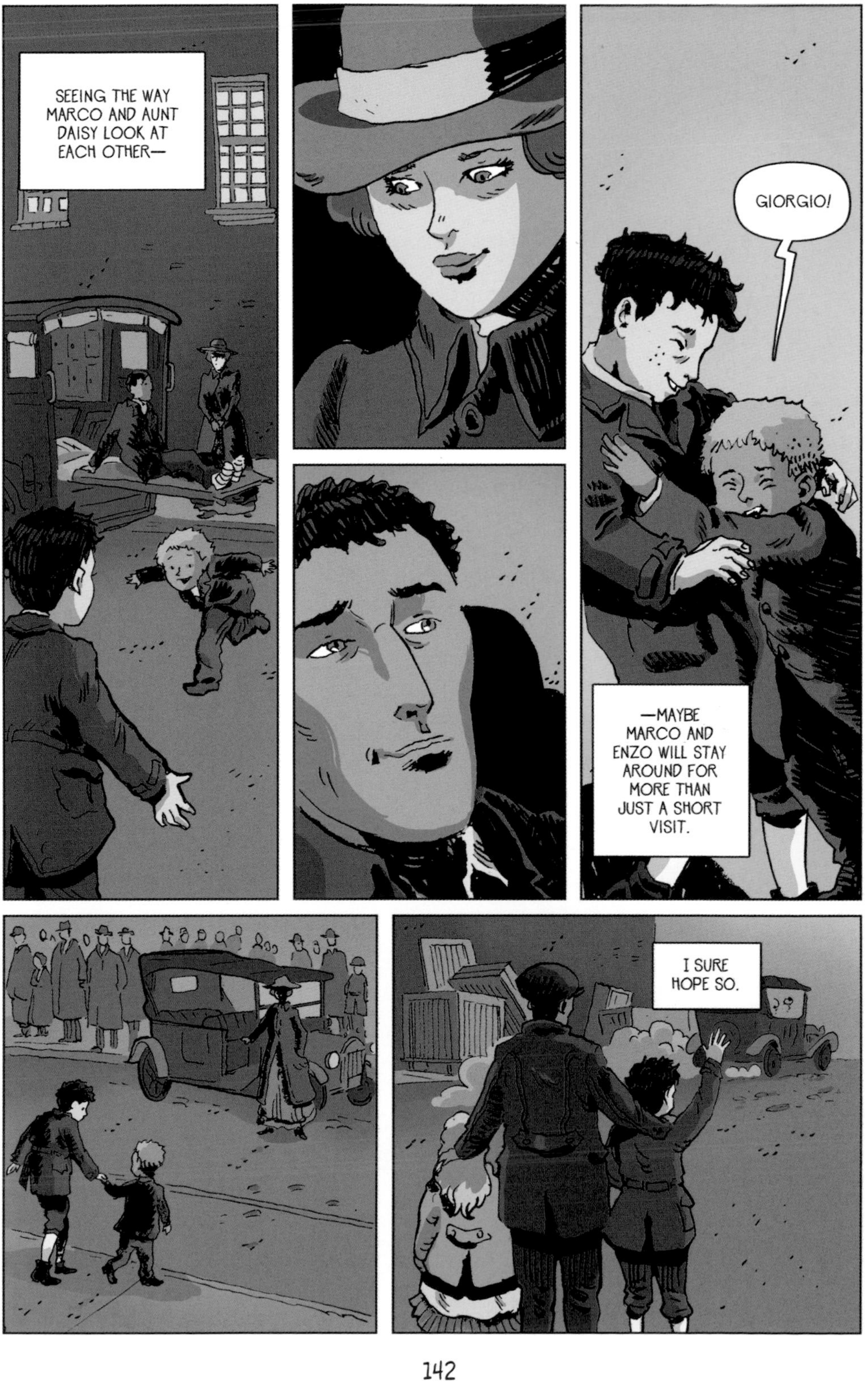
SEEING THE WAY MARCO AND AUNT DAISY LOOK AT EACH OTHER—
GIORGIO!
—MAYBE MARCO AND ENZO WILL STAY AROUND FOR MORE THAN JUST A SHORT VISIT.
I SURE HOPE SO.

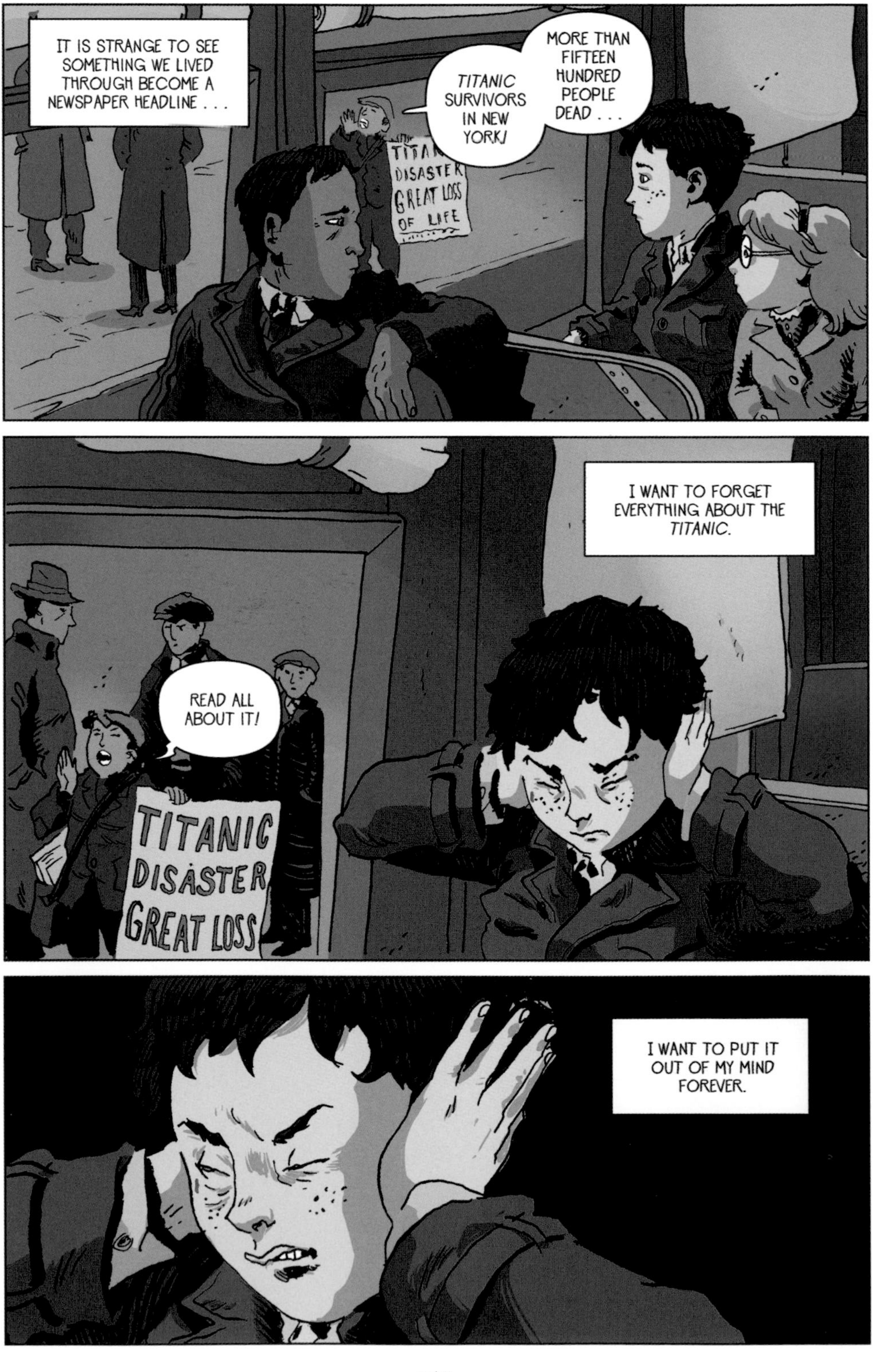
IT IS STRANGE TO SEE SOMETHING WE LIVED THROUGH BECOME A NEWSPAPER HEADLINE . . .
TITANIC SURVIVORS IN NEW YORK!
MORE THAN FIFTEEN HUNDRED PEOPLE DEAD . . .
TITANIC DISASTER GREAT LOSS OF LIFE
I WANT TO FORGET EVERYTHING ABOUT THE *TITANIC*.
READ ALL ABOUT IT!
TITANIC DISASTER GREAT LOSS
I WANT TO PUT IT OUT OF MY MIND FOREVER.

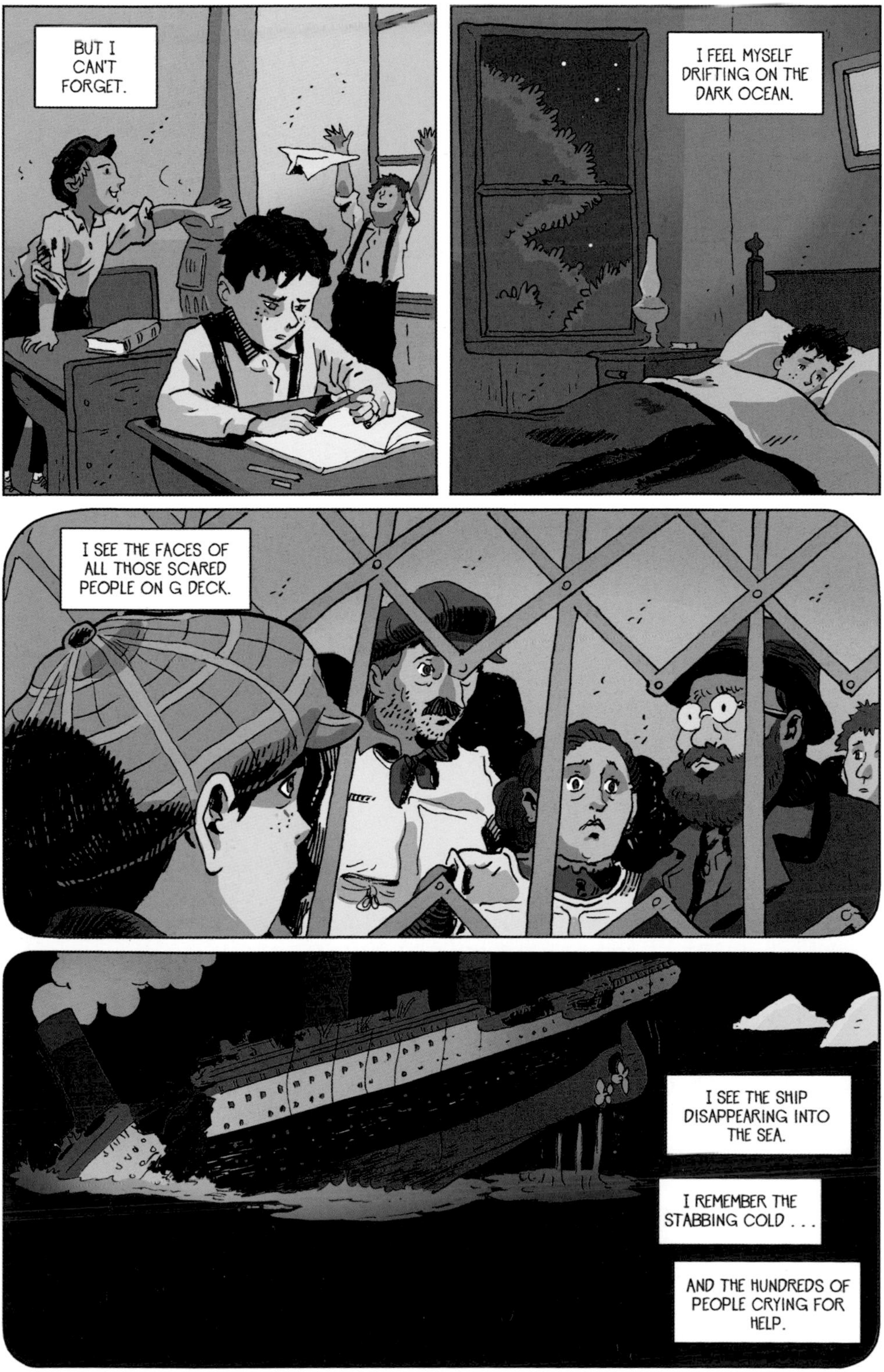

BUT I CAN'T FORGET.
I FEEL MYSELF DRIFTING ON THE DARK OCEAN.
I SEE THE FACES OF ALL THOSE SCARED PEOPLE ON G DECK.
I SEE THE SHIP DISAPPEARING INTO THE SEA.
I REMEMBER THE STABBING COLD . . .
AND THE HUNDREDS OF PEOPLE CRYING FOR HELP.

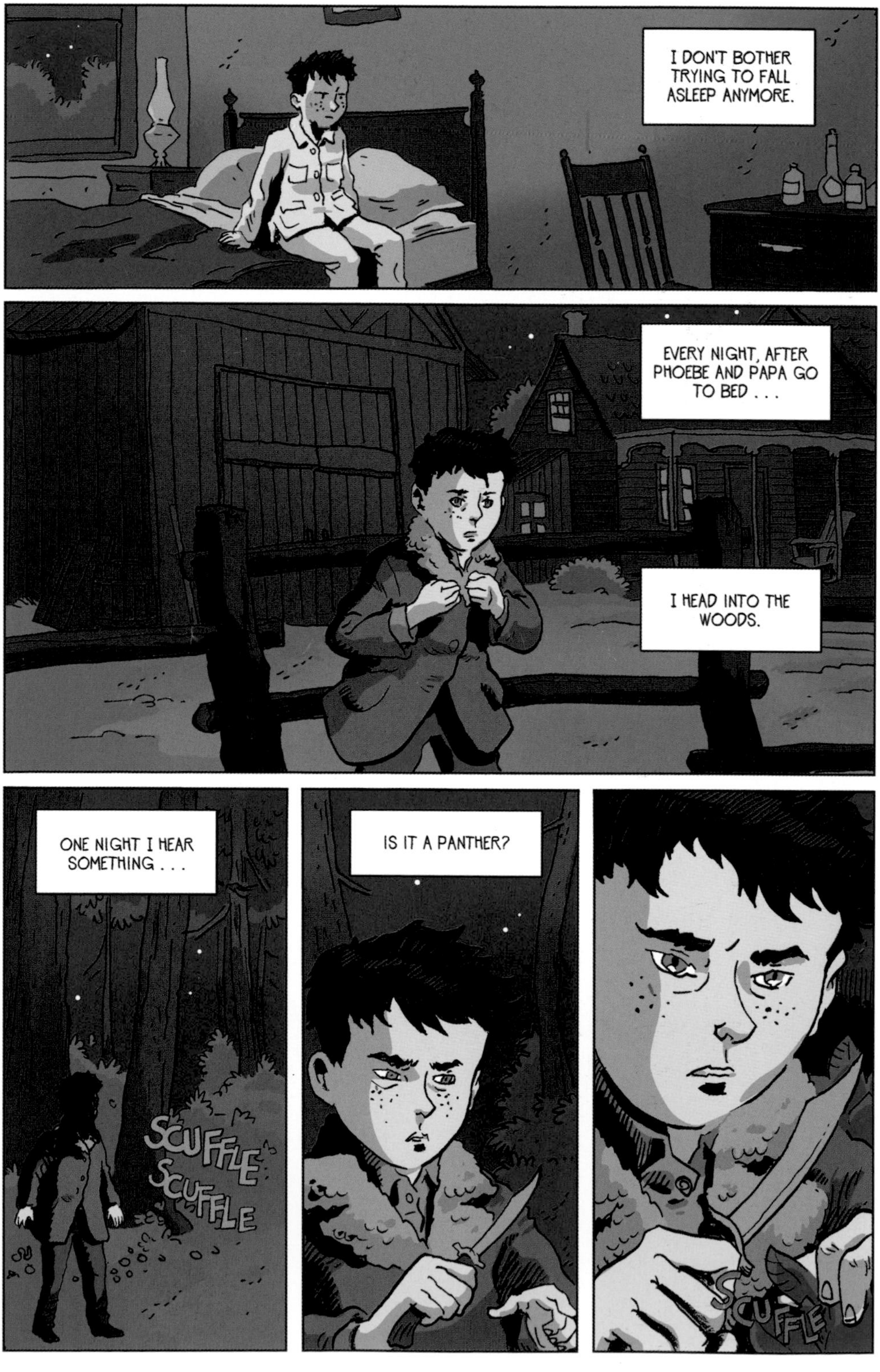
I DON'T BOTHER TRYING TO FALL ASLEEP ANYMORE.
EVERY NIGHT, AFTER PHOEBE AND PAPA GO TO BED . . .
I HEAD INTO THE WOODS.
ONE NIGHT I HEAR SOMETHING . . .
SCUFFLE
SCUFFLE
IS IT A PANTHER?
SCUFFLE

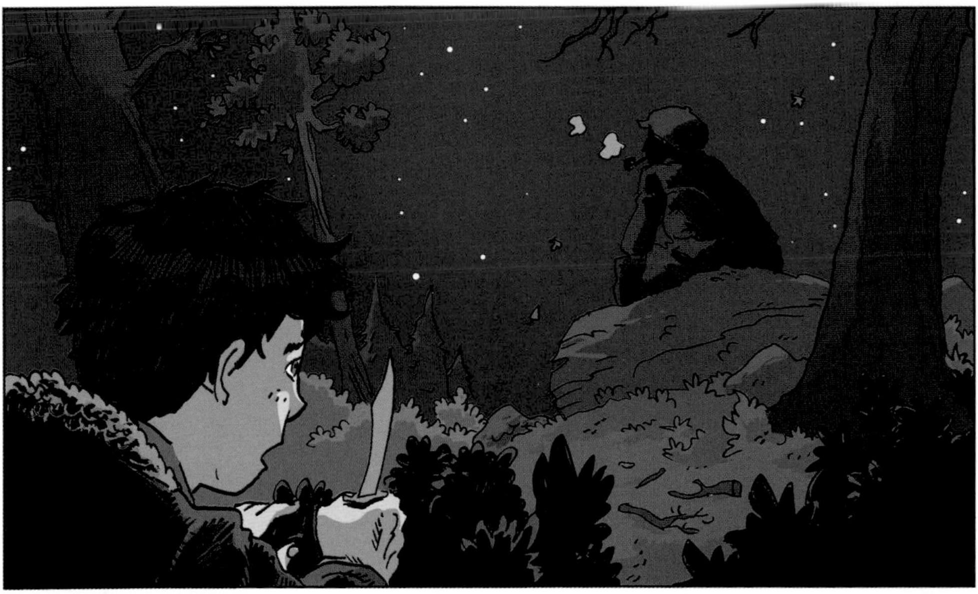

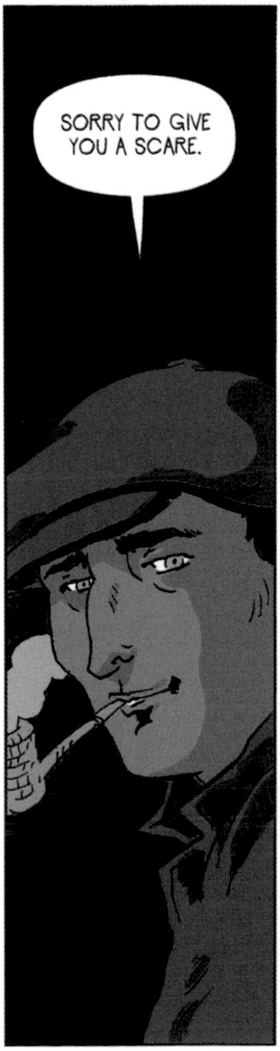
SORRY TO GIVE YOU A SCARE.

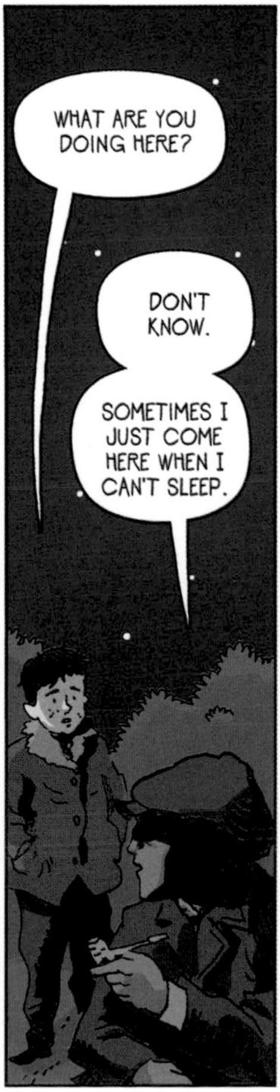
WHAT ARE YOU DOING HERE?
DON'T KNOW.
SOMETIMES I JUST COME HERE WHEN I CAN'T SLEEP.

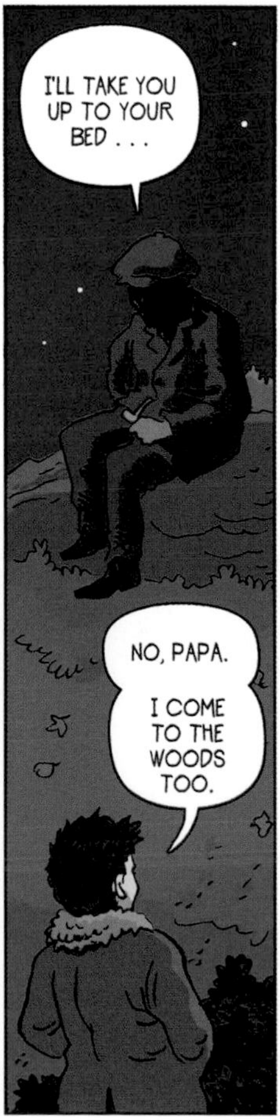
I'LL TAKE YOU UP TO YOUR BED . . .
NO, PAPA.
I COME TO THE WOODS TOO.

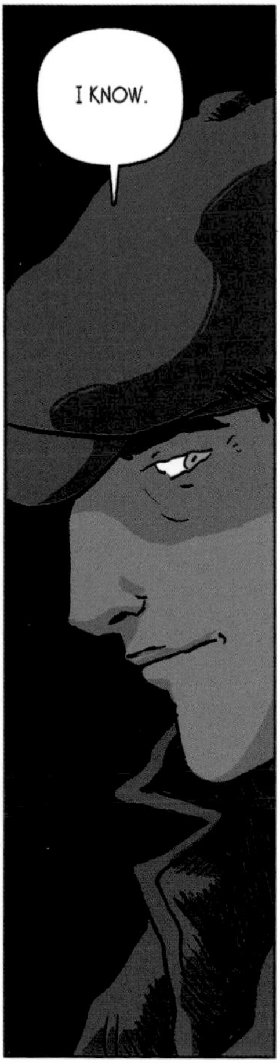
I KNOW.

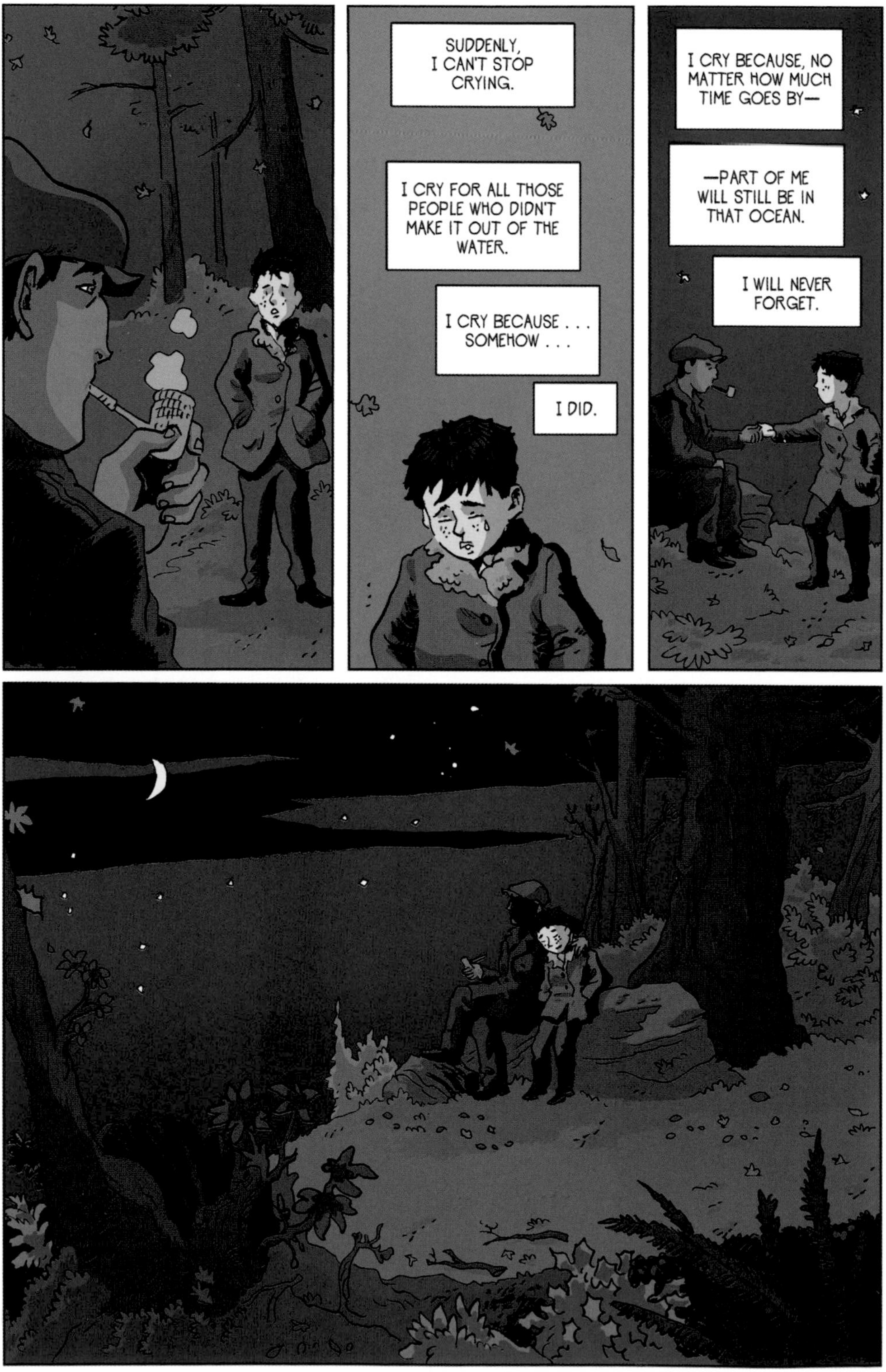
SUDDENLY, I CAN'T STOP CRYING.
I CRY FOR ALL THOSE PEOPLE WHO DIDN'T MAKE IT OUT OF THE WATER.
I CRY BECAUSE . . . SOMEHOW . . .
I DID.
I CRY BECAUSE, NO MATTER HOW MUCH TIME GOES BY—
—PART OF ME WILL STILL BE IN THAT OCEAN.
I WILL NEVER FORGET.

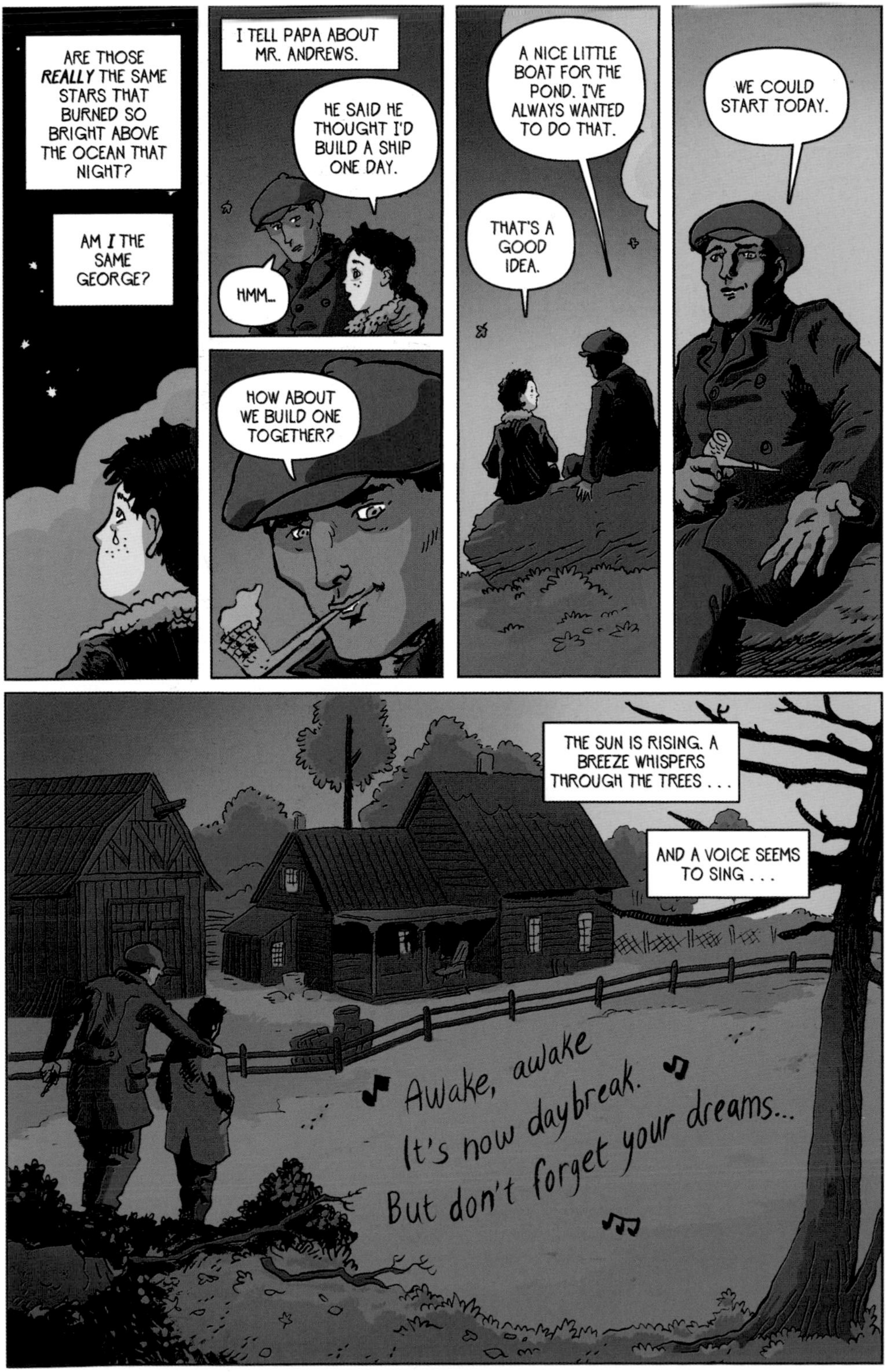
ARE THOSE *REALLY* THE SAME STARS THAT BURNED SO BRIGHT ABOVE THE OCEAN THAT NIGHT?
AM *I* THE SAME GEORGE?
I TELL PAPA ABOUT MR. ANDREWS.
HE SAID HE THOUGHT I'D BUILD A SHIP ONE DAY.
HMM...
HOW ABOUT WE BUILD ONE TOGETHER?
A NICE LITTLE BOAT FOR THE POND. I'VE ALWAYS WANTED TO DO THAT.
THAT'S A GOOD IDEA.
WE COULD START TODAY.
THE SUN IS RISING. A BREEZE WHISPERS THROUGH THE TREES . . .
AND A VOICE SEEMS TO SING . . .
Awake, awake
It's now daybreak.
But don't forget your dreams...

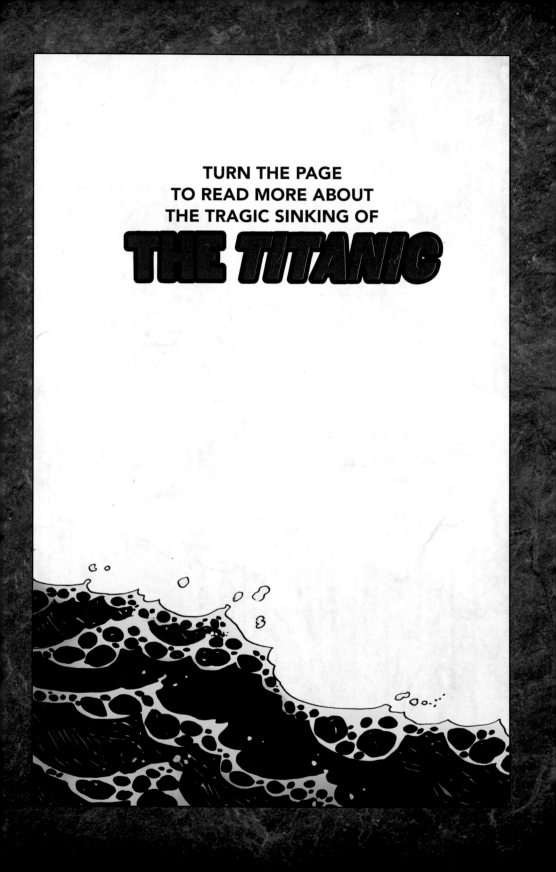

TURN THE PAGE
TO READ MORE ABOUT
THE TRAGIC SINKING OF

THE TITANIC

DEAR READERS,

THIS BOOK IS A WORK OF HISTORICAL FICTION. THAT MEANS THAT THE FACTS ABOUT THE *TITANIC* ARE TRUE, BUT THE MAIN CHARACTERS CAME FROM MY IMAGINATION. GEORGE, PHOEBE, AUNT DAISY, MARCO, AND ENZO ARE BASED ON PEOPLE I LEARNED ABOUT WHILE RESEARCHING THE *TITANIC*. BY THE TIME I FINISHED WRITING THIS BOOK, THEY SURE *FELT* REAL TO ME.

I CAN SEE GEORGE NOW, RELAXING IN THE LITTLE BOAT HE AND PAPA BUILT, ROWING AROUND THEIR POND WHILE PHOEBE WATCHES FROM THE SHORE, READING A BOOK ABOUT DINOSAUR FOSSILS. I CAN PICTURE AUNT DAISY AND MARCO'S WEDDING, AND HOW ENZO WOULD RUN DOWN THE AISLE WITH A HUGE GRIN ON HIS FACE. I'M SO HAPPY I COULD GIVE MY CHARACTERS HAPPY ENDINGS. IF ONLY I COULD DO THE SAME FOR THE 1,496 PEOPLE WHO DIDN'T SURVIVE THE SINKING OF THE *TITANIC*.

EVEN NOW, MORE THAN A CENTURY LATER, IT'S HAUNTING TO THINK ABOUT ALL THE PEOPLE WHO WERE LOST WHEN THE *TITANIC* SANK—THE LIVES FOREVER CHANGED. I'M SURE THAT'S ONE REASON WHY THE STORY OF THE *TITANIC* KEEPS ITS GRIP ON US, AND WHY AUTHORS LIKE ME CONTINUE TO WRITE ABOUT IT.

IN FACT, MORE HAS BEEN WRITTEN ABOUT THE *TITANIC* THAN ANY OTHER DISASTER IN MODERN HISTORY. THERE WAS SO MUCH MORE I WISH I COULD HAVE INCLUDED IN THE STORY. ON THE FOLLOWING PAGES, YOU'LL FIND MORE INFORMATION ABOUT THIS FASCINATING TOPIC, WITH SOME HELP FROM MY FRIENDS AUNT DAISY, GEORGE, PHOEBE, MARCO, AND ENZO TO GUIDE YOU.

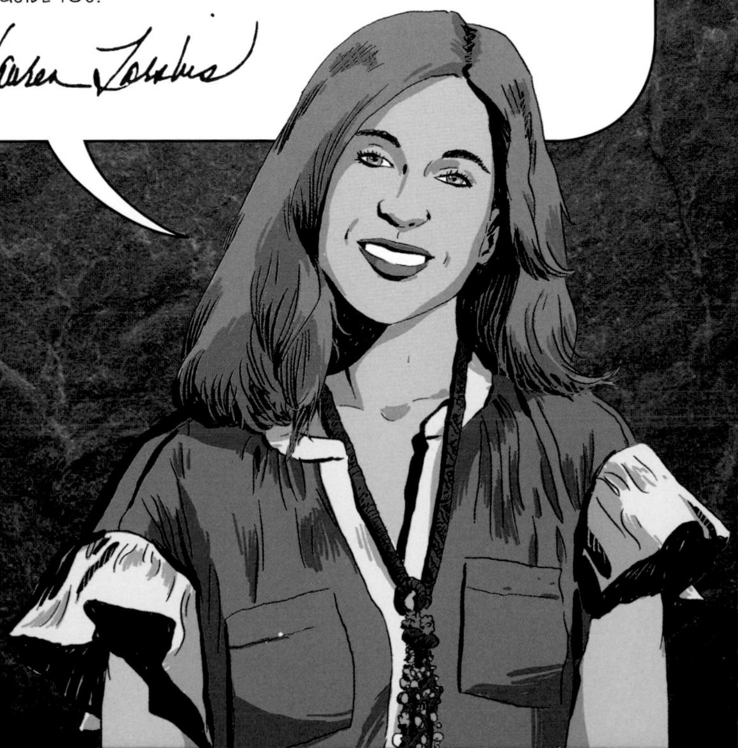

MORE *TITANIC* FACTS

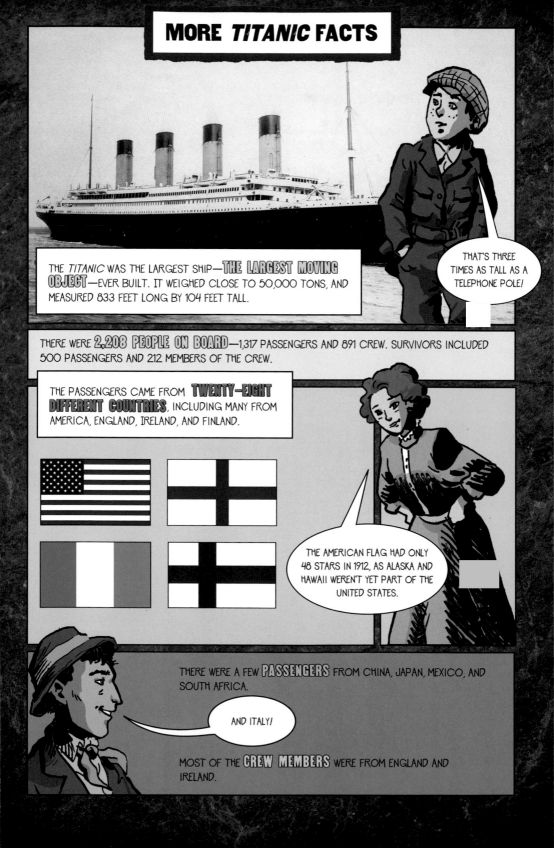

THE *TITANIC* WAS THE LARGEST SHIP—**THE LARGEST MOVING OBJECT**—EVER BUILT. IT WEIGHED CLOSE TO 50,000 TONS, AND MEASURED 833 FEET LONG BY 104 FEET TALL.

THAT'S THREE TIMES AS TALL AS A TELEPHONE POLE!

THERE WERE **2,208 PEOPLE ON BOARD**—1,317 PASSENGERS AND 891 CREW. SURVIVORS INCLUDED 500 PASSENGERS AND 212 MEMBERS OF THE CREW.

THE PASSENGERS CAME FROM **TWENTY-EIGHT DIFFERENT COUNTRIES**, INCLUDING MANY FROM AMERICA, ENGLAND, IRELAND, AND FINLAND.

THE AMERICAN FLAG HAD ONLY 48 STARS IN 1912, AS ALASKA AND HAWAII WEREN'T YET PART OF THE UNITED STATES.

THERE WERE A FEW **PASSENGERS** FROM CHINA, JAPAN, MEXICO, AND SOUTH AFRICA.

AND ITALY!

MOST OF THE **CREW MEMBERS** WERE FROM ENGLAND AND IRELAND.

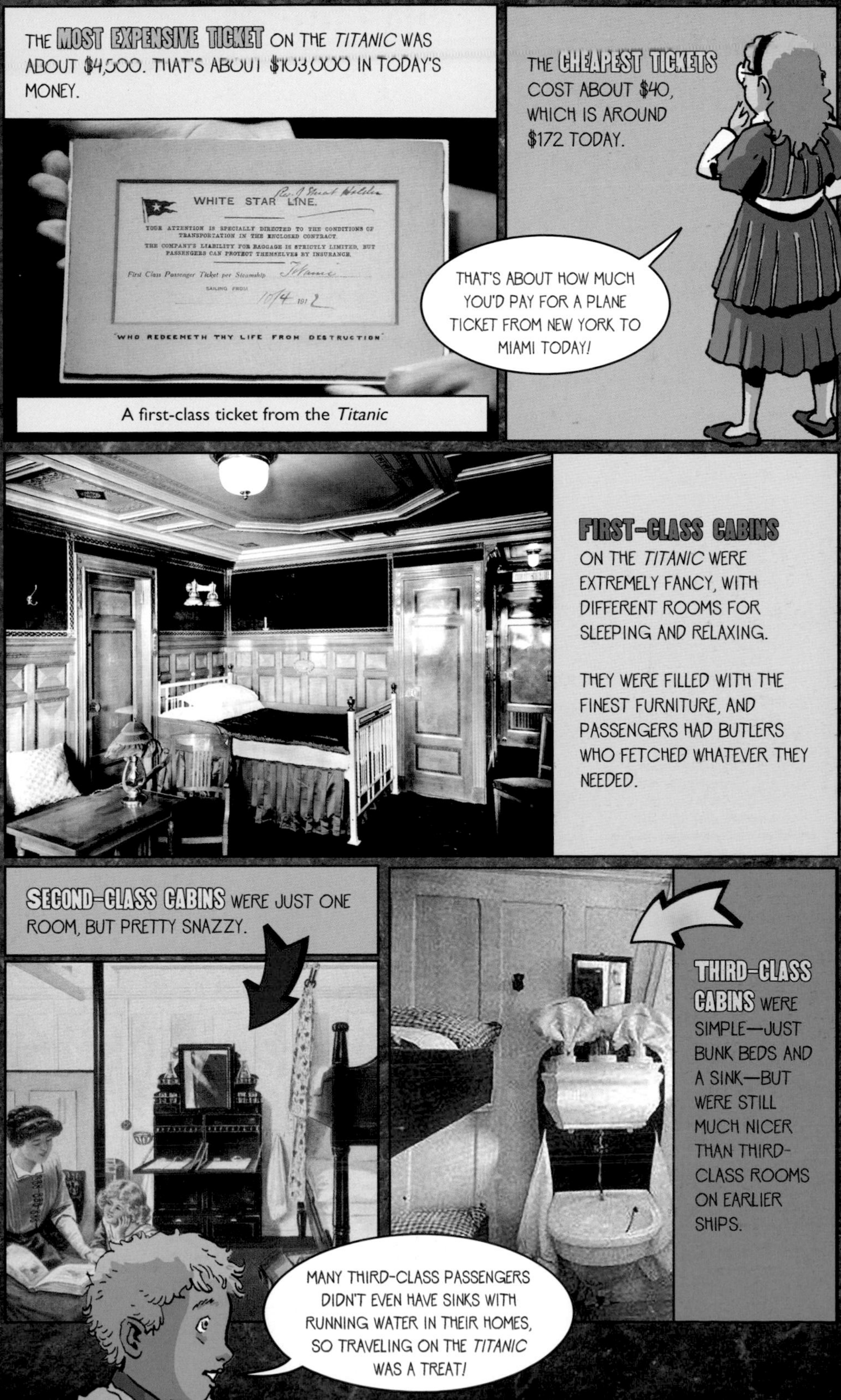
THE MOST EXPENSIVE TICKET ON THE *TITANIC* WAS ABOUT $4,500. THAT'S ABOUT $103,000 IN TODAY'S MONEY.
WHITE STAR LINE.
"WHO REDEEMETH THY LIFE FROM DESTRUCTION"
THE CHEAPEST TICKETS COST ABOUT $40, WHICH IS AROUND $172 TODAY.
THAT'S ABOUT HOW MUCH YOU'D PAY FOR A PLANE TICKET FROM NEW YORK TO MIAMI TODAY!
FIRST-CLASS CABINS ON THE *TITANIC* WERE EXTREMELY FANCY, WITH DIFFERENT ROOMS FOR SLEEPING AND RELAXING.
THEY WERE FILLED WITH THE FINEST FURNITURE, AND PASSENGERS HAD BUTLERS WHO FETCHED WHATEVER THEY NEEDED.
SECOND-CLASS CABINS WERE JUST ONE ROOM, BUT PRETTY SNAZZY.
THIRD-CLASS CABINS WERE SIMPLE—JUST BUNK BEDS AND A SINK—BUT WERE STILL MUCH NICER THAN THIRD-CLASS ROOMS ON EARLIER SHIPS.
MANY THIRD-CLASS PASSENGERS DIDN'T EVEN HAVE SINKS WITH RUNNING WATER IN THEIR HOMES, SO TRAVELING ON THE *TITANIC* WAS A TREAT!
A first-class ticket from the *Titanic*

REAL LIFE CHARACTERS

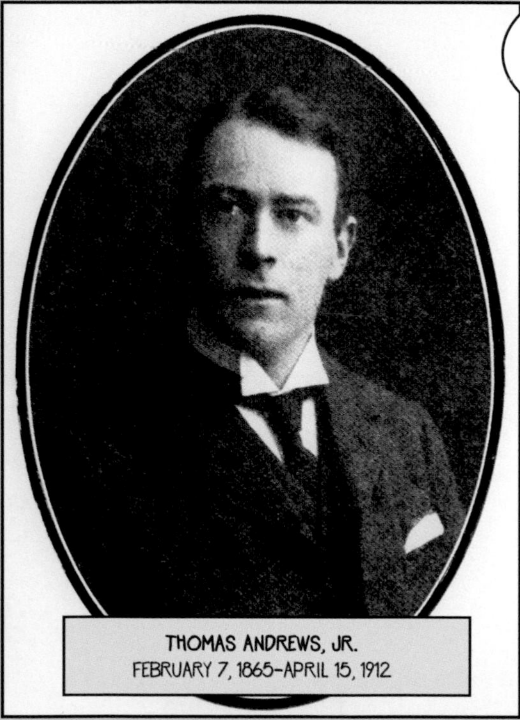

THOMAS ANDREWS, JR.
FEBRUARY 7, 1865–APRIL 15, 1912

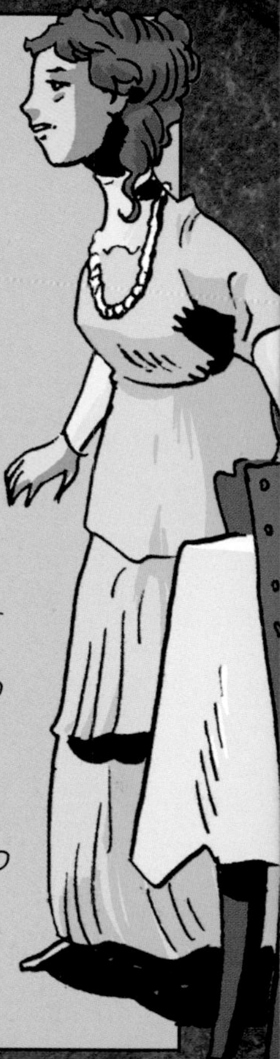
WE MET MR. ANDREWS AND MR. STEAD IN THE STORY. HERE'S WHAT THEY WERE LIKE IN REAL LIFE!

THE SHIP'S DESIGNER, **THOMAS ANDREWS, JR.**, WAS FROM IRELAND. HE DIED IN THE SINKING SHIP.

SOME SAY MR. ANDREWS'S COLLEAGUES REQUESTED THAT THE SHIP TO HAVE 64 LIFEBOATS, BUT THE REQUEST WAS TURNED DOWN BECAUSE TOO MANY LIFEBOATS WOULD HAVE MADE THE DECK LOOK CLUTTERED.

AFTER THE SINKING OF THE *TITANIC*, LAWS WERE CHANGED TO REQUIRE ALL SHIPS TO CARRY ENOUGH LIFEBOATS FOR EVERY PASSENGER AND CREW MEMBER.

WILLIAM THOMAS STEAD WAS A FAMOUS WRITER AND NEWSPAPER EDITOR IN ENGLAND. HE WAS KNOWN FOR BENDING THE TRUTH TO MAKE A STORY MORE EXCITING.

MR. STEAD DID NOT SURVIVE THE *TITANIC* DISASTER.

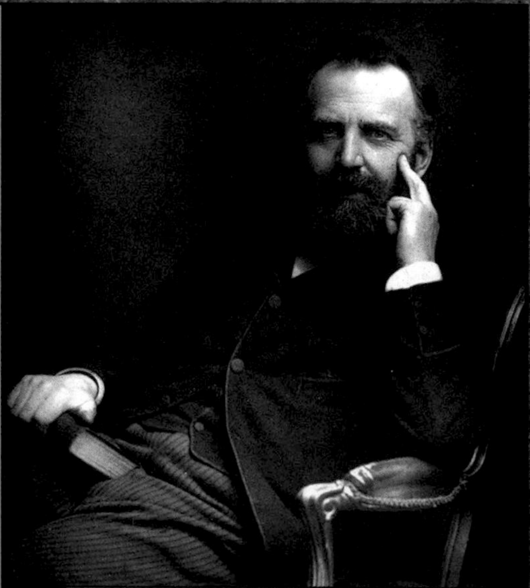

WILLIAM THOMAS STEAD
JULY 5, 1849–APRIL 15, 1912

MEET SOME OTHER FAMOUS *TITANIC* PASSENGERS

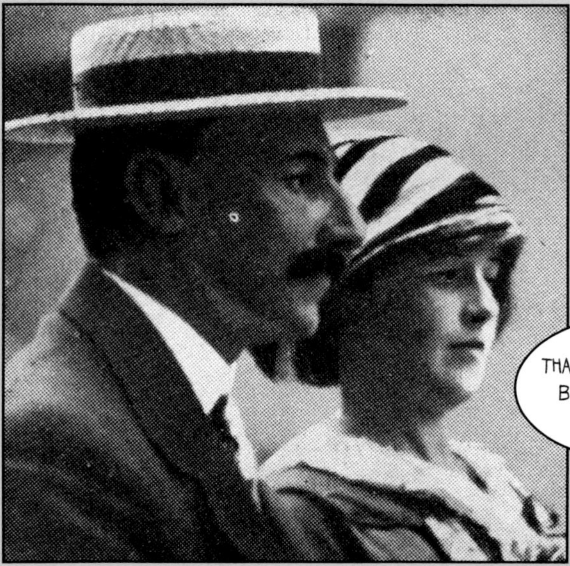

MILLIONAIRE NEW YORKERS **JOHN JACOB ASTOR** AND HIS PREGNANT WIFE, **MADELINE**, HAD BEEN ON THEIR HONEYMOON IN EUROPE BEFORE BOARDING THE *TITANIC*. MR. ASTOR WAS THE **RICHEST MAN** ON THE SHIP—WORTH ALMOST 87 MILLION DOLLARS.

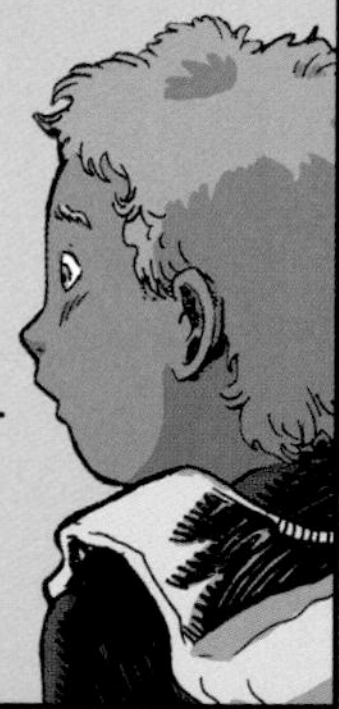
THAT'S MORE THAN TWO BILLION DOLLARS IN TODAY'S MONEY!

MADELINE SURVIVED THE DISASTER, BUT JOHN DID NOT.

MARGARET BROWN EARNED THE NICKNAME **"THE UNSINKABLE MOLLY BROWN"** FOR HER HEROICS DURING THE DISASTER.

THE STORY GOES THAT WHEN SHE REALIZED HER LIFEBOAT WASN'T FULL, SHE TRIED TO CONVINCE FELLOW PASSENGERS TO GO BACK AND LOOK FOR MORE SURVIVORS.

AND WHEN THE MEN IN THE BOAT DIDN'T WANT THE WOMEN TO HELP ROW, SHE TOLD THE WOMEN TO KEEP ROWING ANYWAY.

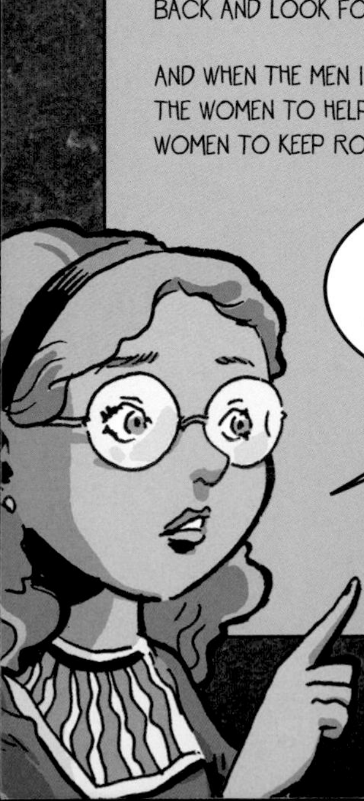
BACK IN 1912, WOMEN WEREN'T TREATED AS EQUALS TO MEN. UNTIL 1919, WOMEN IN AMERICA WEREN'T EVEN ALLOWED TO VOTE IN ELECTIONS!

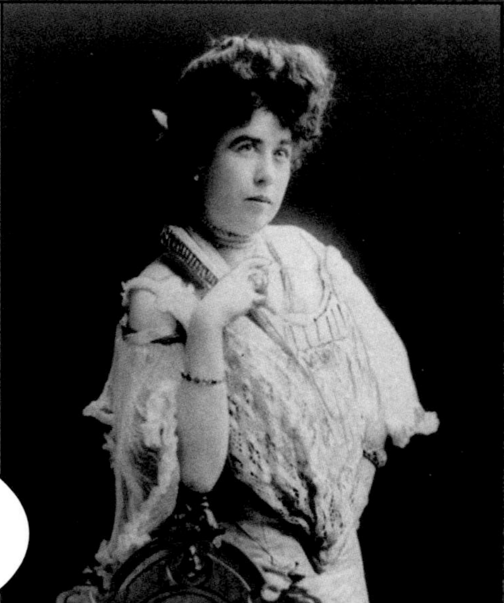

MS. BROWN SURVIVED. SHE USED HER FAME TO **FIGHT FOR RIGHTS** FOR WOMEN AND CHILDREN, AND OTHER CAUSES.

FINDING THE *TITANIC*

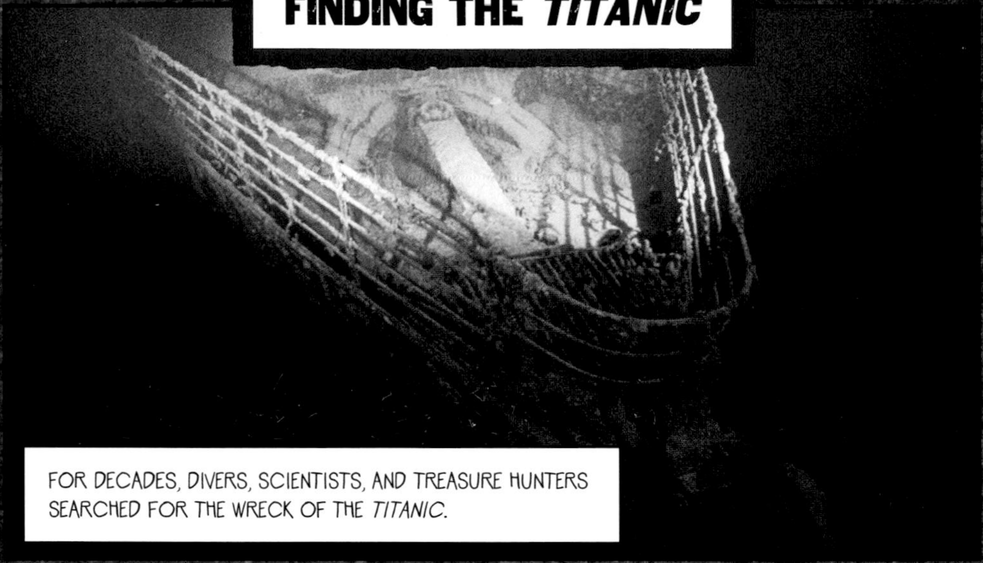

FOR DECADES, DIVERS, SCIENTISTS, AND TREASURE HUNTERS SEARCHED FOR THE WRECK OF THE *TITANIC*.

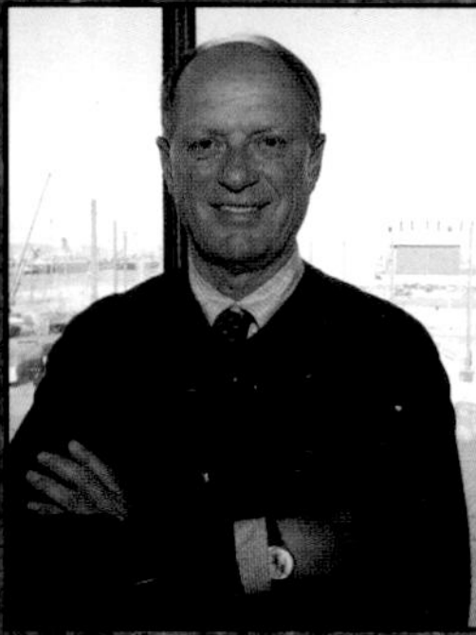

IT WAS FINALLY LOCATED IN 1985 BY A TEAM LED BY U.S. SCIENTIST **DR. ROBERT BALLARD**, TWO AND A HALF MILES BELOW THE SURFACE OF THE SEA.

DR. BALLARD AND HIS TEAM DID NOT TAKE ANYTHING FROM THE WRECK. HE BELIEVES THE *TITANIC* SHOULD REST IN PEACE AS A MEMORIAL TO THOSE WHO DIED.

BUT HE COULDN'T STOP OTHER EXPLORERS AND TREASURE HUNTERS FROM DIVING TO THE WRECK AND REMOVING THOUSANDS OF **ARTIFACTS**: JEWELRY, DISHES, CLOTHES—EVEN THE SHIP'S HULL.

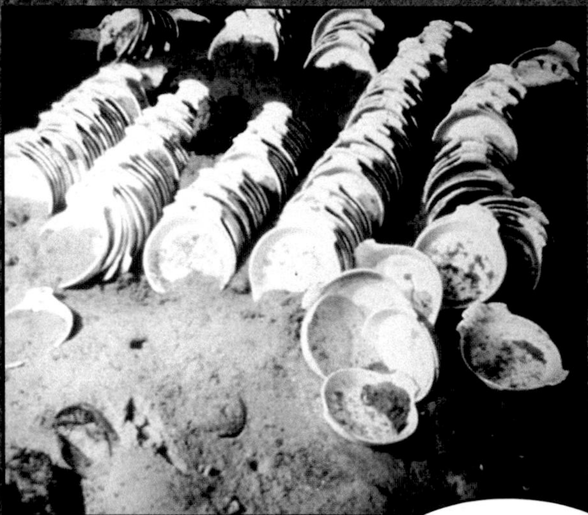

Some of the thousands of dishes found on the sea floor were not even chipped.

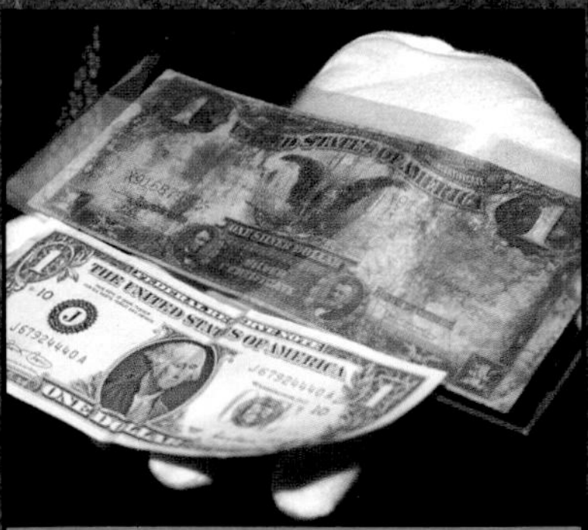

A dollar bill from the wreckage and a modern-day dollar bill.

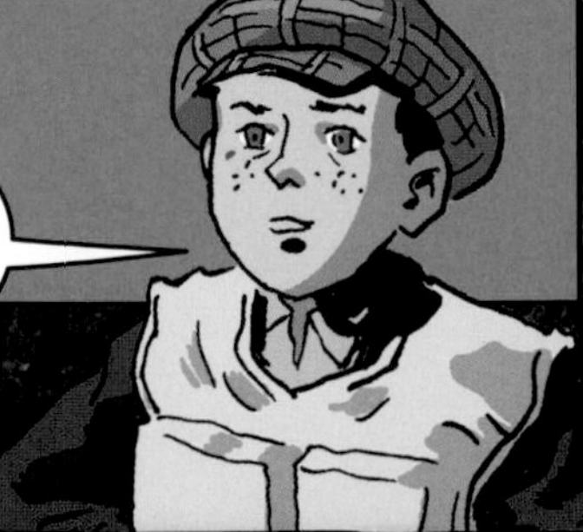
WHAT DO *YOU* THINK? SHOULD THE *TITANIC* BE BROUGHT TO THE SURFACE OR LEFT IN PEACE?

SELECTED BIBLIOGRAPHY

Fitch, Tad, J. Kent Layton, and Bill Wormstedt. *On a Sea of Glass: The Life and Loss of the RMS* Titanic. Gloucestershire: Amberley, 2012.

Forsyth, Alastair, and Sheila Jemima. Titanic *Voices*. New York: St. Martin's Press, 1999.

Gracie, Archibald, and John B. Thayer. Titanic: *A Survivor's Story and the Sinking of the S.S.* Titanic. Chicago: Academy Chicago Publishers, 2005.

Lord, Walter. *A Night to Remember*. New York: Holt, 1955.

Winocour, Jack, editor. *The Story of the* Titanic *as Told by Its Survivors*. New York: Dover Publications, 1960.

MORE *TITANIC* BOOKS YOU MIGHT LIKE

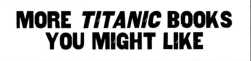

Callery, Sean. *Discover More:* Titanic. New York: Scholastic, 2014.

Hopkinson, Deborah. Titanic: *Voices from the Disaster.* New York: Scholastic, 2012.

Korman, Gordon. Titanic *Trilogy: Unsinkable, Collison Couse, S.O.S.* New York: Scholastic, 2011.

Tarshis, Lauren. *I Survived the Sinking of the* Titanic, *1912.* New York: Scholastic, 2010.

White, Ellen Emerson. *Dear America: Voyage on the Great* Titanic: *The Diary of Margaret Ann Brady, RMS* Titanic, *1912.* New York: Scholastic, 1998.

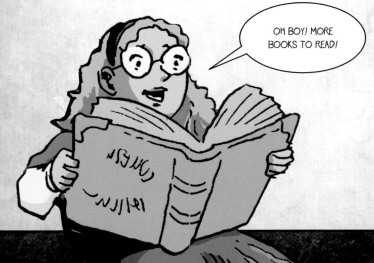

OH BOY! MORE BOOKS TO READ!

STORY AND TEXT COPYRIGHT © 2020, 2010 BY DREYFUSS TARSHIS MEDIA INC.
ILLUSTRATION COPYRIGHT © 2020 BY DREYFUSS TARSHIS MEDIA INC.

PHOTOS : 153 TOP: MARY EVANS/THE NATIONAL ARCHIVES, LONDON, ENGLAND/AGE FOTOSTOCK; 154 TOP: DAVE THOMPSON/AP IMAGES; 154 CENTER: POPPERFOTO/GETTY IMAGES; 154 BOTTOM LEFT: MARY EVANS/ONSLOW AUCTIONS/THE IMAGE WORKS; 154 BOTTOM RIGHT: WIKIMEDIA; 155 TOP: MARY EVANS PICTURE LIBRARY LTD/AGE FOTOSTOCK; 155 BOTTOM: UNIVERSAL HISTORY ARCHIVE/UIG/ SHUTTERSTOCK; 156 TOP: THE TITANIC COLLECTION/AGE FOTOSTOCK; 156 BOTTOM: WORLD HISTORY ARCHIVE/TOPFOTO/THE IMAGE WORKS; 157 TOP: RALPH WHITE/GETTY IMAGES; 157 CENTER: PAUL MCERLANE/ALAMY STOCK PHOTO; 157 BOTTOM LEFT: ALAIN BENAINOUS/GETTY IMAGES; 157 BOTTOM RIGHT: MICHEL BOUTEFEU/GETTY IMAGES.

ALL RIGHTS RESERVED. PUBLISHED BY GRAPHIX, AN IMPRINT OF SCHOLASTIC INC., *PUBLISHERS SINCE 1920.* SCHOLASTIC, GRAPHIX, AND ASSOCIATED LOGOS ARE TRADEMARKS AND/OR REGISTERED TRADEMARKS OF SCHOLASTIC INC.

THE PUBLISHER DOES NOT HAVE ANY CONTROL OVER AND DOES NOT ASSUME ANY RESPONSIBILITY FOR AUTHOR OR THIRD-PARTY WEBSITES OR THEIR CONTENT.

NO PART OF THIS PUBLICATION MAY BE REPRODUCED, STORED IN A RETRIEVAL SYSTEM, OR TRANSMITTED IN ANY FORM OR BY ANY MEANS, ELECTRONIC, MECHANICAL, PHOTOCOPYING, RECORDING, OR OTHERWISE, WITHOUT WRITTEN PERMISSION OF THE PUBLISHER. FOR INFORMATION REGARDING PERMISSION, WRITE TO SCHOLASTIC INC., ATTENTION: PERMISSIONS DEPARTMENT, 557 BROADWAY, NEW YORK, NY 10012.

WHILE INSPIRED BY REAL EVENTS AND HISTORICAL CHARACTERS, THIS IS A WORK OF FICTION AND DOES NOT CLAIM TO BE HISTORICALLY ACCURATE OR TO PORTRAY FACTUAL EVENTS OR RELATIONSHIPS. PLEASE KEEP IN MIND THAT REFERENCES TO ACTUAL PERSONS, LIVING OR DEAD, BUSINESS ESTABLISHMENTS, EVENTS, OR LOCALES MAY NOT BE FACTUALLY ACCURATE, BUT RATHER FICTIONALIZED BY THE AUTHOR.

LIBRARY OF CONGRESS CONTROL NUMBER AVAILABLE

ISBN 978-1-338-12091-2 (PAPERBACK)

ISBN 978-1-338-12092-9 (HARDCOVER)

ISBN 978-1-4071-9687-9 (UK PAPERBACK)

10 9 8 7 6 5 4 3 2 1   20 21 22 23 24

PRINTED IN MALAYSIA   108
FIRST EDITION, FEBRUARY 2020

EDITED BY KATIE WOEHR AND RACHEL STARK
ADAPTATION BY GEORGIA BALL
ART BY HAUS STUDIO
PENCILS BY GERVASIO
INKS BY JOK AND CARLOS AÓN
COLORS BY LARA LEE
ART ASSISTANCE BY DARIO BRABO
LOGO AND FONTS BY CARLOS AÓN
BOOK DESIGN BY KATIE FITCH
CREATIVE DIRECTOR: HEATHER DAUGHERTY
SPECIAL THANKS TO BILL WORMSTEDT

D0043879

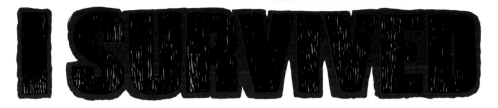

THE SINKING OF THE *TITANIC*, 1912